THE D⁰LLMAKER

JUSTIN ROBINSON

CAPTAIN
SUPERMARKET
PRESS

COPYRIGHT © 2014 BY JUSTIN ROBINSON

Captain Supermarket Press
info@captainsupermarket.com

First Printing, 2014
ISBN 978-0-9892781-2-6

First eBook Edition August 2012, MuseItUp Publishing
eISBN 978-1-77127-142-4

Cover Art © 2014 by Keri Knutson
Book layout and composition by Lauri Veverka
Typefaces: Heavyweight, Trajan Pro, Fanwood

www.captainsupermarket.com

FOR PENNY.
You believed in this book before I did.

CHAPTER ONE

EVERY MOVEMENT SEARED HIS WRISTS like barbed wire. Red seeped through the soaked rags to tap the bare planks of the floor, collecting in treacherous pools. He maneuvered through the stifling attic, slipping here and there. *Don't look down. Know what's there already.*

The air wrapped around him in a python embrace, wringing breath from lungs, sweat from skin, blood from veins.

The wood of her leg was warm, skin-soft, and still sticky with blood. The seams at ankle, knee, and thigh were nearly invisible—the leg could almost belong to a living woman. His gaze crawled up the nude body. She was swanlike... perfect. Her face painted from memory, a memory that would never— could never—dim. White face, crimson lips, black triangles over and under the eyes—a lovely harlequin. She had no eyelids. He could have carved them, but they would have been mere shutters. Unworthy. Let her stare at the world out of those beautiful eyes. They were blown glass, fragile, and nearly transparent. Her hair was black, pulled into a neat bun. Running a finger along her hairline, he caressed the individual plugs attached to the wooden skull, hating that they were even barely visible.

In her open mouth were teeth individually carved from wood. The tongue, a solid block, soaked through with blood, spongy now. And there, written along it—three letters. They were small, though still legible.

The body was lean and muscled, the curves of a dancer. He traced the small breasts, the delicate nipples that took days to carve. They were the same stark white as her skin, the shadows dyeing them oily black.

She lay in the middle of the circles, ruddy light from the candles turning her to lacquer. The symbols were carved on the floor, the calculations done. There was only one thing left to do.

He was nude, and had been since the sun came down, teased by the worst erection of his life for most of the day. Couldn't do anything for it. Wasting power this late in the game would have been the worst kind of stupid. There were others to think of.

His daughter.

Blood caked hair to skin. He held the knife gingerly. Too tight and his slashed wrists burned.

Standing over her head, his cock was entirely soft, a direct contrast to the earlier priapism. He took it in hand, looked over her smooth body, the painstakingly carved breasts, the soft, black fur at the apex of her legs. The plugs there were tiny as well. Through those would be her closed outer labia. A seam would reveal the inner lips and beyond, the rest of her. It had been the same white as the rest of the wood, now stained where spilled blood had collected between her legs. She was flared and crimson.

He stroked himself, not thinking about the culmination of the ritual ahead, unable to tear himself from the beauty stretched across the bloody floorboards. Hard again, he wanted to fling himself on top of her, fuck her now, see how well she had been crafted. See if she was as warm and wet as he hoped.

The knife came alive, slashed the head of his cock once, twice. Red for red.

He tried not to cry out. Failed. The blood tumbled over her in fat drops, falling on her eyes like rain on cloudy windows, cutting across her body in gory streaks. He wanted to hold himself, to grab and cradle until the blood stopped flowing, but the rite was not finished yet. Think of her and only of her.

She needed it.

She did not move.

He wrung the blood out of himself. More. She needed more. That was the only solution.

She still did not move.

Then, doubt.

She lay there, still as death. His hands were ghostly white in the few unstained bits of skin. Like her.

No. He had done everything right.

Hadn't he?

D'Aisecq's diary wasn't complete. Piecing together what was lost had been difficult. There were other sources, after all. Older, even more arcane. There was enough. Enough to do it right. Enough to recreate the ritual.

But she was still.

His life.

Ten years to decode d'Aisecq's secrets.

One year to sculpt her body.

Who knew how many pints of blood.

And she was still.

A waste. All of it.

Hot tears of rage—of fear and desperation—chased the cooling blood down his cheeks. Falling to his knees over her, he took her head between sticky hands. The emptiness bigger than space, crushing him small, making him helpless. What had he thought he could do? Nothing against something this big. This uncaring. This empty.

His forehead touched hers, bloody tears falling on her cheeks. Kissing her softly, he whispered into that still and perfect mouth, "I'm sorry." There was something else he wanted to say, something circling the dark corners of a mind obsessed with her from the moment he, as a child, first saw her. But he couldn't say it. Not where it wouldn't echo.

He stayed there for a long moment, wishing to breathe what wasn't there.

Something caressed the sides of his face. At first he believed they were rivulets of tears. No. They were too strong and much too gentle.

He parted from her, taking in her face upside down. The eyes had something in them. Flickering gold from the candlelight, an expression of wonder.

The pain had vanished. He rocked backwards, fell clumsily on the blood-slick boards.

Now. All of this. An entire life.

Two lives.

She moved, sitting up, turning, gazing at her graceful hand in wonder and then at him—pathetic, bleeding on the bare wood in the breathless attic.

"Is it you?" He hated the question as it hung in the air. Every thought was hopelessly jumbled, entwined, burning bright, and mad. She was there.

She crawled to him. Her harlequin face showed only childlike awe, touching his face, tracing the matted flows of blood down skinny arms to the ruined wrist. Her clear eyes found the soaked bandage, and the amazed expression did change, a brief flicker. Horror? Concern? Could have been something far older, something insect and terrible.

Her gaze fell to his cock, once again soft, hiding like a turtle in its shell, away from the brutal wounds carved across head and shaft. She took it in hand and found it growing eagerly. The agony exploded in white. He cried out. Her other hand touched the fresh tears.

"Please," he said, not knowing what it meant. Invitation? Mercy?

He was hard again. The blood bubbled up through slashes now freshly aggravated. She cocked her head. A question, but there was no question.

"Oh, God." This was every fantasy, every dream, everything, right in a single moment. A perfect angel, made from wood and blood. She mounted him quickly, guiding one crimson body into another. She was softer than he could have imagined. Warm, wet, welcoming. Her body closed around him, wooden mouth on flesh, sculpted fingers digging into weak meat. She sat up, watching him—the ritual circle, the pools of blood still flickering in candlelight—her hips rolling like the sea. Every ecstatic thrust tore him open anew, turned vision to static, body to fire, arms to steel. She was implacable, grinding, pushing, face locked in the same wonder.

Then—black.

* * *

Three beginnings—more than that, certainly. Birth, of course, Stephen James Monaghan, seven pounds, eight ounces. Conception, the rainy night, the good bottle of claret, their daughter sleeping soundly upstairs. Parents meeting at a fraternity party at Stanford, the unexpected chivalry from Charlie, the bright blue eyes of Sarah. And so forth, and so on, back before anything could have conceived of something called Stephen James Monaghan.

But three beginnings—skip the early years. The obsession hadn't shown itself yet, and wouldn't until the metamorphosis to imago. There was the talent. The scores on standardized tests said genius. Teachers knew him as sullen, quiet, and watched every curve annihilated. A surgeon's hands, long, agile fingers, strengthened first on toy bricks, then on clay, alone in the cluttered bedroom, upstairs in a huge gingerbread house. No matter how strange the kid, there was always room for one friend, one person as strange, but only one. Stephen wasn't strange. There wasn't a word for what he was.

Still, three beginnings—three vital steps in the making of him. Three hammers, three anvils. These are only visible in the aftermath, the way it's impossible to tell which stone in an avalanche actually struck the killing blow until you unearth the body, find which rock nestled in the broken skull.

Start with the first. The poster.

The avalanche rumbled, sending the first wave of pebbles. Stephen never saw his sister get it, still managing to pinpoint when and where. Her twelfth birthday, making him eight. It turned into the desire to breed and birth, in the wrong order.

The poster was only the seed. The soil was the intellect itself; intellect that sprouted into three paths—three times three.

Take the desire. Focus it. Strain it. Break it. Remake it.

These two beginnings create the real. The culmination of the Work.

Creation.

* * *

He awoke to a sensation of pinching. Surfacing from a black pond, the room swam into view—upstairs in bed, lying on top of his now bloody sheets, skin moist, warm, clean. A pot sat nearby, washcloth floating in copper water like a piece of flayed skin.

She had found an old nightgown, maybe his mother's, maybe Emily's, now stained pink over her belly and lap. She cradled one ruined wrist, studiously stitching it up. He tried to sit up, and she gently placed a hand on his chest. The hand was strong. There was no arguing with it.

He lay back. She wound gauze around the repaired wrist, turned to the other. Glancing downward, he prayed not to see the ruined thing he pictured between his legs. Thankfully, it was already wrapped, hiding the stitches, threatening to burst if he looked at her too long. She was too perfect—a wooden goddess. Flooding his mind with horrible images, it did nothing to banish the newly living fantasy.

She was staring. She'd finished, cleaning, and bandaging her creator.

She was silent. He searched her face, traced the seams around her mouth and eyes. Maybe another week of sanding and those would have been completely invisible.

She was still staring.

"I'm Stephen. Monaghan."

She nodded patiently. No surprise to her. Of course. She must know the name, right? Or was there already another name for him burned into her mind?

"I'm so glad to meet you."

That seemed to satisfy her. She carefully lifted him, as easily as a grown man would lift a child, and settled him amongst the blankets. Casually, she lifted the nightgown over her head and tossed it aside, settling in next to him, her body molding to his. He was asleep before she stopped moving.

CHAPTER TWO

HIS EYES OPENED, THE DOLL staring into them. Her eyes, translucent, prisms that caught every color and held it in the miniature bubbles floating within. She was nestled in the crook of his shoulder, watching him in apparent fascination. A human's eyes would focus—these never did. It made her gaze, even when it was one of wonder, into something disturbing and alien.

A chill breeze blew in from the open window. He shuddered against the gooseflesh, cuddling closer to the doll's warm body.

Warm body.

He sat up, hands exploring her. She lay back, allowing him to probe. He was looking for a place he could be sure their bodies hadn't touched. In the bend of her elbow... not body heat, but something. A dim flame heated her from within.

"Incredible." The pressure of her eyes was palpable. "I'm sorry. It's..."

He couldn't stop himself from leaning over and kissing her. Her mouth was lukewarm and wet, and she responded. Her hands moved for his face again, and below, the ragged ripping, then the warmth of fresh blood. He struggled, pushed her away.

"No. Not yet. Not yet."

Something so perfect could never be denied. She followed the commands of his belly and balls, ignored the words tumbling from stubborn lips, stopping them with kisses. She could not be resisted.

* * *

It was the beginning of June right before the culmination of the Work. The body of his wooden daughter lay in the attic, waiting for life to be breathed into her.

Part of Stephen feared the ritual. What if the years were a waste? What if the Work was insanity? What if he would spill mind and blood for nothing? What if she would never live?

What if she would?

Stephen wandered the grounds of his house. Living in the past was safer. There were no questions there.

The house was not a mansion, but it came close. It had been in the family three generations, and with each, the money diminished. It reminded Stephen a little of a movie called *Grey Gardens* about two crazy cat ladies slowly being digested by their cancerous home. The Monaghan home wasn't in that bad a shape, though there were places where the wallpaper frayed, where earthquakes had torn cracks, and even a closet where the house's bones had been laid bare.

From the outside, there was no indication. Like most houses built in the early part of the last century, it was a Victorian with two stories, three counting the attic. The front yard was a long expanse of lawn out to a high stone wall covered in ivy. In the spring, monarch butterflies flitted past the little purple flowers growing throughout. There were a few statues—concrete replicas of Greco-Roman figures—a bird fountain, and on the lawn, a hedge maze that would only be baffling to midgets or children. The garden was a point of pride for Stephen, the sole groundskeeper since inheriting the house. A huge semicircular window looked south from the attic, out over Pasadena, and in the distance, the Rose Bowl.

He stood in the garden, looking up at that window. Behind it, his fantasy waited, still and cold. When he was little, the attic had frightened him. The fear remained; the source had changed. The attic was no longer dark and empty. Power lurked within.

A gravel driveway went from iron gate to door. His father had liked to park in front of the door, but Stephen never did, preferring to park near the back of the house. It gave him a chance to walk through the garden.

Stephen left the garden for the back of the house. Hot fog had rolled in from the ocean, thickening the air and promising rain. June always threatened a deluge and rarely delivered.

The house had been built at the edge of the old orange groves. The trees were all gone now, save one, stubbornly growing in the southwest corner of the backyard. Like the last man holding onto the collapsing bridge, the bleeding and battered survivor who refuses to let go. The tree should have been rotten clean through, but it wasn't. Stephen often forgot it for weeks at a time. It never seemed to need watering, no matter how dry and cracked the earth. The tree had given the Monaghans fresh orange juice from time to time, thin and sour as the air. When the house became his, the fruit remained untouched to fall and rot into soil.

At the other end of the backyard was what had once been a coach house. Stephen stopped at the door. His parents had used it as a place for storage, but Stephen cleared it out, installing a large furnace and attendant tools. There were still elements of the elder Monaghans in the rusted nails, in the corner of decaying wood, and in the dusty crates holding more rats than mementos.

The workbench where the first parts of his daughter had been cut was pushed against one wall. It still had some shavings on it—parts that would never know life though they came from the same tree.

The unborn woman called from the attic. He had to return to her.

The house betrayed its age. Occasionally, the walls wept. Every footstep creaked loudly. The pipes groaned. Wind breathed through the front hall and out the back. The house had lasted long enough to develop a life of its own.

He entered through the scarred antique door to find the foyer. Straight ahead, a hall pushed past a dingy half-bathroom with crumbling plaster into the kitchen. On the right, a staircase led upstairs, to a landing. Arches on either side opened to large rooms. The left was the parlor, set aside for guests and holidays, the right was the living room for TV and hobbies. Never feeling much connection to the living room, Stephen often ignored it, even when there were other people in the house. He always preferred the parlor, doing homework at the low table in front of the sofa. There was a fireplace—in Los Angeles, it was almost always cold and dark.

Stephen walked through the parlor and into the dining room, through the swinging doors and into the kitchen, the only thoroughly modern room, and through the farthest door. This was the laundry room, hidden in the back of the house. Then, back toward the front of the house, through the large living room, quickly to avoid waking the ghosts still infecting that place.

The old stairs groaned as he climbed to the landing, turned left and ascended into the upstairs hall. He would not descend again without spilling pints of blood. The hall described an inverted L. The upper half was covered in textured wallpaper and pictures of family, the lower half in dark wainscoting. The two doors facing the stairs were Stephen's on the left and Emily's on the right; between them was the bathroom they had shared. Across from Stephen was the library: shelves of books surrounding a balding pool table. He never went in there anymore. Across from Emily was the office. Also, devoid of life. At the foot of the L was the master bedroom and bathroom, gathering thick layers of dust. At the tip of the L was the trapdoor leading to the attic. He was not ready to move through the trapdoor, into the dark world above. It was still daytime, and the rules applied. At nightfall, they would fall away like snakeskin.

He hesitated at the door to Emily's room. She had not been home for a long time. A slow turn of the knob and the door swung open. Emily's bedroom was as she left it, a strange cross-section of her life. There were remnants of her childhood, then the plague of adolescence, and the few final touches that she had put on it in the lost year after college.

Emily looked like Stephen. Same fair skin, same oily black hair, same problems with acne at temple and hairline, same icy blue eyes. Free of context, those eyes looked aloof, even cruel. When their minds wandered—something they did often—Emily sang under her breath. Stephen's face was blank in times like this, as if he had simply shut down. People thinking they were funny liked to wave in front of his face, but when they would attract his attention, what they saw in those blue eyes—that crushing depth—would make them shudder.

He found himself sitting inside Emily's open closet, looking outward at the place over her bed where the poster used to hang. He had done this many times before, letting it fill him before returning to the attic and to the Work. He could have drawn her from memory, but chose to think of her in stillness before revealing her in motion.

That night was different. As the sun set, he rose, clothes dropping away. The attic called.

* * *

Stephen sat up, turned away from her. Still nude, and had been for five days, there was no reason to leave the precious doll for a moment. Stomach snarled. When had he last eaten a proper meal? The dregs of the peanut butter were gone as of last night when hunger finally eclipsed desire if only for a moment.

He had risen quietly, to keep from disturbing the living dream on the other side of the bed. Hunger drove him to the kitchen. The fridge was nearly empty now. The jar of peanut butter had only scrapings left. In the harsh fluorescence of the fridge, his cock looked a little less angry—more pink than deep red. He had stopped bleeding every time they had sex. She was no gentler, but twelve hours of sleep a night could help even the most worried of wounds, and the wrist bandages were white and dry. He shut the fridge, plunging the room into dark, and revealing a slender silhouette waiting behind the door.

He dropped the jar—thank God it was plastic—and went

to her. He ended up fucking her on the counter, chaining her wide-eyed gaze, only shutting his eyes when the pleasure was too much. He pulled out, nearly collapsing against the kitchen's island, groping for the jar of peanut butter, scraping it clean with one finger. She closed her legs and sat next to him, leaning close, maybe fascinated by the act of eating.

It took the edge off. Nothing more.

Now, it was back. The peanut butter might have caged it, but it forgot to close the lock. She was already sitting up, sensing the change, reaching for him. He touched the lukewarm wood of her skin with wonder, looking into her clear eyes. "I have to go."

She cocked her head. Though there was no change to her expression, the question implicit was obvious. "Not forever. I'm hungry. I have to eat. I'll only be gone for a little while."

He tried to stand. Her hand closed over a still tender wrist.

"Not forever. I'll be back. And when I am, I'll have something for you."

Her hand snaked to his groin. He flinched away. "Not right now!" Anger was cruel, especially when she was only doing what she was taught over five days of life. "I'm sorry. I have to eat. I will be back."

His clothing was scattered across the bedroom. He pulled on a pair of jeans, nearly worn through at the knees, and a long-sleeved shirt that would hide the bandages well enough. Another shirt to put on over that one would cover the stains of varnish and blood. As soon as his head poked from the hole, she was standing in front of him. She made no sound when she moved.

"Wait here. You can read something," he said, gesturing to the bookcases against one wall. Her glassy gaze passed over it, going right back to him. She leaned in for a kiss, held him a fraction too long.

"Damn it!" He pushed her away, not gently. She could have held him fast but didn't, leaving him wobbling.

He found clean socks in a laundry basket and shoes crammed under the bed. "I'll be back, I promise." A stray thought bubbled up; if she decided to keep him there, he didn't have the strength to fight her.

She walked to the bed, and like a murder victim, collapsed onto it. "No!" He ran to her. Her head popped up. "Don't play games." Her head fell back onto the bed.

"One hour."

He picked up a pen and journal.

"Maybe two."

And with that, he left.

The Nite Lite stood at the corner of Fremont and California. It was the kind of place that would have been called a coffee shop before the term had been eaten up by places claiming to serve coffee, but actually served morning milkshakes. The Nite Lite had milkshakes, real ones in tall glasses with broken cookie garnishes, alongside the metal cup filled with the extra. Stephen never remembered a time without the Nite Lite. For years, it was merely a landmark, only starting to go in high school for late nights eating french fries and drinking Coke. The booths were burgundy vinyl, comfortable for resting off the edge of a teenage drunk. He remembered filling his belly with grease until the feeling returned to alcohol-numbed fingers and lips, afterwards making it back up the hill to sneak back into the house.

The Nite Lite had stood since the 1940s. The fact proven

with a few pictures scattered around, hung on the wooden areas between the blackboards that made up the interior walls and bordered the windows on all sides. The photos were old shots of the Rose Bowl, of the neighborhood, of Dodger Stadium going up in Chavez Ravine. There was even one of the old South Pasadena ostrich farm from the nineteenth century. The blackboards had the menu copied out in garish chalks, like something scrawled on a sidewalk. They still had actual menus, making Stephen wonder why they had copied them out on the walls. His mother had chuckled and said "ambience." It took him almost half an hour to find the word in the dictionary. It seemed a useless word at the time and only more useless now.

The Nite Lite was at the bottom of the hill, barely a five-minute drive from home. Grab food quickly and back to her. Even now she was lying in bed—in their bed—apparently dead. He gripped the steering wheel. Kept the hands from shaking. The road wound through trees green enough to be on the east coast.

The parking lot was a relic from old L.A., before they smoothed the ground, back when they let it lump around like a fat girl's muffin top. The driveway into the parking lot was ridiculously steep and the concrete of the lot split anew after every rain. Stephen had to gun the accelerator to get over the hump without the engine stuttering, and immediately ride the brake hard to stop. There was another entrance on California, so cars would be coming at each other head on and before going over the hump an oncoming collision was impossible to see, yet Stephen had never seen one happen.

The parking lot was even laid out strangely. Double spaces

in the front for cars to park front to front with nothing in between. If one snaked past the long spots, the dark back of the lot. No lights back there, despite the name of the place. The lot was flatter in the back, and the trees overhead made a ceiling. Stephen preferred it coming out of the darkness, into the one sickly yellow light of the lot.

What he hadn't realized until seeing the numbers on the dashboard clock was that it was a little after midnight. The cars in the lot were thin, and in the back, nonexistent. He walked across the lot, turning once when a prowl car rolled to a stop at the light.

He pushed the door open and the bell jingled. The counter was in the center of the room, a large U-shape enclosing the kitchen where the heat lamps made the food look like it was on TV. Booths ringed the room with a few tables in between. An old man sat at the counter, sipping coffee in front of a small plate smeared with pie filling. A group of teenagers took one of the corner booths, talking too loud, eating an appetizer sampler, the same thing Stephen would share with Brian and the others back in the day. The cash register was at the front of the counter, with a section that would open up and let the waitresses out.

The woman at the cash register was twenty pounds away from fat and ten years from young. Tattoos covered her bare arms, and she had rockabilly bangs to go with her bottle-black hair. She smiled at Stephen and handed him a menu. "Anywhere you like."

Stephen picked a booth in the back corner as far from the teenagers as possible. A window looked out over Fremont. Stephen sat and ignored the menu, instead opened the notebook to a blank page. The idea wasn't firm, and there would be no need for it, but someone, maybe later, three hundred years later, when he was the Marquis d'Aisecq to another Stephen James Monaghan, this hypothetical person might need it. The first step was a simple sketch of a wooden chair.

"Can I get you something to drink? Coffee?"

"A tuna melt, fries, and iced tea, please," he said.

The waitress made an "oh" sound under her breath as her hands scrabbled for the order pad. Only then did he look up, saw a swirl of bright copper hair as she walked back toward the kitchen. She was dressed casually—the Nite Lite was supposed to be a hip place, so her jeans, frayed white at the knees, and tank top were practically a uniform. A poet might call her voluptuous, an asshole would say chunky. Stephen could only think of how he liked the way her soft butt moved under her jeans.

He realized he was staring, blinked, and returned to the sketch of the chair. In seconds, his gaze was back to the waitress. She was in profile, her red hair, cut in a chin-length pageboy, covered her face from that angle. Freckles dotted her bare shoulders.

Freckles. How do I make freckles? The thought rattled through his mind—a distraction.

Back to the notebook. A wooden chair waited for him. Really a collection of scribbled lines, the barest attempt at perspective kept it from being preschooler's drawing. A couple restraints and a metal cap and the thing could be the electric chair in some backwater prison. But the opposite of its purpose. First, a cushion. No need to be uncomfortable. The arms, too. Fuck it, upholster the whole goddamn thing.

Stephen scratched out the old drawing.

"You know, most people bring a laptop when they want to write."

The glass of iced tea was sweating in front of him. He blinked, squinting up into the waitress's face. WASPy nose, big green eyes, and large expressive mouth. Not a knockout. Cute, reminding him of Chris somewhere deep. The kind of girl he would have loved from afar, maybe even talked to, but never had the balls to ask out. The kind of girl that would have ended up with someone else, God forbid Brian, and Stephen would end up crying by himself, a big old pity party with only a guest of honor.

Worse still would be getting her. Her filth, her stench, would flood into him and the revulsion would lead to mockery and rejection. Finding out what he had wanted wasn't sweet; it was black bile.

He could hardly remember what she said. "Huh?"

"Your notebook. Most people who write bring laptops."

He looked at the journal. It looked old; something Emily bought him at an upscale stationery store, a book with good heft and a better smell. He realized it smelled almost exactly like his dancer. Stephen scrawled over half the pages, stuck Post-Its on pages, bookmarked others with scraps of receipts, napkins, things to hold ideas in trust when the book wasn't handy.

"I don't have a laptop," he said apologetically.

"I always thought it was a little d-baggy, you know. It's like, write your novel at home, you know?"

"Oh. Sorry."

"Not you! Oh, shit. I'm sorry. It's late."

"It really is."

"Let me check on that tuna melt for you."

She scurried back to the kitchen. Stephen watched her, not knowing quite what happened, but pretty sure she would start avoiding him. He downed the iced tea quickly, pen scraping over the page, creating a softer chair, maybe with antique, plush cushions on seat, back, and arms.

There would have to be needles, of course.

He smelled the thick grease before the plate hit the table. "Let me get you some more tea."

She was gone before he could say anything. He coaxed some ketchup out next to the fries, the perfectly cut coffee shop fries, the same wherever there was a counter and a case with hardening slices of pie.

She returned with a pitcher.

"Thanks." He'd meant to say something funny, unable to bring himself to or really even think of anything funny to say. Not with the chair in front of him. Tubes, needles, a collection area attached to the back. It would need an alarm. Wouldn't do to have him passing out in the middle. He shuddered at the thought, pushing it away with a bite of the sandwich, relishing the crunch. He scratched out the tubes and drew a mantle of slender arms around the chair. It reminded him of an el train.

She reminded him of an el train.

He didn't know why he thought of the chair as female, but the thought had wings. It was impossible to think of her in any other way.

He finished the sandwich and mopped up the ketchup with cooling fries. The waitress was gone. Home was calling. Three fives on the table should be enough. If not, she could get him the next time he stopped in. There would be a next time.

Walking to the car, he looked back once and saw her clearing off his table. And only then realized he had forgotten to look at her nametag.

* * *

The front lawn was wet with dew. The houses on the street were utterly still. There was a strange sense of power to being awake when everyone else was asleep, the sense of being somehow special. The rules didn't apply. Stephen could do what he wanted this late because there were no eyes open to judge.

He opened the front door, half expecting her to be there. She wasn't. She was still collapsed on the bed, one leg at a crazy angle. In this position, with the moonlight streaming through the curtains, her seams were apparent. Big brutal lines cutting her into something fake. He should have spent another week sanding, should have made sure she fit together perfectly before making her. He should have picked another material. One that connected better than wood ever could.

All at once, her body collected, stood. Nothing human in the movement. She stared at him.

"I told you I'd be back."

She tilted her head.

"I ate something."

She nodded.

"You don't need to eat. I guess."

She didn't give him a "no shit" pose, but the picture popped into mind anyway. Sometimes he wished he had given her a little attitude. She was created with her personality whole. None of it had been a conscious gift. Still, there was something to be said for someone as pliant, as willing, as welcoming, as loving as the dancer was.

"I'm not a writer. I can barely write a birthday card." Let her be the waitress's proxy in this. The doll wouldn't know.

She smiled as she helped him undress, motioning to the bed, placed one hand over the other, and cocked her head—a question. He nodded. She crawled into bed.

CHAPTER THREE

THOSE EYES NEVER CLOSED. It was Stephen's fault when deciding against lids. That might have been a mistake. Even shutters would have helped. At least now he could find comfort by choosing to believe she slept. Knowing for certain she never did, that she stayed conscious, watching him snoring beside her, might be too much. When a human woman would sort through her subconscious mind in vivid dreams, the doll was a careful blank. But the true question was something he never let himself think. What was worse, that she didn't dream? Or that she might?

Stephen's eyes opened with a start. The window was open, the air itself still and heavy. His skin stuck to the sheets. She lay facing him, wooden skin bone dry. She had been born a little over a week ago. In a way, she was still not complete. She was still not quite the figure he had fallen in love with. The clothes, the costume, were waiting for her.

He wanted to do something more. Beyond the physical acts. She had to be complete.

She had to be loved.

He kissed her on the forehead. She reached for him, but he

was already up, already going into Emily's room. The hairbrush was on Emily's nightstand, still entwined with strands of crow-black hair. He returned to his bed and beckoned to the dancer. She crawled to him, once again reaching. He gently turned her. There was no doubt—had she wanted to resist, she could have. She turned her slender back to him and waited.

The pins came from her hair easily. It fell around her shoulders, caressing him with a wave of lavender perfume. One hand supported the thick, black mane; the other passed the brush through it, as carefully as possible. Her fingers closed around his knee as she leaned back into him. He was thorough, working the tangles from her hair as the act worked the tangles from his mind.

After a hundred strokes, he refastened her bun and kissed the graceful slope of her neck.

"I have something for you." His touch ran from leg to belly to breast to arm to hand. Her delicate fingers closed over his, softly as a moth's kiss, and she let him lead her to her feet.

"You're going to need to be dressed soon."

No reaction. Not a cocked head, not a dramatic fall. She only followed him through the house. "Before I made you, I had an idea of what you... You need to be dressed a certain way."

This she nodded at. Did she know? Did she see it in her mind? There was no brain, no case. Her head was mahogany, through and through. There was nothing to think thoughts, and yet she seemed to.

He opened the door to what had been Emily's room. He had intended to take the doll here first, but sex and blood had stopped him. Now was the time for her to assume her identity. To become the dancer truly.

The outfit laid waiting on Emily's pink sheets. White tights and ballet wrap skirt, pale pink leotard and pointe shoes. She sat down on the bed and touched the clothes. Looked up at him. Still no question. She picked each up in turn, turning them over in her white hands. Stephen left the room and shut the door. He couldn't see her incomplete. She had to be the dancer in total, or none at all.

He sat in the hall, watching the door. In Emily's room the scrape of cloth on wood. She was taking forever. This was it, to see how perfect he made her, in the image of his ballerina.

That she would be imperfect was terrifying; that she was perfect was worse.

Silence.

The twin shadows of her feet waited just behind the door. Was she afraid, too? Terrified to displease?

The door swung open. She was unsure. Clothes, precisely arranged. The costume, the figure, everything was as he imagined.

He stood. She seemed to flinch for the barest moment. He embraced her with desperate hands and crushed her lips to his. She wrapped him in her wooden arms with the strength of relief.

* * *

A surreal landscape of swirling ribbons and checkerboards, everything shone with more depth than the real world. Twirling at the center, a ballerina in clean pink and white, leotard and wrap skirt, black hair in a tiny bun, face painted as an elegant harlequin. The poster hung over Emily's bed, the one solid thing in the flat room. He stared at the dancer before knowing why, eyes following her subtle curves, making him feel strange the way nothing else had, the knowledge to quantify this still many years off. Instinctual shame hung over him like a thundercloud. Don't look at the dancer when Emily was home. Don't let Mom and Dad catch him. He saw the ballerina at all times, sketching her in notebooks and the margins of textbooks, the drawings more detailed and the lines more confident with each passing year. Some part of him knew even then—she could be rendered better in three dimensions.

It changed one day when he was nearly ten years old.

His mother was downstairs, his father at work. Emily with her chattering friends that made him feel small. It was one of those dry summer days that feel somehow phony, when the sky is brown and low and could be cracked with a hammer. In Emily's room, the windows were shut and the air heavy. His mother moved around the living room downstairs, the television spouting muted vowels. His pants moved again. He had heard of this at school from Brian Baniszewski who had breathlessly described getting one while watching one of those movies they showed late at night, with strange looking women and were dubbed like kung fu movies.

Stephen's eyes caressed the poster, hand snaking downward, clumsy, ashamed. The television continued its droning downstairs. He reached in, felt his penis through the cotton tighty-whities unable to bring himself to reach inside. Each stroke burned with the cloth. He didn't know when to stop, or if such a thing was possible, even as it felt as though he were rubbing himself with sandpaper.

The television went silent. He cocked his head, reaching for his mother with terrified ears. The door remained shut. Then, a creak in the hall. He thanked the house for the warning, rolling clumsily off the bed, trying not to make a sound.

The door let out a warning squeak as it opened; the breath of the house flooding into the once still room. He pressed himself against the frilly comforter, becoming small.

"Stephen?"

His mother. The voice was the cry of an owl, freezing the mouse in place. If she walked in, she'd see. The white tent between his legs screamed his shame. It wouldn't go down.

"Stephen? Are you in here?"

He tried to force thoughts on her. *No, I'm not. I'm anywhere else.*

The door made another sound, maybe opening, maybe closing. Impossible to tell without looking. He tried to be the bed, to fall into it. Tried to be Nightcrawler. Tried to be the Invisible Man.

A minute passed. Then two. Three. Down the hall, at another doorway: "Stephen?"

He zipped up quickly, the damn thing stopping halfway. A second later, it turned into a pinch with fingers made of acid. Red was already spreading over the front of his underpants—like a broken pen. His eyes shuddered, blinked, shed water. He wanted to cry out. Couldn't.

He fought the urge to roll into a ball and tried to stand. It ripped, the tears welling up instantly. His fingers found the zipper, fumbling, gripping, yanking. It's a band-aid. Just a band-aid.

Relief. Dull ache following after. Stumbling through the

door into the bathroom, he looked at the damage only there, in the clean sanctuary of the tiles. It burned. There was blood. Not as much as he thought there would be.

A strange thought: *Not as much as there should be.*

It felt right. No bandage; let it bleed. It would scab over on its own.

The day the poster came down he was thirteen. Emily was too old for ethereal ballerinas, and it was gone one day. He ransacked the trash, through tears and cursing. She was already gone; to see her again, he would have to make her.

It was that day he asked to be taken to an arts and crafts place. His father was reading the trades with the same look of resigned disappointment that had been on his face for years. Charles Monaghan wore rumpled shirts smelling of the medicine cabinet, never bothering with a sport coat.

"Dad?"

Stephen's father looked up over half-glasses—bennies, he called them—taking a minute to recognize the breathless boy. "What is it, Stephen?" Suspicious. Saw the red rings around Stephen's eyes, maybe.

"Can you take me someplace?"

His father tossed the paper aside. "Toy store?"

Stephen shook his head. "I want a model."

Stephen's dad paused. "A model? Like an airplane?"

"Like a person."

"Sure, Stephen."

There were cars, planes, spaceships. There were no ballerinas. Wrong. All wrong. Stephen's father took a battleship from the shelf. "This one?"

Stephen didn't respond. He bought paints, cloth, and a genderless wooden doll. After three weeks of carving, painting, and sewing it didn't look like her—the ballerina trapped inside, demanding release. She was the first, and far from the last.

The Work had a long way to go. He was more than willing to do it.

* * *

Stephen snored beside her. She had a name, but she could not speak it. It was within her, and thus within him as well, but he could not know it. In sleep, Stephen scarcely moved: the occasional turn of his head, chest rising and falling, fingers playing an imaginary tune, and, of course, eyes flickering behind their lids in dream.

There was a time when his sleep was violent.

The dancer rose smoothly, letting him fall away from her. She watched him sleep for an hour before drifting from the room. She was nearly silent through the dark halls, never taking a wrong step. Her head never turned. Her feet barely made a sound.

The doll opened Emily's door.

Moonlight, in silver pools, washed over Emily's childhood. The graceful shape, merely a shadow, moved through the room. She paused, regarding the blank space above the bed, before going to Emily's closet and opening the door. Something drew her attention downward. She sat inside the closet, looking toward the bed for nearly an hour before standing again. Her hands touched Emily's clothes, but when the dancer reached the newest ones, her hand recoiled as if burned. She shut the closet almost roughly.

She went to the few stuffed animals leaning against the pillows. Her hand brushed over them softer than a breeze, before picking one. It was a puppy, and it had a name. Loved to rags, it had been Emily's since she was a baby. It caught her tears over her mother, over Dawn Molinaro. The dancer gently placed the puppy back in its position of honor.

She went to the bookcase next, fingers touching each book before selecting one of the larger ones, read, dog-eared, highlighted and loved. *The Collected Works of Shakespeare*. It was impossible to know if the dancer could read anything, but she opened it and brushed her hands over the pages, stopping at *As You Like It*, one finger caressing the cast list for hours. She held the book until sunrise when she replaced it on the shelf.

She rejoined Stephen in bed and waited for him to awaken.

CHAPTER FOUR

STEPHEN BOOTED UP THE COMPUTER that gathered dust in the living room. Somewhere, the dancer was gliding around the house like a ghost. Some nights she even wandered through the yard, back to the lonely orange tree. She would wait there and watch the sky. Stephen would call to her, and sometimes she would come. Occasionally, she would have to be led.

He pulled up his bank records. The insurance money and the inheritance were doing fine, thanks to Brian's help. Budgeting was still important. The thought of the horrible things the money was needed for nearly made him shut the machine down. The chair would cost next to nothing; merely the time combing antique shops to find the right one. Surgical tubing and needles, an alarm, a gauge and a tank, a freezer, and blood bags. The last nearly made him vomit. Total it up—the money was there and more.

He turned to the sketch he had made at the Nite Lite, staring at it for a long moment. A grin tugged at his lip. He scrawled Siege Perilous over it.

Now all that remained was to build her.

The phone rang. Stephen jerked his head up, stared at it. Insomnia had turned it into a screaming monster for a moment.

"Hello?" Days of disuse covered the greeting in rust.

"You're answering!" Brian said.

"Yeah. What's up?"

"Don't be such a cranky little bitch."

"You called me."

"Party at my place this Saturday."

Stephen sat up straight, squinted first at the darkness, then at her. She was watching him and had approached in total silence.

"What's today?"

Brian laughed. "It's Thursday. Man, you're really into something. You ready to tell me what?"

"Not really."

"Well, whatever it is, just wear something nice."

"Why would I want to do that?"

"Why the hell do you think? Because there's some talent coming."

"Talent?"

"Girls, Steve. There will be girls here."

"Oh."

"Yeah, it's a fuckin' tragedy it's not a sausage fest, I know. Come by like ninish. Late."

"Bye."

Stephen hung up the phone, focused on the ethereal dancer. Her eyes held everything. Not only the room, but the sky, the moon, him. The sight of her dropped hooks in his throat. "I won't bring anyone home."

She watched him.

"I have to go."

He found her, but couldn't hold on.

* * *

It was the true pariah who had no friends at all. Stephen wasn't a true pariah, just a pretender that played the role comfortably. He was strange and smart, but Brian Baniszewski was strange in a different way, managing to hide it far better than Stephen ever could. He never knew why Brian had befriended him but must have seen something in Stephen, something that made him feel safe.

Because Brian had let Stephen in.

On the outside, Brian was what people wanted to see. On the short side through most of high school, the growth spurt that finally kicked in senior year even gave him the height. Good-looking, smart but not too smart, contagious smile—he was the kind of person that others secretly resented for not having a dark side. Not true. He kept it in the dark. Stephen saw that dark side. Stephen saw the toll it took to have an opposite persona. Easier to hide, so when night fell, the transformation wasn't complete.

Still, Brian was there for Stephen in the aftermath of his mother's death. There wasn't another person who could make that claim. When Stephen went to a different junior high, Brian never lost contact. And when Stephen went to college two years early, it was Brian that kept inviting him to parties in the old neighborhood.

Brian went to the east coast for school and that was loneliness. With Brian gone, Stephen had only Emily, who left in turn shortly afterward. Those were long years.

In the summers, Brian would return and they picked it up like it had never been dropped, with Brian occasionally needling

Stephen about doing something—a job, back to school maybe, but Stephen demurred. With the death of Charles Monaghan, that kind of talk died too.

But earlier, when they were still kids, they were united in mutual knowledge.

Brian had a sister, Jessica, three years younger. She took more after their mother. Brian got the black hair, skin a shade darker than white, but that was about it. Jessica's eyes were unmistakably Japanese, and her skin was the color of porcelain under an oil lamp. Her high cheekbones and pixie nose were ivory smooth. Her hair was lighter than her brother's, a lustrous chestnut. She was a little tomboy, always trying to follow Brian around and do what he did.

Stephen worried about her. A girl shouldn't do everything Brian did.

Fatherly advice for Stephen was rare, but he got some at age thirteen. Charles Monaghan was driving Stephen home from Brian's birthday.

"Have fun?" Even at this age, Stephen knew his father asked questions as an attempt to connect that was ultimately futile, wanting a link with the last remnants of Sarah Monaghan. There was no link.

"Brian's sister is a pest. She won't leave us alone, and she whines to his parents whenever we try to leave her behind."

His voice growing deeper, the cadence a little clearer, Stephen's father said, "Always be nice to your friends' sisters. You never know which one is going to grow up to be pretty."

"Not Jessica."

"Just trust me."

Stephen didn't, but there was nothing to be gained by being mean to her. Besides, with the way the others treated her, Stephen could identify with her a little. After that day, Stephen tried to be nice. He didn't tease her like the others, giving her things if she asked, even sharing a secret joke or two. When the time for college came, he forgot about her.

They had to leave her behind, that night. They were nearing fourteen. Stephen was sleeping over at the Baniszewski place. Jessica had wanted to stay with them, but Brian kicked her out. They had their sleeping bags unfurled in the living room of the Baniszewski guesthouse and had finished off the home stretch of a zombie movie marathon. The credits on the last movie were rolling. Stephen was exhausted, but still jittery from all the soda. The beginning of the conversation was already forgotten, but it was Brian bragging about something or other and Stephen said the words that he would later regret.

"I saw Dawn Molinaro naked."

Brian was stunned. After gathering his wits, he said, "No you didn't."

Stephen could back out right there, but he wasn't going to let Brian win this one, not when he'd won all the others. "I did."

"Where?"

"At my house. In my sister's room."

"What was she doing?"

And it was at this point that Stephen realized that he shouldn't have said anything, but taking it back was no longer an option. "Uh... I don't know. Hanging out?"

"Bullshit. You're lying." Brian was clearly baiting him, but it worked.

"It's true. She and my sister were kissing and stuff."

"Stuff? Like fingering each other?"

Stephen nodded. Brian's eyes glittered, reflecting the same in Stephen's.

"You saw your sister, too?"

Now he blushed. "Yeah."

"Oh, God. Emily is so hot. I wish I was you right now. I didn't know she was gay, though."

"She's not. They were just fooling around or whatever."

Brian nodded sagely. In the days before the Internet, this phenomenon wasn't widely known, but Brian thought of himself as worldly. "Yeah, I heard that kind of thing happens. Did they see you?"

"Nope. Saw the whole thing. Never got caught."

"How?"

"I was in the closet."

Brian seemed to think about that. "In the closet. What if you had been like a murderer or something?"

"What?"

"Like what if you had a knife? Like Jason or Michael or something?"

"Jason doesn't use a knife."

"I know, but what if you'd had one? Like, they wouldn't have known you were there. Right? Like you could have killed them but you didn't." Brian trailed off, watching some other place in the room.

"I didn't, though."

"But you could have." Brian thought about it some more. "You think they'll do it again?"

Stephen shrugged.

"I wish I could've seen Emily like that. I don't think my boner would have ever gone down." Another pause, as Brian considered the world splayed out before him. "Who lives near me?"

"What do you mean?"

"From school. Girls."

Stephen thought about it. Rattled off some names.

"Risa Douglass," Brian said, as soon as Stephen named her.

"What about her?"

"A mission, Steve. A secret mission."

* * *

Brian was smart, calling Stephen on Friday and again on Saturday morning to remind him about the party. Stephen's inertia was a known quantity. If allowed, he would rot at home, but rob him of the easy excuse "I forgot" and there would be no choice. The knife wounds had healed, leaving slender scars. He hid them with long sleeves, even though it was August. Long sleeves, jeans, wristwatch with a wide leather band, some silver rings, covering as much skin as possible.

His dancer hadn't understood why he was leaving, and there was no way to explain. She returned to her silent vigil.

He knocked on Brian's door precisely at nine. Never got the hang of fashionable lateness. Chances are it would just be them. Fine by him. Brian was the only one Stephen would be past nodding acquaintance with, and besides, most of that crowd probably thought he was a serial killer.

The door opened. Brian was dressed as a corporate shark—

pressed shirt that shined at angles, and black slacks. Stephen abruptly felt underdressed.

Brian burst out laughing. "I was saying, 'either he's here at nine on the dot or he's not coming and I have to call his dumb ass.'"

Stephen chuckled. "Yeah, I kinda figured."

"Is that Stephen?" The voice was feminine. Familiar, and not. Fuller than anything he could recall.

"Come on in," Brian said.

He stepped in, followed by Stephen, and the owner of the voice moved into view. She had a couple more years on her, but that face could never be forgotten. Jessica Baniszewski. The years sat well on her, or else she lived at a gym. The zits and braces were gone. Her body had filled out, no longer just knees and elbows. She was made up for the evening, accentuating those almond eyes with red and gold, rosebud lips in a similar shade of red. She looked, more than anything else, cool—the kind of person who wouldn't want to talk to Stephen under any circumstances.

She hugged him, washing him in the scent of French honey.

"Stephen! It's been so long!"

"Nine years."

"Yeah. I missed you. What are you drinking?"

"Beer's fine."

"Get him the good stuff," Brian said.

Jessica gave Stephen an adorable look. "You're a beer snob?"

Stephen shrugged. "Compared to your brother, I guess."

She giggled and brought him something with a long Dutch name. That would be the end of it. She'd talk to one of Brian's friends who looked like they modeled sweaters, even if those were the same guys that used to torment her.

Stephen would end up out on the balcony, listening to the traffic. It was fine out there. No one talked to him unless they came out for a cigarette, and usually the words drifted away with the smoke. The heat of the day had burned off, and the night was mild.

Stephen downed the dregs at the bottom of the bottle. There had been three people on the balcony and each one had jumped a little when they saw him sitting there in the dark. Resting in the good chair, he stared at the little candles in the glass holders that had to have been Jessica's idea. The partygoers would come out, light the cigarette, half-turn and jump, touching their hearts to get them started up again. Stephen would smile a little and the other person would make some joke Stephen would immediately forget the details of, instead melding all the jokes into a single über-joke, unfunny and stinging with the single message—you're undesirable because you would rather be out here instead of in there.

The door slid open, closing Stephen's eyes. He considered coughing or something to head the shock off at the pass, but that might just make it worse. Maybe start a conversation, if there was any common ground.

"There you are." Jessica? Eyes opened. Jessica. She slid the door shut and plopped herself in the chair next to him, the one he usually sat in. "I was looking for you, but you vanished."

"Yeah. I don't really know what to say at these things."

"Me either."

"I'd think you were over that."

"Doesn't matter what I say. My brother's friends only talk to my tits."

"At least they talk to part of you. They sort of talk around me."

"Some of them think you're retarded."

Stephen smiled and picked at the label on the beer. "I do, too."

She giggled. "What does that mean?"

"I don't know. It sounded profound in my head."

"You *are* retarded." Her smile died on her lips. "I'd rather be with you. Brian's friends creep me right the fuck out."

"Why so?"

"Nothing specific." A lie, clear as day on her face. She smiled, embarrassed and distracted and said, "You want another one?"

He didn't have to think. "Yeah."

"I'll be right back." She was halfway through the door when she said, "I'm not going to have to track you down again, am I?"

"I'll be sitting right here."

"If you aren't, I'll kick your ass."

"I'll go ahead and ignore the paradox in that statement."

She laughed and shook her head. "Promise you won't talk like Spock when I get back."

She was gone before he could promise anything, leaving him with time enough to come up with the perfect response to it. Something to make her laugh again. All he could think of was the smell of French honey.

She came back in a couple minutes with two beers. "I see the threat worked."

"You terrify me."

She sat down and looked out over the balcony. They listened

to the murmur of the people on the street below mixing with the conversation inside. "I can see why you like it out here."

"Yeah. I wish Brian kept saner hours. It's much more pleasant out here after the sun goes down."

"Saner hours?" she said. "Brian told me you sleep all day and work all night."

"That's not entirely true. I don't sleep every day."

"Then I take it all back."

He took a pull on the beer. "So what are you doing out here talking to me?"

"I'm the white rabbit."

He frowned. Decided against asking for clarification. The moment was too delicate; no need to start throwing conversational bricks around.

"You know, my brother is in there talking you up to any woman who'll listen."

"He's been known to do that."

"You might want to get in there. He's laying the ground work and everything."

"I don't know. Have you talked to any of those girls?"

"Dingbats," she said. He liked the archaic sound of it. She might have heard her father or even grandfather say it.

"I know, right?"

"It's not like you're going to find someone you connect with here. You're a genius, after all."

He watched his feet, fighting the glow. "I don't know about that."

"Well, you can tie your own shoes. So you're already ahead of them."

"I can and do."

"Me too."

He grinned at his beer. "The balcony is hereby reserved for shoe-tiers."

"Good call." She watched the traffic.

"Besides, I'm sort of seeing someone." It was out before he could stop it. The dancer was someone, after all, and the beer loosened the words.

"Oh?" Jessica coughed.

"Yeah." Some damage. Someone knew she existed, at least in concept. Track her, find her, she could be in danger. Stephen could be in danger. "It's nothing serious."

"Just physical, huh?" She tried to make it light, but it didn't sound like much of a joke.

"She's a dancer."

"What, like a stripper?"

Blushing: "No, ballet."

"You're fucking a ballerina?" Now that sounded like a joke.

"Jesus, Jessica!"

"Well, you are, aren't you?"

"Look, you're still Brian's little sister. I remember you with that bald Barbie, the one whose head you shaved and painted."

"That was all of them."

"Well, I still remember it."

"What's your point?" She was cheerfully belligerent.

"Sometimes I still think of you as a little girl."

"You probably intended that to sound sweet, but it just sounds creepy."

"In my defense, I am creepy."

She giggled. "That what your little ballerina thinks of you?"

"Probably. I don't know. Look, it's not serious, but don't tell anyone, okay?"

"She can't be ugly. What is she, like a religious freak?"

Stephen saw the lie right there and grabbed it. "Yeah, she's a total Scientologist. That's why it's not going to work."

"That and the eating disorder."

"What?"

"You think they stay that way naturally? Look at her teeth and index finger. Probably all yellow and fucked up. My freshman year roommate was bulimic. She didn't think of it as an eating disorder. She called it being 'pro-mia.' Called it a lifestyle choice."

"That's seriously fucked up."

"I know, right? Well, I'm glad you're getting some, even if it is from a bulimic clam. Brian's always going on about how you need a woman, but you couldn't get laid in a women's prison with sixty pounds of Ben and Jerry's and a skeleton key."

"He says all that?"

"He was extremely specific."

"Seriously, though, don't tell your brother. I'll never hear the end of it."

"Cross my heart." Her posture was weird. She was sprawled on her chair, looking for somewhere to lean, with nothing volunteering. Finally, "Give me your number."

"You're going to call me?"

"Your little ballerina can be jealous if she wants."

She produced her phone. "What's your number?" He gave it to her. "Cool," she said, and let in the night with him.

* * *

The sound of crying melded with the dream he had been having, forgotten as soon as he awoke. For a moment, there was disorientation. The dancer slept on his chest. She was breathing softly and smelled wrong—good, but wrong. He was cold except where their bodies made one. A tiny patch over his heart was soft and wet and nearly frozen.

The crying got louder. Stephen wasn't at home.

A sharp inhale—not the dancer. Jessica, waking up. She wiped her mouth, noticing the small patch of drool she had left on him, embarrassed. A headache pounded in at him. He was rock hard; Jessica's hip was against it. She had to notice.

He remembered the endless drinks with Jessica, her persuading him not to drive home, him settling in on the couch. She must have joined him. There was no memory of that part.

Brian's bedroom door burst open. Stephen recognized the girl from the party, another of Brian's tiny brunettes. She was sobbing, her makeup running in thick tears, clutching some of her clothing to her body. Even in the dim light, the angry stripes across her arms screaming.

"You asshole!"

"Alex, come on. You said okay."

"Fuck you! Fuck you, you fucking asshole!"

And she was out the door, the muffled sobbing still cutting through Stephen's headache. Jessica stared down at the patch of wetness on Stephen's shirt. Brian had already forgotten the crying girl and was glaring at Jessica.

They all had questions. Stephen was afraid the answer to his was already known. None of them had the courage to actually voice them. "I should probably be going."

Brian said, "Yeah, probably."

"I'll catch you guys later. It was nice seeing you, Jess."

She nodded wordlessly and Stephen was left to fear, regret, and the doll.

* * *

He pulled into the gravel driveway well after four in the morning. A ghostly white shape glided through the garden amongst the stone cherubs. Her movements were not quite human, somewhere between the ballerina of her inspiration and religious reverence. She did not seem to notice him, going to each of the stone statues in graceful turn and giving them a delicate bow.

He stopped at the edge of the maze. Her alien attention turned and she moved to him, holding him close, her body finding the same contours Jessica had, although this time they didn't fit.

The erection that vanished with Brian's guest returned. As lovely as the dancer was, Stephen had to struggle to hold on to the guilt of his time with Jessica. He brushed the doll's inquisitive hands away.

"No. Goddamn it."

She watched him with her unblinking eyes.

"I told someone about you."

Maybe there was a flicker in her eyes. Maybe it was wishful thinking.

"She asked me and I lied and said you were a bulimic Scientologist. It was all I could think of because I sure as fuck

THE DOLLMAKER // 51

couldn't tell the truth about us. About me, fucking a goddamn doll every night."

She never blinked.

"Goddamn it! Yell at me! Be mad! Be something! Anything!"

She didn't react. He left her there, in the dark.

That night, he awoke briefly from sleep and found her standing over the bed, gazing down. His eyes closed as sleep returned.

CHAPTER FIVE

BLAME THE SEARCH FOR THE NEW. Blame innovation. Blame the promise of the unknown. The list ran upwards to a hundred items. Anything to keep from the obvious conclusion: blame his cock. Blame four million years of evolution. Blame him for being an asshole. Those truths were obvious and he even let himself think them in fleeting moments while lost in the doll's silent eyes.

The next one would talk. Gears in the throat, some vinyl in the mouth, refillable salivary glands, yes, the next one would talk. His dancer's eyes never left him, ice clear. She knew his thoughts. She had to, even as she drifted away, off to their room. She would lay there, a discarded toy. It was horrible to see her like that. He would fetch the hairbrush and her joints would resolve themselves into a woman.

This one would be different. He knew that much, though not how much of the ballerina's life was due to the fact her body was once alive on its own. Something different, certainly, but alive. Perhaps the life of the trees was the root of her strange consciousness. Maybe the next one would be more inviting, more transparent. More human.

She could scarcely be less.

The original golems were always clay. The symbolism was simple: the Bible said man was created from clay, so any parody of that action would use the same. It presented some interesting ideas. Raw clay wouldn't do—it was graceless, ugly.

Porcelain. Little porcelain dolls were always so exquisite, so precious. And fragile. She couldn't be prone to shatter. Looking into it, he found a handy little link at the bottom of the webpage— "dental porcelain."

Perfect. Almost. First, it was semi-translucent, like bone. A simple change in the consistency of the dentine should be enough. Worse, dental porcelain needed to be anchored for extra strength: gold, zirconia, aluminum oxide. There had to be a better way. The powder arrived in the mail a week later, and he began his research in the attic. Add, change, make something different and better. His dancer sat still on a box, only moving her neck at intervals, to stare at him or out the window.

He knew her face before beginning. The dancer was artistic; lines remembered from youth. She was welcoming, not soft, but forgiving. Not so this one. Cruel, beautiful, distant. Paul Mitchell. Nagle. White, black, blue. Icy. Hard. Razor sharp. Familiar somehow.

He pictured her, made from teeth.

She would bite.

* * *

It began with the poster and solidified with the Marquis d'Aisecq. It wasn't a famous name. There was barely a mention of him in the history books, except perhaps in the tally of

Robespierre's dead. The Aisecq family had been on the banks of the Seine since the Gauls, and d'Aisecq was the last of them, tried and convicted for the crime of aristocracy. From Gallic barbarian to old aristocracy; from fur-clad warrior to powdered androgyne. D'Aisecq was far from divorced from society, but even friends called him eccentric, called him recluse. Enemies called him other things—sorcerer, alchemist, devil-worshiper.

He was one of the first put to the guillotine. After killing those nearest at hand, the rebels stormed d'Aisecq's manor. The stories started earlier. Sift through the names of the usual suspects: Cagliostro, the Comte de Saint-Germain, Adam Weishaupt, try to find the truth.

The most famous story concerned d'Aisecq's bet with Madame Theillac.

She was one of d'Aisecq's only friends capable of luring him from the manor house in the French countryside. She did it with an invitation and challenge. Casanova had once again seduced a woman of surpassing beauty, some virginal daughter or another and would be showing her off like a prize mare at one of the few parties d'Aisecq could be lured to. Theillac had commented to d'Aisecq, her dear friend, that none other than Casanova could have gotten such a beauty, but d'Aisecq claimed she was a trifle and told Theillac he could find a woman to put Casanova's to shame. Theillac gave him a month.

The next month at another garden party, d'Aisecq arrived with a woman of such beauty she nearly killed several men outright. No one had ever seen her, and d'Aisecq claimed she was Bohemian, giving Theillac the impression this was an arcane joke. Though d'Aisecq appeared to walk with a new limp, he had never been happier. More than mere seduction, the woman appeared to love him, and a month later they were married. According to the stories, she never spoke. In her eyes was everything.

They were only together for a short time. The Revolution killed d'Aisecq. There were stories of the murder of the Marquise. They said it took eight men to subdue her, and when the mob threw her on the fire, she did not burn immediately. They said she merely lay there, silently weeping for her husband. Only after several long minutes did her skin start to blacken, split, crumble. They say she turned to dust on the pyre, never once trying to escape.

A creation for him and him alone.

Stephen saw the secret right in front of him. What remained were methods.

Any normal sources for books on d'Aisecq had been leeched dry. Every public library, every major bookstore, Stephen was left to scour every independent place in L.A., and soon, beyond. He spent what he could, and often more. Money disappeared from his father's wallet. Fortunately, by then Charles Monaghan was too far gone to talk to anyone.

Stephen found the other stories. The methods were never complete in any text. It was like piecing together an interstate when only the rest stops remained. Stephen had to fill in the gaps. The symbology was the skeletal diagram, hidden in the same legends d'Aisecq had known. If d'Aisecq had done it, Stephen could as well. Create a life; birth a child.

A daughter.

The word was there, but it took the journal of an Ashkenazi Jew to speak it. Golem.

The legend was in the Talmud, repeated with Judah Loew ben Bezalel. The legend talked about the birth of the creature, echoing the creation of Adam in Genesis 2:6. Adam was formed of dust, given breath by God. From God to man to golem, each form drifting further from perfection. Man was not exactly God.

Stephen had trouble with the idea of dust. Dust was never alive in the literal sense. The symbolic logic of all of it did not make sense. There was something alive.

Wood.

Her flesh decided upon, he started to draw the doll.

He started with a genderless entity. Soon she took control of the lines. They became lithe. The body went from grotesque to graceful. The drawing was sure—she wanted to be born.

He drew the ethereal girl from the poster. The ballerina.

He took her apart, drew each section in exhaustive detail. He bought art books, found pictures of prima ballerinas. Every muscle had to be right, every bone thrusting beneath her smooth skin had to be accounted for. The clothing, precise as well— leotards, wrap skirt, and pointe shoes.

He stopped, looking at the sketches, enough for a book.

The curtains of his dorm room in the Fishbowl of South Dorm at Harvey Mudd were drawn and the room stank of old sweat and wheat germ. Stephen barely noticed odor or the roommate that came and went, puttering off to one useless class or another.

A lot of freshmen got nicknames—"something frosh"— such as Random Information Frosh or ZZ Frosh, describing an easily identified trait or quirk of appearance. Stephen's was the Unafrosh, hardly used outside of the few upperclassmen in

South that knew of the quiet freshman with the unsettling stare.

He had no friends at school, apart from Emily across the street at Scripps, four years older and only two years ahead. She tried to get him to parties, but there was too much Work to do.

He majored in chemistry with a concentration in sculpture. Mudd was the one technical school where a focus in the arts was possible. Humanities, shortened to "hums" by the students, were required. The Claremont Colleges were liberal arts schools after all, and Mudd had to fit in. Most of the students regarded their hums as dodges, as wastes of time. Not Stephen. From the first art classes at Pitzer and Scripps, he was home. Life drawing gave him the skills to reliably draw the human form. Sculpture was where he truly shone.

While the other students tried their hand at clumsy pots, Stephen attempted to mimic the human body. There were no models in sculpture, so he made do. Working the clay with his right hand while staring at the muddy left, or else watching another student and trying to capture the secret curve of her neck.

The one knock against his work was always the same: there was no interpretation. Stephen was trying to recapture something in the inanimate, placing no judgments upon it, giving it no scenarios to exist within. The clay took a singular form to express nothing more than a looming perfection.

At night, he tossed and turned so much his roommate, the one whose name Stephen never bothered to remember, took to throwing shoes. Stephen woke up more than once with a flash of white and a stinking size ten. He could never get back to sleep, and so went down to the common area to work.

He was alone until junior year, back from a semester abroad in Paris, armed with new knowledge. The end of his loneliness was not intentional. He did nothing to stop it. Christine was not a new face. An art major, rather than a mere concentration. Stephen never knew when she noticed him but pinpointed the moment when she became more than mere background noise—the back of her neck, dusted with downy hair, a paint-covered hand brushing a strand away.

He never considered a type. Brian had one, liking them small, with dark hair and eyes. Brian's girlfriends looked faintly frail to Stephen. Unsurprising. He knew what Brian really looked for.

In a way, Stephen did have a type. She did not yet exist.

Christine first talked to Stephen the second week of their ceramics class. Stephen was lost in clay, not wanting to use the wheel to make a pot. Not when there was figure lost within the gray.

Always the same one.

"Hey. You were in my Intermediate Sculpture class, right?"

Stephen blinked, tried to focus on the middle distance. She was pretty, even with the mass of hair barely pinned over her head. Her features were a bit too large for her face, conferring a pleasantly cartoonish look.

He remembered that hand, brushing her dirty blonde hair away from her neck. "Yeah, I think so."

"So you were in my Beginning Sculpture class, too."

He didn't remember her from there, but it stood to reason. "Probably."

"Art major?"

He nodded. "Concentration, actually. I'm a chemist." At

Mudd, they didn't say chem major or math major, it was chemist, mathematician: an element of seriousness, the premature adulthood they had been forced into as soon as their first grade teacher noticed their intelligence.

"You're a Mudder?" she said in disbelief.

"Yeah. Is that weird?"

"No, no, of course not. I figured Pomona or something."

"What about you?"

"Scrippsie," she said.

She had the look—too preppy to be one of the Pitzer hipsters, not quite tightly wound enough for Pomona, and, since she was a woman, not a Mudder.

He almost turned back to the clay, the conversation complete. "I'm Chris," she said.

"Stephen." He offered a hand, realized it was caked white with clay and took it back. "Sorry."

"No, no, it's okay. I thought we should meet. You know, in case one of us misses a class, we can get reading assignments. Same major. Or, um, concentration." It made sense.

They exchanged email addresses. Christine returned to her seat with the scrap of paper, and Stephen thought he saw her grin on the way back to her seat. She was gone, but the figure within the clay was not. Far more important than any living girl.

The next class she sat next to him.

The one after, they talked.

"Your final project in sculpture was amazing. I hadn't seen anything like it."

A female figure, caught in the same pose as she always was, twirling to her imaginary symphony. Only one thought came to mind. "She didn't move."

"She looked like she was. I'd never seen anyone capture a subject in motion so well."

"It's not a matter of catching her as she is, but what she was going to do." He shrugged. "It makes sense in my head."

"No, no. It makes sense to me, too." She looked down at the clay in front of him. It had started to take shape. "Do you use models?"

He jumped. "What?"

"Models. You're always sculpting women. I figured you worked off something."

"Just my memory."

Chris—Christine Barrow, as it turned out—was the only one allowed anywhere close to him, in the single room both lab and cell. Emily had graduated the year before, so he only spoke to her on the weekends she came out to party and sleep on the floor. People buzzed outside, in the halls and across the quad, never seeking out the silent sleepless man. Chris had broken a rule there, the first to see Stephen's lonely room.

Not Spartan, but everything in the clutter had a purpose. The computer. The tools. The drawings. Emily's sleeping bag. Unlike every other room, no posters decorated the walls, instead crowded with drawings in a hand made steady by constant work. She was echoed in whole and in pieces everywhere. The Work was disguised, her form obscured, the symbols and the old alphabets hidden in gibberish. Other images: d'Aisecq and his Marquise; the Golem and Judah Loew ben Bezalel; the drawings of the half-things thumping madly in that room in Paris; and one hidden amongst the others—the one of Christine Barrow.

Chris had broken the rule of isolation on a Friday evening after dinner. Stephen had locked up, ready for a long night of Work. As he opened a notebook already filled with formulae and sketches, trying to design the joint of the elbow, one that would not be visible from the other side, a sudden knock rapped the door.

He checked the peephole. Chris. The door opened on its own, though his hand was on the knob.

"Hi, Steve."

"Chris? How did you know where I lived?"

She blanched. "I called the Dean of Students Office. I told them I was your sister."

"How did you know I had a sister?"

"I didn't."

"Oh." The room was a mess. The bed, torn apart by restless sleep; the desk, covered in papers. D'Aisecq's diary was on the bookshelf, a leather spine amongst the drab schoolbooks. "Come in."

As she did, a plastic bag crinkled beside her. She looked around for a place to sit and settled on the bed. At a loss, he sat down behind the desk, with no idea what to say to this girl. Did she recognize what was on the walls as she gazed up at them? Could she trace the outline of his mind?

She might have been reading it, as her eyes followed the path of the figures to the tools smelling of split wood.

He said, "What's in the bag?"

Once again, self-conscious, something that made Stephen accept her presence. She reached in and brought out a couple bottles of candy-colored liquid. "Boone's."

"What are you doing here?"

She shrugged. "I don't know. I thought you could use some company. I thought I'd come over."

"I don't have glasses." It was the closest he was going to come to asking her to stay and the smile said she knew.

"It's okay. Pick one. You just drink right out of the bottle."

He took the orange one and she the blue. For a reason he couldn't name, her happiness was important. The orange drink tasted like flat soda.

"What were you up to?" she said after taking a swig of the blue one.

"Homework."

"I don't know how you Mudders do it. The workload must be crushing."

"It's not so bad."

"But here you are on a Friday night, doing homework."

The drink made him say what immediately leapt to mind. "Not anymore."

She smiled again, openly this time.

Halfway through the bottles, she handed hers over. "Now we trade." The room was heaving already, so he surrendered the orange without conversation. The ghost of her lips waited on the mouth of the bottle—no artificial fruit, only flesh, meaty and alive.

"I like your décor. What do they mean? The symbols."

He moved closer, picking and choosing which to point at. They flicked away as he hunted them with numbed fingers. "Alchemy. The forerunner to chemistry. More of an art than a science, but that's why it can't be duplicated. Doesn't fit the central definition of science then, right?"

"That's like lead into gold?"

"That was one of the big goals, yeah. Not entirely insane anymore. There are other ideals. And, of course, there's how much of it you consider to be metaphorical. I'm not good with metaphor, though."

She laughed. "Yeah. You're good with technique and form, though."

"You sound like Professor Bodine."

"If the shoe fits. Where were you last semester? I didn't see you in any of my classes."

"France."

"Wow. Study abroad?"

He nodded, wanting to tell her of the things he did there, how much closer he had gotten. The surface of d'Aisecq's diaries had scarcely been cracked. The secrets were there, crouched and waiting.

"You speak French?"

"Of course," he said, realizing too late how arrogant that sounded. He taught himself the languages of the Work: French, Greek, Latin, and Hebrew. Without those tongues, the dancer would never be born. "I'm better at reading it than speaking it."

"I've always wanted to go to Paris," she said and laughed. "God, I'm such a cliché."

"I actually went. That has to be worse."

She shifted, subtly making more room on the bed. He flopped down next to her, not realizing he'd done it until he was close enough to smell sweat, skin, soap, shampoo, clay, and something underneath he had only smelled once before—

in Emily's room. Chris's breath caught. The moment hung in the air and the cheap booze made him seize it. They bridged the meager distance between them and their mouths met. Her tongue forced its way in, mixing the two flavors into something at once phony and real. His body responded, mind locked. She shifted, getting closer. He touched her jaw, feeling it working against his.

She tasted like raw meat. His stomach turned, but he didn't retreat in revulsion. Something craved the blood taste. Something else hated that craving.

The knock stopped it cold.

He blinked. Her mouth pursued, still caught in the moment he had been pulled from. The knock at the door sounded again too insistent to be ignored.

Nor could the erection tenting his pants be ignored. Chris would see it. Unavoidable.

"Who is that?" she asked, still breathless.

"I..." Nothing else came from a throat suddenly fear-dry. Partially doubled over, he stumbled to the door, hoping she wouldn't see his shame. He pulled the door open, shielding himself from Chris and the new arrival.

Emily looked him up and down and grimaced. "Oh Jesus, you weren't jacking off, were you?"

"Emily?"

"Well, zip up. I have to use your bathroom before the party." She shouldered past, stopping dead at the sight of the room. Stephen mentally flicked through the channels, the freeze frames. The bottles. The girl.

He turned. "Emily, this is Chris."

Chris got up, smoothing her dress, limbs tight, expression hard. "Hi."

"I'm his sister," Emily said.

The realization looked beautiful on Chris's outsized features—relief, amusement. She shook Emily's hand almost roughly. "It's nice to meet you."

"Yeah, likewise. I didn't think my brother would have guests. I... uh... I crash here sometimes." She nodded to the sleeping bag rolled up by the bed.

"Oh."

"I can find someplace else."

"No, no. I wasn't going to stay the night."

Stephen felt like an idiot when that disappointed him.

Emily went on, "It's not a problem. I mean, I don't usually come back till late. Stephen loans me his key. Look, I'll be out of your hair in a second." She disappeared into the bathroom.

Stephen sat down across from the bed. The spell was broken. Chris regarded him, her brown eyes impossibly large. Finally, Stephen said, "Are you leaving now?"

She shook her head.

He hid the smile fighting its way out.

When Emily left, they settled back down. Stephen turned out the overhead light, using an old trick from his youth: turning the reading lamp toward the wall and clicking it on. Almost candlelight, with a single shining sun. There was talking. Kissing. Whispers. She left a few hours later, leaving him staring at the ceiling, the once proud erection diminishing into a mass of raw tissue. He awoke once, only briefly, when Emily staggered into the room, asleep again before her sleeping bag was entirely unfurled.

* * *

The phone call was roughly a week after Brian's party. The voice on the other end said, "You free?"

"What?" It took Stephen a second to recognize the voice. Brian. Of course. Who else would it be?

"Are you free?" Brian said again.

"Why?" There were options, and Stephen didn't like them.

"Because you need to get out more."

"What's tonight?"

"Does it matter?"

"For you. Work or whatever."

"Why don't you let me worry about that? Get some clothes on. I'll be there in fifteen."

Stephen stared at the phone, blinking, mute incomprehension. The formulas scrawled over the butcher paper were mere letters, numbers. A hopeless jumble.

He looked down. Naked. Couldn't remember the last time he'd been dressed. His penis still chafed, but not quite abraded. Meant sex maybe twelve hours before. So it was five. On what day?

He stood, stretched, the pain a screwdriver grinding through his lower back. Down from the attic and into the bedroom, stumbling on numbed legs. Clothes went on in blind layers. Then, a realization.

Her.

Couldn't have Brian seeing her. That was not a conversation Stephen wanted, or even could have.

She was at Emily's window, the one overlooking the driveway, looking down fixedly. She didn't turn around when Stephen entered. Brian could look up and see the ballerina staring right back at him. Brian had seen the poster, how dimmed by time the memory was something else entirely. Another chance Stephen could not take.

"I need you to get away from the window."

She didn't move.

"Please."

Nothing.

He moved up next to her, followed her gaze to a bird's nest perched on Emily's windowsill. The eggs were mottled brown and tiny. They looked phony.

"I need you to get away from the window for now."

Nothing.

He drew the shades shut.

Her head bowed.

"I'll be back soon."

He walked down to the foyer. A minute later Brian's car crunched up the driveway. Stephen was out the door and locking it before Brian could invite himself in.

"Jeez, Steve, were you waiting by the door?"

"Just good timing, I guess."

Stephen glanced up at the house as Brian drove away. She had opened the curtains to stare at the nest.

The sullen sun had turned red. "Where are we going?"

"It's a place called Lulu's Petals. You'll love it."

"Bit past your bedtime, isn't it?" Stephen said.

"A couple vodka and Red Bulls and my bedtime is sometime next week."

From Pasadena, it was west, into the towers of downtown, the part of Los Angeles built when they thought it was going to look like any other city, before it spread across the desert as glass and steel kudzu. Brian often said that he liked downtown—the urban decay, the Mexican bars turned hipster hangouts, the weird swap meets only a year away from becoming Thunderdome, the supposedly secret clubs marked by a long line of well-dressed white people in a dingy alley. This was one of those. The converted warehouse didn't even have a sign. A bored man waved them into a crumbling garage.

On the walk to the line, Brian said. "I should have told you to wear something more presentable."

Stephen looked along the line. There were people dressed like Brian—the corporate fratboy with the pressed slacks, the vivid shirt, everything shined from head to toe—cologne in human form. Some like Stephen wore multiple shirts and lived-in jeans, battered sneakers, rings, and wristbands. Others were dressed in suits and tails, with girls in shapeless dresses with pearls—he'd read enough Lovecraft to recognize the look of a flapper.

The bouncer didn't fit the image with his neck as thick as a leg, body wrapped in a black shirt ready to explode off him, Hulk-style. He had an earpiece, a shiny head, and a numb expression. "IDs."

Stephen obeyed. "Stephen Monaghan." The bouncer pronounced the G. Stephen didn't bother to correct him.

He took Brian's. "Brian Banizooski."

"Ban-ih-SHEF-skee. It's Polish."

"Yeah, no shit." The bouncer waved them in.

Lulu's Petals lit in sepias, with furniture lurking in corners like obese stalkers. The decor was 1985's version of the 1920s. Stages, maybe six feet in diameter, were scattered throughout with a larger main stage pushed against a wall. The floors lit up. Poles ran through them. Performing on the stages, the word "stripper" came to mind, though they wouldn't tolerate being called that. After all, it wasn't like they took off clothes. These were lush women, muscled certainly, but many were ten pounds over what would be considered their ideal. They wore lace, garters, stockings, high heels, rings, thin gold chains around waists or ankles, necklaces, panties. They all had the same haircut: a raven black bob, parenthesis for their cheeks, casting kohl-rimmed eyes into subclause. Their lips were red and bee stung. Their skin was porcelain.

Porcelain.

"Stephen!"

"Huh?" Stephen tried to refocus on Brian. The other man was grinning ear to ear.

"You're not supposed to stare."

"Then what the hell are they dressed like that for?"

"That's the whole thing. They're there. The women can stare if they want, call 'em fat, or hate 'em for getting the attention. But we can't look. We have to watch out of the corners of our eyes. See, if you're staring, you get pegged as a perv, and you're going to bed dry."

"Wait, what?"

"You know what I mean or you're a bigger head case than I thought. What are you drinking?"

"Hurricane."

Brian turned to the bartender—could have been the bouncer's

brother—and ordered, "Hurricane and a vodka and Red Bull." Brian handed over two cards. That was the nice thing with Brian—drinks were always on him. Finally, after giving Stephen the same look he was giving the dancers, he said, "You and my sister looked awful close last week."

"Yeah, I guess we passed out."

"She said it was good to see you."

"It's weird to see her all grown up."

"She said you gave her your phone number."

"She asked for it."

Brian was going to say something else when the drinks showed up and then laughed at the bright orange thing in front of Stephen.

"I don't know if I'd have bought that if I knew it looked like a gay tiki party."

Stephen watched the dancer behind him gyrate in the ice cubes.

"She's not all grown up," Brian said.

"What?"

"Jess. She's still young."

"Isn't she like twenty-six?"

"That's young."

His first thought was the simple. *Compared to what?* It was too combative, so a deep swallow of the hurricane bought some time. The juice hid the alcohol entirely. "What are you trying to tell me?" Stephen said.

"Nothing. Just, you know, she's young. Inexperienced."

Stephen frowned, wanting to change the subject. "Why do they call it Lulu's Petals?" The question had been bouncing around his brain since Brian had said it. It sounded familiar, but Stephen couldn't place it.

"It's named after an old movie star, I think."

Stephen watched the girl's hair in the ice. It was so sleek, powerful.

"Hey, bro!" New voice. L.A. accent, nearly stereotypical. Stephen blinked, saw a rumpled Asian guy in a fauxhawk already slapping palms with Brian. Brian's look was unreadable. Not happy exactly, but not mad, something in between, trying to hide one or the other and showing both.

"Tyler. Hey, I'm out with my bud."

Tyler turned to Stephen and stuck out a hand. Instead of a shake, a grab Stephen thought of as Roman, even though it wasn't accurate. "Hey, nice to meet you."

"Stephen," Stephen said.

"Oh yeah, I remember you at the party. You hid out on the balcony."

Stephen tried to see something familiar in Tyler's face, maybe laughing in the living room. It was impossible to tell if this was a real memory or something his subconscious invented to make him feel better. "Yeah, that was me."

"What are you guys doing out here?" Tyler said.

Brian shrugged. "The usual. You?"

"Usual, too." An edge cut through it. When Brian said it, it was vague; it meant "none of your business." When Tyler said it, it said "you know the usual and it's important."

"Probably should get to it."

Tyler grinned. "Unless you know a game."

Brian shook his head. "Sorry, man. Not my thing."

"Yeah, I know. Nice meeting you," he said, before disappearing back into the crowd.

"Fucking Tyler," Brian said.

Stephen's hands and feet tingled through the hurricane; the rums were flooding his bloodstream on a comet of 151. Stephen's eyes found Tyler circulating the room. The guy looked at the dancers, ignoring the real women, talking to the men, and then only the ones dressed like Brian.

He was doing the usual.

Brian didn't talk about anything interesting, never mentioning Jessica again and never mentioning the woman that ran from the apartment. He pointed out the other girls in the bar after catching them looking, asking Stephen what he wanted. The answers were simple, branching into questions. Say the truth: I built a daughter to fuck and she won't be the last. And when there's a new one, I'm going to leave the first in different places and forget her for a time and find her as warm and as wet as when I left her.

Stephen thought each of these things, colored, pushed them from mind, retreating to the safety of the dancers. There was no touching them.

Brian drove him home in silence, broke it only as they passed the Nite Lite. Stephen was looking in the lit windows, the only thing that looked inviting. The wind ripped the trees around like children. "That was fun, right? Maybe next time I'll get you to talk to someone."

"Sure, yeah. Next time."

"I'm gonna hold you to that."

"I know."

She was a ghost in the window as they arrived. Stephen's stomach lurched. Brian never looked up.

* * *

The nametag said AUDRA, bouncing on one breast as she approached Stephen's table at the Nite Lite with a neutral expression. It was a hell of a name, the kind of name to inspire mediocre poets. If she remembered him, she was faking it and hoping he didn't remember her, carrying the problems of the invisible.

"Can I get you something to drink? Coffee?" Rehearsed.

"Iced tea."

"I'll be right back with that."

She was wearing different jeans this time. These were black, or probably sold as black, but they were more of a charcoal and pre-broken in. They cupped her full cheeks perfectly.

She walked behind the counter. The Siege Perilous sketch stared at him from the page of the journal, reminding him of the last time he talked to her. To Audra, that name again, pleasing and round. The formula came out of him in a single spurt. It looked like math, and really it was. When one got right down to it, biology was really just chemistry which was really just physics which was really just math. The art came in making it go the other way.

"Okay, so, it's not a novel." She put the iced tea down. "I'm sorry, I could see you were writing equations or something."

She remembered him.

"Uh... yeah."

"You're a little old for homework, aren't you?"

"I'm a chemist."

"What does that mean? Like a British pharmacist or you operate a meth lab?"

"Neither. I'm making dental porcelain. A new kind that doesn't exist yet."

"Seriously?"

He turned the journal to face her. The equations were all there, all the elements in place. A chemist could read them and see what they made. Still not perfect, though the bones were there. Her bones. "See?"

"What's the chair for?"

He felt the heat rising and pulled the journal back. "A doodle."

"Yeah, I do that too." She knew it was more. She had to. She was gracious and didn't press. "Uh... patty melt, right?"

"Tuna melt."

"I knew it was in the melt family. Let me put that in for you."

Did she mean the innuendo? She couldn't have. It was just something waitresses said. High school entendre meant was clumsy fishing for extra tips. Not an invitation. Even if it was, she was a living and breathing woman. She would taste of meat and foulness. He was back at home, ballerina's hand on his cock, guiding it into her body, glassy eyes fixed on him, mouth parted. Perfect.

"More tea?"

Stephen jumped, painfully hard from the fantasy. Hoped she didn't notice. "Um... yeah."

"Why dental porcelain?"

"How do you mean?"

She was actually standing close enough for Stephen to smell her.

"When someone's doing something weird, it's usually because they have some kind of redemption angle to the whole thing. You know, how Batman is trying to atone for the deaths of his parents."

"You read comics?"

Now she looked a little embarrassed. Stephen wasn't sure how, but he had somehow gained the upper hand in conversation with a woman. "Yeah."

He had no idea what to do with it. "That's cool. Is that what you do?"

"What do you mean?"

"As like, your real job."

Hardness in her face. "This is real enough."

"No, I mean when you're not waitressing. This is a day job. You know what I mean."

"I don't think I do." The challenge.

"I'm sorry. My mistake."

"Yeah." Pause, drawn out too far. "Your sandwich has to be ready right now. I'll be right back."

Stephen wanted to squirm. He'd fucked it up past repair.

He almost wanted to tell her not to go, apologize maybe, but that would have been stupid. Another apology would be trying to put out a tire fire: it was burning and would continue to do so until it was ready to go.

A plate slid in front of him. White-gray tuna between yellow cheese and golden bread. The bottle of ketchup followed. It was one of the old glass bottles. The Nite Lite didn't believe in those new plastic ones. Stephen hated those. They were always half empty and sprat the ketchup in shotgun sprays. "Anything else?" Cold. Distant. The voice of a stranger now.

For you to sit down and keep talking to me? "No, I'm fine."

She walked back to the kitchen. Stephen, powerless to say anything, ate and thought about everything he ever said to her. He was mopping up the last of the ketchup when she put the receipt on the table. Unable to look at her, he instead fished for money.

He peeled off a couple bills, tipping her way too much and walked out before she could fix him with her eyes.

* * *

He found her on the bed, his rag doll. Before she even moved, the clothes were falling away, and he shoved himself roughly into her. She knew what was needed, grinding her hips, milking him, pulling him out in long strands. He couldn't meet her eyes, and only rolled off her.

"I'm sorry."

She put one hand on his belly and watched with clear eyes as sleep took him.

CHAPTER SIX

"HELLO?"

Stephen had the idea the phone had been ringing for some time. It had no larger context until his mind made the leap. Phone. Calling. Someone.

"Stephen?"

He was nude, chest and arms striped with dried plaster. The formula was nearly done. He was so very close. An interruption could send it spinning to ephemera.

It took him a moment.

"It's me, Emily," the voice said. Emily? Sister, right. For a moment, he thought of her by another name, but it vanished quickly and would not return. "Stephen? Are you okay?"

"Yeah, I'm fine."

"I wanted to invite you out here for Thanksgiving."

"What?"

"You know, turkey, family and all that."

"Thanksgiving in Phoenix."

"Come on. It'll be fun." His cock burned along the bloody roadmap of scars.

"I can't."

"Do you already have plans?"

"No, it's just that I can't really afford to fly right now."

"The ticket's on us. Come on, Stephen. It's been too long. I want Adrian to meet his uncle."

"Wow. How old is he?"

"He started kindergarten."

"Weird."

"I'm... I'm pregnant again."

"Oh." He turned to the window, hoping to hear a coyote.

"Look, come out, okay? We'll put you in the guest room. You and I can catch up. I'm the only family you've got and I miss you."

He croaked, "Okay. I'll come."

"Good. I'll call you later to work out the specifics. See you in a month."

* * *

The plane ride was short, and Stephen tried not to think of his dancer. He casually mentioned the trip to Brian, who made a comment about feeding Stephen's cat. A bad joke. Let it be a bad joke. Brian was the only one who would stop by, right? The only one who might discover her.

Her. He wasn't certain she understood. Gone for a week, he had said to those clear eyes. She had tried to get him to make love, and they had, only after explanations had proved futile. At that moment, would she be wandering through darkened halls looking for her creator? Collapsed like a gunshot victim? She was alone, locked in, waiting. The thoughts coursed through a travel-numbed body and he was hard.

The plane landed. He couldn't wilt. Standing was a chore. Impossible—a teenager again. Find something to put in front of it, even if there was no fooling anyone who looked, at least in Stephen's mind. There never was, a glance revealed all sins while others were blank walls.

Shift the notebook into a makeshift shield—Junior High all over again. The old woman in front of him took three years to stand up and for a moment Stephen had the horrified nightmare of poking her in the eye. He stifled a giggle. "I'm sorry, young man." She wasn't, but said it anyway.

"No, no. It's fine." He shifted the notebook, not thinking. Her eyes went to his crotch, seeing everything. Slapping the heavy book back into place, he only succeeded in crunching the head of his penis. The old lady scowled and stumbled her way down the aisle. He gave her as much room as possible before the people behind him got restless and started their insistent shoving.

On the transfer from the plane to the skybridge, Stephen got a blast of Phoenix November, late summer anywhere else. Arizona was only just getting weather every other state had gotten several months ago and had since moved on.

Forget the ghost dancer, even as his cock ached from the impact, the memory of the birthing pains. Think of something else. Emily would be there, so would Dale. Probably... Evan? Ethan? Aidan? Something like that. What would they talk about? Their son. Stephen could talk about his daughter.

He walked into the airport proper. Stephen could imagine a paranormal investigator thinking airports were haunted— air formed pockets, super-heated by bodies, super-cooled by industrial A/C, murmured conversations scrambled off a thousand walls. Unfamiliar faces in the crowd, categorized into the Phoenix Phenotypes—the Mini-mall Aryan, the Assimilated Chicano.

Emily would be neither.

He saw her.

There is a myth that pregnant women are beautiful. This is an attempt to explain a natural instinct. Humans are primates, social animals. Social animals have large enough brains to fit less selfish concepts of survival, places DNA can enforce the idea of it surviving rather than merely its carrier. Stephen had accepted life was really just DNA's way of moving around. In this way, pregnant women represented something greater: the survival of the species at large, and a pregnant wife, daughter, sibling, aunt, cousin—shared DNA carried within her. Calling her beautiful was narcissism at its most altruistic: she was beautiful because there was no other way to express the idea that to harm this woman was to harm oneself; it was to harm the entire purpose of existence, to harm the idea of one's own flesh living into the next millennium.

She was beautiful.

Her face was fuller. She wasn't too far along, though she still had some marks from the last one, new curves, the beginnings of saddlebags. Still, her skin was ivory smooth and her eyes still clear sapphires, even if they were looking out from a pit of tired purple. She probably hated her hair, still no gray, but it looked more greasy than glossy.

She smiled as she saw him. They had the same teeth, white and strong, prominent canines, incisors facing slightly inward.

She waved.

"Stephen!" She hugged him. "You look great! Very handsome."

He frowned, dismissed it. "I missed you." They parted. A little dishwater-blond boy was tugging on Emily's mom-jeans. "Mommy?"

"Adrian." She picked him up. "This is your uncle, Stephen."

The boy tucked his head against her neck.

"He's shy," she said.

"So we know he's a Monaghan."

She offered a brittle smile.

"Emily." The voice was high and male. A flute playing at being a bassoon.

Stephen turned and saw Dale Leitch, a man Stephen had met only once before, at the wedding six years ago. Dale had gained weight too, though less than Emily, settling in a spare tire, an extra chin hidden with a goatee. His brown hair had faded; his skin had darkened.

The little boy looked nothing like his father.

"Steve," Dale said. Didn't offer a hand, didn't offer to take bag or notebook. For that, Stephen was grateful.

"Do you have bags?"

He nodded. They picked it up from the carousel in silence. Emily didn't speak, and Stephen didn't have anything to say, mind at home, in the future.

They were walking to the parking lot, still in silence. Stephen watched them out of the corner of sun-closed eyes. They weren't Monaghan-silent, the way they could drift off into their own worlds to concentrate on the projects more important than each other. Here it seemed everyone was waiting for something.

Dale said, "So what are you doing these days, Steve?"

The first words spoken, and they were in the car, past the gates, almost onto the freeway. Stephen was sitting next to the kid's car seat. Adrian was playing with something small and yellow, something supposed to be cute but made Stephen depressed.

"Doing?"

Dale couldn't know the answer to that question. Couldn't be fishing for it. Could he? Had Emily said something? Something she had no way of knowing?

"Yeah, you know, for work."

"I'm self-employed."

"Fancy way of saying you're out of work."

"Yeah, I guess."

"Stephen's a chemist," Emily said.

"Lot of money in that."

Stephen said, "Before you ask, it's not a meth lab."

Emily nearly chuckled. Dale's voice was stern. "Not in front of Adrian, please."

"Right, sorry."

More silence.

Phoenix was a desert, but unlike L.A., it couldn't pretend otherwise. The baked earth resented any attempt to cover it with something soft and green. Lawns were rocks and cactus. Sidewalks were cracked. And in the hills around the city the ground birthed scorpions. The Leitch home—Emily's home— was there, overlooking the bowl of the rest of the city.

A nice suburban neighborhood, prickled with cactus, marked their community. They pulled into the driveway in the late afternoon.

"You should get settled, and then we're taking you out," Emily said.

Despite himself, Stephen smiled. It felt good to be close to her again. "Sounds good. Where are we going?"

"Steakhouse in town. You'll like it."

Stephen nodded. Neither Dale nor Adrian looked at him. For Dale, it seemed to be a conscious effort. When Stephen glanced at Adrian, the little boy looked through him.

The house was a McMansion. The door, with its panes of angled glass, tried to look antique. As soon as Dale's foot hit the front step, a dog howled, turning into a series of loud barks.

"Be quiet," Dale said.

The cadence of the dog's bark changed from intruder to master. Dale unlocked the door and the dog charged out. It made a futile attempt to kiss Dale's hand, was ignored and it went to Emily, where it got scratched behind the ears. Clearly a shelter mutt, the dog a black-and-tan creature with any number of guard breeds in its genome. "Shh, Eli. Calm down."

The dog suddenly turned and seemed to see Stephen for the first time. It jumped, backed off and let out two snarling barks. Stephen recoiled.

"No, Eli! Bad dog! No! He's not usually like this."

"It's okay."

The dog whined, approached Stephen and sniffed the offered hand. It whined again. Stephen reached out to pet it. The dog shied away.

"Come on, I'll show you your room." With Adrian and Eli in tow, Emily led Stephen through a cathedral-like living room, past the stairs to the second floor. There was a hall in the back, and she took him back toward the front of the house. A side door led into a small bedroom stinking of potpourri. It was the farthest thing he could think of from the house they had grown up in. There was no sense of age, no character, no subtle scents from the years before the house knew anyone still alive. The sun shone inward, and the room was already stuffy.

"This is it. What do you think?"

Stephen put his bags down. "It's great."

"If you wanted to take a shower, it's right down the hall on the left."

"I was actually wanting a nap, if it's okay."

"Of course! If you need me, Adrian and I will be in the back. Dale's office is upstairs. Don't bother him unless you have to, okay?"

Stephen nodded. "It's good to see you, Em."

She kissed him on the cheek. "Yeah. I missed you, too."

Stephen sank into a deep sleep shortly afterwards. It was far from dreamless, but the dreams weren't his.

* * *

When Stephen awoke, throat tight and body covered in a layer of drying sweat, the sun was dying. He sat up and checked the clock, rubbing the crust from an eye. An hour and a half asleep. What now? Calling home. That was what one did when they left behind a girlfriend, a wife. But he hadn't. He'd left a doll. Did she even think when he was gone?

He got to his feet and found the shower. A quick rinse cleared the rest of the cobwebs. The bathroom was clean, past any reasonable expectation of such. Growing up, Emily had been cleaner than he, mostly by virtue of her gender, still, this was antiseptic even for her. There was a distinct lack of character as well; the only art was a framed Bible quote.

That was the only art anywhere; everything on the walls had a direct connection to scripture. Stephen got dressed and started to look around. Odd. Emily had always been an art lover, holding the Impressionists above all others. Though Stephen didn't understand him, Monet always made him think of Emily. There was nothing like this on any of the walls.

Stephen had guessed the Monaghans had been Catholic at one time, but Charles and Sarah were what would have been called Deist and what had become New Age. Any religion in the Leitch home had come from Dale.

Stephen went out into the living room, hair still pleasantly damp. Emily's muffled voice followed by similarly muffled giggling bubbled in from outside. He followed the sound to the sliding glass door separating the kitchen from the patio. Adrian was in a plastic playset, giggling and hiding, while Emily impersonated a T-rex.

"Have you told him T-rexes can't see movement?"

Emily turned and snarled, still in character. Adrian howled with laughter. She charged Stephen and sunk her teeth gently into his shoulder. "And now you're dinosaur food," she said.

He smiled and found a seat. Emily beckoned her son over, the boy ignoring her in favor of the slide. Apparently the dinosaur game was over.

"Feeling better? Up to some red meat tonight?"

He nodded. "Can't wait."

"The sitter's coming over around seven. Adrian should be

ready to conk out by then. I'm trying to tire him out to make sure."

"Good plan. Is that what you've been doing?"

"Being a mom? Yeah."

"Any time for acting?"

"Oh, no. I had to give it up."

"Do you miss it?"

"A little." A lie. Clear she missed it much more. "Maybe I'll have time later."

"Aren't you having another baby?" She didn't answer, but the segue was already there. "How far along are you?"

She touched her belly absently. "Five months."

Five months. Meaning the baby was conceived in June, when his dancer was born. Was there a connection between siblings that drove them to create their children at the same time?

He drifted into himself until Emily broke the silence. "How've you been? We haven't talked in... forever."

"Good. I've been pretty busy lately. New project."

"Top secret?"

"Not exactly. It's dental porcelain. A new kind, should feel more like a real tooth."

She chuckled to herself. "I never understood how you could do those kinds of things."

"What do you mean?"

"You're making something new. Something no one has ever seen."

If only you knew.

He said, "Yeah, well, maybe I wish I had other talents."

"How about girls? Are you seeing anybody?"

"Yeah."

Once again, he'd blurted it. Alcohol was no excuse this time either. With Emily it was pure trust. There was no shield against Emily because there didn't have to be.

"Well, tell me about her!"

He couldn't use the same lie he'd used on Jessica. Emily would see through it instantly. "She's… she's a waitress. At the Nite Lite."

"Explains how you met her. What's she like?"

"She has short reddish hair and green eyes."

Emily opened her mouth to ask something, thought it over, and instead asked something else: "I mean personality wise." She did not sound convincing.

"Oh, she's really cool. She's into comics and stuff. She's not what I'm used to at all." The nametag said Audra. "Her name is Audra."

"Pretty name. I'd like to meet her."

"We're not that far along yet. Not vacationing-advanced."

"Oh! No, no. I mean, we couldn't have brought her out here. You know. Obvious reasons."

Stephen didn't press. The money maybe. That was the clean answer.

"I'm glad to hear everything's going so well. When you dropped out, I was worried."

"So was I."

"I've never seen you so at peace before. This girl is good for you."

* * *

The next morning, Stephen's bowels still full of steak and potatoes, and an unfamiliar male voice: "Rise and shine." Monotone, cutting through the sleep Stephen had only recently found. His schedule was still that of the Work and mornings were something he usually saw the beginning of rather than the end.

He blinked, floundered for his glasses and found the speaker—Dale, in the doorway, wearing a bathrobe, reeking of cologne.

"What time is it?"

"You need to get showered, shaved, and changed."

"What for?"

"Church is in an hour."

"I don't go to church." Stephen rolled over and groped for the rapidly fleeing sleep.

"Yes, you do."

"What?"

"As long as you're here, you go to church."

"I'm sorry?"

"Get showered, shaved, and changed and you won't have to be."

Stephen considered the options. Dig his heels in and piss everyone off, or go and get it over with. No choice really, get up, nod to the man in the doorway, get ready. Dale kept standing there until Stephen stood up and walked to the door. Dale lingered, before letting Stephen by with a cold smile.

Shower, shave, and change, done in simple robotic motions. When Stephen came out in his street clothes, Dale's smile vanished. "Is that what you're wearing?"

"This is the first I'd heard we'd be doing anything formal."

"Your sister was the same way when we first got together. We'll get you fixed up with a suit later; call it your Christmas present. In the meantime, that'll have to do."

Stephen found Emily, but she wasn't looking at him. She concentrated on the fidgeting Adrian, a desperate ignorance to her attitude. Stephen didn't quite understand, though the ignorance felt artificial.

The church was filled with zombies. Staring straight ahead, occasionally nodding, laser-focused on the tall brown-haired man at the pulpit. Stephen let the sounds wander. They wouldn't teach him anything new.

Without warning, it was all over. The murmur broke and washed in. Stephen blinked and followed these strangers who were family, museum-walking to the door. Dale was smiling and glad-handing, Emily right with him. Stephen heard names and introductions before some keywords flashed in his mind's eye and made him come to earth.

He whispered to Emily: "What's happening?"

"Church potluck today."

"We were just at church."

"The service, but there's more to it. Church family and all of that."

The words struck him—family was at home, the girl Emily used to be and the ethereal dancer. They should be waiting together in the dark house, washed in the drafts that felt like breath. The doll did not sleep. She did not eat. What would she do alone? Could she live at all? The need to be back home, look into her clear eyes and see everything he wanted to see in them was suffocating.

Stephen, sucking in gusts of air, silently followed Dale, Emily, and Adrian to their car. The Leitches, they were the Leitches. The name was still unfamiliar, wrong. Go home and change, meet at some park or another. Stephen allowed himself to be led, waited as they changed, as Emily pulled the potato salad from the fridge and loaded them back into the car. Refuge was in his notebook, in the endless streams of chemical equations.

Adrian peered over from the car seat, gaze flickering over the letters and numbers. Stephen held up the notebook. The little boy glanced at it before looking up and meeting Stephen's gaze. There was something in Adrian's eyes, an alien hunger demanding to be fed. It was familiar.

Then the boy turned away to watch the cacti turn to smears of green. They pulled into the park. The faces were the same as those at church, the bodies now in khaki shorts and polo shirts, looking formal in a new way.

Stephen wanted to leave, but there was no leaving, as sure as if there were weeping steel walls all around. So, instead, he ate and watched and shook hands with whomever Dale and Emily brought over. When Dale mentioned Stephen wasn't a regular churchgoer, they swooped and surrounded. Matching faces and names was impossible; they all blurred into a single happy façade with boundless rage beyond. Pestering, hectoring. Stephen's mind at home with his doll.

Two cornered them. One was the brown-haired man from the pulpit, Boyd; the other was Jim, a pale man with bright blond hair. They were concerned with the state of Stephen's soul. Without a guiding influence, there was a single sure destination. Fortunately, Jim and Boyd were the perfect guides, the road they walked leading to light and pain. They told him about God and sin, and what Stephen could do to come to the former and avoid the latter.

The shadows grew long and they lost patience with the silent man sitting and eating cold chicken and cold potato salad in the stifling air that reminded him of the attic.

Soon, Emily came to him. "Could you get Adrian? We're loading up the car."

"Where is he?"

She pointed to a sandbox twenty feet distant. Without thinking, Stephen got up and dumped the greasy paper plate into the oily trash barrel and went to find Adrian.

There were three children, all around the same age. Nearly identical. They didn't notice him. Adrian's specific face was a muzzy memory: all three could be him, all three could be Stephen's flesh and blood.

No way to tell.

"Adrian?" One of the kids looked up. Stephen beckoned him over. "It's time to go."

The little boy stood up unsteadily, the expression on his tiny face pure Monaghan, finally staggering over and taking Stephen's hand. They walked toward the car. As they did, Stephen looked back and saw Jim picking up the other two kids that looked like Adrian.

Stephen turned back and made it to the car.

Dale said, "So, what did you think?"

"Oh, just that I wasn't sure which one."

Dale frowned. "What? I meant the potluck."

Stephen's mind found the track and took it. "It was fine."

"Fine? It's a community, and not just one in this life, but in the next, too. We're saved and it's always good to have one more, especially family."

"Saved?"

"Your soul. It means you get to be with God when you die."

Stephen nodded. "God is already here."

* * *

Thanksgiving, the ostensible purpose of the trip, was a church function. The Leitches went to church three times a week at minimum and expected Stephen to do the same. He went along placidly, the experience null. Time with Emily was welcome, and there was something in him, some growing fear over returning home. What was his dancer doing, along in the house? The question came, again and again, but the one thing worse than the question was learning the answer. So he stayed.

And stayed.

Stephen had taken to wandering around the Leitch house late at night. It gave him power, power Dale took back every day. Stephen wondered if Dale realized the transfer had even taken place. Maybe somewhere in his reptile brain, prompting the need to belittle Stephen at every turn. Or it could be because somewhere Dale knew Stephen had done something great and terrible that made a mockery of Dale's beliefs.

Stephen stepped over the Leitch dog sleeping lightly by the door, going to the back window to watch the night.

* * *

The ringing phone brought her to life.

Collapsed in a heap of tangled limbs on the bed—their bed—she rose fluidly into the shape of the dancer, glided to the door in the half-light, and downstairs, to the kitchen.

One gentle hand lifted the phone from the cradle.

A pause. From the other end of the line. "Hello?"

She tilted her head. Waiting.

"Steve? Is that you? It's Brian."

One nail, glossy and perfectly sculpted yet a part of her finger, touched the mouthpiece.

"Hello? Is someone there?"

The doll ran the nail down the mouthpiece. *Scratch. Scratch. Scratch.*

The voice was softer. Frightened.

"Hello?"

She hung up the phone and returned to the bed. When the phone rang again, she gave no sign of hearing.

* * *

It was early in December. Dale was gone, at the church or with friends. Stephen and Emily were at home, Adrian napping in the other room.

"So what have you been up to? Other than this girlfriend of yours?"

"I wish I had more to report."

"Friends?"

"A couple, I guess."

"Sometimes I wish I stayed in contact with my old friends."

"Sometimes?"

"Sometimes I don't." Her mind switched tracks. "How about

nostalgia? I have some pictures of you around here before you grew into yourself."

"Oh, God."

"Yeah. Hold on."

She came back with the photo albums, the kinds with the crackling pages and faux covers. "You know, we might be the last generation with these."

"Small favors."

She opened one up to Stephen and Emily as small children, at the beach. Emily had her chubby arm around her little brother, who was focused on the sand, looking at something invisible to everyone else.

"I used to hate the beach," he said.

"I know! Remember how mom used to slather us in that gross sunscreen? And then the sand would catch in it?"

"Worst feeling."

"Of course, the way we burn..."

She flipped through the pages. There they were at four and eight. Six and ten. Then, Emily's twelfth birthday, blowing out her candles. Over her shoulder, Stephen. They could tell it was him by the t-shirt—three canine heads, top to bottom, fox, coyote, wolf. His face was blurred, as though his head turned at the instant the camera clicked.

"My twelfth. Remember?"

Of course. The poster. "A little."

She turned the page. This was Stephen, graduating junior high at the age of thirteen. Also there, Emily and Charles Monaghan. Something had happened to the picture. Some kind of mold had rooted over Stephen's face, rendering him nearly unrecognizable.

"Damn—darn it. That was a nice shot of you."

"Not anymore."

"Sorry."

"You didn't put it there."

She turned the page. She was a sophomore in high school, dressed in a Renaissance gown, her face almost clown-like under her thick stage make up. It was right after her last performance of *Taming of the Shrew*. She smiled, holding a bundle of roses. Stephen stood next to her, unsure of what to do. Emily smiled happily into the camera. A flare from the stage light obliterated Stephen's face.

He glanced at Emily. She was frowning. "What?"

"I thought I remembered this one. I guess not."

Turned the page. Stephen stood in front of the Lincoln Memorial. The sun turned his face into shadow. Disneyland— his face was blurred. She turned the page. His face, scratched out. His face, erased from existence.

"What the hell?"

"I thought you had something of me."

"I did. I mean, I thought I did. I could have sworn these were... I don't know." She shut the album.

"It's okay." But it wasn't.

* * *

On Thursday, Emily grabbed her keys off the end table. She was almost out the door when Stephen called to her from the couch. "Where are you going?"

Emily blushed. "I thought you were sleeping."

"I was. Where are you going?"

"My... um... my waxer."

"Your what?"

"My waxer. Come on. You know."

He didn't. He would find out the next night.

Emily came home from her errands with Adrian in the afternoon. Along with the shopping, she had a small box. Stephen watched from the couch as she walked to the mantle, opened the box, and removed something. Gazing at whatever was in her hands for a long moment, and setting it on the mantelpiece and moved away.

It was a glass figurine.

A ballerina.

Stephen sat up. "Em?"

She turned, eyes focusing slowly. "Yeah?"

"What's that?"

"I don't know. I saw her in a window. I liked the looks of her. Why?"

Stephen tried to hide the chill tearing through him. "No... no reason."

He hid it through dinner, thinking only of the unfinished dental porcelain, equations worrying at the edges of him. Minor nudges and the answers would emerge, finished. Returning to the house, to the beautiful doll, and let everything else fade away.

He passed out amongst chemical symbols into a dream where the unseen dolls bore him up and ravens picked at his bones.

He woke up in the middle of the night.

It was a sudden snap to wakefulness, one that kept muzzy fingers on his shoulders, trying to drag him back into the abyss.

With sleep-blurred eyes and a piss-burned bladder, he staggered to the bathroom and emptied himself.

The house settled in around him, wrapping him in the stifling Phoenix night. Back in the moonlit hall, his room was off to the left, dark and warm. In the stillness, the wanting pushed in, the wish he were home in the drafty Victorian, the wish for an ethereal dancer, something not human waiting for him outside. For a second, the silhouette stood in the moonlight, the air was too close to be anything other than the attic, and he was not nude.

The house settled again.

It wasn't the house.

Stephen walked into the living room that connected via archway to the dining room. The center of the house. Another creak. There was something else. Closer. Up the stairs, definitely. He put bare feet on the carpet and moved, stepping over the dog, wide awake but blind to him. On the upper landing, it wasn't the house settling. It was a repetitive creaking.

It pulled to him. He advanced to the door of the master bedroom. Closer. A sudden flash. Emily was in there with Dawn Molinaro, finishing what they had started over a decade ago. Emily had never been happier than in that moment, and in a strange way, he had never been closer to her. Emily would become who she was supposed to be.

No.

A stupid hope. Dawn Molinaro was long gone.

The creaking resolved. Creaking, yes, and slapping sounds, perfectly in rhythm. He took another step toward the open door, putting himself next to the wall, in the deepest part of the smothering shadows.

Emily's face, coming from the darkness like a moon, bobbing in and out. Her eyes weren't shut, but they were lidded, face somewhere between ecstasy and irritation.

Stephen moved closer, hating everything in him, moving his legs.

Emily was on the bed, on all fours. There was a shadow behind her, fucking her.

Stephen took another step forward to the threshold of the door. The shadow resolved itself. It was not Dale. The body was soft, the face screwed up into a toothy rictus. The man from the park. Jim something. One of the men who tried to convert Stephen. The man had a wife, a tired-eyed blonde woman.

The pungent stench of them stung Stephen's nostrils. The wet sucking sounds turned his stomach.

Stephen's eyes probed the darkness. There was another shape, sitting in the corner. The features in shadow, it shifted. Dim light touched the face. Dale, gleefully watching this man fuck Emily.

Stephen wanted to stop them, to do something, anything. Emily. Not enjoying it, having none of the same qualities in her voice crying out for Dawn. She was businesslike. Obligated.

He looked at her face. She was looking right at him.

Now she moved back against the man, eyes never leaving Stephen's, even as he backed away, deeper into the shadows. Emily's eyes followed him, but he wanted to believe she was seeing only darkness. He fought the urge to scream, to attack Jim and Dale, to take Emily away from the man that never deserved her. Stephen wanted to deliver Emily to a brighter and more loving fate. Stomach pinioning him, he couldn't get any closer to the act, the air wet as breath.

He found the stairs and disappeared down them. There was no more sleep that night.

CHAPTER SEVEN

STEPHEN RETURNED HOME THREE DAYS later. He and Emily never discussed that night, and she did not give him a sign she had seen him. Had the shadows been truly safe? The doubt haunted him.

Brian Baniszewski picked Stephen up from the airport in the afternoon. It was the tail end of December in L.A., with the crisp bite of a sore throat. Brian waited beyond the gate and even gave Stephen a small smile as they approached.

"How was your trip?" They walked to the luggage carousel.

"Good."

"How's Emily?"

For a second, Stephen thought somehow Brian knew, but he was looking straight ahead, face innocent. "Good. She's pregnant again."

"Oh, cool. The first one is turning out okay?"

"I think so."

"Not a serial killer yet?"

"Not yet."

They grabbed the bags and walked toward the parking lot.

"Listen," Brian said. "Something weird happened while you

were gone. I called your place and someone answered."

The slash along Stephen's cockhead burned again. "What?"

"Didn't say anything either... it was weird. I thought someone broke in. I drove by your place. It was locked up tight."

"Wrong number?"

Brian shook his head. "No way. Your number's in my cell. Doesn't misdial."

"Maybe... maybe the signal got crossed. Or the wires."

Brian's gaze was withering. Stephen tried to stand firm through it, the urge to quail strong. If Brian came in, found out, what would he try to do to Stephen's dancer?

And what would she do to Brian?

Finally, Brian said, "Maybe."

Brian changed the subject soon after to Christmas spent at home, never mentioning Jessica. Stephen noticed the absence, but didn't bring it up. Brian had given the verdict on Jessica and it was final.

They pulled up the gravel driveway, and Brian said, "I should come in with you."

Stephen's heart stopped. "Why?"

"If there's someone in there, you have to deal with him alone."

"No one's in there."

Brian looked to the dark house, then back to Stephen. "I told you about the phone call. Someone answered. They could still be in there."

"I don't think so." Stephen turned to Brian, saw the cruel grin.

"You got someone tucked away in there?"

"What? No!"

"Got someone to housesit maybe? Don't want me to see her?"

"Brian, come on."

102 // JUSTIN ROBINSON

Brian turned the car off and stepped out. "Now I'm curious."

Stephen followed, fighting to hide the desperation. "It's just that I'm tired. I'm sure there's no one in there, and if there is, I'll call the cops. It'll be fine."

Brian took a step toward the house. "Won't take long. Let me give her a once over and I'll be out of your hair."

"Look, it's nothing. I'm sure of it."

Brian let out a laugh. "Hey, I understand. If you're not worried, I'm not worried." Returning to the car, he flashed the I'm-just-fucking-with-you grin. "Want to hang out later?"

"Not tonight," Stephen said. "But yeah. Soon."

"New Year's at my place. You can bring your housesitter if you want, or you could talk to the five girls I invite specifically for you."

"Sure."

Brian smirked. "Have fun."

He waited until Stephen had the door open to back out and on to the street.

The house was silent. A breeze worked through the widening bones. It felt dead and deserted. Had she wandered off? Could she? There were a million stories of dogs following their masters over hundreds of miles. Had she gone into the deep desert to find him? Was she a pet then? Was he a master? There were no real words for what they were to one another, only shadows that captured a single facet: father, daughter, husband, wife, maker, doll.

He opened his mouth to call to her, but there was no name to call. Could she be waiting? Could she be angry?

The bags fell from nerveless fingers. He strained to catch

some faint footfall. The house was cold.

He took the stairs slowly, letting them creak, to announce he was home. To summon her. She would glide to him, show how much she missed him.

At the top of the stairs, where the open hallway ran back along the house, every door was open, save for one.

Emily's.

His bedroom was empty. The dancer wasn't collapsed on the bed. Into the tiled bathroom, to the door into Emily's room. Something made him knock. A pause. The door opened.

She stood on the other side of the threshold, face unreadable. The room was hers. That much was clear. "May I...?"

She took him in her arms.

He tried to ascribe nobility to what he did in the next few days. There was none. It was guilt. He should have done it before leaving her, should have stayed, should have brought her with him, should have introduced her to Emily.

Emily might even understand.

The dancer watched with wordless wonder as he brought materials upstairs. The old bolts of cloth his mother used to use for sewing projects, bits of wood no longer needed, glass beads wanting only polish. He made the checkerboards that seemed to undulate, braced the silk ribbons with concealed wires, hung everything from the ceiling in an elaborate mobile.

He led the dancer into the room, a hand over those clear eyes. Only then—the reveal.

She stood from the bed and stepped into the midst of the hanging garden. She was in the world of the poster. It was possible he imagined it, but she seemed to recognize the false world, twirling through the wonderland, touching each component lightly, offering her ethereal benediction.

Finally, she went to him, taking his shaking hands, pulling him into fantasy.

He let her guide him, never even having to shut his eyes. A gift given and returned without hesitation. She might have been ignorant of what she was doing. It didn't matter. Holding her cool body, kissing the marks on her face and twirling with her, the hours melted into nothing. As the room plunged into silvery dark, she finally carried him to their bed.

* * *

It was a Saturday, back in college, the night he should have lost his virginity. Emily had stayed at home, almost as invested in his nascent relationship as he. He and Chris had been made more or less official at a party filled with strangers at which she had introduced him as her boyfriend, complete with a glance at him as though to see how he would react. He just took the other girl's hand and gave her a "nice to meet you" and it was done.

On the night that Emily stayed at home, they had come back from the best dinner they could afford, a cheap date at a local Thai restaurant. They returned to his room, and he knew it was going further than it ever had without knowing how. It could have been the look in her eyes, the hunger in her kiss, the burning curry of her tongue, the electricity crawling across her skin. He knew, as soon as the door shut, and every hair on his body reached out for Chris.

They fell into bed, and the undressing was utterly unlike the one time he had witnessed sex before. They were tentative.

He kept waiting—though something in him knew it wouldn't happen—for her to tell him to stop, and move his hands from her zipper to her back, and they would spend another evening rubbing him raw.

She didn't stop him at the zipper. She didn't stop him when he pulled her dress down her body. She didn't stop him as their clothes piled at the foot of the bed. She didn't stop him when he unclipped her bra and saw the first breasts bared for him and him alone. She didn't stop him when he reached into her panties and tried to touch her the way Dawn had touched his sister.

Chris was real. She was alive. She writhed under him. She whispered to him. Stephen breathed in her moans, their lips brushing together.

Chris, breathless, reaching, saying, "Are you okay?"

"What?"

"You're... you're not hard."

Their heaving bodies were nearly one. She held him in hand like a dead snake, soft, limp. Ashamed. Poised above, he should have been ready to impale her, but there was nothing.

"Sit up," she said. She pushed him up, desperate in her movements. Stephen thought there was anger, maybe frustration, but in the aggression of her movements there was no way to tell. She ducked down and took him in her mouth. Her head bobbed, her tongue slathered along the head, but nothing happened. It should have set his nerve endings on fire, but that thing between his legs betrayed him.

She wiped her reddening mouth and looked up at him. "Is something wrong?"

"No. Why?"

"This… this should work."

"Maybe you're doing it wrong."

"Are you okay?"

"Stop asking me that."

"We don't have to have sex if you don't want to. I thought… I thought that we were there. I'm there. If you're not, that's cool. We can wait."

"No. No, it's okay. It just takes me a little while." He had no idea where that came from, no idea how long he took having never done this with anyone else.

He pushed her back down, focused on her body. The image of Emily with Dawn invaded his mind. A flutter, somewhere deep. Then, the poster took hold. The flutter became a storm. The poster faded instantly, leaving Chris. He wilted nearly immediately. Sweat, saliva, blood. He tried kissing her neck, tried feeling the wet places in her body. She responded, but she was venal. Disgusting.

"You're right. This isn't working."

She was panting. "It's okay. We don't have to. But… can you finish? I'm close. I'm really close."

He recoiled. "Finish?"

She pulled his hand to her. She was wet, disgusting. Meat.

He pulled away. "You should go."

"What?" Finally slapped back to earth, but barely.

"You should go."

"Stephen, it's okay. I don't have to finish. I can… we can just cuddle. It's okay. We don't have to go faster."

"Get. Out!"

She stared at him, uncomprehending. He was still.

She picked up her clothes, hiding the body she had only been too eager to show him, but never hiding her tears.

He sat there, in the dark, as she went from the room. That was the last time they spoke.

* * *

Through sleep and nightmare, Lulu's Petals called. He didn't know why.

A lie. His second daughter.

She was conceived in the spirit of that place, incubated in porcelain, and would soon be born in blood. If Lulu's Petals was the womb, Stephen wanted to be there.

He left in the early evening, not thinking of it as sneaking out, even if it probably was. Downtown was bathed in the yellow glow of streetlights beneath a purple sky. The air crackled as though the city itself was trying to give birth to the dolls. They weren't ready. Not yet. The girls were on stage, lush bodies bouncing to the old time music. Stephen went to the bar and ordered his hurricane and again watched them reflected in the ice cubes, studying the faces, each in turn, the floury cheeks, the lips made full and wet, but something was wrong. The features were not right for his next daughter. They were far too soft.

"I know you, right?"

Stephen's hand twitched. The smiling face looked familiar and weirdly birdlike with the cockatoo crest of the fauxhawk. Stephen knew this man, but couldn't put a name to him.

So the other man did. "Tyler. I'm a friend of Brian's."

"Right, Tyler." It came back to Stephen. Tyler had run into them at the last visit, doing the usual. This was Tyler's home ground, though the guileless man wasn't a wolf sniffing after an interloper. "Stephen."

"Yeah, Steve, I remember you. What's going on, man? Brian here?"

"Nope. I'm here on my own."

"Looking for something?"

"Yeah."

"Me too." Tyler waved a bartender over and held up a finger. A minute later a drink appeared that looked like iced tea and smelled like formaldehyde.

Stephen thought it, and almost said it. Tyler's attention was elsewhere. Stephen followed the gaze to the door, found himself as distracted. The woman coming into the club was striking, having what everyone else lacked. Style. She held it effortlessly, wore the vintage dress, the antique drop earrings, the pearled snood, a woman born of the time. That was her trick—there was no time. Her style mixed and matched into a portmanteau at once innovative and classic. Even her features, the strength of her chin and the odd lines of her mouth, were antique. Large brown eyes found Tyler's, and she smiled, coming closer.

Stephen hated the thought, but there was no stopping it. She was exactly Brian's type.

"Hey, Tyler."

"Milena. Let me introduce you to Steve."

"Stephen," Stephen said, tracing the delicate waves of her hair. *How do I make curly hair?*

Milena turned to him and held out a hand. It felt cold and smooth, like glass. "Nice to meet you. Stephen." She said the last, focusing in on him. When Milena put her attention on someone, everything else fell away. She turned back to Tyler and Stephen felt very alone.

"I didn't think you'd be around tonight," Tyler said.

She shrugged. "Here I am. Are we getting together later?"

He nodded. "In the meantime?"

"In the meantime, I need to earn some money."

"Same. You find something, let me know."

She flashed Stephen a brilliant smile. "Nice meeting you," and dove into the press of people, stopping, talking, laughing. Fitting in. Tyler watched her, downing his drink and holding up two fingers.

"What's with her?" Stephen asked. He kept watching Milena.

"She's a gambler. Like me."

"What do you mean, gambler?"

"We're card players. Poker. Professionally."

"You can do that?"

"Sure. We each have our regular games, but sometimes we need a little extra, you know. For unforeseen expenses."

"Unforeseen expenses. Right. So you're looking for something?"

"Not really. If she finds something, we can take turns. Tag-team the bitches. Leave 'em just enough blood so they can still walk."

* * *

Construction of the Siege Perilous began one week later. The materials—the tubes, the bags, the needles, the tanks—had arrived. Stephen found the right chair in an antique shop and set it in the center of the attic, in front of the picture window that looked like a cross section of an orange. A good view to bleed to. He tried not to think of the last, but the chair was a predator, one for whom he would be the only prey.

The knock at the door spun his head around in a meerkat jerk. No car had crunched its way up the driveway. No calls had announced anyone's arrival. He was dressed. Something about clothes felt wrong, though it was a good thing in this case.

He turned to his dancer, sitting in the corner of the attic, head cocked like the doll she was. She brought him her hairbrush once every three days and he brushed her hair for her, enjoying the closeness of it, but it was clear she loved it much more.

"Stay here, please." She was motionless.

He rushed downstairs.

Jessica Baniszewski was craning her head to peer through the small warped windows on the door. She smiled when she saw him. "I didn't wake you up did I? You said you don't sleep."

"I did, didn't I?"

"I thought I'd stop by. Is that cool?" She made a move to come in.

"Now's not a great time."

She frowned. Pretty girls weren't used to being told no.

"The house is a bit of a mess. You know. Bachelor, living alone. Uh... no one really comes over."

"Oh. I'm sorry. I'll go."

"No!" A little desperate there. Wincing inwardly, he said, "I'll get some clothes on and we'll go get I don't know, a cup of coffee."

"Sure."

"Wait here. Right here."

Her face was halfway between a smile and a frown. Maybe it was good, maybe bad. Whatever it was, it was adorable. He had to take that thought and crumple it in the corner and never remember it. But she was still his friend. She was still Brian's little sister.

He shut the door, turning. The doll slumped on the landing, partially collapsed. Was this a threat to Jessica? Or was the doll hurt? Angry?

"I'm sorry. I have to go."

She made no move.

The front door opened. If it opened all the way, Jessica could look up and see the white shape slouching on the landing. "Stephen?"

"Just a sec!"

What would the doll do? Kill the invader? Or merely spawn a thousand questions to which there was no clean answer?

The doll did not move, still as a tree. He grabbed the door, trying to shield Jessica from the revelation, and nearly bowling her over. Her face, on the other side, brow furrowed. She caught his upper arms with a nervous smile. "Are you okay?"

"I'm fine."

"What, did you have porn on or something?"

He let out a brittle laugh that said she was close. "Right, yeah. That's all I do around here."

"Wait. Is she here?"

"What?"

"The fucking clam! Your 'girlfriend!'" She made the air quotes.

"No, of course not."

"Then why are you whispering? She's upstairs, isn't she. Sleeping?"

He saw Jessica going inside. The doll's hands were so strong.

"Trust me, Jess. It's fine. Let's go." Leading Jessica out of the house, she moved closer to him, folding his arm in hers. As he closed the door, the doll on the landing stood. Waiting.

"Sorry I didn't call. I was up and I thought you might be too."

"It's fine. I'm... glad to see you. So... coffee?"

"Where did you have in mind? It's the middle of the night."

Without thinking, he blurted, "The Nite Lite has decent coffee." Audra would be there and their last conversation loomed large.

Before he could take it back, "Fine by me."

Jessica's car was little and Japanese, like her mother. It was ten years old and had the sharp artificial smell that happened when the hard foam lining the doors cracked. A book of CDs and some mystery novel lay on the floor of the passenger side. She reminded Stephen of a David Lynch character, maybe one of the residents of Twin Peaks five years down the line, with a bug up her ass to finally find out who killed Laura Palmer. The car snaked down the hill cautiously. It didn't fit her. In Stephen's mind, she was a wild woman with a lead foot.

"So how's the Scientologist who was totally upstairs?" she said.

"She wasn't upstairs. And she's fine I guess."

"Still seeing her?"

"Not exclusively."

She rolled her eyes. "So basically you're letting her cheat on you. 'Not being exclusive' is basically just code for 'I want to fuck someone that's not you.'"

"How do you know I'm not the one seeing someone else?"

"Are you?"

The word caught, "No."

"That's how. You need to dump this chick now. Sooner if possible."

She hit the upward slope of the parking lot like she was mad at it, guiding the car in one of the front spots. There were a few cars there. Stephen recognized a couple. One of them had to be Audra's. Hopefully the compact with all the indie band stickers, the kind of cool car he'd always wanted to have, mostly for what it said—whoever drove it went where they wanted because people wanted them there.

Audra was writing taking an order at the counter when the bell rang. She smiled at Stephen. It could have meant nearly anything. Her gaze dragged over Jessica. Audra's blonde eyebrows went down for a moment, before remembering she was taking an order.

"I guess you come here a lot," Jessica said.

"I keep odd hours."

She let out an embryonic chuckle. Audra moved over to the table. "Tuna melt, fries, iced tea?"

"The tea, yeah. Can I get a slice of cherry pie instead of the usual?"

"Hot or cold?"

"Hot. With vanilla ice cream."

"Sounds good. What do you want?"

Jessica thought it over. "The same, but sub coffee for the tea."

"I'll get your drinks."

Stephen looked out the window, and turned back to see Jessica watching Audra in the kitchen. "Cherry pie. The innuendo writes itself," Jessica said.

"You ordered it too."

"Oh, I know."

"Well then." Stephen didn't know what else to say, so he didn't say anything at all. Jessica squirmed a little.

"Why do you keep asking me about my not-girlfriend?"

She shrugged. "It's interesting."

"What about you? You have a boyfriend?"

She gave him a hard look. "No."

He paused. "Girlfriend?"

"You wish."

Stephen groped for a reason why this interaction was so awkward. "Does this count as hanging out?"

"I think so. I mean, it's almost coffee. Granted, it's in the middle of the night, and we're in a diner. Take away the fact that I have work tomorrow, it's pretty good."

"You have... this is probably a weird question, but what day is it?"

She smiled. "Nice."

"I'm serious."

"Do you know a ballpark?"

"Now I know tomorrow's a weekday. So I've narrowed it down a bit."

"It's Wednesday. I guess you get to make your own schedule if you're a genius, huh?"

"I don't know if I'm..."

Audra put the pie on the table. "There you go. I'll be back with refills in a second."

"Thanks," Stephen said, turning back to Jess in time to catch her brittle look at Audra.

"You should call the clam right now and dump her. Do you have your phone on you?"

"I don't own a cell phone."

"You don't? Who doesn't have a cell phone?"

"Can we talk about something else, please?"

"Why are you still with her, anyway?"

"It's not like I have options."

She stabbed the pie with her fork.

"What?" he said.

Audra refilled the tea. Jessica was forgotten. Audra had become everything.

"What about her?" Jessica said.

"Huh?"

"The waitress. What about her?"

"She doesn't like me. I said something stupid to her last time I was in here. She's only being nice for the sake of a tip."

"I know that look on her face."

"We see what we want to see."

"Which explains her blonde roots."

Jessica finished off her pie almost cruelly before turning back to Stephen. Talking about Audra with her sitting across the restaurant and trying to pretend she wasn't watching felt wrong.

Stephen took out his wallet. Jessica stopped him. "I'll get it. I picked you up, remember?"

Jessica went to the counter to pay while Stephen waited outside in the chilly night. Jessica joined him. "So, is the clam really not at your place?"

"Really."

"Are you going to invite me in, then?"

"You have work tomorrow."

There was a long pause. "I guess I'll drop you off."

She drove fast. When she dropped Stephen off, she didn't bother to go up the drive, and Stephen was grateful. He had caught the doll on the lawn once before, and that couldn't happen again. Not in front of Jessica.

Holding the car door open, he said, "I'll see you soon."

"Sure. We'll do it again."

He walked toward his house. Jessica didn't drive away. Up the gravel, and Jessica still hadn't moved. Only when he opened his door did the car rev and disappear down the dark street. He closed and locked the door, moving up the stairs purposefully, shedding clothing with each step. Upon reaching the attic, he was comfortably nude.

She was sitting at the feet of the chair that would be the Siege Perilous, looking out over the arroyo, completely still. She didn't react, though she must have heard him coming up the ladder, heard him crossing the beams, and saw him settling next to her.

Bladder and bowels were full, but it wasn't unpleasant. He wanted to talk to her. Back from speaking to the real girl to the graceful enigma cross-legged next to him.

"There are six billion people in this world," he said to her.

Her head turned. Smooth, unnatural. Clear eyes watched him.

"You know one of them."

Somewhere in the arroyo, a coyote's howl spiraled upward.

"Ever want to meet another one?"

There was a long moment of silence. She left the room, returning with her hairbrush, handing it to him. He did as she liked. The answer was clear: there was no need for anyone else.

CHAPTER EIGHT

THE SIEGE PERILOUS WAS FINISHED by the beginning of February. An antique chair, modern medical equipment rising off the back in a mantle, a metal parasite. The alarm was calibrated to sound when the bags hit a pint. Stephen didn't want to give more. Not at a single time. The Siege was grotesque and horrible, the dark sister of the graceful dancer.

He tried to step toward the Siege Perilous. He could not. The thought of her nailed him to the floor. Those velvet cushions soft under his bare ass, sinking her metal teeth into the tender skin on the inside of his elbow. There would no longer be Stephen Monaghan and the Siege Perilous. For a single moment, they would be united by blood, a single organism of meat and wood, pumping living tissue through dead passages. The alienation of that simple act was crushing. The inanimate predator would feed on him, supplant him, and store him. What was taken would be neither dead nor alive, hanging in plastic to be spilled on future daughters, granting life to the unliving.

There would be no more life without the sacrifice. The harvest was the cleanest option. Otherwise, it was the knife. His entire body recoiled around his groin, protecting the target of the genesis rage.

He forced himself to sit, placing his right arm along the arm of the chair. Soft on one side, sharp the other. He took the IV in one hand and tried to find a vein. His fingers rebelled. The IV fell. He tried to pick it up, but couldn't hold it delicately. It had become a cudgel.

He swore, tried to make his fingers behave. They had a clear image to emulate, but ignored it. His hand, for whatever reason, was no better than a clamp. Fear did not do this. It was something far older. Something that had fallen away and could never be regained.

A hand, soft and comforting, stroked his hair.

He looked up into the beautiful face of his harlequin. She took the needle gently in hand and expertly placed it—a single red pinch followed by enervation. The plastic tube became part of him as it turned red and bled him into the bag. The chair was hungry.

He settled back into the Siege Perilous and waited for the alarm to sound.

* * *

It started the night Stephen revealed Emily and Dawn's secret by the bluish flickering of the television. Right after Brian said "a secret mission," they snuck out of the yard, suppressing thrilled giggles. The walk to the Douglass house through chilled streets was quick, the mournful calls of wild peacocks following them.

If they had seen something that night, it would have been the perfect capstone and maybe it would have calmed the thing that had awakened in Brian. But Risa's window was dark, so Brian turned inward, imagining what could have been.

Brian slept over at Stephen's the next weekend. The conversation was perfunctory, just a breathless prelude to what Brian really wanted to know. "Tell me about Emily."

And Stephen did. There was a part of him that hated himself, but there was a stronger part that needed to relive it. He omitted only one thing: the role of the poster. The dancer was not Brian's. She would never belong to any other.

The weekend after, they returned to the Douglass home. The weekend after that as well. On the third in a row, they found themselves camouflaged in the greenery at the edge of the Douglass backyard, having hopped the fence. They marked Risa's window easily, the golden light showing next to nothing as she got ready for bed.

Brian's breath came quicker, hand absently rubbing at his groin. Stephen was not interested in the girl in the window. She was pretty, but she was a creature of the here and now. She had makeup and acne cream. She bled and carried.

The night adventures did not stop there.

As they walked home on that third night, Brian was flushed, eyes not really looking at anything.

"Steve? Can you, you know, work locks?"

Stephen shrugged. "Probably." Mentally he took the lock apart into its components, found the vulnerable spots and put it back together. "Why?"

"I have to get closer."

"Closer?"

"I want to be close enough. You know."

Stephen did know. Risa Douglass was a substitute for Emily.

A sacrifice. It was one that he was willing to make. Feed Brian to pacify him. It was the starving animal that was dangerous. The starving animal that lashed out.

Stephen and Brian ditched sixth period, Stephen from high school, Brian from junior high, walking to the Douglass home in the early afternoon. The air was soft and breezy like a bad lie. The street had only a few cars, but the boys were aware of their vulnerability. Stephen knew on a purely intellectual level that they were committing a crime. If Brian were caught, there was no telling what would happen to both of them. Instinct consumed intellect. It had to be done.

They hopped the back fence. Stephen felt completely exposed in the backyard, wanting nothing more than to slink back into the foliage, to climb the fence and run until his lungs burned to ashes.

They snuck up the porch, a wide and comfortable place to spend a sleepy afternoon. A cat watched them lazily from a white wicker couch. Stephen knelt by the door, while Brian watched the cat.

The makeshift picks took the lock on the knob quickly, and Stephen went to work on the bolt. Brian approached the cat. "Hello, puss. Come here, puss."

The cat flicked its tail.

Brian took another step.

The cat bolted.

Brian turned back to Stephen, disappointed. "Just wanted to say hi."

The bolt clicked. "It's open."

Brian dropped his backpack and unzipped the top to remove

a kitchen knife. The sun played across the large silver blade, turning it into a shard of glass.

Stephen's eyes got big. "What the fuck is that?"

"Calm down. I'm not going to use it. I just want to have it."

"I'm not gonna let you hurt her."

"What do you care? You don't even know her."

"It doesn't matter. I let you in. That means that it's my fault if you do something."

"I won't do anything. I just want to watch."

Stephen shouldn't walk away no matter how exposed, but the eyes of neighbors were in every darkened window, behind every sighing bush. "Promise?"

"Promise. Take my backpack home. I'll see you tomorrow."

"Yeah."

Stephen picked up the pack. Brian disappeared inside. Risa would be home in an hour or so, and it would be too late. Trust that Brian wouldn't do anything, and if he did, at least it wasn't Emily.

Stephen double-timed it from the neighborhood, only slowing at Brian's street as though that would somehow exorcise the deed, arriving right as Jessica was coming home. She was in the fifth grade, still pudgy with baby fat. Her face lit up at the sight of his approach, but the expression fell a bit when she saw her brother's backpack over his shoulder.

"Steve! Where's Brian?"

"Don't worry about it."

She rolled her eyes. "You guys don't tell me anything."

"When you're older."

"You're barely older than me."

"I'm in high school."

"Only 'cause you skipped. I should skip some grades too. You want to come in? We have Girl Scout cookies."

"Sure."

Stephen spent the afternoon there finishing his homework over the thin mints, letting Jessica chatter on about the girls in her class, occasionally, grunting some agreement. Risa Douglass wandered through her room, oblivious to the knife in her closet. She was alive, sleeping. She was dead, bleeding.

"Are you okay, Steve?"

"Huh? What?"

He blinked at Jessica. She looked scared more than concerned, convinced she had done something to provoke his melancholy.

"No. I'm just worried, you know? Just worried."

"Wait here."

She ran upstairs. Shaking his head, he returned to work. After a minute, Jessica pounded down the stairs, then slowed in the hall. She came in, face flushed and watching the floor, cradling a small stuffed animal. She hesitated, then set it down in front of Stephen.

It was a little black bird, the fuzz on its neck smooth from endless petting.

"Whenever I'm worried, I tell him. Then I'm not worried anymore."

"Jessica, I'm not going to—"

"You don't have to talk here. Take him home."

"I can't take your stuffed animal."

"I want you to have it."

Stephen picked the bird up and turned it over. It had been loved nearly to death. "What if you get worried?"

She shrugged. "Maybe I'll just tell you."

"I'd be okay with that."

She looked at the floor and barely made it back into her chair, not speaking again, but when he got up to leave, she pressed the bird to him. The protest died in his throat at the hope in her eyes.

"Thanks, Jess."

Just before sundown, Stephen walked home, leaving the latchkey girl home alone.

The next day, Stephen was relieved to see Risa Douglass walking to school. Brian hadn't done anything. After school, a grinning Brian held up a small glass unicorn.

"What's that?"

Brian didn't bother to hide the pleasure that bubbled up behind every word. "I waited until she got home. I could have gotten out when she went down for dinner, but I waited. I watched her get ready for bed. I waited until she was asleep. I could have killed her if I wanted to. She's mine now and she doesn't even know it. Maybe I'll show her this and tell her sometime."

* * *

Sculpt her in negative. The mold was the first step. The body would be easy. She could be solid through and through. Her head would be hell. The seam could be concealed in the scalp, under the Louise Brooks bob, but a part of Stephen would always know it was there. The other seams in her joints would have to be cast carefully and sanded with precision to render them smooth and invisible.

When he tried to sculpt the molds, his hands betrayed

him. Palsied fingers tore huge rents through her thighs, slashed her face. Every strike was murderous on his unborn daughter. Working until spiders washed through nerveless hands, the only fruits of futile labor were bitter tears. The chisel clattered across the attic, cast away for its uselessness.

The dancer picked it up, went to him, and without glancing at the sketches, got to work. Her hands were sure, as sure as her father's had once been, his knowledge of anatomy moving her, helping create her sister. When the mold was finished, she set the tools down and returned to the window to contemplate the arroyo.

He looked after her, wanting to say something, but couldn't know what.

The next step was filling the molds. He was able to do that, at least. This was done in the coach house, at the site of the new furnace. There were no illusions. This would take at least a couple tries. Air bubbles would kill many pieces during conception.

The third step would be joining the pieces.

The eyes would have to be constructed on their own. This one would have more human eyes, bright blue. Stephen would blow the glass himself.

The hair would be black. Same as the dancer's.

Not everywhere. Emily's appointment would make her look cleaner. Perfect. Smooth between the legs, a living doll. A perfect cleft. Unashamed.

The labia would be four separate pieces. The vagina could be created with the insertion of a small steel rod in the molding stage, and the resulting genitals lined with soft velvet.

Her proportions would be more feminine than his dancer's.

Her skin would be the uniform ivory of the porcelain, with none of the ebb and flow of a human woman's complexion.

Her mouth would be intricate. Soft tongue, inscribed truth in Hebrew: *aleph-mem-tav*. Gears and pistons concealed in mouth and cheek to make it work. This one wasn't a mute ballerina. This one would be the mistress of the house. This one could entertain.

None would know her. She would be kept hidden away. Design her for sociability and hide her from the world. It never entered his mind that she would have the needs he had designed in her.

He tried to go into Emily's room to lay out the costume, as he had with the dancer. The closed door stopped him. This was not a place for his new daughter. That room belonged to someone else. Going in was a violation. Other rooms were not as bad, but none were perfect. Everything had to be perfect. Something pulled him down the creaking stairs and into the parlor.

Stephen's breath came more quickly as he laid the costume out on the couch. Where his dancer was simple, this new one would be as frilly and complex as a woman, all soft spikes. His dancer was effortless grace, this one would be mannered and studied and built.

Stephen laid the newest doll's costume inside-out.

He placed her panties in the center of the bed, imagining her behind the fabric. They were tiny and white, the thong barely there at all.

He framed it with the garter belt and stockings. White again, with black straps and borders. Clean connected by dirty. The shoes were white, heeled, strapped at the ankle. There was a theme of straps with this one, strapped into her complicated clothes, strapped into her complicated life.

White satin elbow gloves would mirror her legs.

The corset was white, with black embroidery. It would hold her breasts in place, pushing them up, though they would stand up proud and fake.

Below, a frilly black and white half-skirt. Open in front to frame the white triangle at the apex of her legs.

The black choker with the white cameo at her throat. The pearl-drop earrings. The collection of bracelets and rings over the gloves.

This one would be covered nearly head to toe, and yet show every feminine curve, from neck to ankles.

She would be perfect.

* * *

Working in the dental porcelain was easy. That is one of the things Stephen designed it for. Unlike wood, it did not have its own stubborn grain. It was never alive and so had no desire to remain as it was. The symbolism bothered him, but there was no more room for doubt. It would work because he wanted it to. Clay had never been alive, and had worked, at least in the distant past. This was a different kind of clay, one always intended for life of a sort.

The body was finished. She was not yet dressed, lying on the floor, inside the ritual circle, ringed in black candles. She was still clean, not yet covered in blood.

He was nude—his ritual garb.

The dancer lurked in the corner, watching, her eyes clear.

He imagined a thousand things running through her impassive stare. At turns she was hurt, aroused, angry, prideful, lost. Really, she was inscrutable, and had been since her birth in that same attic nine months ago. Perhaps it was merely alien interest in the circumstances of her creation. Stephen couldn't know how much she remembered, if anything at all. Had her consciousness sprung into being there, or it had been summoned?

This one would talk. She could tell him what came before and what came since. She would be so much closer to a real woman. But not too close. She would be clean and smooth. She would not have the past to haunt him. She would not sweat, nor excrete, nor bleed.

She lay still. The three bags of blood, drawn over the course of the last two months, were at her head. Stephen knelt by her body as the doubt flooded into him. This would not be the same ritual. He had changed it. It was horribly possible this doll would remain lifeless.

He lifted the first bag, bringing the knife to the plastic skin. The head of his penis throbbed in poison memory. The knife tore through the first bag. The sharp tang of pennies hit him as blood splashed over her body and ran off in meaty streaks. He tossed the empty plastic aside, picking up another, slashing it and spilling the blood up her smooth legs. As the drops poured into the fold of her vulva, he nearly retched. It was almost too close to reality. She was not a woman. She was a doll. She was a new creature. Far more perfect than anything living could be.

He slashed the final bag, dumping a pint of himself over the doll's mouth and chin.

All birth needed pain. Stephen opened his mouth and

grabbed hold of that piece of meat so like a writhing slug. Two slashes, two agonizing, white-hot slashes, and blood flooded into his mouth.

Blinking away tears, bringing mouth to mouth, to give the last part to her in a kiss, a deep red breath into her body. In his mind's eye, the blood trickled past the clockwork gears of her throat, soaking into porcelain bones.

He rocked back on his heels. Some part of him was disgusted. Mouth drooling sticky strands of red, his hands were wet to the wrists in blood and even as his erection throbbed painfully.

The doll's eyes opened. The lids were mere shutters. This one could open and close her eyes. This one could blink. Maybe this one could sleep.

These eyes were glass, closer to marbles. The irises were not perfect. Neither were the pupils. From far away, they merely looked slightly odd. From close up, the uncanny valley turned them into something more horrible than the dancer's blankness, for there was something within those eyes, looking back at Stephen.

She lifted one bloody hand up. The dancer had done the same, caressing his cheek in comfort at the moment failure had seemed his only prize. This one looked first to her own hand. Her body moved, not as graceful as the dancer, but languidly, sensuously. A knee came up, the thigh folded under in a gesture of unconscious proto-modesty. Only then did she fix her eyes on Stephen.

"Maker?" she said.

He tried to speak. It came out in a crimson bubble.

The doll rose up, resting on an arm and hip, casting an eye

around the room. She appeared to be concentrating, trying to remember words, or else conjure them where they had not ever been. "I... I am here now."

He spat out a mouthful of blood, wincing as it tore through the fresh cuts. He considered taking her there and then, penis erect and at her eye level, but it wasn't right. Instead, he reached for her hand. She took it, allowed herself to be guided to her porcelain feet. She was unsteady for a moment, catching her balance, learning to stand and walk in seconds.

As her eyes swept the room, she said, "Firstborn."

The dancer stepped forward from her corner. The new one, his concubine, fixed the elder with the alien gaze.

Stephen tried to speak the other doll's name.

The concubine nodded. "The Firstborn."

He placed a finger on the new one's chest and gave her a questioning gaze.

She smiled and moved closer. Had this been Christine Barrow, there would be hot breath on his neck. With the doll, he felt nothing at all; just the closeness of something that was—but was not quite—alive. There was a brief rush of terror. She was the other. She was not alive, and yet she moved. She stepped into him, her hands lightly on his hips.

He pointed to himself.

She said, "The Maker."

He pointed to her.

"You can't ask that." She shifted uncomfortably, turning away, trying to hide her nudity from him.

He frowned.

"Don't be stupid." She took him by the hand, pulling. She

was stronger than he was, though not as strong as the dancer—
the Firstborn, she was called the Firstborn. His concubine's
hand felt like cool ivory. Their palms, both covered in blood,
stuck together, a scab forming between them. When it fell away,
their flesh would be joined forever.

He turned to the Firstborn. Her back was to them, disappearing
into the shadows. The concubine pulled him to the ladder.

He looked back into the darkness.

"You created me," she said. "I'm here now."

He nodded.

"Come on."

She pulled him into bed, and when they finished, he drifted
to sleep on sheets streaked with gore.

* * *

The newest doll waited until the Maker was fast asleep,
motionless, like a corpse. She laid him on his side so he would not
choke on the thick blood sluggishly flowing to form a crimson
blossom on the pillowcase. There was not quite enough red
around him to make a convincing crime scene. He could have
been a body moved from elsewhere, if not for the gray rise and
fall of his chest.

She rose. Even alone in the moonlight, in the room of the man
who had created her and with whom she had just made love, she
seemed self-conscious. Her porcelain flesh had softened a bit
with the transformation, but she still made light clinking noises
with each step. She moved into the hall, found the stairs to the
attic, and took them up.

The Firstborn stood in shadow.

"You should come down. Join us."

The Firstborn was still.

"He hasn't forgotten you."

The Firstborn was still.

"The Maker wants us both." Her words were certain, but her voice wasn't.

Finally, the Firstborn stepped into the moonlight, approaching her sister, stopping only as the shadows of the window fell through black bars over white flesh. She turned and walked to the window, looking out into the night.

The concubine left, curious about the house. Part of her knew it before she saw it. Still, she wanted to explore the connection. To know she truly belonged, even as she felt like an afterthought.

First she went to the Wretched's room. She did not belong there. That was for the Firstborn and the Firstborn alone. Downstairs perhaps. Only the dead had claimed it. She drifted into the parlor. Closer. The chair by the front window. That was right. That was her place, something she knew without knowing, and felt almost right. She settled into it delicately, crossing chiming legs.

Near dawn, she returned to the Maker, still in the same position she had left him.

CHAPTER NINE

IT WAS PAST MIDNIGHT WHEN Stephen made it to the Nite Lite. The new doll's second week was nearly finished. The cuts on his tongue had healed partially so speaking barely hurt. The Firstborn had not left the attic since the night her sister was born, but there was scarcely time to notice it, not with the constant wet presence of the new doll. She was not as pliable as the Firstborn. Stephen often wondered if that was a good thing.

The parking lot was not empty. The cars belonging to the cooks were lined up by Audra's.

He rubbed exhaustion from his eyes as he strode across the lot. The dolls were back at the house, doing God knew what. They had been scattered throughout, each in their little worlds. That they should have little worlds was horrible enough, that these worlds were big enough to get lost in was even worse.

Best not think about it.

Audra was in the front of the restaurant, taking a slice of the banana cream pie from the refrigerated display case and frowning at it like it had just lied to her. She looked up as the bell rang. Quick smile, look at the pie, put it back and poured him iced tea. He slid into his usual booth, feeling the heat of her behind him.

"Just you tonight?"

"Yeah."

"Girlfriend stand you up?"

He stuttered, "I... I don't have a girlfriend."

"Oh. That girl you were here with the other night. I thought..."

He laughed. "No, no. She's my best friend's little sister."

"So?"

"So, we're not dating."

Audra looked like she wanted to say something provocative. Instead, she said, "The usual?"

He nodded.

"Be right back."

She was, filling up the iced tea again. "So how's your project coming?" The venom within the statement might have been manufactured and it might have been real. He had never apologized to her for the stupid thing he had said before and the incident had been forgotten into something huge. Bring it up, and it was back, worse than ever. Be content it never happened and maybe it never did.

"It's okay. I'm trying to make complete molds. Um... this may sound creepy. Could you smile please?"

She did a cute little curtsy, her eyes up, shoulder tilted, adorable and retro. Her teeth were slightly yellow, but more importantly, straight and even.

"Your smile is perfect."

Blushing, she said, "Never had braces."

"Can I take a mold of your teeth?"

"Does it hurt?"

"You bite two chunks of wax. One for upper, one for lower.

The worst thing you're going to get is a bit of a bad taste in your mouth, but I'll buy you that piece of pie you were looking at if you'll do it."

She made a face. "I'm on a diet."

"Since when?"

"A week."

"Why?"

Quickly, words tumbling out, she stammered, "I have to go to a wedding. High school friends. I want to be a little closer to my old weight."

He shrugged. "Okay." She was lovely. Soft, vital. Alive. A mystery. He didn't know every inch of her body before touching her. Which would mean slick fumbling, which would mean embarrassment, which would mean her laughing which would mean never coming here and seeing the slope of her neck.

"Sure. I'll bite your wax." She made a lame joke face, but bulled on, "Is it at least tadpole shaped?"

"No. It sort of looks like a boxer's mouth guard."

"No, because when they tried to market Coke in China, they called it 'Bite the Wax Tadpole.'"

"That doesn't make any sense."

"Well, you try to write a gibberish word phonetically in another language. It'll come out weird. It's like when they tried to sell the Chevy Nova in Mexico. 'Nova' means 'won't go' in Spanish."

He smiled. "Is that true?"

"Of course," she said. "I read it on Wikipedia."

Laughing a little too hard, he loved the way her eyes sparkled when she said it.

She grinned, "Do you have the wax on you?"

"I have to run and get it. You mind if I eat first?"

"'Course not. Let me get your sandwich."

A moment later she handed him his fried fish and mayo. Fifteen minutes later, he said, "I'm going to get the mold. I'll be right back."

He drove fast—too fast—and thundered into the house. Quiet, only the soft sounds of the dolls moving. No voices. He could not face his newest creation, not with the flush of another woman on him. Upstairs, the shadows drank the Firstborn's pale silhouette. Ignore it. He pulled the attic trapdoor down and climbed upward, found his table and clicked on the fluorescent. Two unused tooth molds waited on the desk. He grabbed one and turned.

The Firstborn was standing there. "Jesus, you scared me."

She did not move.

"Okay. I'm going to go." He moved around her, down the stairs and out the front door. The clock in the dashboard said 2:10. Audra sat outside by the door of the Nite Lite. When he came from the shadows, her face brightened and she walked out to meet him.

"I have it." He waved the wax at her.

She took it and bit into it, making a face.

He said, "Keep biting for thirty seconds and, I don't know, I'll buy you a Diet Coke or something."

She made a sarcastic thumbs-up gesture, bore down for a half minute and took it out of her mouth along with a clump of saliva. She spat it out awkwardly and wiped her mouth. "Sorry."

"Happens. So, want to get the taste out of your mouth?"

She laughed and nodded. "Do you buy them ass-flavored or is that included?"

"I add it myself."

* * *

Dawn Molinaro kept Stephen from kicking Emily out the night she interrupted him and Christine.

He was one of three people that knew the whole story and the only one of those on the outside, having watched it through the wooden slats of Emily's closet, ringside seats to her desolation, and nothing to be done for that. Comfort would become betrayal.

He was thirteen, a year after his mother's death and only a week before the poster was gone. Things had begun to normalize. It didn't hurt quite as much or as constantly. He could be sane for long stretches before the grief would break through the membranes and bring him down.

The Work helped. It was not fully formed, but it had begun its long gestation. The sketches were secreted around his room, in desk drawers, in notebooks, under the mattress. His father no longer cared, Emily was wrapped up in her own mind, but there were guests. The Baniszewskis and Emily's friends. He couldn't have them accusing him of playing with dolls. Not when the truth was the other way around.

The Work was taking shape. The dolls would have to move, but that was impossible. Not in the books he read. But in reality. There had to be a way to bridge that gap.

But he was also thirteen and easily distracted, body and mind lashing out in all directions. He wanted to get to the time and place in which he could fuck the world. No matter how beautiful the girls at school, or browning on the hot sand of the beach, or laughing on television, their faces would quickly be covered with the pancake makeup of the dancer. He often would find himself in Emily's room, looking raptly at the poster, feverishly masturbating. He had almost been caught on several occasions since that first time, but luck had made him cocky. That day, he sat on Emily's bed, penis in his right hand, tissue in the left, locked in a fantasy of a swanlike neck, harlequin eyes and sleekly strong legs.

He didn't hear Emily until it was too late.

She must not have been talking. Had she not hit a loud creak in the hall, she would have caught him. The bathroom door was across the room; the closet was closer. He rolled off her bed, hand gripping the waist of his pants, and stumbled to the closet, ripping open the door and hiding amongst the girl-smelling depths of Emily's clothes. The room was visible through the slats of the closet, though any movement made it flicker like a silent movie.

Emily's door opened. She was seventeen, four years older but only two grades ahead of Stephen. Her face was bright red— blushes showed easily on her Black Irish complexion. Before Stephen could see the field, the hair on the back of his neck was already standing up. Something was happening. He couldn't be sure what, but knew the electricity spiking from Emily was not his imagination.

He saw why in the figure that followed. Dawn Molinaro was Emily's best friend. Stephen's eyes fell from Dawn to Emily to the dancer that seemed to watch over them, *en pointe* in her candy paradise. Emily pulled Dawn to the bed and their lips met. Dawn pulled away for a second.

"Em, please."

"Don't worry about it now."

"We talked... we don't do this anymore."

"You always say that. One more time."

"Not this time."

"Like always."

As if to prove her right, Dawn attacked Emily's mouth hungrily. Jaws worked, hands gripped in a desperate sort of kiss, both girls trying to hold on. Dawn seemed to push away with her arms, even as her hands grasped Emily.

Stephen felt himself harden again.

He wanted to take the grip again, but it was Emily. He couldn't watch her.

Emily pulled Dawn's shirt over her head. Her flesh was smooth.

He could watch Dawn. Or his beloved dancer.

The choice was made. Clothes vanished, nearly torn from soft skin. Lips played over bodies. Hands worked secret places.

Stephen's eyes fell from Dawn, then from the dancer in that crucial moment when he went entirely white, eyes falling to the contours of Emily's ivory skin, where Dawn's hand pressed into the apex of Emily's thighs.

He gasped, terrified that the sound carried through the slats of the closet door.

But Emily and Dawn were making noises of their own.

Stephen tore his eyes away, wracked with self-loathing that was nearly overwhelming. Tears wobbled in his eyes, but they would not fall. He hadn't earned that.

He watched the ground instead as each girl cried out.

Breaking the thick silence of the room, Emily said, "I love you, Dawn."

"I told you not to say that."

"It's true."

"We're just fooling around."

"I know." The tone said otherwise.

There was rustling. Stephen looked. Dawn had stood up, was gathering her clothes from the floor. She was hunched over, back to Emily, trying to hide the nudity that she'd brazenly shared. Emily reached for her glasses, put them on, magnifying those blue eyes.

Dawn said, "We're stopping. We're not doing this again."

"I know."

"No, you don't. I mean it."

"You always mean it."

"Em, stop it. We're not dykes."

Emily reached out. "Come on."

Dawn flinched, an instinctive reaction. "No."

Emily was silent.

Dawn bulled on, pulling her clothes on. "We're never doing this again. We never did it in the first place."

"Yes, we did. We made promises."

Dawn looked away. "I was confused."

"No, you weren't. Come on, my dad won't be home for a couple hours and my brother won't bother us. Come here."

Dawn bit into the comment. "No. This is not happening. When your mom died, I thought you needed some, I don't know, a shoulder or whatever and it got out of hand. That's all this was. A mistake that lasted too long."

"It wasn't a mistake."

"Whatever it was, it's stopping. Forever."

"Don't."

"It's over, Em. Just don't... don't talk to me for awhile."

Emily's voice was suddenly small. As she moved into a supplicant position, Stephen hated what grew between his legs. "Don't talk to you?"

"You used me."

"I wasn't—"

"You did. And it's stopping."

After Dawn left, Emily waited to hear the front door slam before she started to cry. In that room that stank of sex and the closet that stank of him, both Monaghans cried in their helplessness, never closer and never farther from one another.

*   *   *

The Firstborn watched the Maker's car peel out from the attic window.

She left the attic shortly after. Her purpose was not obvious. She did not walk as a human being did and did not appear to be searching for anyone or anything. It was the graceful pace of a ghost, wandering the same paths for centuries. And she was a ghost, of the Maker, of the house itself and of one not present but always so.

The Firstborn didn't follow the sound, and it was not clear if she even heard it, for it was soft. If she did, and if she could have drawn the comparison, it would have sounded like fine china being scrubbed. It was coming from the parlor.

The Firstborn traced the path of the hall, and then slipped

through the dining room on the way to rendezvous with the hypnotic sound, passing through the darkness and stopping, path ended.

Her sister lay back on the couch, legs pressed together over her right hand, digging into herself. On the table, fixed in her glassy gaze was a small stuffed toy—a blackbird.

The Firstborn did not move. Her sister let out a small moan accompanied, shuddering with the sound of soft chimes. She opened her eyes.

"Hello."

The Firstborn took two steps forward and knelt. Her sister reached out, fingers wet, smelling gently of fresh clay.

"It feels nice," her sister said into the silence.

The Firstborn touched her sister's cheek. The other doll moved closer, the two harlequins leaning in for a satin kiss.

"Do you want to know?" her sister asked when they parted.

The Firstborn stood, stripping out of her ballet costume. There might have been eagerness in something more human, but the Firstborn undressed with the same alien grace with which she did everything.

Her sister ran a white hand over the fur between the Firstborn's legs, up the dancer's belly, before hooking her around the slender waist and pulling her down, guiding the Firstborn to the couch. The concubine knelt between the other doll's legs. "I think you're going to enjoy this."

* * *

Audra had fetched two pitchers, one of iced tea and the other of Diet Coke. They refilled their glasses as they emptied.

Stephen tried to ignore the insistent pressure in his bladder. To leave, even for a break, would be to lose the moment, maybe forever.

He poured another glass of tea for himself. The restaurant was empty, except for the single cook dozing in the entrance to the kitchen. Outside, the streets were dead.

"I love this time of night," Audra said.

"So do I."

"Yeah. Because you feel powerful, right? There's something about being awake when everyone else is sleeping. You feel like you're something... I don't know."

"Like the rules don't really apply."

"Yeah."

"I work through the night, usually, except when I'm down here. My friends think I'm crazy."

"My friends tell me I should work normal hours. I mean, they offered me the day shift. Much better tips, but I don't know. It would mean giving up the night, and once you do that, you can't really get it back."

"I know exactly what you mean."

"You do." She was looking into his eyes, seeing something there.

His eyes traced the smooth curve of her bare shoulders. Freckles. She was fairly covered in them. Close up, they were blotches of color. Ink, shot into skin, spreading like a bloodstain. Dots. Different sizes, irregularly spaced. Impossible to do it in wood. Porcelain would be beyond impossible. Latex. Some kind of latex.

Then maybe she wouldn't smell of the grill.

"Where did you go just now?"

"What?"

"You were thinking of something. I saw you. You were listening, and your eyes went all far away and you were gone."

He blurted, "A new kind of latex, I think."

"Weren't you working on dental porcelain?"

"It's finished. I just need to file the patent."

She shook her head, chuckling. "You're, like, crazy smart aren't you?"

He thought that was a particularly good way to say it. "I guess so."

"God, the sky's getting light. How long have we been here?"

"I wasn't keeping track."

"Me neither. I have to be getting home."

"Yeah, probably a good idea." He reached over to the bill, still unpaid.

"Come on, Steve. It's on me."

"I'm not going to make you lose your one ticket of the night."

She went behind the cash register. "I'm not going to talk you out of that." Closer, he could see what Jessica was talking about. Farther down, her hair was bright, unnaturally red. Along the scalp, it was a lighter strawberry blonde. Neither shade was perfect. Something in the middle. Closer to blood.

"What are you doing Friday?" Audra said.

"Nothing, I think."

"You want to come to a party at my place? It's nothing big. Just some friends."

I'm a friend? "Sure. Yeah."

"Cool." She wrote her address on a restaurant business card. "Here you go."

He handed over the receipt and the credit card. She scanned and handed it back to him, followed by the receipt to sign. He took the pen in hand and put down Stephen Monaghan.

Or tried.

The signature went haywire. It was chicken-scratch. A series of spiders. He had even misspelled his own name. Scratched it out. Tried again. The same.

"I'm... I'm sorry," he said, fleeing the diner. Looking at Audra, seeing the mixture of confusion and disgust that had to be on her face, was impossible.

Stephen floored it on the way back to the house, rushing up the drive, and barreling in the door. Through the parlor, through the dining room and into the kitchen. He grabbed a pen from a drawer and the blank pad off the fridge and wrote his name.

Worse than the first time.

He wrote it again. A scrawl. A child's writing. And again. Another misspelling.

One of them was behind him, making no sound. The concubine's hand slid over his.

"What's wrong, Maker?" she said.

"I can't write my name."

"Shh," she said. "It's easy." She lifted the pen and signed in his old handwriting—Stephen Monaghan.

He spun away from her. "How the fuck did you do that?"

A smile spread slowly across her face. She was still nude, but now she was unashamed, flaunting her body at him. "It's easy," she repeated, explaining everything and nothing.

"No! No, it's not. I can't fucking sign my name!"

"I can. That should be good enough."

He nearly reared back and struck her. Would violence have broken whatever hold he had on her? Would that have freed her from this bondage and given her the will to strike back?

Instead, a familiar form behind him, the lightly warm body of the Firstborn coming closer. Her arms slid across him, inhumanly strong, but gentle as always. It was her skin caressing his, not the leotard. She was nude as well. Something flickered across his brain, vanishing as quickly. One perfect harlequin in front, the other behind, thought of Audra, talking to him when she didn't have to.

"Let the Firstborn take care of you." The concubine stepped from the room, her porcelain skin vein blue in the moonlight.

The Firstborn let him go only enough for him to turn into her. She returned the embrace and allowed him to lead her upstairs. He wanted the comfort and intimacy of their bed. She was willing to be led.

She fell back onto the bed, knees open. He fell on top, ready to enter her. Her powerful hands landed on his shoulders. There was no clue to her intent in those clear eyes. She pushed him, gently but firmly, and with her strength there was no resisting, until his head arrived at the folds he had sculpted. They flared, blood pulsing through the unnatural tissues. Unlike a living woman, she smelled clean and beautiful. He leaned in and tried his best to please her.

* * *

Stephen and Brian were fourteen when it happened. By then, a confrontation was inevitable. Stephen knew it, and Brian probably did as well. Stephen had worked hard for the past year and a half to keep the thing inside Brian fed. Such action was only a delaying measure. Brian's vision was clearly on a single prize.

Emily.

Ever since Stephen told about Emily and Dawn's encounter, Brian had not gone a week without mentioning her. How hot she was. How the thought of Emily and Dawn together made him feel. How Emily was the perfect thing. That was the word he used.

Thing.

Stephen would not let Brian have her. Stephen wished it were entirely altruism, but something linked Emily and the dancer, a moment of release bonded them, leaving them spinning over the darkness entwined.

Still, he couldn't keep the thing inside Brian at bay forever. Denials were no defense against that knowledge. They were fourteen when the thing could no longer be caged.

It was a Friday, of course. Those were the prime hunting nights. Neither Stephen nor Brian slept as they should. The creatures inside kept them both awake. Stephen was in his room, working by the reflected light of the reading lamp, turned to face the wall, bathing him in soothing twilight. He sketched the dancer again, trying to get the proper angle on the left side of her face. The side turned away from the viewer, so there was no way to it, forcing him to conjure it with symmetry, to give her what she was. There was no thinking. It had to be simple knowing.

Emily was out. She was always out on Friday nights these days. Those were game nights and it meant she would be with her boyfriend.

One of them, anyway.

Stephen went through dozens of iterations of the picture without getting the perfect one. The perfect one was a mystery, perhaps an impossible goal, but in chasing it, Stephen defined himself. The pencil scratched to a halt on the page. He didn't know what made him stop. The house had its way of warning the people within, as the boards rumbled with the hunger of a colossal stomach. He set the drawings aside and stood, picking up an X-Acto knife sitting amidst the plastic frames of some modeling kits.

He was still dressed, except for bare feet; perfect for moving against this phantom prowler. He didn't believe it was anything, but wanted it to be something. Something to do. Something to make a lonely night important.

Stephen realized all of a sudden—the intruder was Brian. Had to be. Stephen was Brian in reverse, a defender rather than an invader, and knew his reflection.

The hall was silent, empty, but somehow pregnant. In front of Stephen, the door into the game room yawned open, black beyond. The time for games had passed when Sarah Monaghan died. The hall was perfectly dark. No looming shapes, no shadows thrown against the wall. He ducked back into his room.

He thought of sitting back down, of returning to the Work. The dancer wouldn't let him. She called to him from Emily's room and the summons could never be ignored. He opened the door into their shared bathroom, clutching the knife in a white-knuckled hand. He pressed an ear to Emily's door, straining to hear anything.

Nothing.

He opened it. Moonlight was the only illumination. Eyes still adjusting to the silver light, he turned to where the poster used to hang. Instead of the image of perfection, Emily had replaced it with an image of Dave Gahan and Martin Gore, pouting at the camera. Along the borders, she had added pictures of her and her friends, drunk, mugging, miserable. At the top, a scarf hung like a parted curtain. He was still able to come to it for comfort, to know his ballerina was ready to cross the barrier and be real. Merely a matter of replacing the lie for the truth.

Something was wrong. The hair on Stephen's neck stood up as he turned to the back of the room. The closet where he had watched Emily and Dawn stared back at him. He took a groaning step toward it. Then another. Another.

He pulled the Venetian door open with a creak.

Brian stared back at him, holding a butcher knife, point down.

For a moment, neither boy spoke. Stephen was the first, saying, "What are you doing here?"

"You know. I want to see Emily."

"Get out."

Brian grinned. "I'm gonna stay, Steve. You're gonna close this door and go back to your room and keep your mouth shut."

Stephen's eyes went to Brian's knife. In the moonlight, it looked six feet long and dripping with quicksilver. Stephen's was tiny, weak. Obeying Brian would be so easy. Emily would be safe. Brian had never hurt anyone. Not yet.

But Emily was special.

Stephen felt his feet working on their own, backing him toward the bathroom. The moonlight flashed off Brian's blade. Stephen turned from the reflection.

Into the image of the dancer. The poster was years gone.

Stephen's mind never let it go entirely, sketching it there in exacting detail.

She wouldn't let him walk away. She wanted Brian away from this sanctum. This room was hers, and she would keep it inviolate. Stephen turned back to Brian and took two steps forward.

"I said get the fuck out."

"What?"

"You heard me."

Brian's voice shook. "Stop fucking around. If Emily catches you in here, we're both fucked."

"Get out, Brian. Not going to tell you again."

"What are you gonna do?"

"I'm not sure yet." Stephen pushed the tiny blade of the X-Acto knife into his palm. "I can think of something."

Brian's eyes went big at the sight of the blood welling up from the meat of Stephen's hand. "Holy shit, dude. Don't do that. It's cool."

The blood looked black. Stephen felt the water growing in his eyes. He wouldn't let it fall, fixing an implacable gaze on Brian. "I told you to go."

Brian ran for the door, retreating into the game room. The shed was directly below the window, making it the easiest way into the second floor from the outside. Stephen heard Brian go back out the window, and the other boy was gone to the night. Stephen went into the bathroom to look at his hand.

The puncture was a little less than an inch deep. The blood was thick and every time he flexed the hand, it burned up to his forearm. It was hypnotic, watching the blood slowly drip into the porcelain sink.

"Oh, shit. I'm sorry, Stephen." Behind him, Emily in her Friday clothes: heavy makeup and a short skirt. Her tights were gone. Her hair was mussed in the back and her mascara had run. She stank of flesh.

Her eyes got huge. "Stephen! What happened?" She ran to him and cradled the hand in hers. The sink was splattered in blood.

He held up the knife.

She said, "You shouldn't do your projects in the dark! This kind of thing was bound to happen." She didn't look into his face, just put the hand under the tap and washed it. "You might need stitches."

"I don't want stitches."

"You might not stop bleeding."

"That's good."

With those words she met his eyes. "Don't say that." She looked back down at the cut. "It looks like the bleeding is slowing down a little." She bound the wound carefully, disinfecting and pressing on it with gauze. "I'm checking on it every day. If it looks bad, you're going to the hospital, okay?"

"Okay."

Brother and sister were silent. Stephen wanted to tell Emily what he'd done, that he loved her, and he was sorry for the trespass she still didn't know. More than anything, he wanted to warn her about Brian.

The words wouldn't come. She hugged him and filled his nose with her pungent backseat stench. She said, "You're such a spaz. Get some sleep, okay?"

"Goodnight, Em."

He tried to sleep, but the wound burned too much.

* * *

The rash was growing. Jessica scratched at the raised welts along her forearm, wishing they would go away. It wasn't the only outbreak. A strip ran up her right thigh. Another came over her shoulder. She had an appointment with the doctor who would say it was only eczema.

She sat at her desk, absently scratching at the irritated patches of skin and thinking of Stephen Monaghan.

Mooning over him was stupid, though it grew less so by the day. The night after the party where she had slept pillowed on his chest, the night they had gone out for pie together. It had been a schoolgirl crush at one time, but she wasn't a schoolgirl anymore. And he was no longer older and unattainable. There was nothing between them she could see.

Other than Brian.

She thought of that day often, when she saw what she was never supposed to. She was promised to others, those she would never want. Not after that. Even if she couldn't understand everything she witnessed, it had been a metamorphosis, not outside, but in. Brian held those boys, and they were boys, no matter their actual ages, in such patriarchal contempt. To them Brian promised to give Jessica. She was never supposed to see that, and though she didn't quite understand everything that had happened, she would never completely trust her brother again.

And perhaps worst of all, was Brian's tacit believe that she was a thing to be given.

Brian had tried to warn her once, of Stephen specifically, and men in general. It hadn't made much sense. She wanted Stephen and would get him, if she could only work up the courage to fail.

Jessica had thought of him often over the years—the one boy who had always been nice to her when no one else was, who listened when she spoke, responding in oddly wonderful non sequiturs. He was beautiful, in his strange way, with graceful hands and eyes almost too blue. He was ethereal, never completely there, merely on loan to this reality.

More than anything it was the one thing he had said to her. He probably never thought of it again afterwards, just said it and drifted away into the air, not knowing she had taken it and made it into a safe cocoon.

"You'll be going places."

An office in Pasadena, doing meaningless paperwork and answering phones. It was not what Stephen had in mind with those words and it wasn't what she wanted for herself. It was nothing, a holding pattern. It had held since she got out of college with her useless English degree.

He had wanted more for her in that moment. She wanted him, wanted to be the person those words were meant for, the person worthy of his gallant rescue. Become her, and she would be the woman he could love.

More than anything, she needed a purpose.

* * *

He slept through the day. For some of it, both dolls stayed in bed with him, one on either side. At other times, they took turns wandering the house. Stephen's concubine picked up the

Firstborn's ballerina costume from where it lay at the foot of the bed and turned it over in her hands. The Firstborn watched the nesting birds.

Stephen finally awoke well after dark. They were with him, watching with inhuman eyes. "Good night," the concubine said.

He wiped his eyes. "What time is it?"

She didn't answer. The clock did. Making freckles was long hours of Work ahead. The question of whether it was possible to duplicate something so human was a fascinating one to him. His first two daughters could not pass as flesh and blood under close inspection, but with the skin he had in mind, this one might. That would be the test.

He emptied his bladder and got dressed. The house would not help his thinking. The Nite Lite would lead to him talking to Audra, although she would ask him about the previous night and he didn't know what to say. He needed to be alone. Needed the night air.

The dolls seemed to sense it, letting him go with scarcely a glance. The air was chill, but he felt better in it. The streets were dark. In the hills, streetlights could be few and far between. Walks at night in a neighborhood with small or absent sidewalks could be considered a death wish.

Stephen set out with no destination, working through the equations in his mind, wandering down streets claimed more by flora and fauna than people. Houses peeked from behind curtains of foliage. He couldn't appreciate the scenery. Not with the puzzle worrying at him.

The feeling was a slow one. Something soft, bobbing alongside. Following the smell—a skunk, but lesser. He looked down.

A coyote was walking alongside him, blithely brushing against him.

Stephen let out a yelp and jumped backward.

Only then did the coyote turn with a surprised yelp of its own, turning to a snarl. They faced each other for a moment, before the creature ran off into the underbrush.

Stephen walked home very quickly.

CHAPTER TEN

THE MONEY DIDN'T ADD UP.

Dolls were expensive. That's what the dwindling accounts said, the effect compounding every time Stephen pulled money out. When it was spent, the money no longer bred. Without money there could be no Work.

Part of him was aware of the diseased irony that still thought of it as the Work. He had proven life could be created, had duplicated God's feat, twice over, with no indication there was a limit. A race, perhaps, forms varied as snowflakes, all created in the image of his mind.

The concubine had his signature. What else could they take?

He could not create without money. The planned body, sculpted from the wholly artificial, would cost more than the wooden dancer and the porcelain concubine. She would be a creature free of the symbols of the others. Never alive. Not even hinting at it, and he would bring her to life as well. Concentration was hard when the image of warm freckles and welcoming thighs entered him.

A job was unthinkable. To leave the dolls alone for nine hours every day would be torture. For a brief, insane moment, he thought of becoming a supervillain with his powerful daughters as a militant arm and nearly laughed out loud.

He thought of ways to get money. Brian was the obvious choice, still an honest man when it came to finance. Stephen rattled off the questions in Brian's badgering voice. What do you need the money for? I'm making people. No. Not people. Something better.

Money. Quick money. The realization was a slap to the face. *It might work.*

Clothes first. He was spending more and more time nude, even as the drafty house turned his skin into the surface of the moon. It was not entirely sexual. It was contact with the outside, at once increasing yet growing distant. There were friends, more than ever before; Brian, Audra, Jessica, friends for the deep of the night when even the most normal person felt like something apart from human.

As he dressed, glassy eyes found him.

His concubine stood in the doorway, aristocratic face cruel, especially behind the harlequin flourishes on her skin. Her pupils were hourglasses. She was elegant in her costume. Part of him wondered the judgment he'd receive if anyone glimpsed that part of his psyche given form.

"You're leaving us then."

"Not forever. I'll be back soon enough."

"It must be nice to leave when you like."

He burned, shrugged. "I have to."

"See your friends."

He thought it over. "Do you ever want to meet anyone else?"

Her posture closed. One leg moved in front of the white triangle at the apex of her thighs. Her arms crossed, one hand playing with the ring on her middle finger. "You want to bring people here?"

"I don't know."

"Maker, we aren't natural."

"How do you know that?"

She was silent.

He repeated, "How do you know that? I never told you. You only know me."

"I know it," she said. "I don't need to be told what is and what isn't."

"You knew I was the Maker."

She nodded.

"You knew your sister was the Firstborn."

She nodded again.

"Who are you?"

"I can't... I can't say it."

"I don't understand."

She crossed to him, her posture opening up, closing him within a cage of her arms and skirt. There was something living within her that knew things she had no way to know. "We are different. Others would fear us."

"I love you."

Her face changed, but only for a moment before descending back into stone. "No one else will. They would hurt us."

"You can't know that."

"Yet I do." Her odd eyes met his, close enough to see just how strange they were. She was right. She could not pass for human. A look into those eyes, a touch to her cool skin, and she would betray herself.

"I won't bring anyone inside. This place is ours."

She touched his cheek. "Good. That's safer for all concerned."

The concubine left the room. He couldn't escape the nagging threat within her words. Struggle against their meaning, and have it return, even stronger. Leave, begin the plan for the next doll, give the silent house to them. It seemed to be empty. In a way, it was.

His footsteps made the house moan.

* * *

Lulu's Petals was the goal, Tyler's presence was the hope. Stephen wished he had gotten Tyler's number. Something seemed dangerous there, though whatever danger Tyler represented was a mystery. Maybe it was simply because Brian didn't like Tyler and that was enough.

It was still early in spring, the air sharp. Stephen got past the bouncers, beginning to wonder if he had become a regular. There were worse places to frequent.

The air of the club was close. It made him think of his attic, the way it felt like the throat of a giant. It was crowded that night, with groups of people pressed against the stages, studiously ignoring the nearly nude soft-shoe. Stephen snaked over to the bar. It was slightly raised, and a good vantage to try to catch a glimpse of Tyler's birdlike crest. The dancers were far too distracting. The kohl-rimmed eyes were pale echoes to him; the hair disheveled when compared to the perfect bob of his doll.

His gaze fell from them to a pair of brown eyes looking directly into his. The tunnel fell away to reveal the rest of the face—Jessica Baniszewski. They blinked in unison and she raised a hand to wave. Waving back, he took in the rest of the tableau. She was with her brother and four of what Stephen guessed were Brian's friends, the J. Crew models. There were always four of them, maybe the ones who taunted Jessica at that party so long ago. Stephen imagined so, or else Brian warped people around him to fill those specific roles. Brian would always have his pack of four. In the dim light of the club, the shadows gathered at the corners of their faces, sharpening brows and twisting mouths. The four men were beasts in human form, but only barely.

Jessica dove into the crowd for Stephen immediately. Brian did not notice, and Stephen was grateful. Explaining he was looking for Tyler would raise more questions than it would answer, almost as bad as asking Brian for the money.

Jessica, sweaty and tired, popped through a wall of black. Despite her flushed cheeks, she was wearing a cardigan over her dress. "What are you doing here?"

He responded with simple half-truth. "I like it here."

"I thought you didn't leave the house."

"I don't always tell your brother when I do."

"I'm surprised he hasn't seen you here."

"He took me here. Actually, to talk to me about you."

Jessica was distracted, not by anything present, but still, she caught that. "About me how?"

"Big brother stuff, I guess."

"He's an asshole. Doesn't care if he's pimping me out to his creepy friends, but he's got a problem with you."

It was as though Brian could sense those words because Stephen looked up, right into the other man's face. Brian's expression was first confused, then something between realization, relief, and anger. He took step toward them, but the pack enveloped him, unconsciously conscious.

"Is that what he's doing? Pimping you?"

She rubbed her right arm. "That's what it feels like sometimes."

Stephen saw the cockatoo crest moving through the crowd. Tyler.

"Jess, are you going to be okay? I have to do something."

"Umm... okay?"

"I'll be back. I promise. Stay here."

"Okay."

He slipped into the crowd, catching Tyler by one of the stages, talking to someone, and immediately losing interest as soon as Stephen materialized from the crowd. "Hey... Steve! How are you?"

"Good. You?"

"I'm glad I ran into you. I was hoping I could talk to you."

"Yeah?"

"I was hoping I could borrow some cash from you. Not much. I just need a little to get through."

"No."

"Look, Steve, I'll pay you back. It's not..."

"No. I won't loan you money. But you can win it."

"What?"

"You teach me poker. I pay you with what you win off me."

"That could get expensive."

"Only if I'm a slow learner. I'm not a slow learner."

"Where?"

Stephen remembered his promise to the dolls, but were they

actually dangerous? A dry run, with Tyler, someone who didn't really matter, might work. Tyler's life wasn't worth Emily's. Or Jessica's.

"My place."

"Give me your address."

Stephen did. "Tomorrow night?"

Tyler said, "You want to hang out, maybe get me a drink?"

Stephen turned around and found Jessica. Let Tyler serve his purpose, if he indeed had one. Better keep Jessica company. Brian had made it to Jessica's side, moving in front of her protectively as Stephen emerged. "Hey, Stephen," Brian said, trying to be casual. Stephen caught the tension under the voice.

"Brian."

Jessica squirmed behind him, nearly pouting.

"Were you talking to Tyler just now?"

"Yeah. He's a good guy."

"No, he's not. You shouldn't be talking to him."

"No? I shouldn't talk to Tyler. I shouldn't talk to Jessica. Who should I be talking to?"

"That's not what I meant."

"Yes, it is." Stephen walked past Brian and addressed Jessica directly. "You want a ride home?"

Brian's grip was a vise. "Stephen. Talk to me."

Stephen pulled away and a gunshot blasted across his mind: hit Brian, bludgeon him with one of the bottles across the bar, or grab an ice pick and puncture the soft flesh over the aorta. No feeling colored the flashes. Brian recoiled, but only slightly. In that moment, Stephen saw the same thoughts in Brian's mind, only reversed.

Brian said, "Jess, stay here."

She looked from Brian to Stephen. In Stephen's mind, it was an impossible choice. Brian was right—Jessica should stay far away from Stephen. A promise made to Jessica would inevitably be broken. That couldn't stop the need to bring her home, to introduce her to his dolls. To bring her in and never let her go. But she was flesh and blood and he could not love her.

"No, I want to go home."

Stephen said, "I'll drive you."

She took Stephen's hand and pulled him away. Her hand was hot in his, their breath quick. He understood now what Audra had thought. What Brian meant.

Stephen glanced back at his best friend. The hatred in the other man's eyes was far from invisible.

The night air hit Stephen and Jessica in a cold blast. They did not speak. Stephen's stereo kicked in, softly playing a wall of symphonic noise as a soft feminine voice whispered a dirge. Jessica turned up the volume. He drove too fast, needing to get little Jessica Baniszewski home as fast as possible. She was half-turned in the passenger seat, hands tracing something on the arms of her sweater.

They were nearly alone on the road. The only light was the sickly yellow of the streetlamps. The Nite Lite shone like a beacon. Tonight it was only a distraction.

Jessica's voice was so low, he barely heard it over the music. "You don't have to take me home if you don't want to."

Turning it down, he said, "You want me to drop you off?"

"I could stay over at your place."

He let that hang, never slacking the frantic pace of his

driving, pulling them up the back streets, the curves snaking them through the back parts of the city. The streetlamps were no longer balls, but smears of yellow light fighting to close his eyes.

She said it again.

"I heard."

Her hands went back to her forearm, fingers probing at the rough softness of her sweater, picking as though at a scab. "I'd rather not be alone."

"Then you should have stayed with your brother's friends."

"I mean I'd rather be with you."

He couldn't think of anything else to say. "Why?"

"So we can... I want to be with you."

They were on her street, the houses nothing more than blurs. Her complex was just ahead. Jessica was too close. Her breath, her perfume, natural and artificial, permeating every inch of him. Braking in front of her place, he wanted to grab her like one of his dolls, to lean over his seat, kiss her, tear her clothes from her, take her. What would happen next would be inevitable. It had happened before with Christine Barrow, and it would happen with Jessica. The problem was Jessica wasn't someone who could be surgically excised from his life. She would always be there, just like her brother. Humiliation with her would dog him until the end.

"I can't."

He heard the tears in her voice. "You're serious."

"I'm sorry, Jess."

She leaned over, her hand hard on his groin, and realized he was fully and painfully erect. He strained against the stroking hand, trying to push through the fabric, joining flesh with flesh.

No. He would not flay himself in front of her.

She said, "You don't want to leave me. You can't fake that."

She climbed partway over the parking brake. Her breath smelled heavily of bourbon, but there was blood under it, hot and spurting. She sucked his bottom lip into her mouth and flicked her tongue lightly over it. For a moment, he gave in, grabbing the back of her head and pushing, too hard, and their teeth clacking. She was real. So real.

He pushed her away.

"Jessica, you're too drunk."

Her breath, coming fast and heavy. "No, I'm not."

"Yes, you are."

"What does it matter? I want to do this when I'm sober. I've wanted to do this for a long time."

"We can't, Jessica."

"Why the fuck not?"

"Because I don't want to lose you."

"You'll only gain me. All of me."

He pushed her gently away.

"No."

She gave him a long look before opening the door and getting out. "You're an asshole sometimes, you know that?" She slammed it.

Stephen couldn't be with her, even as he burned with memory. The refusal guaranteed she would never speak to him again. Excised, leaving a Jessica-shaped hole nothing would ever fill. She would have rejected him regardless. This made it worse.

He tore up his driveway and nearly leapt from his car, flinging the front door open, hungry, animalistic. The concubine was downstairs in the parlor, sitting by a window, legs crossed primly even as every curve she had was on full display.

"Are you finished for the evening, Maker?"

He pulled her to her feet and crushed his lips to hers. She responded knowing what he needed and taking what she did. She did not embrace him. When they parted, she was grinning.

Her hands played at the porcelain skin of her forearm. No scabs. No rashes. No imperfections.

"She wasn't what you hoped for."

"She? Who's she?"

"Don't play games. The Heart. You were with her. We know it, you know it, and now you want to fuck."

"Shut up."

"I've been wondering about her. Does she smell of tuna fish?" The doll seemed to be surrounding him, even though she was only one person. No. Not a person.

"Shut up!"

"I know you. You want me because you think I'm not real. You want me because you can't have a living woman. You want me because you can't bring yourself to fuck who you really want."

"Shut your fucking mouth!" Stephen lunged at her. She caught him by the wrists. For one insane moment, he imagined biting her. Instead, their lips met and she was moving under him. He growled and tried to turn her around. She resisted for a moment—to show him she was stronger—before acquiescing. He lifted her skirt and ripped her panties from her.

She braced on the chair. "See? Fuck me, Maker. Prove me right."

He gripped her hips and shoved himself into her. She made

an odd sound, something between a gasp and a chime. "Is her skin greasy? Does she sweat?"

He thrust into her brutally. She continued to taunt him, even as the chiming took her voice. She was shuddering beneath him now and he lost control, emptying himself into her.

For a split second, the black wad of hair he now held in balled fist was chestnut brown.

He pulled out of her, lurching toward the couch. "She would never do that for you," the doll said. She stood gracefully and smoothed her skirt down. "Do what you've been thinking. Make us another sister. Someone as soft and pliant as you need."

There was an unspoken part of her sentence, but Stephen couldn't know if it was the human statement, or something arcane and immortal behind it. Where was the source of his concubine's rage?

She picked up her panties and smiled. "Torn. Don't think I can quite fix these."

She left him in hatred.

* * *

It wasn't Brian's last party, but it was the one Stephen remembered that way. It happened the year before Christine Barrow. Stephen should have been a senior in high school, instead finishing sophomore year in college.

Brian was having an after prom party at his old place, the huge craftsman sitting almost on the lip of the arroyo. Brian hadn't invited Stephen exactly. Those things didn't have to be said between them. The Work wasn't going well, and Stephen needed company or at least alcohol.

He started driving at eleven from Claremont, knowing he'd be in Pasadena by midnight. The bass rumbled up the street in crashing waves, slapping him in the chest. Nearly every window blazed with gold light. Shapes moved past windows, drinking, holding, laughing—an alien intimacy. Stephen, slinking up through the dark, was a parasite.

He walked up the front steps, didn't bother to knock, and barged in through the front. The guys were in tuxes, the jackets gone, the vests unbuttoned, bowties hanging in two lazy halves. The girls were in gowns, still beautiful. Their hair had fallen, their makeup was three touch-ups into the evening. Everyone looked alive. Not like him.

Familiar faces loomed in the crowd, but none looked at him with anything approaching pleasure. He tried to ignore it, couldn't, let the horrid taste of cheap beer wash it away. Two bottles went with him to the empty study. He settled down in one of the high-backed leather chairs and got to drinking.

After a minute, the door opened in on him. It was Brian, holding Risa Douglass in a drunken headlock, two other guys behind him. "That's not a crasher. That's Steve Monaghan."

"Whatever, man." The guys disappeared. Brian came in, not as drunk as he was pretending, his grip a vise on Risa's neck. She kept her face plastered with a fake smile.

"Risa, you know Steve, right?"

"Yeah, I think so. You went to South Pas Middle School, right?"

"For a little while." Had Brian ever showed her the glass unicorn he'd stolen from her room? Or was it still a sharp promise?

"Steve skipped some grades. He's a genius."

"Really?"

Stephen nodded. "That's what the tests tell me."

Brian laughed too loud, and when Risa tried it, it came out brittle.

"Come on, Steve. We're doing a shot."

"Sure."

Stephen pounded the last of the second beer. The room swayed underfoot on the way to the kitchen. The liquor was set up in rows of cheap tequila, vodka, and rum. No need to ask where it had come from. The Baniszewski parents hardly cared what the kids did. They were probably out of town.

Brian let Risa go. She waited until she was free of his peripheral vision before rubbing her neck. Brian poured two tequila shots and handed one to Stephen.

"To graduation."

"I already graduated."

"To my graduation and to you finally getting some pussy."

Stephen blanched, trying not to show it. "Sure."

He swallowed the burning liquid.

Brian said, "Shit, it's great to see you. I didn't think you were coming."

"Wouldn't miss it."

Brian grinned and grabbed Risa by the neck again, dragging her from the room. "Hang out if you want."

Stephen took another beer, heard laughter coming from the living room and followed it, if only to feed from the outside. He crossed into their living room, a usually bright and open space, and it was dark, barely lit with guttering candles. The four boys spread around the room were nothing but barking heads, the girls strips of frosting laid across their laps. For a second, the boys' eyes shone like wolves in the dark. They had honed in on a solitary figure in the corner. She was a skinny thing in shorts and a t-shirt, hugging her coltish legs.

Jessica Baniszewski.

One of the guys said, "Anybody order pizza? She brought some on her face."

They howled, even though it wasn't funny. Jessica sat there and took it.

Another of the guys said, "Stand up. I want to know if those toothpicks go up to an ass."

Stephen came into the room, the beer burning in his belly in lieu of courage. "Shut the fuck up."

The guy looked up at Stephen and laughed. "She's got a boyfriend? You gay or something?"

"Lay off her. I'm not going to tell you again."

Maybe if they were alone, the challenge could have gone unnoticed, but their dates were there. Stephen was attempting a castration, and the guy had need of his balls later. He shoved the girl off him and stood up. "Tell me again."

Stephen would have backed down on any other night. Something in him wouldn't allow it. "Should I say it slower? Shut the fuck up."

He never saw the fist fly until it exploded in a bright flash. The second one was right on top of the first. More laughter rattled through the room, now infected with something animal. Swinging blindly, Stephen's fists slammed into meat, barely feeling the impacts from the other boy's punches. He kept throwing fists in violent answer. The other boy would know he had been in a fight. He'd touch those bruises and remember the words spat at Jessica.

Hands covered Stephen's shoulders, yanking him away. The impacts stopped. His vision returned on a rolling thundercloud. The other boy, mouth bloody, was being pulled backward as well. Stephen looked over behind him and found the boy who belonged with the hands.

Stephen never struggled, and the other boy let him go. Stephen's opponent snarled and spat like an alley cat. "Come on, Jess," Stephen said.

Mute, she rose up on her toothpick legs—Stephen hated that he saw them as the other boys did—and followed him from the room. The adrenaline evaporated, leaving blossoms of pain over his body. Replace beer with adrenaline. He'd left his mostly full beer in the living room. Two more from the kitchen replaced it. Jessica stayed behind him, head bowed like his feudal bride.

He led her to her room, the room of a girl trying too hard to be a woman. Posters of brooding boys were slicked over the pink wallpaper. Softball trophies turned a shelf into a glittering gold army. Stephen shut the door and collapsed into a wicker chair. Jessica settled on her bed.

Only then did she start crying.

She was fifteen and it wasn't being kind to her. Glittering braces and a tragic complexion, a body entirely made of knees. The boys downstairs were assholes, but they were right, and that was the worst part. She admitted it with every sob she failed to hide. He reached out and laid a soft hand on her elbow. She turned her face away from the pillow. Tears matted hair and eyelashes. She looked at the hand, her body contracting into it. Too close for him. He leaned away, pulling on the piss warm beer.

"I'm sorry," she said. "I didn't want to cry."

"Fuck it. Cry if you want to."

She looked up at him. The braces split her face in a railroad.

He went on. "Those guys are idiots. Fucking morons. They're never going anywhere. You? I know you. You'll be going places."

She sniffed.

"I've been there too. Brian's party, everyone is a dick. People like us... we're invisible until they want to fuck with us. We don't need them."

She said, "We don't need them."

"Damn right."

"Can I have some beer?"

"Fuck no."

"Why not?"

"You're too young."

She gave him a sobbing laugh. "You're not twenty-one yet."

"Yeah, but I'm older, so I can make up rules I want to make up."

She flopped on her bed, hiding her face amongst the stuffed animals. "I'm sorry I cried."

"Stop apologizing. It's okay. Girls cry."

"Do you?"

He looked into the murky depths of the bottle. He murmured, "Sometimes."

"When does it stop hurting?"

"I don't know. It doesn't hurt now. Does it?"

She whispered so softly it was nearly inaudible, "No."

The silence that followed drifted back into words, but they returned to something safe, ephemeral nothings until she fell asleep. He left as the sky was turning red, boys and girls passed out around the house. The sun would disturb them before Stephen did.

He didn't see Jessica for many years.

* * *

Stephen had not slept when Tyler knocked on the door the following morning. There was too much to do, and there could be no sleep over the sounds of Jessica and the concubine. As soon as his eyes closed, Jessica would taunt him in the doll's words as the doll drunkenly begged him for sex.

He tore open the door. Tyler flinched. "Hey, Steve. I'm here."

"I know." Stephen blinked and looked out at the night sky. He put his attention back to Tyler. The house groaned behind him. This had been a mistake. The house hungered, and spurred by the ivory dolls within.

"For your lesson." Tyler held up a pack of cards, still wrapped in shiny cellophane.

"Right."

Stephen was still wearing his clothes from the previous day, shirt unbuttoned and sweat stained, eyes ringed in purple and a chin covered in patchy black stubble. Tyler followed Stephen inside. The house smelled strange—not quite mildew, but something far more vital.

Stephen led Tyler through the parlor and past, into the

dining room. The inner wall drooled. Stephen sat down at the head of the table, Tyler nearby.

"So what's with you and Brian's little sister?"

"Nothing."

"Didn't look like nothing."

The house moaned. Tyler glanced at the ceiling. Other flowers of moisture bloomed up there was well. "Is she here?"

"No."

He opened the pack. The house moaned again. "Is someone upstairs?"

Stephen thought of the dolls moving through the hall upstairs. "We should go."

"There's someone upstairs?"

An unshakeable image: the dolls coming downstairs, ready to enforce Stephen's promise for him. "Come on. We'll play somewhere else."

He practically pushed Tyler out the door and tried not to think of what had almost happened.

* * *

Stephen returned in the evening. His fight with the concubine haunted him. Partly for the venom with which she had cut right to the soul of him. She had to know there was more to it. He loved her as he loved her sister, as he loved... The end of that thought was too terrible to finish.

Proof. Show the concubine what she meant. He expected to find her awaiting him in the parlor. She wasn't. Listen for her, find the sounds of her footsteps, a toast being made over and over. There was nothing. He ran upstairs, fighting panic. Nothing.

Had he dreamed it all? The Work, the dolls, everything? Jessica? No. It was too real. Scars throbbed within a body far too altered for that kind of thinking.

He opened his closet, digging into the detritus of youth—old journals, a greasy license plate scavenged from the 110, a roll of stolen police tape. He sifted through this to find the real treasure: the old prototypes.

Before sculpting his precious dancer, the perfect Firstborn, there had been dry runs. He sculpted her in clay, carved her in wood, cast her in porcelain. It was this last he fished from the pile. She was dusty, but the joints still worked.

At the time, she had been a failure. The face was wrong. Instead of the welcoming Firstborn, she was closer to the cruel face of the concubine. That face had been with him for much longer than he had thought.

He brought her into the bathroom. The gift should not be dusty. Behind him, Emily's door opened.

The light footsteps belonged to the Firstborn. She stopped next to him, peering down at the tiny her in his hands. She brushed a fingertip along the doll's forehead.

"This was you."

The maquette bewitched her.

He cleaned the tiny Firstborn as best he could. The dust had taken root high on her white thighs. Hopefully the concubine wouldn't notice. The Firstborn had vanished, back into her wonderland.

Stephen went down the stairs and into the kitchen. Dinner was tomato soup and crackers, taken into the dining room. He set the doll on the table beside him and had built her well enough so that she could sit upright and even have a modicum of grace while doing so.

"Our sister is small this time."

He looked up. The concubine stood in the doorway, one hand on the frame, the other between her legs. Her panties had been destroyed. She had no others.

"Please, sit down with me."

"You promised."

"Promised what?"

She took the chair at the other end of the table. Looking at the doll through the candlesticks made her somehow more real. It was the view he had once had of his family, the ones living and dead. It grounded the doll in reality, making the breathless creature burn with life.

She said it again, "You promised."

He pulled another saltine from the column and ran it through the tomato soup. "Tell me what I promised."

"No one would come to our house."

"I know."

"The Monk was here."

"The Monk? You mean Tyler?"

"The Monk was here."

"He wouldn't have seen you. I got him out quickly enough."

She shifted in her chair. "It worried me. The Firstborn likes to watch them out the windows. If they look up..."

"I know. It won't happen again."

She touched the lacy tablecloth.

He considered her. The question was in front of him, black and terrible. It was impossible to say what frightened him more, that she would demur or that she would answer. "Where did you come from?"

"You made me."

He waved the sentence away. "Not your body. Your mind. Your personality. Everything else about you."

She watched him with hourglass eyes. "Where did yours come from?"

"I don't know. Answer me."

"You mustn't ask."

He looked at his soup, thick as the blood that had made her. He would need more for the others. There would be others. Even at this moment, with the concubine, having their first real conversation, the knowledge there would be sisters was ever present.

"You're right."

She started to stand.

"Please. I have something for you."

Her look was quizzical. She put her hands up, gloved fingers curling, ready to pull her top down. He shook that off, standing himself and picking up the doll.

"I wanted to give you this. I made it when I was nineteen. It's not very good, but I thought you might want it."

He placed it in front of her.

Her face was blank. Finally, she reached out and picked the doll up. "What is it?"

"A doll. A test. I was still trying to sculpt you."

"You sculpted me second. She was first."

"Look at the face."

She did. She did not speak, setting the tiny doll down on the table. "Clumsy. You've gotten better since then."

He returned to his seat. The anger from the argument roiled beneath the surface, rendering him mute for the rest of the meal. She was silent as well. Finished, he took the food back into the kitchen, leaving her with her hated gift.

When he returned she was gone. As was the little doll.

* * *

The call was surprising. Stephen thought he had ruined things the way when he ran away. There was no explaining why. He couldn't tell anyone.

Her tentative voice asking him to come was too soft, sweet, and genuine to refuse. The dolls were silent on the point, each taking their places and pointedly, it seemed to him, looking at nothing in particular.

Audra wanted him at her party. Would it be a reunion of the late nighters? The old man who ate peach pie every Thursday. The two teenagers who wrote pop-punk songs and guzzled Coke by the liter. The cop who slurped coffee through his mustache and watched Fremont Street.

Or would Stephen be the only one who had passed that point for her?

He drove west. Audra's address was in Highland Park, one neighborhood over and one socioeconomic class down. The green of South Pasadena faded into corn yellow. Dirt turned to dust. Antique turned to old.

He followed the directions scrawled on a scrap of paper in further decayed handwriting. It looked like something a child would write and was only getting worse. The letters no longer quite came together. He tried to avoid thinking of it, only to have it slap him in the face in the form of an innocent note.

He turned down her street—a short hill terminating in a drop off from above. A single, decaying, concrete staircase disappeared upward to that ledge where the houses were invisible from Stephen's vantage. They could live their lives without ever knowing the other was there, right below.

She lived in a bungalow up a short flight of cracked stairs. Moths whirred around the porch light. A low *wallah* came from inside, sounds Stephen associated with ostracism. He considered getting back in his car and driving home. The dolls were waiting for him. The dolls accepted him. They had to.

He forced himself up her stairs, forced his hand on the railing made from an old pipe, forced his fist to rap on her door. The *wallah* faded to approaching footsteps. He could bolt, vaulting the railing and getting to the car. She might only see the back of him. Never know what a coward he was.

The door opened, Audra on the other side. She squinted, seeing Stephen free of context for the first time in her life. For a single, horrible moment, he thought she would send him away, maybe laugh with her friends that a joking invitation had been taken seriously.

But then she broke into her perfect smile. "Stephen! I didn't think you were coming."

"Me neither."

She opened the door into a small living room packed with people. These were the artistic types, with thick glasses and tattoos peeking from underneath lived-in clothes. They smiled at Stephen, aware they weren't seeing one of their own.

"Hey everybody, this is Stephen." There were waves and

hellos. "Stephen, this is everybody."

"Hi." His shell was so inviting, so safe. Retreating would defeat the purpose of coming. Be normal for an evening. Try it on. See how it feels.

"Can I get you a beer or something?"

"Sure."

Stephen looked around her living room. Audra was a reader. Books were everywhere. She had an old record player and a good chunk of vinyl next to it. How had he come to a place like this? Audra was far too interesting, far too alive, to know.

He turned to another wall. She had put up shelves, and on every shelf, toys. Some were vintage ray guns, others were plastic robots. Toys of every shape and size. All bore marks of use and decay. She had arranged them in no order he could see. His eyes transitioned from one display smoothly to the next, spiraling to the center like a whirlpool.

Seven baby dolls. Each in different styles, all grimy, all nude, all with crayon carving their faces into waxy death masks. Stephen reached out, but couldn't quite bring himself to touch them.

Audra came around the corner and handed him an open beer.

"What are these?"

"I collect toys." She paused. "Only used ones. Some of them are from dumpster diving. Others from garage sales. I've been to the dump a few times."

"Why?"

"There's something about a discarded toy. Someone loved it, but threw it away anyway. These are my favorites." She gestured to the baby dolls.

"Why them?"

"Because they're precious trash. See, when a kid outgrows her doll, she can't just give it up. She has to destroy it first. Usually strip it, take a limb or head. Sometimes they vandalize them too, to make them look even less human. It's a desperate plea to themselves. Like they're trying to convince themselves they don't love the doll and never did."

"What would you think of someone that did the opposite?"

"What?"

He shrugged. "I don't know."

"Come on, let's be social."

She found Stephen a seat and made room for herself on the couch by making a joke at the expense of her big ass. It took Stephen a while to speak up. The conversation spanned important things. Stephen didn't understand politics as such. He could only comment on the definite.

They seemed to accept him.

Several hours later as the evening was almost gone, Audra walked him to the door. "Thanks for inviting me."

"Thanks for coming."

"I had a good time."

"You don't get out much, do you?"

"It's that obvious."

"No, no. I didn't mean it like that. Just that you shouldn't make this a one time thing."

He thought of what she said on the way home, especially the look in her eyes and the smell of her breath. The fingers of her words caressed the nape of his neck. As his headlights splashed through the gate, the fingers turned into a vise.

Brian stood in the driveway.

Stephen got out of the car, mind slammed with desperate thoughts. Did Brian go into the house? Had Brian seen the dolls?

No. He must have stayed outside. If he had gone inside, something would have happened. They would hurt him. Stephen couldn't stop them if they decided to do something to Brian. No one could.

"Where've you been?" Brian said.

"At a friend's house."

Brian laughed. "I'm your only friend."

"Not anymore."

Brian's smile looked demonic in the headlights. "Who's inside the house?"

Stephen's blood went cold. "No one is in the house."

"I saw someone at Emily's window. I looked up, and the curtains were moving, like someone backed away quickly. Like they didn't want me to see. So who's up there? It's whoever was housesitting, isn't it? Whoever you didn't want me to see."

"Brian, I promise you, there's no one home."

"You don't want me to see because I know her."

"No."

"It's Jessica."

Stephen croaked, "Jessica isn't here."

"Maybe you should show me."

"I can't."

Brian turned and walked for the house. Stephen ran after him.

"Brian, wait!"

Brian whirled and shoved Stephen backward. He hit the

gravel, hard. Was the blood running over his palms on the inside or outside? Regardless, it burned.

"Don't make me hurt you."

"You want Jessica? Call her!"

Brian looked toward the house. Emily's curtains twitched. What would it take to launch the Firstborn from the house, ready to tear Brian apart with her bare hands? How close was she to that already?

Brian took his cell phone from a pocket and hit a few keys. "Jess, where are you, right now? Answer me. Just do it! Okay. Bye." Looking up at Stephen: "She says she's at home. I'm going to check. If she's not, I'm coming back and we're having a talk."

"Brian, don't do this."

"I'm not doing anything. You decide where this goes." Brian took several steps from the house. "If she is at home... what's inside you don't want me to see?"

Stephen didn't answer. Brian let out a chuckle. "Don't try to hide things from me, Stephen. I know everything about you."

Brian walked back to the gate before Stephen got up, brushing himself off. "That road goes both ways."

Brian stopped. Stephen thought the other man would turn and come after him. Shut him up for good. But Brian started moving a moment later.

When Stephen went inside, he found every knife in the house stabbed into the doorjamb.

* * *

For the next several weeks, Tyler and Stephen met at the Nite Lite for the poker lesson. Audra kept their drinks full and flirted with both of them. Stephen tried to concentrate on the game, and ignore the insistent thoughts of his next creation. The new doll lived in the twirl of Audra's hair, in the swing of her hips.

By the third week, Tyler wasn't taking anything home. It was time. Stephen told Tyler to find him a game. A week later, the call came.

Stephen was sitting down at a table in Griffith Park forty-five minutes after the phone call. Milena Franco, Tyler's girlfriend, was across from him. She had a look on her face for the first hour like she was trying to remember Stephen's name. Eventually, she dismissed it, got into the cards and proceeded to clean up. The game broke up five hours later, and Stephen was up four hundred dollars. By his count, Milena had done a lot better. It was fine for a first time out, even if the shuffling had gotten to him, cramping sore hands. They did that more than ever these days. Rubbing the cramps barely helped. Flexing pushed the cramp into a hungry background at least for a little while.

As he walked to the car, her voice, behind him, "Excuse me?"

He turned. Milena did not jog to catch up. She didn't seem the type. Others would adapt to her, never vice versa. She pulled on her cigarette as she fell into step next to him.

"You're Tyler's friend, right?"

He had to think. "Yeah, I suppose I am."

She let out a little chuckle. "Most people seem to have the same response to that question. I didn't know you played cards."

"I'm just starting."

"Really? You did pretty well for yourself."

"Not as well as you."

"I do this professionally. I'm supposed to do well." They paused at Stephen's car. "Do you have a plan?"

"What?"

"What are you doing now? I usually like to get a drink or three afterwards. There's a bar a couple blocks past the overpass."

It wasn't a come on. There was no need in her voice as there had been with Jessica in the car. The invitation was entirely innocent. He couldn't remember the last time anything was.

The bar was a faux-lodge, a kitschy reminder of the early '90s when the Pacific Northwest had been in vogue. She drank PBR. He ordered a girl drink. They slid into a booth together and faced off. Every person Stephen had ever met was hard to read, but Milena brought it to another level. He could often get broad strokes off others. With her, she could have been fantasizing about fucking or killing him and it would have looked entirely the same.

"What brought you down to Griffith Park today?" she said.

"I needed a way to make a little money. My patents are taking a little longer than I thought they would."

"Your patents?"

"I invented a kind of dental porcelain."

She raised an eyebrow, a rehearsed reaction. "That's a new one."

"That's the whole point."

"Cute." She took a sip of her beer. "Before you ask, I'm only a card player. No day job. I'm not an actor or writer."

He wasn't going to, but he was glad she told him anyway. "A professional gambler."

"Like you."

186 // JUSTIN ROBINSON

"I don't know that one game makes me a pro."

"It can. Depends on where the hooks go in. Know where they are, so you're the one using them rather than the other way around."

"I thought you were going to warn me off your beat."

"I wouldn't be much of a mob enforcer. No, there's more than enough for everybody. Remember that you can get an egg from a chicken as many times as you want, but you can only wring its neck once."

A sip from his drink gathered Stephen's thoughts for him. The alcohol was pleasantly invisible. "So how long have you and Tyler been together?"

She chuckled. There wasn't any humor in it. "We're not, really. Tyler's not with anyone."

He left that statement alone until she was on her fourth beer and he was working on the second fruit cup, asking, "What did you mean, Tyler's not with anyone?"

She was skilled at hiding the telltale lag to her thought processes betraying that she was closing in on drunk. "He'd kill me if he knew I told you, so keep it under your hat." Milena lowered her voice. "Tyler's asexual."

"What?"

"It means he doesn't have sex. No boys, no girls, no nothing. No desire. At all."

Tyler, in the mind's eye, to try on the revelation. It fit. The sexuality went into something inanimate. Stephen could easily identify. "It sounded like you two..."

She grinned. She wanted to reveal it, not to unburden herself of guilt, but as a point of pride. "He has a thing with sleeping.

He hates to sleep alone, so he pays me to sleep with him. The first time, I figured there would be sex, you know, he wakes up in the middle of the night, we're spooning or whatever, and we have that half-awake half-asleep sex where we can pretend it's a dream. He was the tablespoon, and when he pulled me close, I expected to feel him. You know, wandering hands, an erection, something. Nothing. So I shifted a little, kind of wiggled my ass a bit. Still nothing. So I went to sleep and I woke up the next morning and Tyler was sleeping like a baby. It's easy money. Hell, I've done a lot worse."

She let that hang, an apple for Stephen to pluck, but he didn't.

* * *

Stephen spent the first semester of junior year, the semester before Chris Barrow, at the École Supérieure d'Ingénieurs en Électronique et Électrotechnique in Paris. There were better programs for chemists, but Stephen convinced his advisor of two entirely true things. First, that Stephen's focus was too narrow on chemistry and the ESIEE could expand it to elements of engineering and computer science. Second, a concentration in sculpture demanded a semester in France. Both were true. Both were lies. He spent little time on his studies in Paris, doing the bare minimum for passing grades. They probably expected it for a young man's first time abroad. Though not for his actual reasons.

His true purpose was the Work.

The name that came up again and again in the research was the Marquis d'Aisecq. To learn more, Stephen would have to walk the same paths as d'Aisecq, seek the breadcrumbs the Marquis had dropped.

French was a problem. Self-taught as soon as the name d'Aisecq surfaced, Stephen's French was academic, used to read, not speak. Time could forge it into a tongue worth speaking, a process that cursed him with an accent both thick and halting.

Every researcher kept a diary. No matter what the subject, banal or wondrous, the creator would keep track of it. This was Stephen's quarry. The usual places, libraries and old shops, yielded nothing. For something that rare, private collections were likely the only possible hiding place.

There was a market for those documents saved from the fires of the Revolution. An underground pipeline, whose blood was grimy paper, its skin leather and worn. The entrance was through the bookshops, and Stephen used every bit of meager French to gain passage, contacting people by phone and email, asking for viewings, paying what he could, being polite and gracious. Every week, another appointment to view a private collection somewhere in the Paris environs, for stilted conversation and a search that would find only dust.

He had lost count of the private libraries he searched. Every time it was the same—arrive on a large, decaying doorstep, cash in an envelope, hand it to a gnomic Frenchman and be waved in. The air was still and dense in all, the weight of the ink and paper palpable even from a distance. Stephen would don his white gloves to protect the pages from the acids sheathing human hands, and peruse the various diaries for some evidence of d'Aisecq, be it mentions of the great man, directions to any remaining diaries, or records of friends and associates.

Stephen's spoken French grew stronger. No one would ever take him for a native, but entire conversations would pass without a smirk or misunderstanding from the other.

By December, time was growing short. Rain was nearly constant, a perpetual reminder that home was far away and friends were scattered and forgotten. Stephen would be home in Los Angeles within the month, empty handed, no closer to the culmination of the Work than when he left.

Until Gregory Sorg.

The email was simple. "Mr. Monaghan. You have visited several of my fellow collectors and I believe I might have what you are looking for. G. Sorg."

Though Stephen was getting the smallest of reputations amongst the rare book collectors, this was the first time one had contacted him. He made an appointment for the following day.

Sorg lived in one of Paris's nicer suburbs, a metro and cab ride away. A cold rain fell from the gloomy skies. The sun would set soon, unnoticed by nearly all. There was nothing in the sky except for gray.

The path toward the house was made from cobblestones, slicked by rain. Icy rivulets traced paths through his hair, down into his clothes. The streaked windows were dark. Had Sorg forgotten? Stephen knocked on the heavy door with a half-frozen hand.

He waited for long moments, the house beyond a soundless void. Without warning, the bolt was thrown, with no footsteps on the other side announcing the arrival of anyone. Had someone been standing there dormant the whole time? The door swung open. "Mr. Sorg?"

At nearly seven feet tall, the man behind the door looked like a dead tree—skin gnarled, fingers grown into fleshless claws, a misshapen head almost brushing the shadowed ceiling. It was possible he smiled. There was no way to tell. One of those bizarre hands held a flashlight, pointed at the floor. "I am Gregory Sorg. You must be Mr. Monaghan. Please, come in." The man's voice was odd, but Stephen could not identify how.

"Thank you," Stephen said, coming in and dripping on the dented hardwood floors. In the darkness of the house, cavernous rooms became yawning mouths.

"I'm sorry for the state of things. My home is old. The storm has turned out the lights." Sorg had some kind of accent, mostly French with older, unidentifiable parts. That was not the oddness tugging at Stephen's mind.

"It's fine. I wanted to thank you for this visit."

"You don't even know why I contacted you. Your coat?"

Stephen shrugged off the dripping jacket and handed it over to be hung on a coat rack by the door. "Please, follow me."

Sorg moved with a limp, his right leg apparently paralyzed. Though a heavy man dragging one long and useless limb, he made no sound at all lurching over the wooden floors. Stephen's footsteps echoed loudly off bare floors and vaulted ceilings.

Sorg said, "You are a rare book collector?"

"Not exactly."

"You look young."

"I'm eighteen."

"Very young to be so far from home. You're American, correct?"

"I am."

"Have you ever seen a twin speak to herself?"

Ice water ran down Stephen's spine. "I don't understand."

"Mr. Monaghan, you pose some strange questions to those to whom you have spoken. Word gets around about the young American who seeks out very specific people and yet shows no interest in the usual things."

"What are the usual things?"

Sorg turned, a tree swaying in a violent wind. "Not the Marquis d'Aisecq." The pits where Sorg's tiny eyes hid glittered in the gold flashlight.

Stephen fought to keep his voice level. "What do you know about d'Aisecq?" The question bounced off wooden walls, chasing itself down the mysterious hallways.

Sorg turned and shuffled deeper into the house, a place both menacing and familiar. They emerged into a library, shelves floor to cathedral ceiling, a table in the center. The lamps were dead, with several lit candles shedding light, blinding at the core, but quickly fading to gilded shadow.

"You won't tell anyone I had open flame in here, will you?" Sorg let out a groan that might have been a laugh. "I heard of you, asking about the Marquis, always quietly, always obliquely. Word gets to me, the way any words of the Marquis do."

Others involved in the Work? "How often does that happen?"

"Rarely. Tell me. What do you do?"

"I'm a student. Chemistry and sculpture."

Something washed over Sorg's features. Expressions were almost impossible to see on the man's face, but this seemed to contain elements of relief and joy, followed by deep thought for a moment stretching to awkwardness. Before Stephen could speak, Sorg shuffled to one of the shelves. "I have something to show you."

He turned, holding a small wooden chest, banded in iron, the wood red as blood. The scents of the room swirled over Stephen, trying to drown him. The box radiated power, but he could not put a finger on what that meant, knowing for certain something important was inside. Something wonderful.

"What is it?"

"I thought so."

Looking away from the chest was a battle, and when Stephen looked up, Sorg was staring right back. The old man had a look of recognition—a junkie seeing the same need in another. Stephen felt sheepish in Sorg's sight, even if that knowledge came at the same price.

Sorg set the box on the table, reverently. Angry scars crisscrossed the old man's leathery wrists, the tissue collecting in points like nipples that crinkled as Sorg opened the chest. Stephen leaned forward, not sure what was inside, knowing only he had to know. Nestled in velvet, a burned wooden right hand, fingers charred and partly consumed, only the ring finger somewhat intact. It was expertly sculpted, the articulated joints nearly invisible. A woman's hand.

Stephen's first thought was... *I could do better.*

Sorg said, "Do you know what this is?"

"This is the hand of the Marquise, isn't it?"

"Yes." Sorg's tree face split in what might have been a smile. "They say parts of her survived the fire. Lost over the years. All except this one."

Stephen wanted to doubt this. The scientist in him knew rationally this was merely a wooden hand. It could have come from a puppet, tossed in a fire the week before and trotted out to entertain the gullible. The lie was far more seductive, whispering promises requiring only belief to repay. Refusal meant the Work was a fool's errand.

Stephen said, "What do you know of the Marquise d'Aisecq?"

"I know the name. I know what the Marquis made that night."

"What night?"

"That is the second thing I wish to show you."

Sorg went to the same shelf and removed a leather-bound book, placing it in front of Stephen. The gloves went over his fingers unconsciously. The book was a treasure.

The writing was longhand, nearly calligraphy. Stephen read it with difficulty at first, then with increasing ease. Something about the candlelight, reading it by the same light by which it was written, made the words writhe with life.

It was the diary of the Marquis d'Aisecq. Stephen's goal, in front of him.

Stephen wanted to read it, cover to cover. References to the Work leapt out, even at a cursory examination, to one who had eyes to see them. Meaningful insight, though, would come only with time, long hours sifting through the long-dead mind of a genius.

Stephen looked up into Sorg's knotty face. "You're certain this is his?"

"As are you." Sorg shuffled away, the flashlight clicking off and the darkness swallowing him. From the shadows, impossible to tell if he was five feet distant or fifty, he said, "Tell me, how far have you gotten?"

"In what?"

"You are trying to duplicate his work. You are trying to create false life."

Stephen let the comment hang, bristling at the implication. False life. That was admitting defeat right at the start. The goal wasn't false life; it was something altogether clean and perfect. Snapping at Sorg was foolish with d'Aisecq's diary finally in hand. "Not far. I don't even know it's possible."

"It is. It has to be!" An edge of hysteria crept into Sorg's voice. "The Marquise was real, Mr. Monaghan. She lived. She died."

"What's in this book, Mr. Sorg?"

Sorg ignored the question. "I know your look. I have seen it before."

Stephen realized he had as well.

"I need to study this."

"Of course."

He was returning to the States at the end of the week. "Can I come back?"

"I would expect it."

And so it was. Stephen would rise and make the trip out to Sorg's home. The electricity was back on by the next time, and warm lamplight illuminated d'Aisecq's diary. Sorg left Stephen alone for long stretches to pore over the diary, sifting through the self-aggrandizing ravings of a madman. D'Aisecq spent pages railing against the allegations of devil-worship, claiming repeatedly the Work's goal was precisely the opposite. Stephen didn't care for this, only wanting to find the secrets certain to lie within.

Sorg returned periodically to check on him. The large man made no sounds on the old floorboards of the house. He would say one or two words in that oddly muted voice, and Stephen would jump. The question was always the same. "What have you found?"

The answer was variations of "nothing yet."

The diary was too dense, the secrets too well hidden. Time ran short. Stephen would return to America and leave a wealth of secrets behind. He would not do that. He could not.

His thoughts had a life of their own, trying desperately to turn down the same unthinkable alleys. Even as Stephen rejected the option presented, he began to pay more attention to the house looming large around him. Sorg would be wandering silently through the halls making no sound. Occasionally, Stephen would hear something else—the shuffling of old paper, the scratching of tree limbs, unsure if they came from inside or out.

Two nights before the flight, d'Aisecq's spidery words wobbled and danced. Concentration was impossible. It would be gone, lost in two nights. Those thoughts returned, whispering promises. Take a walk around the house. Leave the books. That would fight the thoughts calling out to him. Stephen tapped the open notebook, a few scraps of d'Aisecq's rite scribbled over the page, listening to the night. Silence, nothing more. He crept to the door to the library where it led into the hall. Empty.

Stephen snuck along the hall, peering into rooms. Every one of them was stuffed with old things. Sorg lived his life between stacks of the past and beneath Old World gentility. The tiled kitchen was small and cold. Stephen found a staircase to the upper floor, paused and listened at the bottom. Silence.

Gingerly, he took the stairs one at a time, remembering what it took to sneak up the wooden staircase at home—stay at the edge, plant the foot then add the weight. The stairs led to a landing and turned. As at home, a landing stood at the center. For a moment, Stephen was at home, resting at the landing.

Gregory Sorg's massive silhouette loomed at the top.

Stephen froze, stuttering, "Mr. Sorg. I'm sorry. I was looking for the bathroom."

Sorg said nothing.

"Mr. Sorg?"

Stephen waited for a response. Getting none, he took a few more stairs. Sorg was still.

Closer now, Stephen approached the hulking man, close enough to smell. A gentle stench of rotten wood wafted outward. Sorg made neither move nor sound.

Stephen got closer. The old man was a statue, not appearing to breathe. The chill working through Stephen started at the base of his spine. Two options sprang to mind. He could return downstairs and forget this, pretend it never happened, and Sorg would never know. Or venture deeper into the shadowed house and look for answers.

In the dark, the sound of long fingernails ripped across wood.

A thumping sound accompanied it. Stephen wanted to flee, but the rational part of his brain drowned it out. The thumping was not getting any closer and the rip did not repeat.

He squeezed past the paralyzed man. A hall stretched out to a shaft of moonlight the only illumination. Stephen stopped at the first door and listened. The sounds, the shuffling, the scratching, the thumping, all rattled outward from behind the old wood.

Stephen opened the door even as his body screamed at him to run.

The light was dim, the bulb flickering, dying. Still, the waning light was enough to see them:

A crudely-fashioned dummy, one arm paralyzed, the other trying to lift itself up and failing, over and over—*thump thump thump*.

Another dummy, half human, half animal, its claws tracing deep trenches into the wooden floor as it desperately hauled itself in mad circles.

A third, only a head, supported by poorly sculpted fingers, twitching and rolling and skittering in blind patterns.

They had no eyes, just pits barely hollowed out on the skulls. They had no mouths, just slits torn into their faces. They were not golems but some failed half-things that would never know the sublime glory of d'Aisecq's dream. Stephen felt at once terror and loathing, wanting to burn them to ash for both realizing and mocking his dream. All of them, crippled by a shoddy maker.

Somehow with their false hollows, they saw Stephen, flopping and floundering toward him. To punish him for the trespass or to fuck him in misguided gratitude, he couldn't know. The hypnotic sight of these broken dolls flailing in the dying light pinioned him. This could not be the true culmination of the Work.

The clawed one's hand bit into the floor, pulling its dead bulk toward the open door. The one-armed one flopped closer. The head skittered forward on its fingers. Stephen slammed the door and turned.

Sorg was beginning to move. Whatever had put him in the stone trance was calling him out of it. Perhaps the inane babbling of the half-things had called him with some awful burbling cry.

Stephen ran past the giant man.

Sorg called out, "Mr. Monaghan?"

Stephen fled into the library, grabbing the notebook. He hesitated for a moment, but it was a foregone conclusion. Sorg was unworthy of the diary. If the half-things were exemplars of Sorg's skill, the diary was best in someone else's hands. That helped Stephen not say the word labeling him now and forever. Thief.

He grabbed d'Aisecq's journal and fled. Sorg was halfway down the stairs, limping slowly on his dead leg. "Mr. Monaghan? Mr. Monaghan, don't be frightened!" The voice was muted, even in the cavernous hall. It was at that moment Stephen realized what was wrong with the man's voice. It never echoed.

Stephen hit the door and fled out into the cool night air, running until lungs burned and feet bled. Every moment, he expected red and blue lights to flash behind him, the theft dooming him to prison and worse. Either Sorg was slow or the police were. Stephen didn't care which, grabbing a few things from his apartment to spend a sleepless night at Charles de Gaulle, clutching d'Aisecq's diary, certain Sorg would track him.

* * *

Stephen received the call several weeks after his first professional poker game. "Mr. Monaghan, my name is Henry Tessier. We have a mutual friend. Mr. Gregory Sorg." An invitation and an address followed. Henry Tessier's accent was slight, elements of Paris shining through. The man's tone was friendly enough, but Stephen was nervous.

A friend of Gregory Sorg, the man from whom Stephen had stolen the d'Aisecq diary, meant danger. Sorg would want the diary back, maybe a pound of flesh beyond. Still, Tessier knew Stephen's number. With that much, Tessier might know more. Not going to meet him could be as dangerous as going.

There were two things to protect—himself and the Work; and two protectors—dolls, both stronger than any man.

He found the concubine in the parlor cradling her dolly by the window. Her neck swiveled smoothly to him. "Could you come with me, please?"

"What's wrong, Maker?"

"Come upstairs. I want to tell the Firstborn as well."

She stood, placing her dolly carefully on the vacated seat, and went to him. Her hand, encased in the silk glove, was cold and hard in his. He held it, feeling safe in her. He knocked on Emily's door and opened it, to find the Firstborn amongst her mobile flitting from item to item. She didn't react to their entry.

"Firstborn," he said. She stopped, her alien eyes meeting his. "I wanted to tell you both. We may be in trouble. A man has called me and asked to meet. He knows someone who has good reason to hate me, someone who might want revenge. I need to meet with him, but I can't go alone." The concubine stayed close, never letting go of Stephen's hand, fingers ivory hard and smooth.

The Firstborn cocked her head. "I want you to stay here in case someone comes." He turned to the concubine, "I want *you* to be with me."

"Maker, I can't leave. They would know I'm not human."

"We'll disguise you."

"Maker…"

"Please. I need you there."

His concubine looked to the Firstborn for approval perhaps and then back to Stephen. "I'll go."

He wanted to kiss her, to hold her, to touch her cool cheek and close his eyes. Instead, the feelings coursing through him were enigmas, leaving him paralyzed. Weak flesh would yield. The concubine's porcelain hand did not.

He barely managed "thank you," turning away before she could say anything, letting his hand fall away like a November leaf. He moved to Emily's dresser, removing things and throwing them on the bed. His sister had gone through a girly phase right after Dawn Molinaro. Some of those might do for the concubine's disguise.

He turned. The Firstborn was behind the concubine, delicately undressing her. She covered herself, turning her head away from him. The clothes fell away from her porcelain skin and Stephen was struck. She was perfect. Life, walking and talking, from nothing. And beautiful. It was not enough to merely create life, not when there was a chance to make something exquisite. The culmination of the Work was before him, lovely and strong.

And he was already thinking of another.

He went to Emily's clothes, trying to think only of the task ahead. A pair of tights. A skirt with an elastic waist. A hot pink Blondie t-shirt. Em's old leather jacket. A pair of leather gloves. Finally, a black silk scarf and a tiny hat with a heavy veil that dipped below the chin.

His concubine, now undressed, approached the costume with trepidation, picking up the jacket first, putting it on. Then she tried the shirt.

"No, no." She turned to him, confusion plain on her face. He

THE DOLLMAKER // 201

removed the jacket and selected the tights. "These first."

"I don't understand, Maker."

"It's easy. They're like your stockings."

That didn't help her at all. He knelt, opening the tights. Desire uncoiled within. She was so perfect he wanted to take her immediately, on Emily's bed. Her scent, the scrubbed china aroma, cut ever so slightly with fresh clay, was intoxicating. Unable to resist, he held her close and inhaled. Her fingers snaked into his hair. "We don't have to go. We could stay."

He kissed her lips once, making her body ring. "No. We need to."

He held open the tights and guided her smooth white leg inside, then the other, unrolling the thin material up her body. "These feel wrong," she said.

"It's a disguise."

"I know." He put the shirt over her head, helping her arms into it. It was the first time she had ever worn either garment. She looked down at it, smoothing it. "It won't hang like my corset."

He smiled and helped her with the rest. Piece by piece, she donned the clothes, all a little too small for her. She was tall for a woman, nearly the equal of the swanlike Firstborn. Emily wasn't quite so statuesque, and the clothes fit tight over the concubine's porcelain form. She was still beautiful, though it was a forbidding beauty. Her face, obscured by scarf and veil, could only be seen in abstract.

He took her hand and led her outside. It was April, and a light rain fell over Los Angeles. She drew closer to him. It wasn't the warmth a human woman would seek. It was merely a connection from the one person who knew what she was. He led the way to the car, opened her door for her and got behind the wheel.

Though frightened, she didn't fidget, instead sitting extremely still. Perhaps turning into a statue would cause the danger to pass over her and around her. He drove in silence, not knowing how to comfort a ceramic woman.

The address the man had given was downtown. Much of that had changed from the post-industrial wasteland it had been into upscale lofts. Stephen headed toward one of these, through rain-slicked streets and clashing headlights. The building in question was an old bank, gothic and stone, the loft near the top floor. Stephen parked a block away, and escorted the concubine through the rain.

People walked through the same soaked streets, brushing against man and doll. Stephen waited for one to point to the porcelain woman, to recognize her for what she was. Stephen imagined the mob, burning him alive as a sorcerer. Was that even what he was? They would kill him quickly and shatter her into a thousand pieces. What if they only managed to tear him apart? Flesh was weak. Wood and teeth were strong. Would the Firstborn collapse for a final time and remain inert until she rotted into nothing? Or would she continue her alien existence?

But in the cold rain, flesh and porcelain felt very much the same.

They passed through the tiled foyer to the large elevators. As they neared the top, abruptly the concubine stepped forward, ahead of him. She was out the doors first, looking both ways. The right apartment was down a white hall with concrete floors and artfully chipped paint. He was going to knock when she nudged him aside and did it for him, stepping outside of the view of the peephole.

First, there was the barking of a dog, followed by, "Who's there?" The voice was the one from the phone call, down to the slight accent.

"Stephen Monaghan. You called me."

The locks clicked open and the door swung wide. The man was a gnome, tiny and balding with a ridiculous push-broom mustache and thick glasses. He held a large Rottweiler by the collar and smiled up at Stephen. "So I did. Please, come in, Mr. Monaghan."

Stephen entered. The dog ignored him, just as Emily's had, concentrating instead on the unfamiliar china scent out in the hall. Tessier lived in a large loft, with picture windows looking out over downtown. Bookshelves covered every available piece of wall. Stephen recognized the looks of both Tessier and his home from the time spent perusing collections.

Tessier nearly closed the door on the concubine, until she put a hand on the corner and pushed it open. The dog snarled at the new arrival. The doll's face was unreadable behind the scarf and veil. She stared at the dog, perhaps angry, perhaps fascinated.

"No, Lisa. Bad dog." The dog took a step back, momentarily cowed. "I didn't realize you would bring a guest." Tessier turned to the concubine. "I must apologize for Lisa. She can be overly protective. Henry Tessier." He held out a hand to the doll.

She continued to stare at the dog, before her head turned smoothly toward Tessier. "You are the Herald."

Tessier frowned. "Of course. And you are?"

"You mustn't ask that." She moved into the apartment and took her place by Stephen. Tessier went to the door, fastening the three brass locks securing it. Stephen seized up. If Sorg was in the apartment, they were now trapped. Yet Sorg was an old man over ten years ago. He would be older now, and Stephen had someone with him far stronger than any man could ever be. Sorg would be no match for the concubine. The crippled half-thing stood even less of a chance.

"You're a friend of Gregory Sorg's," Stephen prompted the old man.

He turned, still holding the dog. She had calmed, her expressive eyes still locked on the doll. Stephen wondered what the dog was thinking. It had to know, to smell that this was not a human woman.

Tessier said, "I am. I was. Gregory passed away last month."

Unbidden, a thought rushed into Stephen's mind. *...when the concubine was born.* "I'm... I'm sorry to hear it."

"He spoke very highly of you."

...of a thief. "I don't know why. We didn't part on the best of terms."

"He said you and he were the same."

"How so?"

"He didn't elaborate."

"How did Mr. Sorg die?"

Tessier shrugged. "I never received any official cause. Just a package from him to be sent in the event of, and he hasn't responded to calls or email. Gregory had a bad heart, so..."

Tessier released the dog and shuffled toward a dining room table nearly bowed under a mountain of mail, sifted through it, and selected a something wrapped in plain brown paper, tied with string. A present maybe, down to the small note nestled under the bow. Tessier handed it to Stephen. "The package.

Gregory asked that it be given to you."

"What is it?"

"He never told me. I got the impression it was some kind of joke only you and he would get."

Stephen accepted it.

Tessier looked at him expectantly. "Would you open it, please? I must admit, I'm curious."

Stephen first opened the note and unfolded it. The letters ran together. It spoke only insanity. Stephen smiled, looking up at Tessier. "It was a joke. This letter is gibberish."

In the corner, Lisa approached the concubine gingerly. Her attention was squarely on the dog. Stephen hoped the animal wouldn't attack. Even if it didn't, would the doll move to violence?

Tessier accepted the letter with a wilting smile. "Mr. Monaghan, I assumed you read French."

"I do."

"Then you're having a joke at my expense."

Stephen's attention left the concubine and latched onto Tessier. "What are you talking about?"

"This letter. It's French. Quite clear. 'Dear Mr. Monaghan, this gift might be unexpected, but you should know that I neither regret nor reproach your theft of the...'" Tessier paused. "'Theft?'"

Stephen snatched the letter. Gibberish. The letters were empty spirals. A gloved hand took the letter from his. The concubine was next to him, looking at it.

"Mr. Monaghan, what did you steal from Mr. Sorg?"

She read it in a clear bone voice: "Your theft of the first d'Aisecq diary. I hope you discovered his methods better than I could have. From everything I heard from my associates and acquaintances, you are precisely the kind of man who could. The chances you could duplicate or even exceed d'Aisecq's material were worth the loss of the book, which had already told me everything I was equipped to understand. I must thank you for leaving me that piece of the Marquise. Had you taken it, I would have had a different opinion of you. Please accept this, the Marquis d'Aisecq's second diary. Yours, Gregory Sorg."

Tessier backed away. "What was Gregory talking about?"

Stephen ignored the old man. "I can't read that. Why can't I read that?"

Behind her veil, the concubine was serene. "You no longer need to."

"What was Gregory talking about?"

The dog, master agitating her, started to bark. The cacophony pounded at Stephen, the letter, the package, everything was overloading him. Get out, back onto the rainy streets, let it wash him clean. The dog punctuated Tessier's pleading.

Stephen fled.

In the elevator, the groan of the cables brought him back. Stephen struggled to remember any of his French, but it was gone, as was his Greek, Latin, and Hebrew.

"Did you take it all?"

"What are you saying, Maker?"

"My languages. Did you take them along with my signature?"

"They were freely given."

He didn't remember driving home, finding himself in the parlor, holding the useless diary in front of him, dripping rainwater in an expanding dark stain on the couch cushions. The concubine joined him on the sofa, taking the diary, opening it to the first page. "Now, Maker, I'll read it to you."

She did. From beginning to end. He never fully slept, experiencing d'Aisecq's words as a dream. The diary detailed the Marquis's escape from the mob. The Marquise was the first doll. The second was intended as a double, a doppelganger to burn in d'Aisecq's place. Though this second doll was born to die, d'Aisecq was oddly linked to it, something pages of meandering writing tried desperately and futilely to explain. The creatures slew both the double and the Marquise, bond be damned. D'Aisecq retired in anonymity, creating a third and final doll, to love as much as he loved the first and needed the second.

Something had changed.

He spoke of his body and spirit fading from the world. The dolls were life, but with them, they brought slow death. Each doll cut deeper into the cord connecting d'Aisecq with the waking world. As Stephen heard d'Aisecq's words, spoken in the clean rhythms of the concubine, he knew their truth. The fading had begun, slowly enough as to be invisible until it was too late. The two had already taken things that could never be given back.

And there would be another.

CHAPTER ELEVEN

AS STEPHEN'S SKILL GREW, THE money started
coming in more quickly, allowing him to begin the mold for the
newest one's body. She was shorter than the other two; he could
not say why other than it felt right. She would be the closest to
reality. She might be able to pass as human.

The thoughts came quicker. Jessica's hand on him. Dawn
Molinaro's hand on his sister. The two dolls that shared him. He
felt as he had the first time, sitting in the pregnant attic, before
bringing the dancer to life. The erections were nearly constant,
forcing him to tie himself down when he went out. The pain
would sometimes stop the arousal.

Sometimes.

He began extracting the next doll's blood from his veins in
May. The Siege Perilous was hungry. Even after he filled the
required three pints, he continued, extracting a pint every month.
There might be an emergency. An accident. Not another doll.
After this one, there wouldn't be enough of Stephen Monaghan
to make another.

The Firstborn turned one year old in June. He brought her
a cupcake with a single candle. She watched it burn all the way

down, covering the icing with a coat of wax. When it finally guttered, she looked up at him, taking him by the hand, pulling him into bed with her.

He guided the Firstborn to sculpt the new doll in negative. The mold was in two halves and fitting them precisely would be the most exacting part. This one could not have mold lines. Those would ruin her. This one had to be a perfect facsimile of flesh.

The concubine would stand by him and she wouldn't stop talking. "Another sister," she would say each time. Whether the judgment was actually in her voice or was the product of an addled mind he could not tell. The Firstborn hollowed out the thighs, sanded the heart-shaped face.

The concubine picked up a pair of real-looking blue glass eyes and swirled them through jingling fingers. "She's beautiful."

"She will be. If I can get the mold right."

And he would. He mixed the first batch of plastic that stank like the action figures he and Brian had melted when they were nine and carefully colored it, giving her living skin tone. Stephen injected the molten plastic into the fitted mold, let it cool and a day later, cracked the molds open like an egg. An air bubble had bitten a crater into her sternum and left breast. The mold lines were webs. He discarded the body in the corner of the attic with the rest of the cast-offs.

The second set of molds was flawed. And the third, fourth, fifth, and sixth.

The seventh set was perfect.

He went to work on her skin. First, the nipples. It was like tattooing, putting the realistic color beneath the skin, making them pink and delicate, and then moving onto the freckles. He regretted it, but the thought of Audra's shoulders spurred him. The eyes went into the blank sockets and she blankly looked outward.

He took a knife to her vagina and opened her up.

He moved onto the hair. The most expensive part as it turned out. Human hair would not come cheap, especially when it had to be red. He put it under her skin in plugs, first at the scalp, then between her legs.

Her mouth next. The Firstborn had sculpted it in the mold, adding porcelain teeth made from Audra's exemplar. Upon the tongue, the word.

The final touches were the tiny white triangles beneath her eyes. They would look like greasepaint and would be the only harlequin flourish on this one.

He dozed in the Siege Perilous, waiting for it to bleed him enough. Seven pints of his blood hung inside the freezer in ice-crusted bags, far more than she would ever need. D'Aisecq's second diary stopped him from completing the ritual, even as Stephen's needs demanded the new doll. What would the newest one take? He had already lost his signature, his skill, and he hadn't even known they were gone. The dolls had taken those things for their own. And would keep taking, as long as he had something of himself to give.

The voice behind him said, "She's finished."

"Almost."

"The important part is there already. For this one."

He didn't answer her because she was right. Something in this new one frightened him. He couldn't say what. She was born in desire, nothing more. There was not the dream there was with the Firstborn, nor the love as there was with the second. With this one, there was only base desire. Desire could not be controlled.

He wondered if she could be.

He existed in a daze; neither fully asleep nor awake. The air had grown dry and chill with the coming of fall. Emily and Jessica haunted his fitful dreams, and so did others with blank faces and soft flesh, speaking in languages excised from existence. Some of the conversations seemed almost real, an invitation to Emily to stay, a plea to Jessica to leave forever.

The dolls continued their rituals. The Firstborn brought him her brush. The concubine joined him for dinner. Sometimes he heard them making love downstairs, the music of a treebranch scratching a window during a storm.

The body of the newest doll lay in her cradle, ready for the first rite. She was with him at all times, no matter how he fought against it. Her life would be some kind of tipping point... enough of him would be lost that he would no longer be entirely human. Maybe there was still time to go back. Foolishness.

It was noon on a Saturday according to the computer. He had to do something to block out the maddening desire to go upstairs and make her.

He dialed the number.

"Hello?"

"It's me."

The pause was a long one. "I'm glad you called. I need to see you."

He waited for her on a wooden bench outside the house.

The dolls were inside, nothing stopping them from stepping into the sunlight, except their alien inhibitions. The hope simmered within him that they would stand revealed and he could tell all his secrets.

A raven swooped down from a tree and landed at the other corner of the antique wooden bench from Stephen. It watched the street, never once looking at him or protesting the presence of a human.

On the street, a car's brakes squeaked as it pulled to a stop, followed shortly by the slamming of a door.

Jessica walked into view from the hedges and turned, stopping almost immediately. Her eyes were hidden behind a pair of chunky sunglasses, but Stephen could tell she was taking in the sight of the bird. She reached into her purse, removed a camera, and snapped a picture. The raven croaked at her.

She took a step forward, the wonder writ large on her face. "How is that thing not flying away?"

He shrugged. "Beats me."

The raven's attention was entirely on Jessica. She kept coming forward. It squawked again.

"Did you train it or something?"

"Nope."

The raven hopped and cocked its head, black doll eyes on the woman. Jessica got closer.

"Seriously?" Closer.

It took flight.

"That was weird," she said.

"I'm glad you came over."

"Are you going to invite me in?"

She could catch him with the dolls, tell him he was insane, stop him from bringing the newest doll to life. The concubine couldn't resist revealing herself, not to a new intruder. The secret would stand bare. Jessica would know. Someone flesh and blood, someone who could stop this.

"So you want to come inside?"

She started. "Um. Yeah. Please."

He stood from the bench and opened the front door. It was cool inside, black. His eyes went up the stairs, expecting the Firstborn at the landing. It was empty. The hope that one of the dolls would make a telltale noise, make Jessica investigate, died when the only sounds were the groans of the boards beneath human feet.

She came in. "I remember this place from your birthday parties when we were little."

"Does it look the same?"

"It should look smaller. It doesn't. It's so much larger."

He led her into the parlor. The air seemed blue, light diffuse, marking shafts of whirling dust. The antique furniture, the same that had been there when they were little, was waiting. The dolls were absent.

She sat down on the chair by the window, setting her sunglasses and camera on the table.

He said, "Can I get you something?"

She shook her head.

He sat down on the couch, eyes going to her arms, covered again with a cardigan, this one buttoned to the neck. Her hair was down and her legs were covered. She crossed her legs and picked her camera back up, fidgeting with it. There was a welt on the back of her hand, maybe a healing cut. She wasn't picking at herself as she had before. "You said you needed to see me."

"After the other night. I wanted... I wanted to apologize."

"Apologize?"

"Yeah. I acted like a drunk slut. I'm sorry. You must think I'm an idiot."

"Of course not."

"You don't hate me?"

"God, no. I knew you were drunk. I didn't want to do something you'd, you know, regret."

"So we're cool?"

"It would be a little stupid if we weren't. These days, you're my best friend."

She blushed. "I am?"

"Yeah."

She clicked her camera, looking at the pictures she had taken. It wasn't a response, but she was too self-conscious to think of anything else. The screen threw green light across her face. "Dammit," she said.

"What?"

"The picture with you and the bird didn't come out." She showed him. The upper part of the image was fine, but the bottom, where his image should be, was only a sheet of digital green. Like the pictures at Emily's house.

"Take another one."

"The light in here..."

"Humor me."

She held up the camera, and with a flash, clicked another one. She turned the camera over to check the picture. "It happened again." She showed him. The green wiped him out of existence again. The waiting corpse of his daughter lay in the attic, ready to rob him of more.

"Do you have to get back to work?"

Stephen shrugged.

"What are you working on, anyway?"

That could be it. She could see the sickness in him. She would make sure he wouldn't fade away. "Do you want to see?"

Her breath caught. "Sure."

"It's this way."

He walked into the hall. Her feet squeaked on the boards behind him. There was no explaining the plastic girl in the attic. Her still form was perfect. She would be so soft, so willing. She would do whatever he required, the whole time smelling of clean plastic.

With the second step, the erection was agony.

She would never be brought to life. She would stay the way she was, useless. Unfulfilled. He was obligated. Her birth began as soon as the first chip had been made in the mold. To rob her of life would be cruel.

The sickness had its desire and could not be denied.

He turned. "I'm sorry. I can't take you up there."

"Why not?"

He thought quickly. "Dangerous chemicals. I just realized some of the porcelain is setting. The gas rises, so it's safe down here, but up there..."

"Oh. Okay."

He guided her downstairs, suddenly terrified she would see the dolls. She would stop him. That couldn't happen. Not with so much more of the Work left to do.

"Can you show me later?"

"Yeah. Maybe. It's hard to find the right time."

"Okay."

"I'm sorry. I'm glad you came over, but I have to get back to it."

"Let's hang out. Soon."

"I'd like that."

They were at the door. "Goodbye, Jessica." He meant it.

"I'll see you."

He watched her disappear up the driveway and turned. The concubine was at the landing. "Did you get what you needed?"

"Get the Firstborn. We have a life to create."

"I suppose you did."

* * *

Brian returned from senior year in college on a Thursday. None of the Baniszewskis had made it to the graduation ceremony. Jessica felt bad she hadn't gone but couldn't afford a plane ticket across the country if her parents weren't footing the bill. They, of course, had other things to do.

Jessica had just finished frosh year at Occidental, having gotten home a few days before. The house was empty. Gone from the vital dorms to a tomb. Already she could not wait for school to start back up. Summer in Pasadena was unbearable anyway, the way the mountains pinned the smog against the San Gabriels and turned green streets into the surface of Venus. Outside, feet dangling in the pool's cold water, rereading the same fantasy novel she read at the same time the previous summer, she wondered if she could muster the energy to go back inside and put on a bathing suit.

Jessica set the book down after reading the same page three times. Her side of the pool was shaded by several elderberry trees abutting the house, casting dappled shadows that only partly blocked the sun. Her father detested the trees and the leaves and berries that peppered the pool area, but not enough to do anything about them. Jessica was fond of them because when she went swimming, she ended up with something like wine on her feet. Tracking it into the house, if only so her father would yell at her, was better than being ignored.

The backyard went upward into the slope of the hill, with the property line being level with the second story of the house. The guesthouse lurked back there, shielded by several more elderberry trees. It was ostensibly an office, but more often it was for the kids, first as a place for sleepovers, later to smoke pot. Jessica hated it. Her father, an avid fisherman, had decorated the walls with trophy fish. Their dead eyes scared her, and some part of her carried that totem to adulthood.

The sound of a car pulling up in the front—it had to be Brian, and even if it wasn't, checking wouldn't hurt any. Nothing else to do. Leaving her book by the pool, she rushed inside to the front of the house, peering through the floor-to-ceiling windows in the living room

It was Brian, bags beside him, leaning into the window of a black Honda, speaking to the driver. Jessica craned her neck trying to get a glimpse. As Brian ducked to pick his bags up, she saw the driver's face—Stephen Monaghan. Her heart stuttered, telling her to run out to the lawn, make a show of hugging Brian. Be girlish, carefree, full of life. "Oh, hello, Stephen! I didn't see you there! You should come on in!"

218 // JUSTIN ROBINSON

The tank top and shorts showed off some skin. Maybe enough for Stephen to notice. She nearly hitched the shorts up to show more leg. But by the time she looked up again, the car was already moving away. It was a silly thought anyway. Stephen probably still envisioned her as that crying little girl with the braces.

Jessica opened the door before Brian could unlock it. His face lit up at the sight of her, setting the bags down to accept a hug. "Hey, Jess. Were you waiting for me?"

"Nah. You're lucky I heard your ride." He picked the bags back up and moved past her. As she shut the front door, she said, "Was that Steve Monaghan dropping you off?"

"Yeah, he picked me up from the airport."

Brian headed up the stairs, Jessica following.

"You should have invited him in."

"Didn't think of it. I'm surprised you remember him."

She shrugged, trying not to blush. "You guys were like best friends forever."

"He's gotten a little strange since he dropped out."

"What?"

"He dropped out of school two years ago. You didn't know?"

"Who was going to tell me?"

"Well, now you know."

Brian opened his bedroom door and headed inside, the conversation over.

Following him in, she blurted, "Strange how?"

"What's this sudden interest in Steve?" he said, putting the bags on the bed and opening them up.

"Nothing."

Brian opened his mouth to say something, but swallowed

it, turning back to his bags. He removed a small leather valise and unzipped it. Staring into the dark hole, his voice was serious, "Jess, you need to stay away from him. Trust me, as your big brother."

"You do know I'm not a little girl anymore, right?"

Brian's face turned to stone, dropping the valise, and when he took several steps toward her, Jessica thought the advance would end in a punch. She fought the urge to flinch. "What's that supposed to mean?"

"I'm in college now," she said, stumbling over her nerves.

"Are you dating anyone?"

"Dating? No, not now."

"But you were?"

Dangerous ground, but Jessica unsure of the way through. Of course she had been dating. She was a normal freshman. Two boyfriends, one a sophomore and the other a senior, and had dumped them both when they didn't display any interest in her beyond as a sex object. "Well, yeah."

His words were sharp and measured. "Jessica, did you sleep with anyone?"

"Sleep?"

"Are you still a virgin?"

Brian loomed large over her, face a mixture of pain, anger and something else that took her a moment to understand—fear. Jessica didn't know what would happen if she told the truth, so she lied. "Yeah. Yes. I'm still a virgin."

Brian let out a long breath, held since the first question on this tree, turning back to the bags, picking the valise up and unpacking it. Jessica assumed it would be toiletries. It wasn't.

220 // JUSTIN ROBINSON

It was an odd assortment of objects: a small picture frame, a woman's hair clip, a tiny toy soldier. He held each one of these things almost reverently before setting them carefully on his desk, one by one. There seemed to be a specific order to these items, but not one based on anything rational.

When Brian spoke again, the naked honesty in his voice staggered her. "Jess, you should know... men aren't nice. Men will want things from you that you shouldn't ever give. They'll try to take it if they can."

"What are you trying to say?" There was something in it of the older brother not wanting to imagine his little sister fucking; yet something larger looming over it that Jessica could not glimpse.

"Stay a virgin. For you."

"For *you*," she said.

His voice was firmer. "For you. It's better if you keep away from guys."

"What about girls? Because my roommate drinks a lot and I could totally hit that."

He almost snapped but caught the glint in her eye and chuckled. "I'm serious, Jess."

"I know. No sex, I promise."

He looked from the things from the valise and back to her. "Good girl."

She waited until she was in the hall and out of sight to flip him off. After the almost attack, she wouldn't do it to his face. She looked forward to throwing her sex life at him one day. Once she moved out, maybe. On her wedding day. Sometime when she was untouchable. Whatever made his little world crash down the quickest would be perfect. That was Stephen Monaghan, the one person who would do the same for her. Get Stephen and do all the things Brian would hate. The thought filled her with dread. What would happen when Stephen rejected her? She would lose everything. Except a brother who hated her and a first love who pitied her. The first was bad. The second nearly brought her to her knees.

Jessica was feeling too gloomy to return to the pool. Instead, she fetched her book and went upstairs to her bedroom. The heat inside was stifling, sticking clothes to skin. The fan by the window didn't do much to stir the air. Distantly, she heard Brian on the phone, barking orders at one of his friends. She never bothered to remember their names. Some were new, others had been with Brian forever. At some point, they changed to become what Brian wanted. When that happened, it was almost as though they had no names at all.

They had given their names to Brian.

There was a time when Brian spent more time with Stephen. They were the odd couple, the awkward genius and the golden boy. They never stopped being friends, but there was a point when Brian cooled on Stephen. Jessica was around eleven when it happened and she never knew what, if anything, had caused the distance.

It was a little after that point Brian gained his first follower. And another, and another. They always circled her like wolves. When she was young, it was to mock. Later, it was to leer. Brian encouraged it with inaction, never once defending her.

The thought flowed cleanly into the next. The party four years ago. She had been struck dumb when Stephen stood up for her. He hadn't been much of a fighter, and still wouldn't give the other guy an inch. Stephen would fight for her and had proven it in blood.

The afternoon haze crept deeper. That night had sparked fantasies. She had seen him only once since then, when she and Brian went to Charles Monaghan's funeral. She didn't feel right saying much to him other than expressing condolences and offering a hug, wishing it could be more. She was left with the ghost of him, sitting in the chair in her room and comforting her. The chair remained empty. No one was allowed in it. Not even her. The chair would be waiting when he came back to claim his place.

Her hand went to the nightstand. She paused, listening. Brian's voice, closer, then farther, disappearing downstairs. Her door was locked. With a flick of her fingers, the drawer on her nightstand opened. Her fingers groped for a second, before closing around what she wanted—her magic wand. She listened again. She couldn't hear Brian, meaning he was probably outside. She squirmed out of her shorts and panties and clicked it on.

She thought of Stephen on that night. Part of her wished he had gone to bed with her then. He was too old for her and she too young, but she wished that had been her first time and not the drunken embarrassing groping in a dorm room stinking of pot. She imagined kissing the blood from his lip, smothering objections with her mouth, taking him out and into her. They would have belonged to one another, at least for a night.

Her magic wand knew her perfectly, every corner of her body, every movement of her hips before she made them. It was plastic and inanimate, but it was filled with a form of life, the closest thing to Stephen's touch. In her mind, she had linked the two when she purchased it in high school. It had kept her a virgin longer than Brian's glowering had.

She fought her mind, trying to keep the fantasy alive long enough to finish. She pushed out the thoughts of Brian, thinking only of Stephen saying the things she had wanted him to say, letting her into his labyrinthine mind, making her the one and only person who would understand him. Eyes closed, her breath came quicker. The sensation worked inward, lighting her body on fire through her spine up and out of the crown of her head. She was with him in her mind, and she always would be.

With that thought, she exploded into helpless tremors. She lay there on top of the covers, gasping the still air. The heat pressed in on her still, and she radiated it back, the core of a new sun. She looked at the toy and nearly laughed. There was one way to pass the boring summer months.

Then, the knock on her door. "Jess?" It was Brian.

She nearly swore. She jumped up off the bed, grabbing for her shorts and panties. "Yeah, what's up?"

"Can I come in?"

"Just a sec," she pulled the shorts up and zipped them before going to the door. She had it open before she realized the magic wand was sitting on her nightstand and the room probably stank of sex.

Brian stood in the doorway. "Hey, I'm ordering pizza. You want some?"

"Yeah. Hawaiian?"

"No problem." His flickered over her flushed face, then into the room. She shifted uncomfortably. "I'll let you know when it gets here."

"Thanks."

He was down the hall a few steps before turning. "Oh, I'm having some friends over later. So you know."

"Okay."

"We're taking the guesthouse. So make yourself scarce."

"Sure."

She returned to her room, shut the door and had to laugh. She straightened up, splashed some water on her face and joined Brian downstairs in time for the pizza. They ate and half-watched *Die Hard*. Brian was distracted, looking at his phone and fidgeting. Jessica watched him. The phone buzzed, sending him shooting off the couch.

"Yeah? I'll be right out."

Jessica rolled her eyes, sharing a small moment with John McClane, who had just killed a terrorist with feet smaller than his sister's. Jessica didn't want to be around for Brian's friends, so she grabbed another slice of pizza and her Diet Coke and retreated upstairs.

She was halfway up the stairs when Brian came back into the house, three of those leering assholes surrounding him in an honor guard. She had met them all on many occasions, but couldn't tell them apart. Once they entered Brian's orbit, they all started to look alike. Brian looked up at her, and as one they followed did the same.

"Hey, Jess. Going up to your room?"

"Yeah. Think I'll take a nap."

Their eyes crawled all over her. She wanted to close the legs on her shorts, throw on a burqa, turn into a shadow.

"Thanks," Brian said.

There was an odd energy in the four men. They were definitely excited about something, but Jessica had no idea what it could be. She had three options for what to do with the rest of her evening, and she had already exhausted two of them. She might as well fight boredom in the tradition of bratty little sisters everywhere. Brian still owed her a pound of flesh for being an asshole. At the top of the stairs, she went one step into the hall and sat down, eavesdropping into the large front room.

"He's on the way?" Brian said.

"Yeah. He did it," one said.

"I thought he was pure pussy," one of the others said.

"He was," Brian said. They all laughed. Their attitude, celebratory and predatory, disturbed Jessica. She knew for certain she wasn't safe in her own home. She didn't know why, but it was there, the fight-or-flight of the animal inside. She got up, bare feet silent on the wooden floor, and snuck into her room. The murmuring downstairs exploded into another horrible, knowing laugh as the doorbell sounded. The front door opened, and there was more susurration. Jessica found her softball bat. It was stupid. Still, holding it made her feel a little bit better.

Her conscious, reasonable mind should have provoked another laugh. It was ridiculous. These were her brother's friends. He wouldn't let anything bad happen to her.

He already had.

This time there was no one to defend her but her.

She heard them coming out of the house, right below her room. Their voices were low, dangerous. From her vantage, she saw them climbing the rock steps to the guesthouse, Brian in the lead, the other three around a single late arrival. The new one looked nervous, his shoulders hunched, posture meek. The others were pure predator, gleeful in raw manhood.

They disappeared into the guesthouse.

She looked at the bat. This was silly. They were probably in there watching porn and playing poker. Farting and telling sexist jokes. Stupid guy shit. Her rational mind told her this, even as her animal mind begged her to take the bat into the closet and wait them out. She wouldn't be a slave to fear. She would go, see they were doing exactly nothing, and come back to her room, once again safe and sound.

She leaned the bat against her bookshelf, opened the bedroom door silently and snuck back down the hallway. At the top of the stairs her pizza hardened next to the glass of soda. She crept outside onto the pool patio. She would be visible from the guesthouse for a quick moment as in the mad rush from the patio to the stairs, where the hill would once again hide her. She climbed the stairs, body hunched and hands almost touching the ground, animalistic in her movements, subconsciously becoming the perfect counterpoint to the men inside.

One more step up the stairs and she would once again be visible. Elderberry trees dotted the top of the hill, and she would have to move from tree to tree to make it to one of the windows into the big room making up the bulk of the guesthouse. If they were watching porn on the big plasma in there, they would be facing her direction. Through the mostly glass door, she would be almost completely exposed.

Jessica peeked over the top of the hill, over the stone path leading to the front door. She could see nothing from that distance, only hearing a distant murmuring from inside. She broke cover, sprinting for the closest tree, the ground chewing her bare feet. She paused behind the tree, certain her brother had spotted her and would burst out of the guesthouse. To yell or something worse, she was unsure.

Nothing came.

She moved to the next tree, making her way toward the side of the house. The angle would make it harder for them to see her. The closer she got, the safer she would be, until she got too close—the seductive paradox of spying.

The words grew louder, but she couldn't make them out. They were slow, halting, submissive. It was not Brian. One of the others, the late arrival from the sound of it, the one they called half-pussy. As the man fell silent, Brian began to speak in words with the cadence of a speech, the weight of a sermon. She couldn't understand him. She had to get closer.

The dying sun turned the white walls of the guesthouse bloody. She pressed her back to it, looking up at the window. Closed. The next was open. She slunk to it and rose, pausing in a half crouch. If they were facing her, they would see. She closed her eyes, evened her breathing. They were playing poker. They were watching the game. They were smoking out or getting drunk.

She peeked.

They were in the middle of the guesthouse's large room. All around them, dead fish were the silent chorus. Brian was standing, back to the window. The new arrival, on his knees, faced Brian. The others were arrayed behind the new arrival, cutting off escape, consciously or unconsciously. Brian said, "Do you have the trophy?" It was a ritual question. There was only one answer.

Jessica craned her head, trying to see what it was. Four of them could see her if they only looked up. She prayed they wouldn't. Curiosity spurred her on. It was not poker or porn, but something altogether more sinister. The new arrival reached into the pocket of his jeans and removed something, holding it up. It was soft, dark, with a splash of color. Jessica couldn't see what it was from her vantage point. She would have to get another angle. The front door.

She looked over at it. It was almost entirely glass, with only a thin grid of wood supporting the large panels and at the farthest point from any trees. The nearest cover was a breathless sprint around the side of the guesthouse. It was entirely exposed.

Ignoring the parts of her mind screaming at her to run, to get her bat, to get to her room and lock the door, she crept closer. Sound was muffled, but clear enough to understand.

Brian accepted the token reverently. "This links us together. These are the spoils, and the spoils are mine."

Jessica was right outside the door, low to the ground, peering upward without looking into the room.

Her blood turned to ice. "My sister, Jessica."

She almost ran, but the animal fear stuck her to the spot. She saw them boiling from the guesthouse, grabbing thick handfuls of her hair, holding her, ripping the clothes from her to rape and consume.

Instead, the kneeling man said, "Yes."

Brian went on, "She's in her bedroom now. You want to fuck her, right?"

"Yes."

"She's ripe for it. She's keeping her virginity for one of you, but she doesn't know which one yet. The one of you that brings me the most of these."

The words turned to iron. She hated Brian. She wanted to fuck every man she met in front of him, wanted to break his head open, wanted to scream at him. She wanted him to understand what should have been self-evident: she was human.

"Now, to consecrate."

Jessica had ducked out of sight. Then, the sounds of zippers and belts being undone. Despite herself, she looked.

Brian and the three other standing men had their pants down, penises out and erect. Even those were oddly similar. Same sizes, same circumcision scars, same angry red. They began to masturbate. The man in the middle remained on his knees, looking upward in a mixture of horror and anticipation.

Brian held the token out in one hand, the other furiously working on his cock. The other men stared at the item, working themselves into a dank lather at the very sight of it.

Jessica still couldn't see what it was and couldn't leave until she did.

The first man came. Soon after, the second and the third. They ejaculated into cupped hands. Brian's strokes moved quicker, grunting, still staring at the offering.

"Drink of me and become my brother," Brian said, grabbing the back of the kneeling man's head and pulling it in. For a moment, Brian's penis pressed against the man's lips as he fought it, but Brian pressed harder. The man's mouth opened, and he gagged. Brian grunted, ass flexing, fingers gripping. Eyes watering, the man tried to pull away, even as his throat worked, swallowing everything Brian gave him.

Brian pulled out. The other man was stunned. Something was different. Human consciousness had fled, burned away by Brian's seed. The man knelt, deflated.

The other men dipped fingers in their semen and touched first the kneeling man, drawing something on his forehead and cheeks, then the item in Brian's hand. The kneeling man looked up, eyes dark and glittering, lips parted over teeth that seemed sharpened—a red animal grin.

"Now it belongs to all of us," Brian said, kissing the item.

It was then that Jessica identified it: a lock of hair tied with a swatch of cloth. As they reached for their pants, she finally obeyed her body's demands. She sprinted back to the house, into her room and locked her door. Over time, she convinced herself half the memory was dream and the other half embellished. She pretended there was nothing wrong with a brother she knew at heart was something much worse than she had imagined. Brian hid that other side well, and she stopped looking for it.

But she never slept behind an unlocked door again.

* * *

Stephen stared down at the unliving doll. As always in times of birth, he was nude. Hard as well and had been since throwing Jessica out of his house. He didn't wait for the sun to go down. There was no need for it. The power of the symbolism was waning as he grew more comfortable with the raw power of the ritual.

The new one's pink body lay within the circle, ready to receive life. The Firstborn stood exactly where she had when the second doll was born. The concubine stood by the trapdoor, clown face impassive. It was almost too painful for Stephen to see them this way, both dolls keeping their distance. Maybe they knew it was sacred.

Maybe they were waiting for the point to be reached.

The blood was cold and syrupy from the freezer. The blood that had brought the others to life was warm. The X-Acto knife punctured the first bag with a wet thump, drooling the blood across her belly, breasts and face. The second bag was frigid as well. Hateful.

She was beautiful. More than the others, and they were perfect. This was a living, breathing woman, but it was one lacking in the venality of the human. Her birth had reached the point of no return. The doll would soon burst into the world as a fully formed creature.

Stephen sliced the final bag open. Blood flowed from it, chunky with partly melted ice, onto his hands in ropy streams. It squelched and crunched as he covered his belly, torso, cock, and balls. Then, he knelt between her legs, spreading them roughly, entering her, gore slicking the way in.

She was still not alive yet. Her mouth was open, still nothing more than a soft hole. Thrusting deeply, he brought his mouth over hers and exhaled, turning that into a kiss. Again. And again. Brutal. Frenzied.

As Stephen shuddered with the ecstasy of birth, the woman below turned her glass eyes upon him, gasping in his breath. He rolled off her, their bodies wet with blood and semen.

She sat up awkwardly as he dripped from between her legs.

"Hello, Maker," she said. It was an innocent statement at odds with her position. She turned one hand idly doodling designs in the blood on her belly.

"Hello, Firstborn. Hello, Knife."

The concubine, the Knife, smirked. "Welcome, Poem."

Stephen turned to the second born. "You're the Knife?"

"Yes."

"Why?"

"You mustn't ask that."

He turned to the newest, the libertine covered in the cold blood of birth. "You're the Poem?"

"Of course." She stood up. "Do you want to fuck me again?"

The erection returned instantly. He nodded, mouth dry, not noticing she had drawn the symbols of the rite all over her body. He couldn't see past the skin beneath.

* * *

"Your clothes," Stephen said.

Blue stockings, blue elbow gloves, blue choker. Cover arms, cover legs, leave her nude from thigh to neck. The Poem held each one in hand, as testing weight and texture. She didn't alter her expression as she did this. As with most things, what the Poem saw was what she wanted.

"Thank you, Maker."

She slipped them on, strangely childlike even as she dressed the whore. She was barely warmer than the others, a dim heat trickling through the softest touch. Her skin was indistinguishable from flesh, though it smelled and tasted so much cleaner. The mold lines were utterly absent. He had created something as close to life as could be made. She was a masterpiece.

He kissed her and she responded as she always would. Her body formed to his like melted wax as she reached to him and took him out. He let her do whatever she wished. There was no difference in the desires of either man or doll.

* * *

"What are you doing in here?" the Knife said.

The Poem sat in the bathtub, suds still clinging to her body.

"The Maker told me to bathe. He said he would come in and get me when he was ready."

The Poem was shivering. The Knife felt the water. Lukewarm, leaning to cold. "How long have you been here?"

"It was daytime," she said, gesturing to the dark window.

"It's nearly morning. The Maker is sleeping."

"Oh." The Poem looked hurt.

"Come on," the Knife said, picking up a towel.

The Poem shook her head. "The Maker wants me in here. This is what I'm to do."

"He forgot you. Come on, don't be stupid."

The Poem shook her head emphatically. "No."

"You're disgusting."

"I'm his favorite."

"The newest always is. Pretty soon, he'll make a new one and you'll be forgotten, if you haven't already been." The Knife stormed from the room. She glanced back, but the Poem's head was down, patiently waiting for the Maker to remember her.

CHAPTER TWELVE

THE POEM DRIFTED THROUGH THE hall, tracing the soft wallpaper, with the raised scallops, all pale pinks and creams, faded with age. Her delicate fingers would dip to the black walnut paneling, the kind that looked like it should hide a secret door.

The Maker was asleep, the Knife in bed with him.

Her eldest sister lurked in the Wretched's room.

The Poem padded down the stairs. At the front door, she stripped out of her gloves and stockings, leaving them in a blue puddle, and stepped out the door, nude. The breeze caressed her skin pleasantly. She ran hotter than the other dolls, but it couldn't compare to the furnace inside the Maker.

She made her way down the gravel driveway, enjoying the shallow cuts the rocks opened in her soft skin. She kept to the shadows, a flitting phantom, following the winding hill downward. Houses were dark. The only light came from the bottom of the hill, where the Nite Lite emitted its firefly glow. The Poem's senses reached out. A flash of red inside the Nite Lite called.

The road whispered the approach of a car. She moved off the road into the front yard of a small house, stepping behind a tree. The car moved past, headlights splashing along the tree, not finding the freckled ghost.

The Poem approached the house, peering into the front window in fascination. It was quiet inside. To her eyes, boring. There was nothing like the large and clunky furniture of her house. There was no sense of the place being alive. It was no home of wonder.

She turned and kept to her original destination. There was so much outside, and yet the Firstborn and the Knife never ventured out. It was too bad, but their indifference left more of the world for the Poem.

She made it to the bottom of the hill, slipping into the back of the Nite Lite's parking lot. There were two cars—one a black and white that took her a moment to recognize as a police car. She didn't understand police in a human way—she saw them as they were. Enforcers of the cruel and arbitrary. They had no authority other than what was granted by the blind. She wondered what they would say if they found her, if the Maker was committing any crimes in their eyes. Probably. In their vicious minds, miracle was ruin.

Her eyes moved along the wide glass window, finding the source of the call: the Seeker.

She was bringing a pot of coffee from the kitchen to the booth where the two men in uniform sat. The men said something under their mustaches and the Seeker laughed. The Poem laughed too, but she didn't know why.

The Poem settled into the shadow beneath the pine tree. Briefly, she wondered what the Maker would do if he woke up and wanted her. His desires were secondary to watching the

Seeker. The Poem would wait with the Seeker as long as it took.

The Seeker moved around the Nite Lite, unaware of her doppelganger. The Poem traced her face with light fingers. The shapes were in the Seeker's face, more exaggerated in the Poem—eyes were bigger, nose shapelier, hair longer, curlier, redder, brows more arched, cheekbones more pronounced, chin more pixyish. The Poem was smaller, sleeker, firmer. She was the Seeker transformed into something elfin and strange. An exemplar from the Maker's mind.

The Poem wanted to touch the Seeker's skin to see if it burned as the Maker's did. Could the Seeker have the same spark? The mere thought sent shivers through her body, tracing an absent nervous system into the molten center of her form.

The uniformed men left the Nite Lite. The Poem hid from them. No other car took their place.

The Nite Lite was empty of customers. The Seeker settled down on one of the stools by the counter. The Poem crouched down underneath the pine tree in the middle of the lot to watch her echo. The Poem froze in that faintly animalistic pose, never twitching, never checking her balance, never blinking. The only movement was the faint breeze ruffling her hair.

Hours later, the Seeker emerged. The sky was still dark.

The Seeker's breath quickened. The Poem moved her chest in time, trying to breathe with her echo, gulping lungless breaths and holding the bubble of air in her mouth. When the Seeker released her breath, the Poem did the same, hoping the air would mingle. Pieces of themselves, the bits of the Maker's breath the Poem had made her own, bits of the Seeker's dying flesh, joined into one.

The Seeker's manifold scent—grease, soap, and beneath, life—pulled the Poem and caressed her hackles. She compared it to the smells of the Maker: the life scent weaker by the day, the tang of wood, stone, and plastic growing ever stronger. The Poem craved both in different ways. The Maker she loved. But the Seeker's smell was the second half of her.

The Poem's hands fell to her breasts. The sensations were new. Her light touch burned in paths of raw power, blood pulsing, and moving within plastic tissue, alive of its own accord, a great flowing amoeboid globule. Her vulva flared, lips opened, right hand nestled between her legs, finding the furnace within her. The Seeker was there with only fear and shadow separating them. The Poem explored herself for the first time, her hand a reflection of the Seeker's. It was a collapsing spiral—reflection fantasizing a dream, the bodies belonging to both and neither.

The Poem was not a human woman. She never blinked. Each caress produced something new, wonderful, revelatory. She lost herself in the touch between her and her inspiration, etching sigils of power across the labia the Maker had given her, swirling over a plastic clitoris stuttering to an inhuman heartbeat. In this act, there was power. The Seeker was so close. She was nearly a participant.

The sensation coalesced into something raw and red: blood, power, pleasure, fantasy. It sizzled upwards, flashing and undulating, forging a bridge between the Poem and her echo. Crackling fingers reached into the Seeker, connecting nerve endings to living plastic. The Seeker could not see it, but something in her would know it was there, tugging on her spine. A connection forged in blood, bridged in lust, bolstered in times to come.

The Seeker paused. The Poem did not.

The Poem reached for ecstasy, moving her other hand to join the first. She was entirely open, not letting the Seeker in, instead consuming her whole, knowing her inside and out. The Poem's body seemed to melt, to reform around the Seeker in a pink chrysalis until there was no difference. The Seeker could hatch in imago, wings sticky and wet against her back. They would be a single creature, something alive, powerful, and wonderful.

The Seeker peered around the lot, shuddering in time with the Poem, as each stroke sent another pulse of energy along the bridge. Her spine shivered, knuckles turned white, blood rushed and boiled, trying to free itself of vascular tyranny.

The Poem's body wracked and heaved. She did not breathe. Even in her ecstasy, her face was stone, gaze fixed on the Seeker. The Seeker sucked in quick, tiny mouthfuls. The touches merged, pounding through the Poem's insides. For a single moment, the Poem looked through the Seeker's eyes, seeing herself across the parking lot, face flushed and body shaking. Then the bliss broke, a single pulse of red washing from doll to woman. The shock slammed into the Seeker and she nearly doubled over. She stood in its path, let it flow around and through her. Her breathing slowed. Her glassy eyes opened, heart returning to its human beat. The Poem felt all of this and more through their bridge.

Finally, the Poem pulled her hands from her body. They still burned, wanting to find the same places. She would not yet. She would return later and do it again. And again.

The Seeker shook it off. The Poem felt the denial through the fading connection. They would always be linked in the Maker's inspiration, but their direct line would have to be maintained.

The Poem would haunt her echo.

The Poem calmed herself. Finished, she moved into a crouch as the Seeker quickened the pace to her car. She gunned the little compact from the parking lot. The Poem watched the car fade into the night and made a plan. Retracing her steps up the hill, she was inside before the sun was up.

The Knife was waiting in the parlor. "Where have you been?"

"Where I wanted to be."

"You're filthy. Clean yourself up before the Maker rises."

The Poem considered skipping the bath just because the Knife ordered it, but she wanted to soak herself. She got into the tub and turned the faucet on, hotter than she should have been able to stand, wanting to melt. The Seeker would be doing the same. The Poem wished she could bring the Seeker into the house and to join the others. The Seeker could be a doll, too. She would understand.

Her feet burned distantly. A little blood seeped from the cracks the gravel had made. There was no flesh in them, thin blood leaking directly from the soft pink plastic. The wounds would close over the next few days and before long, the fleshless skin would be perfect and smooth again. She ignored her wounds and found the bar of soap, soon turning the bath into something like milk.

The Maker came into the room, rubbing his eyes, still tired. "You're bathing."

"I was dirty."

He dipped the washcloth into the water and rubbed her soft back, liking the way the bubbles glided off her false skin. "Thank you."

"I love you, Maker." There was no lie there, even if she didn't understand the word.

* * *

When Brian called, part of Stephen still responded instinctually. It took him back to the time when they were little, when Brian was the leader and Stephen was the follower. Things were the way Brian wanted them because Brian wanted them that way. Stephen kept those pieces that had changed well hidden.

Stephen knew going over there was a bad idea. The question remained—was there was anything left of the relationship they'd had as children? It might have been bruised and rotting, but it was the one friendship Stephen could lean on. So he left the house on a chilly fall day to go to Brian's.

It led to the glass unicorn Stephen stared at.

He was in Brian's apartment. Nothing had been said yet. The pleasantries.

"Thanks for coming, Stephen. I wanted to clear the air."

"Yeah, I think that's a good idea."

Brian waved him inside, shoulders relaxed as he turned his back on Stephen, unafraid. "You want something to drink?"

"Actually, I could use a bathroom."

"Through the bedroom."

Stephen followed the directions and found the unicorn sitting proudly on a little shelf over Brian's bed. The glass unicorn Brian had stolen from Risa Douglass's room. The unicorn he took instead of her blood.

It wasn't alone.

There were other trinkets. Stephen recognized a few of them from the other trips that occupied them until the night Brian waited in Emily's closet. There were far more with no connection to anything Stephen had done. Brian had been busy. Stephen couldn't tell ages from the combs, or the figurines, or the scissors, but something told him Brian's trophies did not stop there.

Something had been hidden in the apartment.

As certain as there was something hidden in Stephen's house, Brian had other trophies. He had gone further than mere lurking. At some point, probably beginning when Brian left for college. And there was no bringing him back.

Stephen couldn't muster the strength to piss and went back into the living room with urine straining against him. It was agony, and he deserved it and much more for helping free the thing in Brian. That thing had a twin in Stephen, and when they broke chains on one, the other had come from the dark as well.

Stephen came back into the living room, aching from the piss, and froze. Brian had four of his friends now—there were always four—arrayed as an audience. Stephen hadn't heard them enter the apartment, but they were predators, and predators move without prey hearing. All four watched Stephen without trying to watch, the way Brian told Stephen how to watch the dancers at Lulu's Petals. They hunched behind their master, their alpha. Wolves. In Stephen's mind their features had changed and were barely recognizable as human. Eyes flashed red, sharp teeth poked into lips, hands twisted into claws. The thought lingered and altered the images of the men.

He understood how the dolls assigned names.

"Hey, Steve. Hope you don't mind. I called some guys over to have a beer with us."

"Why would I mind?" Stephen's mouth was completely dry.

"Good. About that night... Jessica was at home. You probably figured that out by now."

Stephen resisted the comment that sprung to life.

Brian went on, "Still, I can't help but wonder. I mean, you disappear for months and months. You're doing something."

If only you knew. "No. I'm just keeping to myself. Like you asked."

Brian grinned. "I didn't ask you to do anything. Funny thing. I spoke to Jess the other day and she mentioned she saw you."

"She stopped by. We talked."

"Did you tell her what's going on in your house?"

"There's nothing going on."

"Yes, there is. You can lie to me if you want, but it's not like I can't see through you. I've known you long enough."

"We have known each other for a long time."

"What's that supposed to mean?"

"You know what I mean."

Brian's pack exchanged gleeful looks. Stephen understood—he had raised on a pair of tens. Brian had no secrets from the pack. They knew more than Stephen, even the location and purpose of the trophies Stephen sensed in the other man's room.

Brian didn't bother to smile. "Go on. Shout it out, if you want."

"No. It's fine. I should be going."

Brian got up. "You started this. You can finish it. Tell me what you think you know."

Stephen quailed. "This is all about Jessica? She's a friend. That's it."

"That's not it. You're trying to fuck her."

"I can promise you, I'm not."

"Please stop lying. It only gets worse when you do. Now, are you going to tell me what's going on in your house?"

"There's nothing, Brian."

Brian turned to his friends and smiled as if to say, *See? What did I tell you?*

They smirked and chuckled. One of them leaned forward, anticipating something.

Brian was across the room before Stephen could blink. There was no memory of being hit, just a flash, then being on the floor with Brian standing over him and reaching down.

Stephen thought of the dolls. They were perfect, strong, powerful. Once he had been afraid they would hurt Brian. If only they were there now. If only Stephen were strong like they were, a woman of wood, of porcelain. If only his unclean flesh were pure and false. Deep in the wolf's lair, he was naked and helpless.

Brian hauled Stephen to his feet. "What's going on in your house?"

One of Brian's friends let out a laugh. Another pulled on his beer like he was watching the whole thing on TV.

Brian hauled a haymaker into Stephen's chin.

Stephen fell backward into a chair, knocked it over and tumbled to the floor. He tasted blood. Blood was creation. Suddenly he was hard.

"What. Is. Going. On. In. Your. House?"

Stephen drooled blood from a smile. "Fuck you."

The piss burned in his guts, the erection locking it in place.

Brian kicked him in the ribs, hard. Kicked him again. The pain was bad, but it was nowhere close to what he had visited upon himself. He wanted to lose control, to wet himself all over Brian's floor. Even that impotent freedom had been taken from him. Brian kept asking the questions and kept hitting. Distantly, Stephen wondered how much of a beating would kill him, how much pain had become background noise. Could he be beaten to death and not care? The fists kept falling. Vision began to iris closed in red shadow.

What would happen to the dolls? The ones he had birthed and the ones who had not yet been made? There was still Work to do.

Audra's words. A joking comment. Chemist. Stephen spat out the words along with black blood. "Drugs."

Brian stopped, chest heaving. "What?"

The room swam. Brian looked so far away. "Drugs. I'm making drugs."

"You called it," one of the friends said.

"Who are you making them for?"

"I supply a couple people."

"Now it looks like I know something about you."

Stephen slowly rose, ribcage moving, ripping through his insides with a molten blade. His erection wouldn't drop.

Brian righted the chair Stephen had knocked over and sat down, inspecting bloody knuckles. "You want to hang out, Steve? A beer might make you feel better."

Stephen limped out of the apartment, staggering into an

alleyway, finally pissing. It came out thick and red.

He didn't remember driving home, just the feeling of the Firstborn gently carrying him, washing and binding him. The dolls gathered in a vigil around the bed, Firstborn cradling his head, the Poem stroking his belly, the Knife holding his hand. Their words went unheard by human ears as they talked of ancient and horrible things.

* * *

Stephen was able to leave the house two weeks later, still with a black eye, but a mouth no longer tasting of change. The broken rib would never fully heal. During his convalescence, the Firstborn often sat on the bed, brushing his hair. The Knife fed him soup. The Poem bathed him.

He slept on his bed of razors, the dolls arrayed around him, facing inward in mourning. He awoke with their unblinking attention upon him. There was a time when the terror would have gripped him, now it was only comfort. The eldritch things within them would keep him safe until they devoured him.

Life returned to normal, but he never worked on his garden again, leaving it to the spiders. It was not a conscious decision. The garden was merely forgotten.

In two weeks, he went to his regular game, ribs shifting with every bump, despite the tape the Firstborn had applied. Every bump on the road, every limping step into Griffith Park was a new agony.

Tyler and Milena were at separate tables. Tyler's eyes bugged out when he saw Stephen, hopping up from the table and rushing over, followed by Milena.

"Holy shit, what happened? You look like you got hit by a truck you owed money to."

"That bad, huh?"

Tyler threw a thumb at the other card players. "They might let you win out of pity."

"Lucky me."

"I heard you and Brian had a falling out. I didn't know it was like that."

"Neither did I until it happened."

Milena said, "Who's Brian?"

"A friend of mine," Stephen said.

Milena looked him over. "I don't think so. How are you feeling?"

"I think I look worse than I feel."

Tyler said, "I was gonna hit you up for money, too. Brian said some things."

"Said what?" Stephen tried not to let the fear shine through. Brian didn't know about the dolls, but he had the potential to ruin everything. Anyone coming to the house, for drugs or otherwise, could expose the dolls.

"Said everyone should stay away from you. Hinted you had some kind of income you shouldn't have, you know?"

"I don't."

"Yeah, whatever. Not my problem. Brian's an asshole."

Milena said, "Come on, ladies. Let's make rent."

They each sat down at a different table. Nearly everyone in the park was there for the same reason. It was sharks hunting other sharks. Stephen preferred that kind of opposition. It made the winning all the more satisfying. Easier marks were fine, but preying on the weak was never a good thing. The Work could proceed without it.

He played for over an hour, mind wandering from the game. It helped leaving the house at least for a time. Part of him still felt vulnerable. He entertained the thought of bringing the Firstborn, but she was different enough to notice, even if disguised. Tyler and Milena would recognize the Firstborn's inhumanity, and they would fear her. He cared what Tyler and Milena thought. That surprised him.

Stephen noticed the Benz as soon as it rolled to a stop in the parking lot. It was a hundred yards out of the way, something in its movement reminding him of Brian. The smoothness, the way each joint was running on oil made of adrenaline.

The doors opened and the men that got out had the same wolfish posture. There were two, both swarthy and muscled, wearing tight shirts to show off ape arms. Gold jewelry flashed at wrists and throat, showing where to cut. One had a shaved head and goatee; the other had short, wiry black hair. They started to the games in a predatory, quick stride. Stephen followed their attention to land squarely on Tyler.

Stephen glanced back, and saw that Milena had seen them, too, and had taken a phone from her vintage purse. Tyler was taunting the dealer while collecting a big pot. He frowned when the dealer didn't respond to the bait. Only then did Tyler see the two guys.

Tyler ran.

He ignored the money on the table and ran.

The two men broke into a run after him.

The games were already breaking up—the rabbits scatter once the coyotes have made their choice. Milena headed right for Stephen. "Come on, we're going."

"What's going on?"

They were clearly faster than Tyler, expertly boxing him in against the wall of the hill beyond. The longer he ran, the worse the beating. Stephen knew the equation.

"I'll tell you if you move." Milena grabbed Stephen under the arm. The rib shifted and Stephen winced. "Sorry," she said.

She took him to her car. They were driving for five minutes before she said, "I'll give you a ride back here to pick up your car later. We just need to wait it out."

"Wait what out?"

"Their blood will be up. After they're finished with Tyler, no telling who or what they'll do next. We wait, give an anonymous call to 911, and forget it."

"What's wrong with Tyler?"

Milena drove him to their bar, but she didn't order alcohol. The drinks weren't a comedown this time. These were funereal.

Stephen shifted uncomfortably. "Are you going to tell me what happened?"

Milena sipped at her Shirley Temple. No longer difficult to read, this time the anger boiled from her. "His name is Karo Minasian. The guy with the hair. Tyler owes him money. Time ran out."

"Fuck."

"We all borrow from Karo at one time or another. The question is… what are you willing to pay?"

"I see."

"Not yet. At some point, you'll go to him and you'll find out."

* * *

While Stephen learned about Tyler's debts, wondering if this would have happened had Stephen kept playing for money, the Knife sat in her place in the parlor, cradling the dolly the Maker had given her. She had finished brushing its hair and redressing it, holding it like a sleeping baby, although neither of them ever slept.

There were none around to hear what she said. The Firstborn danced through the halls upstairs while the Poem paced off the ritual circle in the attic.

The Knife silently watched the front yard. A raven hopped through the tiny hedge maze, looking for lizards to eat. Spider webs pulled at its papery wings.

The Knife spoke. "What did you do?"

A pause.

She spoke again. "I don't need you protecting me."

Another pause.

"What I do with him is my own business. Not yours!"

A final pause.

"Fuck you."

The Knife fell silent again.

* * *

Jessica arrived not long after. The house was dark. She debated entering, knowing somewhere to do so would be wrong. The house was watching, even though there could be no one home. Beyond the darkness and silence, the house paradoxically felt empty even as it stared deep into her. The chipped paint and the spider webs said Stephen had stopped caring.

She wondered what had happened while writing Stephen a

note and sticking it to the door.

As she walked away, the house called to her in simultaneous need and hate.

CHAPTER THIRTEEN

THERE WAS NO WARNING. Not even a knock. Stephen was in bed with the Poem. The other dolls were somewhere in the house, but there was no telling where. His wounds still hurt enough to keep him from responding to Jessica's note, taped to the bathroom mirror. The Knife never reacted to it.

Below, the front door opened.

"Steve!" It was Brian's voice—angry or not, Stephen couldn't tell.

The Poem was already up and moving, a reminder she was not human and needed no time to struggle through the veil of sleep. Stephen stumbled to his feet and pulled on a pair of shorts, rushing to the top of the stairs.

Where were the others?

He reached the landing before realizing Brian might be back for another round. Let him. See if the dolls allowed it. Stephen turned the corner to see Brian just inside the front door.

Brian glared at Stephen. "We need to talk." Stephen took a step down the stairs. Brian seemed to get taller.

"Again."

"Yes, again. You talked to Jessica. She came to my place to fucking yell at me."

"I haven't said a word."

Stephen took several more steps down the stairs into a shaft of light whirling with motes, the house groaning with every step. Brian's face changed to amusement. "You don't look so hot."

"Is that what you came to tell me?" Stephen made it down the stairs, regarding his friend distantly. He was somewhere else, watching Brian bully a complete stranger.

"No. You need to tell me what you're doing with my sister."

"Why's that?"

"Because she's my sister."

"I have a sister, too, you know. There was a time when she was fair game."

Brian blinked, fumbling for the memory. Catching it, the flaw was apparent. "Christ. We were thirteen. I had a harmless crush."

"So does Jessica."

"That's fucking bullshit and you know it. Nothing's harmless anymore."

"You should know."

"The fuck I..." His voice trailed off, eyes fixed on the landing above, past Stephen. The Poem stood at the landing, one smooth leg in front of the other, body plainly exposed, long red hair falling over one eye. She stared back at Brian with naked curiosity. "Who the hell is that?"

The front door shut. Brian whirled. The Knife blocked the now closed door. The Poem walked smoothly down the stairs, taking the hand of the Firstborn, suddenly present in the archway to the parlor. Brian was surrounded.

He couldn't hide the fear. "Steve? What the fuck is this?"

The Knife said, "He's seen us."

Brian went from harlequin to harlequin. The initial shock was beginning to wear off. He was surrounded by three women. Women were nothing to fear. A mistruth—Brian had never been in greater danger. His gaze lingered on the Knife a little longer than the other two. "What's going on?"

"Go on, Maker. Tell him," the Knife said.

"Maker?"

Stephen took a breath. "I made them."

"What do you mean, 'made them'?"

Stephen thought it over. Brian had to see the Work. It was true power. Brian would never, could never, imagine anything close to this.

"I'll show you."

Stephen turned to the stairs. The Poem went first. His eyes found her shifting buttocks and he was hard again. This was Brian at Risa Douglass's house, looking up into the windows, trying to work up the courage to satisfy the thing within him.

No. Brian couldn't create.

Brian's creaking footsteps followed him, and behind, the soft tread of the Firstborn and the Knife. The Poem reached for the cord to pull the attic stairs down, too short to reach it. Stephen pulled the trapdoor down and let his newest creation go first.

Brian emerged into the stifling attic. The Siege Perilous was the most obvious thing in the room. Her back was to the trapdoor, showing only the sharp insect limbs reaching forward. Her hunger was palpable in the still air.

"You're fucking with me, right?" Brian's voice was starting to shake. Consciously, it was possible to ignore that these were not women but alien things standing around him, Brian's animal mind would pick up the little differences. The strange eyes never focused. The way none of them would fidget or rock when they were at rest. The sounds of their bodies like nothing flesh had ever made.

"No. I'm not."

Stephen turned on the light over the worktable. There were sketches of the Poem still on it and a few early attempts at her limbs.

Embryonic freckles on the smooth peach-colored skin, a severed arm without blood, meat or bone, just flat plastic like sliced cheese. Brian flickered from the Poem's body to the limbs.

"And then there's those." Stephen pointed to the far corner, deep in shadow. Brian followed the finger, moving closer to the pooling shadows.

The Knife joined Stephen by the worktable. She put her hand on his. It was smooth, cool, and very strong.

Brian whispered, "Holy shit." In the corner of the attic, war crime piles of limbs and incomplete bodies. These were the cast-offs. The mistakes. An errant hit with a chisel. Momentary carelessness when handling them. Bubbles not purged from injection. Flaking mold lines. Evidence the three living dolls represented the pinnacle of the Maker's skill.

Brian knelt and picked up the Knife's face from the pile. Hollow on the inside, almost a mask, cracks spider webbing from her left eye. He put it back down and turned. "How?"

"Magic."

"I believe it." Brian approached, looking more confident. "Do they work? I mean, are they like real women?"

"Mostly."

"Can you fuck them?"

Stephen turned away. "Yes."

"Nice." Brian's eyes crawled over the Poem, scarcely noticing the others. "Can I borrow the little one?"

The Firstborn stepped between Brian and the Poem.

"No, you can't," Stephen said.

The Knife said, "He's going to tell. We should stop him."

"Stop me?" Brian said.

The Knife toyed with one of Stephen's blades. "He doesn't have to leave."

Brian tried a laugh. The dolls were silent, watching him. His eyes worked crazily for a moment, before he moved closer to the exit and lunged at the Poem. The Firstborn was much quicker, grabbing a wrist and pulling Brian smoothly off his feet, slamming him into the floor face first. She placed a pointe shoe on the back of a torqued shoulder, still holding the arm. Brian cried out in pain. The Poem knelt, heedless of what showed, and inspected the hyper extended limb.

Stephen realized for the first time he could easily kill Brian. A nod to the Firstborn and she would tear him apart. A word to the Knife and she would cut his throat. Brian writhed under the Firstborn, weak, helpless, belonging to Stephen and the dolls.

Stephen let the idea enter him, shuddering only when it found a home. "Let him go."

The Firstborn dropped Brian, gently taking the Poem's hand to lead the smaller doll away. The Poem put her arms around the

Firstborn, molding to her body. Brian got up unsteadily, rubbing the wrenched shoulder, and glaring at the Firstborn. She had torn the teeth from that hound.

"You shouldn't have tried to touch her," Stephen said.

"Fuck you, Steve. This is what you say to me? You're trying to fuck my sister and you have a house full of living sex dolls?"

Stephen's cheeks burned. "There are rules here."

The Knife said, "I could end him if you like."

"No!"

Brian's eyes were big, but his mouth was still in a growl. "That one is right. I could tell someone. I could tell the cops."

"Tell them what? I haven't killed anyone. I haven't stolen anything. All I did was create."

"I could tell Jessica."

The Knife's head whipped around. "You tell her nothing!" She had taken two steps before Stephen caught her by the cold arm.

"Brian. Please, shut the fuck up."

"Control them."

"I don't know if I can."

The silence nearly swallowed both of them.

Finally, Stephen said, "What can I do?"

"Make me one."

* * *

Brian and Stephen were downstairs in the dining room at either end of the table that was much too large for them. The stain on the wall had grown. Stephen never noticed, a pad of paper in front of him, ready to sketch. He was a police artist in reverse, asking Brian for the description of the woman who didn't yet exist.

The doll Stephen had given to the Knife was in front of Brian. As they spoke, Brian twisted it into contorted positions. She was bound by invisible rope, in agony, unable to resist. Brian's fantasy.

Stephen thought of the woman running from Brian's room, the trophies over Brian's head when he lay down to sleep. There had been a lot of them. There would be more. Stephen should have created Brian a doll a long time ago, as soon as the Work had reached the point of birth. It was already impossible to go back to the moment Stephen had released that creature on Risa Douglass.

"Okay. What do you want?"

Brian's eyes went to the Firstborn, standing in the doorway behind Stephen, unwilling to leave Stephen alone with the other man. Her clear eyes stared past Brian, refusing to acknowledge his presence. Even when Stephen asked her to go into the other room, she stepped beyond the threshold of the door and stayed there. No use in asking her to go further and Stephen wasn't certain he wanted her to.

"Brown hair." Of course. Brian preferred brown hair. The crying girl. Risa. "Can you do other colored eyes?"

"Like the Poem's?"

"What?"

Stephen looked up. Brian's face was a picture of confusion. "Like the, uh, redhead?"

"Yeah, but brown."

"I can do that."

"Fair skin. Pale. No freckles. Smooth."

Stephen thought of Jessica's skin. Nearly a perfect description. Stephen went fishing. "Sort of silvery?"

Brian nodded. "Perfect. Make her face heart-shaped, you know? Narrow chin. Big eyes. Make her small, too. I want her around five-two."

Stephen's pencil scratched at the page.

Brian went on, "Small nose. Almost a button nose. Cupid's bow lips. And, uh... none of that clown shit, okay?"

"I figured." *Not clowns, harlequins. Show some fucking respect.*

"It's cool, I mean. For you. I mean, whatever."

"Build?"

"Soft. Young. Small boobs, small waist, small hips. Small."

"I understand."

"And tight. She has to be tight."

"What style hair?"

"None."

"On her head, I mean."

"Oh. I don't know what you call it. Give her bangs like the psycho bitch with the X-Acto knife. But pull the hair tight into pigtails. Curly pigtails."

Like a little girl. "Ringlets?"

"Yeah."

"And what do you want her to wear?"

"A dress. Like *Alice In Wonderland.*"

"Shoes? Socks?"

"Knee socks. Mary Janes."

"Jewelry?"

"None." A pause. "One more thing."

"Yeah?"

"Give her bruised knees."

Stephen's pencil scratched to a stop.

Brian said, "Can you do that?"

Stephen's voice caught. "Yes." He finished the sketch with some dark splotches on her exposed knees and turned the pad around for Brian. "How's this?"

He looked at the tiny woman on the pad. Stephen had given her a fearful air, looking up at Brian with tears welling in her eyes. Brian swallowed, mouth dry. "Make the nose a little smaller and she's perfect."

"Good."

"You haven't asked me about personality. I want her like that. Submissive. Willing. Pliable."

"You can't design personality. They awaken with whatever will they have."

"Awaken?"

"Born. I don't know the word for it."

"Where does it come from? The personality."

"I don't know."

Brian nodded, looking at his hands.

Stephen broke the silence. "Ten thousand."

"What?"

"I need ten thousand dollars. Making dolls is not free."

"You got some balls. But I'll get it to you. This is worth it. When will it be ready?"

"She'll be born in a month."

Brian paused, birthing a thought, and for a moment, Stephen saw the best friend Brian had once been. "When you create them, how does it feel?"

"You know how they say amputees can still feel a missing limb? This is the exact opposite of that."

* * *

The newest doll, the one he would never fuck, was beginning to take shape upstairs. She was created in the same manner as the Poem, who was fascinated by the whole process, staying with Stephen constantly, sitting on the floor, legs crossed, splaying her body lewdly. She never asked a question, her presence enough to absorb the knowledge. The only sound was the constant scratch of the Firstborn's chisel.

As Stephen sat in the Siege Perilous, banking the blood for the new one, the Poem held a perfectly cast forearm, turning it over in her gloved hands. "I was once this. No face."

"No face."

"The Sorrow," she said.

"What?"

The Poem's soft blue eyes caught him. "You're making the Sorrow." She kissed the forearm and returned it to the worktable. Her hand went to his hair.

He said, "What does that mean?"

"Merely what is. It's been dark for hours now. Are you staying in?"

His stomach, mostly dormant these days, let out a little rumble. "No. I was going to eat."

"When you come back, will you fuck me?"

"Of course."

"Good."

The Firstborn, as though summoned, came to him and

removed the needles, expertly bandaging him, leaving him to hold the wounds until he was fairly certain the blood had stopped flowing, and finally rolling his sleeves down to hide the track marks. The Siege Perilous didn't bother him as much anymore.

He touched the Poem's hair. She crouched by the Siege Perilous, looking out over the arroyo. Stephen left the attic, and then the house, for the Nite Lite. Audra was there and being with her felt normal.

She was clearly visible from the parking lot, filling up the coffee cup of a late night writer. Audra was in bad shape, staring listlessly out of twin pits, her skin looking faintly yellow under the lights. She jumped at the sound of the jingling bell, and offered Stephen a relieved wave. Taking his normal booth, the one facing home, he pretended he could see it, even as all the lights were off. The dolls didn't need light, and never turned them on of their accord.

Audra stopped by the table. "Usual?"

He nodded. "Are you okay? You look… tired."

"It's been… let me put your order in. I need to talk to somebody. You of all people might understand."

She went back into the kitchen and brought him a glass of iced tea and slid into the booth across from him, rubbing her eyes. "I haven't been sleeping much."

"Me neither."

She smiled, tired and humorless. "I knew you'd understand. Do you have nightmares too?"

Stephen had to think. He couldn't recall the last dream he'd had. "No. I don't think so."

"I have this dream I'm lost in this creepy house. I can't find my way out. And somewhere, outside, there's another me, and she's doing all the things I'm supposed to be doing. Everyone I know thinks she's me. The longer I stay in there, the more lost I am. And the longer I'm lost, the more damage she does." Audra shook her head.

"Sounds horrible."

"It is. It's so real, too. When I wake up, I wonder what the other me is doing."

"So you haven't been sleeping."

"Yeah. And that makes it worse. You know in *Fight Club* when Jack says when you have insomnia, you're never really awake and you're never really asleep? It's like that. So when I get off work, I have these flashes. I don't know. Like she knows where I am." She stopped, breaking into a brittle laugh. "I sound crazy, don't I?"

"I'm probably not the best judge."

"Thanks for letting me talk about it."

"What are friends for?"

She paused, the first real light flickering into her eyes. "Yeah. Listen, can I call you? If I feel weird? Of course, now I feel weird, so can I call you now?"

"Whenever you want."

"Thanks, Stephen."

"It's my pleasure."

* * *

By the beginning of February, Stephen had assembled the creature the Poem had named the Sorrow. That was not accurate. The Poem had not named her. The name came from somewhere else, the same place that had spawned the names of the others. Some black place into which Stephen had reached blindly, not knowing what he had drawn back.

They weren't really names.

The Sorrow was taking shape. She was breathtaking, but that was hardly noteworthy. They were all creatures of exquisite perfection. She was not interesting to Stephen. She was identical on the inside to the Poem, an already boring design. He could do so much better. Making a creature that looked human had been done. What remained was to create something plainly beyond.

Of the others, this was the closest to the human conception of daughter. He would not touch this one, and instead send her off to be married. That was almost normal.

He was not only her father. He was mother as well.

He treated the knees with a dye made mostly of ink, subtly blending the edges of the phony bruise. The joints were fitting together nicely. She would be a worthy doll. The Poem relentlessly shadowed him, smiling guilelessly. "The Hide will be pleased."

Stephen shuddered, thinking of Brian and the knife. The way the other boy had wanted to hold life in his hands. What would he be when he emerged from hiding? "I'm glad."

"You don't mean that."

"No, I don't. Where are the others?"

"Below."

"They don't approve."

"The Knife worries someone will come and hurt us. Take us away."

"You don't worry about that."

"No, Maker. You wouldn't let them."

264 // JUSTIN ROBINSON

"And if I couldn't stop them?"

The Poem shrugged. "We stand with you."

Another question surfaced before Stephen could determine whether her assertion was as futile as it sounded. "Why do you call her the Sorrow?"

"Because she is."

"Why?"

"Because she is. How long until she will be done?"

"I'll bring her to life tomorrow night."

"The Hide will be pleased."

"Come with me. It's time for your bath."

* * *

For the first time at a birth, he was dressed and flaccid. Barefoot, only because the blood-slicked floorboards of the attic no longer felt right without skin against them. The Sorrow was nude, a temptation-that-wasn't. Nothing lurked in him for her.

With all the preparations made, he paused, trying to bring the rest of the rite to mind. He grasped for what happened next, but it flitted out of reach, an occult butterfly.

The Poem stepped up next to him and calmly took the chalk from his hand. She made the circle, lit the candles, rained the cold blood from the bags onto the Sorrow's body. Stephen merely watched. The ritual she performed didn't jog a single memory within him.

That was the most horrible part of all.

When she had finished, she beckoned Stephen over. "Now give her breath."

He knelt before her and blew a single gust into her mouth,

then stood and turned away. The Poem nodded, happy. There was no worry that this time it wouldn't work. There was no need to see her eyes open for the first time.

"Maker?"

"Yes." He looked out at the night. The other dolls lurked in the corners of the attic.

"Maker?" She stood, never coltish. Like the others, she was smooth, confident, graceful.

"What is it?"

She took one light step toward him. Two. A tentative hand on his shoulder.

The Poem shouted, "No! He's not for you!"

Stephen turned to see the Poem push the Sorrow away. He expected the Firstborn to come to the Sorrow's defense as she had done for the Poem, but the Firstborn moved past the Sorrow to stand at Stephen's shoulder. The Sorrow stumbled, righting herself. "Maker? I'm here now."

"I know. Your..." What was he supposed to call Brian?

"Master," the Poem said.

"Husband," the Knife said.

"He'll be... happy to know you're here."

"What?"

"Someone asked me to make you. So I did. You're not mine."

The Poem said, "I told you."

"Of course I'm yours. I am as you made me."

The phone rang.

"No. One of you, get her dressed."

On the way down the ladder, he answered the phone. "Brian? Good timing."

266 // JUSTIN ROBINSON

"Stephen?" It was Jessica's voice, quavering, terrified.

"Jess? What's going on?"

"Can you come over?"

Something in her voice said it was horrible. "Yeah. I'll be right there."

* * *

The dolls listened as the Maker left right after the phone call. The Sorrow was in the center of them, not exactly standing, plainly terrified. The others stood in a triangle, the same one inscribed inside the Maker's ritual circle.

"What does he mean? Where is he going?" The Sorrow's eyes went from doll to doll.

"The Maker goes sometimes. He always comes back," the Poem said.

"For now," the Knife said.

"Why did he say that about me?"

The Poem's voice was even, never bothering to hide the malice. "He doesn't want you. You weren't made for him. It's why you don't have these." She pointed to the white triangles on her face.

The Sorrow looked from white triangles to black.

"His mark," the Knife said.

The Sorrow got to her feet, backing toward the ladder out of the attic. The Poem took a step forward. "You shouldn't leave. You should stay here until the Hide takes you home."

"I am home."

The Poem shook her head, a radiant smile on her face. "You have no home."

The Sorrow made a fast move to the ladder. The Firstborn

caught her shoulder. A human would have squealed or squirmed, but the Sorrow froze.

"Take your hand off her, Firstborn." The Knife took a step forward.

The Firstborn hesitated, wooden fingers digging into the soft plastic. Only when blood ran from beneath them did she release the Sorrow, whose terrified gaze went to the Knife. "Come on. Your costume is downstairs."

The Sorrow paused, waiting for the Knife to betray her. She took a single, tentative step. Then another. And another. And she was with the Knife.

The other dolls waited across the attic, the Firstborn tall and regal, the Poem hunched, hair wild. They were as statues. The Knife gently ushered the Sorrow to the ladder and let her down first. No doll spoke.

The Sorrow finally broke the silence when they went down the front stairs. "Thank you, Knife."

"Don't do that."

The Knife brought the Sorrow into the parlor, where her little frilly dress was laid out on the sofa, lonely and fragile. The Knife smoothed the half-skirt underneath her as she took her seat in the antique chair, primly crossing her legs. She remembered getting her outfit from the Maker. The complicated snaps and garters had gone on smoothly. At first sight, she knew where everything went, even liking it above and beyond the obvious way it pleased the Maker. It was right.

The Sorrow approached her clothing with trepidation, picking up the socks, regarding them, putting them down. Then the dress, turning it over in her hands.

"It goes over your head."

The Sorrow found the way in and let it fall around her. She collapsed onto the couch with the rustle of fabric. A human woman might have cried. The Sorrow stared straight ahead at nothing.

* * *

Stephen drove too fast on the way to Jessica's. He had never heard someone that sounded as scared as she had. The dolls wandering through his home faded into the background, replaced with flashes of Jessica—as a child, then older, desperately groping him, smiling on Brian's balcony. Each flash drove his right foot down a fraction of an inch, a new curse for every driver blocking his way.

Jessica's apartment building was covered in crows. Croaking and feeding, fluttering their wings only to reposition. When Stephen parked his car a few of them flapped away in surprise, settling quickly. They were thick on the ground. Someone had spilled garbage all over the tiny front yard, making a banquet for the carrion birds.

He took a step forward, waiting for the murder to take flight. They croaked and cawed around him, feasting on the trash. There was no path through the sea of black feathers rubbing together. Even nudging one with his foot did nothing more than make the thing squawk, and peck at him half-heartedly. He had to step amongst them. None took to the air.

They couldn't see him.

Like Emily's dog, like the coyote. He paused in the midst of the birds surrounding him and wanted to scream, just to see what would happen. If they didn't react, that might have been too much. Instead, he pushed through the croaking mass.

He went to the second floor of the apartment complex and raised a fist to knock on Jessica's door. It opened to Jessica's haggard face. The rings under her eyes had darkened and looked grayish rather than purple. The silver-gold of her skin had paled to stark white. All he could see of her was her face. The rest of her body was covered, dressed like she thought she was Audrey Hepburn in *Funny Face*.

"Stephen." She hugged him. Fear regressed her to childhood. After a moment, she started shaking.

He didn't know what to say.

She parted from him, the tears on her face thick as mucous. She pulled him into the apartment and shut it.

"What's wrong?"

"I don't know." Her tone said that wasn't the whole story. She sat down on the sofa, and Stephen knew enough to sit beside her and hold her hand.

She winced, pulling the hand back. Angry welts, like a bad cat scratch, crossed the back of her hand. She covered it with the other.

"What are those?"

"I've been to the doctor. She didn't know. Said maybe an allergic reaction to something. But that was before... I don't know how..."

"Jessica, please. Tell me what's wrong."

She wiped her eye. A moment later nodding, a decision made. She rose, and stripped off her pants, pulled the turtleneck over her head. He recoiled.

Across Jessica's smooth skin more of the scratches. Some were welts, some were bloody. They covered her, disappearing into her panties, cut off by her bra. They looked familiar.

She said, "First, they were tentative. Just little welts. Never any blood."

He thought of her at the club, picking a nonexistent scab.

"They cooled off for a while, but they've come back. They've gotten worse. Much worse."

She stank of fear.

One of the scratches, up her thigh. Closer, so close it filled his nose. The scratch was a word.

HEART.

"A week ago, they started spelling words."

The words were clear, etched in a cruel, sure hand.

ALONE. BLACK. NEED. LOVE.

She collapsed into his arms, crying. "Stephen, I'm so scared."

He tried to comfort her, to stroke her hair and whisper babble into her ears. Eventually, she slept, but only fitfully.

He stayed the night.

CHAPTER FOURTEEN

STEPHEN LEFT ONLY AFTER MAKING Jessica take something to sleep in the early hours of the morning. Carrying her into the bedroom, she was light in his arms. He promised to stay when she asked him not to leave. She climbed under covers flecked with blood and fell asleep. He watched her for a time before it sunk him under its weight.

It was different, sleeping with a woman. She made little noises in her sleep. She turned under the covers. She smelled of sweat and of blood, hair sticking to her forehead. She slept.

He looked her over on the many occasions during the night when sleep was impossible. She was more real than they were. Her skin was smooth, marked by moles, something he had never bothered to put on even his most human doll. She had imperfections. The scar on her shoulder from when she broke it skiing. The way her armpits were already dusted in black. The small pimples forming at the corner of her mouth.

She was disgusting.

And for a moment, that didn't matter.

Then there were the words etched on flawed skin. Jessica, terrified, in pain—his fault. There could be no other explanation.

Find a way to spare her pain, heedless of the price. There were consequences to the Work. He forgot them thinking of the cool thighs of the dolls, but they were there, racking up a toll he was too blind to see.

The Sorrow waited at home. She needed to be given away, to go to Brian and feed that thing inside him. Jessica was sleeping peacefully. Stephen entertained the thought of coming back to Jessica, letting her wake up with him and know he was there for her.

He wouldn't be.

He entered the house. Immediately, the Knife and the Sorrow turned to him. The Knife was sitting primly in her chair by the window, her dolly on the table beside her, expression unchanging. The Sorrow was on the couch in that outfit Brian had asked for, a sick hope in her face.

He said to the Knife, "What are you doing to Jessica?"

"I don't know what you mean."

Stephen advanced on her, voice low and dangerous. "You're marking her somehow. Writing on her skin."

"Maker, I have never touched the Heart."

"Heart?"

The Knife nodded.

"One of the words on her."

The Knife was still.

"Goddamn it. Whatever it is, it stops! You don't hurt her! You don't touch her!"

Her eyelid shutters closed, opened, too slowly to be a blink. "I will never touch her."

The Sorrow opened her mouth but didn't speak.

Still angry, Stephen said, "She needs to go." The dolls didn't often show recognizable emotion, this time the despair on the Sorrow's face was heartbreaking. He had to turn away, going to the kitchen for the phone.

"Hello?"

"She's ready."

"Seriously? She's alive?"

"Yes. Alive, dressed, and ready to be taken home."

"I'll be there in fifteen."

Stephen hung up the phone, mind turning to Jessica, softly bleeding in her sleep.

"You're giving her up."

"What?"

The Knife stood in the doorway. "You're giving the Sorrow away."

"I didn't make her for me."

"It doesn't matter. She's still yours."

He thought it over. "Are you mine?"

"You know the answer to that, Maker. I could reverse the question on you, as none of us truly know the answer. The Poem might think she does, but it's a belief. Not a fact."

"Are you worried I'd give you away?"

She didn't answer.

"Is that why you're hurting Jessica?"

She still didn't answer.

"I made you for me."

"As you made the others."

"Except the Sorrow."

He wished the Knife's face was readable. She was even more

closed to him than most people. He had created her and the workings of her mind were a mystery. There was nothing to say. Could a doll be comforted? Should he even try?

Brian tore the front door open and shouted, "Steve!"

Stephen came out of the kitchen into the front hall. Brian's attention was already on the parlor, no doubt seeing his living doll for the first time. The force of cruel joy, the need to possess was written large on him, nearly rocked Stephen after focusing pinpoints on the closed books of Jessica and the Knife.

"That's her," Brian said. "It's like you went into my head and pulled her out."

Stephen got closer. The Sorrow stood with the couch between her and Brian, hands crossed over the apex of her thighs. Her eyes went from Stephen to Brian and back to Stephen, pleading, terror, pleading. "Her name is the Sorrow."

"Fuck that. Her name is Tabitha. You ready to go now, Tabby?"

The Sorrow went to Stephen. "Maker. Please don't send me away. I can make you happy. I promise."

"I'm sorry," Stephen said.

Brian snatched the Sorrow by her arm. "Let's go. I have something for you."

The Sorrow grabbed at Stephen. "No! Maker, please!"

Stephen said, "You're not mine."

Brian wrestled with her, far stronger than the little doll. The plastic ones were so much weaker than wood or porcelain. Had she been born of those, she would have torn herself away with ease. She reached for Stephen, making a horrible sound in her throat, something awful and inhuman. He turned away, eyes shut tight.

The door slammed, the sound hitting him with the force of a gunshot. The Knife was with him, just out of reach.

He heard her chiming footsteps, felt the coolness of her skin, "I could never do that to you."

"I don't believe you."

He took her by the hand. "Please, Knife. Come with me."

After a moment, she accepted his hand and let him lead her upstairs, into bed gently, let him try to show her what she could never believe. There was an element of desperation to her touch, terrified of him leaving her. He fell asleep with his cheek on her smooth breast, and she let herself stay until sleep truly claimed him, before finally leaving to resume her post downstairs.

She heard the Poem padding upstairs to replace her in bed, to wake the Maker and reaffirm their bond. The Knife wanted to scream, but she didn't know how.

* * *

The Sorrow would try to forget the things Brian Baniszewski did to her that first night, but she never would. When the Hide finally slept, she stripped out of the hated costume and abandoned him for the living room. The couch carried the scent of the Maker, when he smelled like a man, and that is where she stayed.

* * *

Stephen was in his deep slumber, laid out peacefully on his back. A human would think him dead, until they noticed the infinitesimal rise and fall of his sunken chest. The Firstborn seemed to enjoy watching him sleep, but she was elsewhere. The

276 // JUSTIN ROBINSON

Poem kept Stephen company that night, pretending to sleep. Her pubic ruff matted from the night's lovemaking, she wore only her blue velvet choker the Knife thought of as a collar. The Knife lifted the plastic libertine easily.

The Poem's eyes flew open, soft hands grabbing at the Knife's arms. "What are you doing?" she whispered.

"Shh. Don't wake him," the Knife said.

The Poem glanced back at Stephen and turned a glare on the Knife. The red one would be quiet, but she wouldn't like it. The Knife only set her down in the hall. The Poem folded her little arms and glared. "What do you want?"

"We need to talk." The Knife smoothed the skirts that fell around her waist but did nothing to conceal her body.

"Talk."

"Not without the Firstborn."

The Poem's attention was now undivided. She frowned, though remained silent. The trapdoor was open and the ladder down. The Knife led the way, the Poem's soft feet padding behind.

The Firstborn sat in the Siege Perilous, facing the window, watching the moon. She didn't stir. All of them could be still, but not like the Firstborn. In her stillness was the barest minimum of movement, the subtle sway of an oak in a breeze.

"Firstborn," the Knife said.

The Firstborn stood in a single motion, turned gracefully, and was still again. The Knife moved over and all three stood in their triangle: the ballerina, the concubine and the libertine.

"The Knife wants to talk to us," the Poem said.

This Knife flicked hourglass eyes at the Poem.

"He is reaching out," the Knife said.

"The Knife loves and hates the Heart," the Poem said to the Firstborn and giggled.

"He wants to bring her here, but can't. What does he say about us?"

"If she would make him happy, she should join us."

"A flesh and blood woman? She would call us monsters."

The Poem pouted. "We're women, too."

"We're things to them."

"Not to the Maker. He loves us."

"He gave the Sorrow away. What's to stop him from tossing us aside once he's done with us?"

"The Sorrow was an ugly little mistake. Of course he gave her up. But one of us? He'll never be done."

"What if someone else came? The Maker is one person. If they came to take him away, if they found us, they could destroy us easily."

The Poem turned to the Firstborn. "Tell her."

The Firstborn watched them both with her glassy eyes.

The Poem turned back to the Knife. "What is your solution?"

"Another doll. Someone who could protect us."

"How can we make another?"

"He has spare parts from all of us. Pieces that weren't… what he wanted. There is enough stored blood, and the rites are in his notes."

"I know the rites," the Poem said.

"We make another doll. A special one."

"No," the Poem said. "If he wanted one, he would make one."

"Firstborn. Do we?"

The Firstborn waited a long moment. Nodded.

"Get back into bed with him, Poem," the Knife said.

The Poem paused. Shook her head.

"What if he wakes up with wood and wants to put it in one of us?" the Knife said.

"What if he wants you or the Firstborn? No. If we're making a doll, it has to be all three of us. She has to be our baby, not only yours and the Firstborn's."

"We can't risk him finding us before she's complete."

"Fuck you, Knife." The Poem said the word as an insult, though her tone made it a ragged command.

The Knife took a step toward the smaller doll. The Poem shrank. The Firstborn stepped to the Poem's side and was still, watching the Knife.

The Knife could only seethe, "Fine."

She resisted the urge to tromp down the stairs. If the Maker caught them, he could be distracted, taking the desired doll to bed. Usually, they could choose, go to him as they wanted. There were times where only one would do. On those nights, he was forceful and wonderful. Those nights turned the Knife's skin to razors. Those nights made her almost believe him.

She led the way to the heap in the corner of the attic. They instinctively quailed at the piles of parts, though nonetheless spread around it like coyotes at a kill.

The Maker called these failures. A perfectionist, the dolls blessed their Maker for it. They existed on the backs of hundreds who never would. The Firstborn's limbs with tiny chisel marks, The Knife's faces with gentle black veining, the Poem's skin pockmarked with minute bubbles.

The Knife didn't have to speak. They were not scavengers;

though they were vultures, it was an act of creation. They knew the limbs they wanted. The Poem crouched like a child, completely unaware of her nudity. The Knife sat primly on a stool, sifting, lifting, setting. The Firstborn would simply glide.

The pile grew, and as one they stopped. It was finished. In there—

"The Innocent," the Poem said.

* * *

The Sorrow waited until the Hide left his lair. She always slipped back into bed with him before it was time for him to wake in the mornings. Her skin crawled as she moved back. He taught her such revulsion was better than the punishment for catching her out of bed.

When the Hide left into the blue morning, the Sorrow rose and promptly stripped the costume from her body. She felt somewhat normal, but it was still not right. She knew nothing would ever be.

She spent the first several hours standing in the bedroom motionless. If anyone were to see her, they would assume she was an incredibly lifelike statue.

The Maker sent her to be with the Hide. There had to be a reason, and she would find out what. Without a twitch, she was moving, first to the bed. There were tiny objects on the shelf above. She took one in hand and turned it over. A talisman. She felt it, moving to the next, and the next.

And she knew.

She replaced each where it had been and went to the closet, drawn by something she could not name. She used a chair to reach the top shelf. The cigar box she found, cheap wood and faded lettering, did not look remarkable. She took it back to the bed and opened it.

Locks of hair, bound with scraps of torn panties. Thirty-six talismans used to summon horrible memories.

The dark mass was the same color as her hair.

* * *

The body of the creature lay out for them. They had brought her down in pieces through the night, hidden her in the dark corners of the coach house where the Maker never went. The Poem carried the last part of the thorax to the back, moved a box, and found a rat looking up at her. It froze. When she moved, it tracked, but didn't flee. She plucked it from the ground and crushed its spine.

She laid the Innocent's body down and took the rat outside. The sun was rising on her, casting her in gold. She squinted up at it, wondering in the warmth, and walked to the orange tree.

Stephen found her there, his libertine, girlishly kneeling beneath it. The sun made her nude form glow, picking the freckles out in stark relief. Her hair blazed bloody red in this light, her body small and sleek to the soft cleft of her ass.

He walked to her to find her brushing the black soil at the base of the tree. "What are you doing?"

The Poem looked up at him. She didn't sweat, even in the heat. "I wanted to play in the dirt."

Her stockings would run. She was probably due a new pair anyway. He touched her hair and left her to it. Jessica was waiting.

He abandoned his dolls, and they went to the coach house

to find the pieces of the Innocent. They started with her body. Each doll had the same thought, though none of them spoke it to the others. They knew they were creating something of beauty. She would be the loveliest doll of them all. The Maker might be momentarily annoyed when they took the act of creation from him, but when he finally beheld this new doll, rapture would be the only possible response.

He didn't return at nightfall. It took all three of the dolls to bear the Innocent to the circle in the attic. They placed her, coiled up in the center and lit the candles. They disrobed, one by one, stacking their clothing in the corners of the attic, observing the proper ritual garb. Each one had clean memories of her moment of birth. The flood into the lungs, the flash into the eyes and the Maker, looming large for them. The Poem guided them in the rite itself. The Poem was the one who spilled the Maker's blood across the segmented body of the Innocent. The Poem was the one whose hands turned red, whose body clotted with the Maker's ichor. The Poem was the one who knelt over the Innocent's heads, each in turn, and whispered into them.

The Innocent opened her eyes. "Thank you, Poem."

* * *

Jessica was awake when Stephen made it back to her apartment. She looked better, once again covered from neck to ankle, smiling wanly at him.

"How are you feeling?"

"Better," she said. "No new..." she trailed off. No word sounded right and they both knew it.

"Can I come in?"

She nodded. "You're the one that looks bad."

"I've felt better."

"Brian hit you."

Stephen nodded. "It's solved now, I think."

"I don't know. He doesn't... he thinks..." she trailed off. "I'm just glad you're here."

He stayed with her on her sofa, watching movies in silence for most of the day. She would chuckle at the jokes, snuggle with her pillow, and offer the occasional sleepy smile. He only got up to make popcorn and to get fresh drinks. She drifted off several times. The dolls were forgotten. An afternoon on the couch with a real woman. It was normal.

When she slept, Stephen inspected what little skin was showing. There was no blood on her, and the few scabs looked at least a day old. The sun set and he continued to put movies in for her, so that when she opened her eyes and blinked at the screen, something new was happening. She drifted in and out.

Jessica was sick, and Stephen was caring for her. He tried to imagine one of his dolls falling ill. Could they? Would human diseases hurt them or were there no contagions to be found? What were their lifespans? Whether they were equal to humanity, equal to what they were made of, or limitless. The wooden Firstborn could last easily into her second century, the porcelain Knife a thousand years and the plastic Poem would never die.

Jessica murmured, her voice thick, "Not going to put another movie in?"

The DVD menu cycled through the same snatch of theme music. He hadn't noticed. "I should probably be getting home."

"You aren't going to stay the night?"

"Not tonight. I'll be back. I promise."

She closed her eyes.

He drove home thinking of the serene look on her face as sleep claimed her. Joining her on the couch, holding her close and breathing the scent of her hair would be so easy. Never return home, leave the dolls to fend for themselves in a fantasy in a life conquered by them. Instead, he rolled up the driveway.

Three ghosts stood by the door, freezing him in place. All three of his creations were waiting in the front for him—the Knife in front, the others flanking her. They could have been standing there since he left, still as statues in the cool night. All three, even the Firstborn, wore smiles.

He got out of the car.

"Maker, we have something wonderful we want to show you."

The tone of the Knife's voice chilled him to the bone. "What?"

"Please, Maker, come with us."

The Poem and the Firstborn turned as one, followed by the Knife. Smooth as choreography, the Poem moved slightly ahead at the stairs. Stephen could not help himself. He had to follow his precious dolls. They led the way into the attic, and as soon as its black maw opened above, the Knife's stark white ass disappearing into it, he felt something wrong. There was no name for it—for the first time since childhood, the attic was home to fear.

The Poem called down, ghoulishly girlish, "Maker! Come on!"

He took the ladder slowly. Every step pushed the dread deeper into his body. The attic would swallow him whole, digest him.

He moved through the trapdoor. Moonlight cascaded through the main window, throwing the arachnid shadow of the Siege

284 // JUSTIN ROBINSON

Perilous across the wooden floor. The dolls had once again arranged themselves, this time leaving an opening to the darkest corner of the attic. The woodpile, where he kept the defective parts that would never be alive.

Something large shifted in the darkness.

"Maker, we've made something for you."

The shadow moved. Stephen took a step back, but it was too late.

She skittered into the light. Stephen knew instantly the thing before him, the smiling abomination, was a she. Her curves were feminine, even if what they added up to was insect. Revulsion drove him backward, fascination made him search for something to make this thing in some way human. He had to pick it apart, recognize the pieces. The face was the Knife's, with cracks spiderwebbing from the left eye. Its thorax was the chests and shoulders of the others, three from each, all flawed in some way. Her eighteen legs were their graceful arms, the wood scored, the porcelain chipped and the plastic seamed. Her segmented body tapered to the nine curved buttocks in the thing's scorpion tail, rising to three soft expanses of flesh Stephen recognized as bellies from each. The tail was tipped with an early attempt at the Firstborn's face, the jaw horribly joined like Howdy Doody.

The thing reared up. Stephen nearly screamed. The tail snaked around. On every horrible link in the tail, flawed genitals clacked their molars at him. At the base, the Poem's face stared at him from empty sockets, her lips in a welcoming smile, irising open from the vulva beneath.

"Maker," she said, the three mouths echoing in a cascade.

Stephen ran from the attic.

CHAPTER FIFTEEN

STEPHEN DIDN'T REALLY REMEMBER THE phone call, having not had a full night of sleep in the house since learning about that thing in the attic. He could sleep only at Jessica's apartment. Over the last two months, there were no new cuts, and most had faded to pink. She nestled into the crook of his shoulder, her breath tickling his skin like nothing the dolls could ever give him. It was not quite sleep, though it was dreamless, leaving him in both worlds, marking time with Jessica's breaths, wondering if they were the cause of mortality.

The month after the abomination was created, Stephen celebrated the Knife's first birthday. The enthusiasm he had with the Firstborn was gone, staying with the Knife for the day, mostly in silence.

The phone call was an abstraction he initially believed to be a dream, even as his last dream was a distant memory lost in gray snow. He must have been in the kitchen staring at nothing when it came.

Until she called again. The Firstborn brought the phone and her hairbrush into the bedroom. The other two dolls stayed with him in bed, just laying there, all three of them statues. The thing in the attic moved, her ninety fingers scratching along the floor, most horribly, singing softly in a childlike voice. The Knife and the Poem stared at the ceiling, enraptured.

He looked blankly at the brush, having forgotten what it was for, putting it aside where the Knife picked it up and gently undid the Firstborn's bun.

He picked up the phone. The voice on the other end was tinny and far away. "Hello? Hello? Is anyone there?"

The Firstborn gently pushed the phone toward Stephen's head. "Hello?"

"Stephen?" It was Emily's voice. "What was that?"

"I... uh... I dropped the phone. What's up?"

"We're at the airport."

Airport. The floodgate of memory lifted. "You're here to visit. I thought I'd dreamed that."

"No. I'm here at Burbank Airport and I need a ride."

"Are you staying here? With me?"

"Uh... yeah."

He looked from face to face. The dolls were all watching expectantly, none more so than the Firstborn, who had settled at the foot of the bed, fixing him with her glassy gaze. Emily would find the dolls immediately. They wouldn't hide.

Would Emily want a doll, too?

"I'll be right there."

He hung up the phone and pulled on clothes as quickly as he could. The Poem said, "You're bringing the Wretched here?"

"Don't call her that. She's my sister."

"We call her what she is," the Knife said.

"She's staying here."

"And what will she say when she sees us?"

For the first time, the Firstborn's expression was something approaching human. Her normally impassive harlequin face almost afraid.

"I think… I think she might understand."

In unison, the Poem and Knife said, "We trust you, Maker." The Poem was genuine, the Knife mocking. Stephen wondered if it was in them to hurt someone, especially someone like Emily. The scratching started directly overhead. The thing was above him, separated only by a layer of wood and plaster.

He ran from the house to his car, driving quickly, finding Emily and little Adrian at the roundabout, waiting for the ride. There was a surprise in the form of a baby car seat sitting on the sidewalk next to her. Emily picked it up by the thick handle. Of course, she had been pregnant. Had there been a birth announcement? The Knife dealt with the mail, as she had his signature. Perhaps there had been, and the Knife never understood what it was.

All three, Emily and children, were flushed in the late afternoon sun. Adrian half-delirious, maybe all cried out, the baby asleep. Stephen pulled over, and Emily opened the back, lifting the kid in and placing the sibling next to him.

"Did you forget?"

"Like I said, I thought the whole thing was a dream."

She shook her head and fetched the luggage, throwing it into the trunk before getting into the passenger seat. She buckled the baby's seat into the back, followed by Adrian, who promptly passed out against the cool plastic of the car seat.

"We're starving. Could we stop somewhere?"

"Let me make it up to you. I'll treat."

"How did you think it was a dream?"

"I haven't been sleeping much."

"You don't look good."

He turned to her, regarding the dark circles under her eyes, hair hanging in clumpy strands, and enervated skin loose and sallow, and said, "I'm not the only one."

She chuckled, the sound unclean. "Why do you think I'm here?"

Guessing was easy, but he wanted her to say it. Not then, once they were home, when the myriad shadows turned into the one that swallowed the world. She would know the dolls by then. Told or shown, the dolls wouldn't hide. He hoped the thing would stay in the attic, knowing it—she—wouldn't. They hadn't hurt anyone. Something in Stephen made him think it was only a matter of time.

"It's weird. Whenever I come back home, I keep thinking everything's going to look different, and nothing ever does."

"No. Nothing changes."

She glanced at the back seat. "Some things do."

"Oh, yeah. Adrian looks older."

"He's almost seven now."

"It's been awhile. And… um… the other one?"

"You don't remember. You're worse than Dad was. Her name's Hannah. She's thirteen months."

"Do they need anything special?"

"Like what?"

"Food, that kind of thing."

"Just let me borrow your car and I'll go shopping when we get home."

Stephen pulled off the freeway, heading for the Nite Lite without thinking. He couldn't really imagine eating anywhere else, not this close to home. As they pulled into the parking lot, Emily said, "Oh, God. The Nite Lite. It's been forever. I remember coming here in high school."

"Is it okay?"

"Oh, sure. You probably want to see your girlfriend."

Stephen's blood turned to ice water, groping for the thought and finding it amidst the clutter of the discarded. On the visit to Phoenix, he remembered lying to Emily, telling her Audra was his girlfriend. That lie was going to end within a day, regardless. "We broke up," he croaked.

"Are you gonna be okay coming here?"

"She works late. We should be fine."

Emily watched him. She knew him better than any, probably knew the lie when she heard it, but unable to guess the motive for it. No one would guess the lives of his dolls.

They left the car and went inside. The kids were waking up, getting fidgety, Emily expertly placating them. Adrian hardly noticed Stephen, except when Emily specifically re-introduced them. The little boy was surprised, turning back to his chicken fingers quickly when the feeling didn't take root. The baby closed her eyes again and drifted off.

They were deep into the meal when the bell rung at the door. Audra walked in. She went behind the counter and grabbed an apron. For a moment, Stephen had a crazy thought of hiding, maybe running out.

"That's her, isn't it?"

He turned to Emily. She went from Audra to him. Of course,

the waitress matched the description. "Yep."

Audra waved, taking in Emily and the family before coming over. "Hey, Stephen. How are you?"

"Good. You?"

"Fine. Hi, I'm Audra." This last to Emily.

"I'm Emily. Stephen's sister." They shook hands. "It's nice to finally meet you," Emily said.

"Finally?"

"Stephen told me about you when he came to visit."

Audra blushed. "He did?"

"Well, yeah. I mean, it was the Thanksgiving before last."

Audra had to reach for the memory. "Okay?"

"You know, back when you guys were together."

Stephen wanted to find a nice small hole to die in. Audra was flabbergasted, eyes going from each of them, trying to find the practical joke. "Together? We're not together. Never. I mean, he... uh... yeah, we're just friends."

"Oh. I'm sorry, that's my fault."

"No, no, it's fine. I... I have tables. It was nice meeting you." Audra fled for the rest of the restaurant.

Emily watched her go, a speculative look on her face, before turning to Stephen. She didn't bother hiding the amusement. "Never together?"

"Um. No. Never."

"Why'd you say you were? You don't have to brag to me."

"I didn't want you to worry."

"There's something else. You weren't lying when you said you were with someone. I'd have known."

"I wasn't lying about that."

"Why her? Because she's cute?"

"She's a friend. I guess I wanted something more."

"She likes you. At least enough for a date."

"Yeah. I'm spoken for."

"Tell me about her."

"You'll meet her. Them. At the house."

"Them?"

"I am your brother."

"What's that supposed to mean?"

"Nothing. There's... there's a lot you don't know. You're going to know. Just promise you won't..."

"Won't what?"

"That you won't."

He paid the bill and tried to wave to Audra but she was in the kitchen. On the short drive to the house, his heart thudded in his chest. He was certain they could all hear it, reverberating off the walls of the car. Each thunderous beat wrung more sweat from him. It was not salty, tasting instead like clean bottled water.

He went up the driveway and pulled to a stop, helping Emily out of the car. She took the kids in hand and let out a little laugh. "I'm sorry," she said. "I'm a little nervous. After the whole 'them' thing."

"It's okay." He didn't mean it, and knew she could hear it in his voice. It probably only made it worse, but there was nothing to be done.

The door was closed. He had locked them in without realizing it. Expecting the Knife or maybe the Poem waiting in the threshold, Stephen opened the door slowly. The house sighed. He looked into the parlor, at the Knife's chair by the window. Also empty.

Emily came inside. Adrian was whining, quieting as soon as he came in, eyes going round as the big drafty house loomed around him. "Where is this?"

"Mommy's home when she was little," Emily said.

Adrian retreated a few steps, putting his mother between him and the carnivorous house.

"Where should I put you up? Mom and Dad's room? Your old room?"

"I figured you'd be using the master bedroom."

He shook his head. "Same room as always."

"Where do... where do 'they' sleep?"

"They don't."

She frowned, trying to figure out if that was a joke. He picked up one of her bags.

"My old room should be fine."

The Firstborn's room. He led her upstairs, every step a blade waiting for the dolls to come from their hiding places.

"Are 'they' home?" she asked.

"They're always home."

The open upstairs hallway was empty. His bedroom door yawned open. He strained to hear some sign of them—footsteps on the stairs, scratching on the attic, the whisper of sheets. There was nothing. Adrian stayed between. The baby was quiet in her padded chair. Emily opened her bedroom door.

And screamed.

Stephen moved to the doorway. The Firstborn was in the bedroom, arms out, harlequin face blank.

The Knife said, "This is the Wretched."

He and Emily whirled. The Knife stood at the top of the

stairs. There had been no sound. Adrian started to cry. The baby woke up and joined him.

The Poem said, "Why do they make that noise?"

She stood in the doorway to the master bedroom, her body molded to the doorframe like a *frotteuse*.

Stephen's hackles rose. The dolls, consciously or not, had cut off every avenue of escape. If the Innocent came down from the attic, she could slaughter them at once.

"What does she mean, 'Wretched'?"

"I don't know."

The Knife took a step forward. "You share the blood of the Maker. As do we."

The Poem's predatory eyes were on little Adrian and Hannah. "They're so small. I've never seen someone so small."

Emily took both children in her arms. "Stephen, what is this? Are you in some kind of clown cult?" The Firstborn reached out and touched Emily's hair. She yelped and jumped away. Adrian and Hannah kept up their crying.

"Poem, go to the bedroom. Knife, go with her. I need to speak with my sister."

The Poem said, "Can I play with the little ones? I can show them the orange tree."

"Just go. We can talk later. Firstborn, I need you to leave, too."

The Firstborn took several steps backward into the room, then froze into a statue, head cocked. Knowing she would not leave, he sighed and brought the bags into the room. Emily followed him, comforting the children, and trying to keep her eyes on all three dolls. Stephen closed the door, blocking two of the dolls out.

"What about that one?"

"She won't leave. Trust me."

"What have you gotten yourself into? Who are these women? Wearing clown makeup and dressing like that?"

"It's not what you think."

"That's what anyone would say in this situation."

"It applies here. It's not what you think because it couldn't possibly be. It's not a cult. I'm not in any trouble."

"Who are they?"

"They're my dolls."

"Stephen, that's disgusting." The children had calmed down. Adrian's eyes, now red and watering, were glued to the Firstborn.

"Mom. Mom, your dancer. Mom, it's your dancer."

Emily shushed him, stopping mid-comfort as the words struck her. She looked at the Firstborn with new eyes, from the hanging ribbons and checkerboards to the doll at their center. Emily turned to Stephen. "She's familiar. Like... like..." Her gaze went above the bed, where the poster had been. "Her."

Stephen nodded.

"You recreated my poster and got her to dress up like that? How do you even remember it?"

"I'll explain everything, I promise. We need to talk, but not with the children around. Let them sleep and I'll tell you everything."

The Firstborn went to the bookcase her fingers playing over the spines of the books.

Emily said, "And her?"

"I don't think she wants to leave you."

"Does she talk?"

Stephen shook his head, leaving Emily and the Firstborn together. "I'll see you downstairs when you're ready."

Emily turned to the dancer, her posture making it clear that she was ready to defend her children if it came to that. The dancer moved, and Emily jumped. The Firstborn was moving toward the bookcase. With sure hands she selected a book and held *The Collected Works of Shakespeare* out to Emily. She accepted the book and it fell open. *As You Like It.* She had read that one so many times, the spine was permanently broken. Emily gasped once, looking at the Firstborn with new eyes.

The Firstborn's body folded into a seated pose worthy of a lady. The children had already accepted the odd dancer. The mobile held Adrian's attention and Hannah was dozing.

"When you're ready," Stephen said, leaving his sister with the doll.

* * *

It was not in the Sorrow to cry. She wanted to do something to let some of the feelings go, but there was nothing, so they welled up inside and turned to black poison. She hoped the Hide would leave her alone eventually. Every waking minute he was reaching, touching, slapping, hurting, penetrating. Every moment was agony. She wanted him to go away. She wanted to be with her sisters, with the Maker. Failing that, she wanted to be nothing at all.

It was worse that day.

The Hide raped her once when he got home. He rolled off her, interest vanishing for a single blessed second. "I have some friends coming over. Don't shower. I want them to smell me on you."

She made a move to wipe him off.

"No. That stays too. Let it dry and get dressed."

She put the costume on and waited for him to demand her. A half hour later, she was serving drinks to the Hide and his four friends, trying to ignore their vulgar words. She knew the Maker never did this to her sisters. She tried to place her mind elsewhere, in the big drafty house with the other dolls, but it kept returning to the box filled with human hair the Hide kept in the closet.

The Hide's friends were animals, sniffing around scraps and snarling at his enemies. They would purr and howl as he commanded. Though they had the same shape, the Sorrow couldn't see them as human. They had nothing in common with the Maker. They were lesser things. She knew the Hide had warped these creatures as he had warped the Maker, but while they degenerated, the Maker had evolved. Perhaps they had become something else—creations of the thing within the Hide.

Perhaps in some way they were the debased cousins of the dolls.

"Tabby, come here."

She looked up. The Hide reclined on the sofa, grinning. She wished she could melt into a puddle, back into the Maker's furnace and have him make her into someone worthy of keeping.

"Tabby. Come here."

She mumbled, "That isn't my name."

He turned to his pack, laughing. "See, I told you. She has something else she calls herself. What is it, Tabby? What's your name?"

Her flesh bubbled underneath smooth skin. "You mustn't ask that."

"Why not?"

She shrugged, watching the floor.

"Tell me your name, Tabby."

Every time he said the hated name, she wanted to scream. She had the breath for it, but no one would hear except the other dolls. "I can't."

"You miss Steve, don't you?"

She nodded.

"I'll tell you what. If you tell me your name, you can go back to him."

She saw it in her mind's eye. It was more than a name. It was what she was. It was the only thing she could ever be called.

She couldn't say it.

It didn't even stick in her throat. It never got that far. The words were unknown even as they were known. She would fumble over and around them without ever saying them.

"Come on, Tabby. Your name. *The* something. I remember that."

She shut her eyes. A woman could have wept in frustration. A woman could have shouted at him. She could do neither, standing helplessly in the center of the room with the Hide and his pack laughing at her, egging her on, taunting her. She knew she would hear it when the Hide brutalized her that night. They would echo through her sleepless mind when the Hide tossed and turned and she tried to smell the last traces of the Maker.

She came back to earth only when the Hide answered the door. The Hide's pack continued the scattered taunts, but without their leader, they were already losing the will. The Sorrow focused on the girl coming through the door. The Heart. She was hope, wasn't she? The Heart loved the Maker. The Heart could not turn her back on a doll. Heart and Hide were locked in conversation when the Heart turned and saw the Sorrow for the first time.

"Who's she?"

"Stephen introduced us."

"Why is she dressed like a doll?"

The Hide burst out laughing and walked back to his friends. "You want to stay and have a beer, Jess? Or are you done nagging me?"

The Heart was momentarily still. The Sorrow scurried to her. "Please. Tell the Maker what's happening here. Tell him—"

The Sorrow tried to make the Heart understand, but the human woman was entirely nonplussed.

"Tabitha!" The Hide was stern. "Come here. Now."

The Sorrow went back to the Hide, head bowed, hands out.

"Get on your knees."

The Heart curled her lip in disgust and left, taking the Sorrow's hope with her. She fell to her knees that always hurt and did as the Hide ordered.

* * *

Stephen heard Emily's bedroom door open. His sister murmured something, and then the door shut, bringing him out into the hall. Emily and the Firstborn waited, both looking right at him, the Firstborn clear, Emily pale blue. He transposed the harlequin markings from the doll to the woman. They were indistinguishable.

Emily said, "They're asleep. Let's talk."

The sun had been down for hours and the house had already cooled off. Stephen went past the parlor that belonged to the Knife now and forever, instead settling in the dining room with the long table. Unconsciously or not, they took the seats they had as children, regarding one another across the table, through the maze of tarnished silver candlesticks. Stephen faced the stain he never noticed. The Firstborn didn't enter the room. Instead, she stood just past the doorway into the kitchen.

Emily watched her hands.

Stephen said, "Ask me."

"Who are they?"

He told her at length, explaining the process of design, of the science very much like magic, of the need within him. He told her he was not finished.

She did not interrupt a single time, face locked in the Monaghan mask. She was listening, the gears whirring behind her eyes, shaking off the rust of a decade. She could see the edges of it at least.

Finished, he fell silent.

She took a breath. "Why?"

"Because I can. Because I have to. Pick one."

"No, Stephen. This is the Lord's power you're taking here."

"Who is the Lord, Emily?"

"God."

"No, I mean, who is He?"

"The all-powerful creator of Man."

The words were partly d'Aisecq's, internalized, understood. "Who's to say He's all-powerful? What if God was just something else, some other kind of mortal being, no more or less powerful than we are? Not quite human, maybe, but close, and He made humanity. Well, I've made something not quite human."

"You're saying you're God?"

"No. just that He hasn't done anything I haven't."

She stared at him in shock for a second and burst out laughing. "Dale would freak out if he heard you."

"I'll bet."

She looked back to her hands, stealing glances at the Firstborn from the corner of her eye. In the moonlight, Emily looked younger, the soft blue light washing the years from her.

He said, "Now, are you going to tell me why you're here?"

"Later. I promise."

* * *

"The little people. The Testament and the Apostate. They are ours." The Poem touched the door, listening to the soft breathing through her fingers.

It was in the dead of night. The Maker and his living family were fast asleep. The Knife waited outside the Maker's open door. The Firstborn stood across from the Knife, motionless, the Poem close by.

"Same blood," the Knife said.

"The Maker's?"

"The Wretched's. Hers is his."

The Poem touched the Firstborn's chest, to check for a beat both knew wasn't there. "And she is yours."

The Firstborn's head swiveled back to the door.

The Innocent saw it from her place in the attic. She had opened the trapdoor and sat in the shadows, watching from her foremost head, tail reared up behind her to regard only shadows. The Knife's words echoed in her heads, "Hers is his."

As the night evolved, the Poem and the Knife returned to the Maker. The Firstborn stayed by the door. She would not leave the Wretched.

The Innocent waited for the others to vanish before she heaved her bulk from the attic, scuttling down the ladder and into the hall. The Firstborn must have heard, but didn't turn. Gingerly, the Innocent approached on the tips of her fingers.

"Firstborn?" She spoke from the head on the end of her tail, the head intended for the Firstborn, positioning it at eye level to the other doll.

The Firstborn turned, meeting the empty sockets of her twin's face. She caressed the cheek with her graceful hand. The Innocent pressed into the contact.

"What did she mean 'yours'?"

The Firstborn paused. She closed her hands over her chest: love, death, or both.

The Innocent said, "Like the Maker?"

The Firstborn touched the door again, and then placed her fingers on the triangles below her eyes.

"I don't understand."

The Firstborn knelt to bring the Innocent's porcelain face to hers, kissing the Innocent lightly on the cracks spiderwebbing across her face, straightened and was still. The Innocent crept past to the master bedroom. She had to rear up to open the doorknob.

Inside, the dust was thick. The bed was made, the comforter stained gray. One end table was nearly bare, with only a picture of the Maker when he was as small as the little ones, and a girl that looked very much like him. On the other end table, a stack of books, a reading lamp, and a dry glass.

A window overlooked the backyard. The Innocent watched the orange tree sway in the breeze before settling back to the floor.

She shut the door. The others had their places and she had hers.

* * *

Emily woke up when Hannah stirred against her breast. Emily shifted, lifting her shirt and allowing the baby to latch on. While Hannah sleepily suckled, Emily stared upward, the huge mobile twisting above. She fought the thoughts welling up. What had her brother done? She knew when he was lying. This was not one of those times. So either he was crazy or he had created life.

Or both.

She winced as Hannah bit down and tried to think of anything else. It was difficult. The house felt different than it had—alive again, though it was a different life. Not new, exactly. Whatever blessing Stephen had given, it was something ancient.

She pulled her breast away from Hannah and sat up, pulling her shirt back down. Hiding nudity felt a little odd, especially with two of those strange women more naked than clothed. She briefly thought of asking Stephen to dress them. Dale talking. There was nothing to be seen that Adrian wouldn't see soon enough, or already had. God knew Dale hadn't been discreet.

She peered over the side of the bed to check on her son.

Adrian was already awake, dreamily looking up at the mobile, unconsciously mimicking his uncle. She wondered if she had gotten another Stephen. She liked the thought of that. "What are you thinking about?"

"Uncle Steve makes things, huh?"

"Yes."

"He's quiet. Sometimes I barely see him."

"What do you mean?"

The boy shrugged. "I don't know. I don't usually see him coming or going. He's just suddenly there and then he's gone. He doesn't make any noise when he walks."

Emily wasn't sure what to say. "Like a ninja?"

"Yeah." Adrian considered this. "How long are we staying here?"

"I'm not sure yet. What do you think of it?"

"It's okay. Those ladies were a little weird. I was scared at first. Not anymore."

"Good."

"Maybe if we stay here for a little time, when we go home, you and dad won't yell at each other so much."

"I hope so." She didn't feel the word.

"Can we have breakfast?"

"Yeah, of course. I picked some stuff up from the store yesterday." She got up and opened the door, jumping when the Firstborn came to life on the other side. Emily instinctively shielded Hannah, saying, "Please, don't do that."

The Firstborn fixed her with clear eyes. The entire creature was Other. After what Stephen told her, she knew the dancer wasn't human. And now it was obvious. There were the completely clear eyes that held everything and nothing. There was the way she never moved unless she intended it, and then a joint at a time. There was even her smell—clean and polished wood.

The Firstborn looked down to Adrian, now hiding behind Emily's leg. The Firstborn inclined her head and turned her attention to the infant. Blearily, Hannah focused on the doll. Emily tensed, ready to fight this thing.

Hannah yawned. The Firstborn touched Emily's brow and stepped aside.

"Mom, she's weird."

"I know, honey."

"Is she Uncle Steve's wife?"

Emily didn't know quite how to answer that. She decided on, "Yes."

"What about the other ones?"

"I don't know. Let's get breakfast."

She made the children their meal. Stephen had nothing in the fridge when she arrived, none of which surprised her. He was exceptionally good at not caring for himself, focusing instead on his projects to the detriment of anything else. In this case, the projects had taken over.

She glanced up and found the Firstborn lingering at the door to the dining room. It should have been creepy, but something in the dancer's attention felt right.

She fixed Hannah her formula and Adrian got bacon and eggs, one of only three meals the kid would eat. She bought hot dogs, baked beans, and macaroni and cheese for the other two. She got a little extra for Stephen to eat once she returned to Phoenix. If that was where they were going.

When they were finished, she took the kids into the front hall. The dancer shadowed them. Emily emerged into the sunlight, unsure what to do with the kids today. Dale would have the day mapped out to the minute. She wanted to let them go wild, but spite was no way to raise children. The park, maybe. The zoo, if they were up to it.

There was also the question of her brother. She didn't want to think about what he'd done. Blasphemy, certainly. The old Emily, the one who had looked after Stephen when their mother had died, she whispered that there was no such thing as blasphemy. An act of creation was a good thing. It was the new Emily, the one who Dale had made guilty and fearful that was fretting. The Emily she wanted to escape.

She sat down on the bench with Hannah. The baby wiggled and Emily gently set her down on her feet. Hannah held onto her mother's fingers, staggering forward, and then paused, taking in the garden.

It was beginning show signs of neglect. The hedges were shaggy past their squared-off edges. Spider webs patched the sides of the walk. Dandelions sprouted in the flowerbeds. Strange. Stephen used to love to take care of the garden. It appealed to his meticulous nature.

She glanced around again.

"Adrian?"

He had come outside with her, but wasn't in sight.

"Adrian?"

Those dolls were around. They wouldn't hurt him. Adrian was Stephen's flesh and blood. Old and new Emily were silent. Only mother Emily mattered.

She scooped Hannah up. The baby whined, sensing something. The garden was empty. Emily ran toward the side of the house.

A loud thump ahead made her move faster.

She rounded the corner and found the dancer standing between a gaping Adrian and the little redhead, who was on the ground, getting up. In confusion, she [the Poem?] said, "I only wanted to show him the orange tree."

The dancer did not move.

"Mom!" Emily ran to Adrian. "That was great! Your dancer bounced her right off the wall." To the dancer he said, "Do it again!"

The dancer was still. Emily looked from the impassive face of the familiar doll to the other, now in a lewd crouch. Blood dripped from beneath one blue eye. "I only wanted to show him the orange tree."

Something in that statement made Emily's blood go cold. "You don't show him anything."

She backed away, holding onto both children. As she did, the dancer once again stepped between Emily and the little doll. The little one's head swiveled to track them. "You can come back. It's safe."

Emily didn't speak until they were around the corner, turning to her dancer and saying, "Thank you."

The dancer—the Firstborn, the doll had a name—looked into Emily's eyes. After a moment, she placed the tiniest of kisses on Emily's cheek. It was acceptance, pure and perfect, expecting nothing, offering everything. After that moment, Emily knew for certain her children were as safe with the Firstborn as they would be anywhere.

* * *

The Sorrow waited in the bed until the Hide had gone. When he leered at her, told her he would be back, told her they would be doing something new that night, she lay completely still. She wanted to appear as a dead thing. But she had lain still for the last few rapes, and it had not stopped him. Something had to be done.

When the door slammed, she got up, finding the hated costume strewn around the bedroom where he had made her take it off for him. She put it on with difficulty, still unsure where everything went. The Hide got some kind of pleasure from watching her struggle with it. Anything to hate.

She wished she could know where the Maker was. It had to be a mistake. He couldn't have intended this, wouldn't do this to a faithful doll.

The Knife. She might understand. She might be there, at the house where they were born. The Sorrow pictured the Knife in her mind, impossibly beautiful, the Maker's runes blessing her face. The Knife might accept the Sorrow, intercede with the Maker on her behalf.

The Maker could be reasoned with. The Maker had kept the other dolls. He hadn't meant to send her home with the Hide, couldn't know the horrors of living with that monster. She would tell the Maker and he would see the depths of her love and have mercy and she could be with the Maker as was her right.

She went to the door.

What if he sent her back? What would the Hide do? He was endlessly inventive when it came to anguish and humiliation. Nothing pleased him more than to find the Sorrow's plastic body felt pain, loving it when she hurt in the same places as a normal woman, loving it even more when she found agony in a place that should have been dead.

What was worse? What the Hide had already done or what he might?

Stay and he would rape her again. Would torture her. Would do all the horrible things he desired, and would do them until the day he died.

She crossed the threshold and was outside.

* * *

Emily had been with Stephen for a week when Brian finally came over. She had gotten somewhat used to the dolls. The children even didn't seem to mind them and Adrian downright loved the Firstborn. Emily would not let them near the Knife or the Poem. The former was aloof, the latter fascinated. Both were dangerous. The Firstborn spent her nights outside of Emily's door, maybe standing guard, maybe waiting for Emily to wake up and join her.

They were in the front yard when Brian came through the gate. Adrian was running through the little hedge maze, while Emily sat close by with Hannah. The Firstborn stood in the shadow of the house as still as a statue. Stephen watched it all—his family, partly born, partly made.

Brian frowned when he rounded the corner, trying to figure out when Stephen had gotten a normal family. Upon recognizing Emily, confusion turned into a smug smile, one Stephen read easily. *You'll never have a real family.*

"Emily?"

She turned, shading her eyes from the sun. "Who is that?"

"It's me. It's Brian."

"Brian Baniszewski? I haven't seen you in forever."

"You look great. Always did."

Brian got closer, and Stephen saw the same fire in Brian's eyes that was there for the Sorrow. Stephen reminded himself why he had given the doll to Brian. What might happen if Brian didn't have a doll of his own. What might happen to Emily.

Brian went to embrace Emily and she accepted it, revulsion naked in her posture. The Firstborn took several quick steps toward them before Stephen put his hand out. The doll's head turned smoothly as though on a swivel.

Stephen murmured, "Don't. It's okay. I promise."

The Firstborn did not settle back as a human would. She merely froze, apparently off balance but perfectly at peace.

Brian let Emily go. "You had kids? God, they look exactly like you."

Emily introduced Brian to Adrian and Hannah, the boy was suddenly shy. Brian's attention went to the Firstborn, still standing exactly where Stephen had stopped her. "So you told your sister."

"He doesn't have secrets from me," Emily said.

"Really now?" Brian's tone was dangerous. Emily almost responded, but Brian cut her off. "Makes me wonder what he has on you. I actually came by to talk to your brother about his birthday present to me. Wanted to thank him. Wanted to ask him if I could get more of the same for Christmas, with a couple minor alterations."

Stephen nearly retched at the thought.

Brian turned to Stephen. "Up for it?"

Bile flooded into Stephen's mouth, tasting of clean chemical acid. "You know the deal."

Brian put a strong hand on Stephen's shoulder, gripping hard into the flesh. Stephen winced, holding out a palm to the Firstborn, stopping her before she tore Brian apart. It would be so easy, like a child plucking the legs off an insect. Stephen let Brian lead him to the shadows of the house.

"What the fuck, Steve?"

"My sister is visiting."

"Not that. Tabby. What are you trying to give me?"

"I don't know what you mean."

"I was fucking her last night, and it was great. But then I turn her over and... nothing."

"Your access to her vagina shouldn't change..."

Brian laughed. "Vagina? I was trying to fuck her up the ass. She's just smooth plastic back there. You made her without an asshole!"

Stephen's stomach turned over. The bile rose in the back of his throat again. An anus was for... the dolls would never need them. They were clean and perfect. "Of course."

"Won't do. I need anal every now and again. Keeps them from getting too comfortable, you know? So I was thinking I could bring Tabitha by and you could open her up." Brian gestured with a pantomime knife.

"She'd bleed."

"They all do."

"No. It would be a wound, not... what you want. She would heal."

"You could do it again. And again." Brian grinned.

"No. I won't."

He shrugged. "Fair enough. I can do it for now. The next one you make me had better have an asshole. Something tighter than a drum. Something to hurt."

Stephen wanted to vomit. Brian grinned again and walked away, waving to Emily as he left. "Don't want to interrupt family time. I'll bug him later. We can sketch it all out." Brian was gone as abruptly as he arrived.

"I didn't know you still knew him."

Stephen walked back out into the sun, wishing it would wash Brian away.

"Yeah."

"I never liked him."

"I can't be picky about my friends."

"You could be a little pickier."

He watched her, wondering if she knew Brian stalked her. Maybe she had caught him another time with a knife and hadn't told Stephen. "Why don't you like him?"

"He gives me the creeps. It's the way he looks at me, like… like I'm naked. And he stands too close, leaning in, like he's trying to intimidate me. Does the same thing to you. I always got the impression there was something else going on with him."

"Like what?"

She shrugged, the solution in front of her, too horrible to say. "I don't know. What did you get him for his birthday?"

Without meaning to, Stephen's eyes flickered to the Firstborn. Emily said, "You made him a doll?"

Stephen nodded. The words would not come.

"Why?"

"Because the alternative would have been so much worse."

She knew it—all she suspected and worse. She gave Stephen a grim nod and turned her attention to Adrian, chasing locusts through the overgrown maze. She picked up Hannah and went to her son. They spoke the language of mothers and children— amazement and the wonder of the same. Stephen watched them, their shadows playing over the front yard. Then down at himself, standing alone in the sun.

There was no shadow.

* * *

When the sun went down, the Sorrow was walking south, a vague idea that this was the right direction. She felt her sisters pulling at her, the Maker the bright star at the center of the constellation of dolls.

* * *

Stephen found himself with Emily that evening, sitting on the bench in front of the house, the baby monitor next to her playing the soft breaths of both children. The dolls were silent, Stephen straining to hear the sounds of Emily's bedroom door opening. What would he do? Flesh couldn't stand against the dolls.

"You realize if you go public with this, you'll be the most famous person who ever lived," Emily said.

"I don't care about that."

"I know. You did it for you. No one else."

He wished it were true.

"Are you ready to tell me why you came here?"

She let the question simmer before she said, "I know you saw me."

Stephen's mouth went dry. Did she mean her and Dawn? In some ways, that was the Firstborn's true birthday, who even now was likely at the window, looking down at the Maker and his sister, thinking whatever unknowable thoughts passed through her mind. There was no easy response to Emily. A denial would ring hollow. An affirmation would be worse.

"It was a couple nights before you left. The night Jim Dornan... fucked me."

He saw it. Nothing would change that.

She went on. "You probably wondered what was happening. Maybe you thought I was cheating on Dale."

"He was in the room."

She looked at the ground. "He was. He's always in the room."

"What's going on, Emily?"

"He likes to watch me with other men."

"Do you like it?"

"No. No, I don't."

"Then why?"

The response was rote. "Love, honor, and obey. They're not just words."

"Yes, they are."

"Not according to my beliefs."

"Beliefs you got from Dale, right? They're not ours."

"When you get married, you make certain compromises."

"Not that kind."

"What would you know? You don't even date! You had to

make your..." Emily stopped herself as she saw the look on his face. "Oh, God. Stephen, I'm sorry. I didn't mean it. It's just this is kind of raw territory."

He saw what she was thinking—she wanted to be with someone like Dawn. The names Dawn called her, what had happened, had hurt. Emily had tried to be normal, as she saw it, and couldn't be. Would never be.

"It's okay, Em. We're all in places we didn't see for ourselves and when we finally look around to see where we are, it's too deep to ever get out."

"Yeah. That's it. That's exactly it."

They waited in silence.

Finally she got up. "I think it's almost bedtime." She paused in the doorway. "You know, you're smart sometimes."

"Sometimes."

She went back inside. For a long moment, Stephen was alone. After a time, the Knife joined him on the bench. She took his hand in hers and sat with him.

* * *

The Wretched went up the stairs, fighting tears. Anyone with eyes could see it. She was tense, perhaps frightened of the dolls lurking in the dark places. She stopped dead in her tracks at the landing.

The Firstborn waited for her, arms out.

Without thinking, the Wretched went to the embrace. Somewhere, the other dolls felt a wash of incandescence over their skins. In the Maker's bedroom, the Poem arched her back against an imaginary lover. On the roof, the Innocent clattered and snapped. At the front of the house, the Knife shut her eyes and grasped the Maker's hand harder. On the street, the Sorrow collapsed to her bruised knees and nearly cried out in agony.

The Firstborn took the Wretched up in her arms and carried her back downstairs. The moonlight streamed in through the windows. Somewhere, both of them could hear distant music. The Firstborn carried the Wretched into the living room, before giving her feet back. The two were silent. Then, by some mutual desire, began a slow dance around the room.

The other dolls could not fight through the reaction, nor did they wish to. They let themselves join with it, tilting faces to the sky.

The Wretched's lips reached for the Firstborn's. Bodies born for one another joined. Wood and flesh molded into one, the Firstborn accepting the lead of the Wretched, doing whatever was required of her. The Wretched shuddered and cried, holding onto this doll.

The only creature who could love her.

* * *

It took the Knife some moments to realize, after she had opened her eyes, the Maker was dozing peacefully against her shoulder. She was unsure of what to do. This level of tenderness was foreign to her. The Firstborn or the Poem would have the perfect reaction. She merely stayed completely still, hoping the moment would not end.

But it did. A shape came around the corner, between the high walls. It staggered, trapped in some horrible juxtaposition of sensation. The Knife sat the Maker up straight. Eyes fluttering, he had to catch himself as the Knife got to her feet.

It was the Sorrow. A human woman might be crying or screaming. The Sorrow's face was a blank mask. The Knife went to her, stopping short. The Maker followed, rubbing his eyes in confusion.

"Maker. I'm home."

"What the hell… you're supposed to be with Brian."

"I'm supposed to be here. Maker, you don't know what the Hide did to me."

"I don't care what he did to you. That's what you're for, to do whatever he wants."

The Knife took the Sorrow in her arms. "I know. I know what must be done."

The Maker said, "You're going home."

"She's staying home, Maker."

"What?"

"This is her home and she is staying. Tell the Hide what you care to. The Sorrow is home." The Knife took the smaller doll in hand and led her back inside.

Stephen followed. Wet, close sounds bubbled from the living room. He peeked, finding Emily with the Firstborn. Emily lay back on the couch, clothes carelessly discarded; the Firstborn knelt between her thighs. Emily, eyes closed, sucking in shuddering breaths, as her fingers wove into the Firstborn's hair.

The Knife put her hand on Stephen's arm. "Leave the Joyous to the Firstborn."

"I thought my sister was the Wretched."

"Not any longer."

He left them to be together and went to his bedroom and the Poem.

* * *

Emily left the next day. She smiled and kissed Stephen goodbye, the joy spreading to both her children. She said she had to have a talk with Dale. She said she would be in touch. She finally was what she was always intended. She would deny herself no longer.

She would be free. Adrian and Hannah would stay with her, far away from Dale. Divorce. Beginning a new and happy life with her children. They would be what they wanted, as would she. Only once did she worry, when she realized she had left the book—*The Collected Works of Shakespeare*—at the house. Something made her open her bag to check. There it was, sitting on top, placed by the Firstborn's loving hands.

CHAPTER SIXTEEN

THE NIGHT WAS FULL AND THICK. The Maker slept alone, though he had not started the night that way. The other dolls had spread through the house: the Knife in her chair, the Firstborn in her room, the Poem in the garden, the Sorrow waiting outside the bedroom door. Only the Innocent, shifting and clicking and massive, lurked in the darkness by the Maker's bed. She watched him sleep, hypnotized by his breath.

The Innocent watched him nearly every night. It was the one time she could be close. Sometimes, she would reach out one of her legs and nearly stroke his face, withdrawing before she made contact, each time wondering if the next time would be the time they touched.

Outside the door, the Sorrow waited. She had stripped the costume off as soon as she returned home and had thus far refused to put anything on. She stayed on the periphery of the Maker's sight. Let him get used to her and maybe he would love her as he loved the others.

The Firstborn stood over the bed where the Joyous had slept. She never moved, never touched it. She merely stayed with it.

Down the stairs and into the parlor, the Knife sat primly in her chair. She could hear the scratching of the Innocent above, merely waiting for what she viewed as inevitable.

Under the night sky, the Poem played in the moonlight. To human eyes, she would appear as some kind of wood nymph, nude and happy. There was something in her movements hinting she was not playing, but hunting.

All of them moved inward as one, though there was no signal, toward the place of their birth. They went into the attic, waiting for the proper order: the Innocent, the Firstborn, the Knife, the Poem, and finally the Sorrow. They took their places—the Innocent in the center, surrounded by the Maker's three concubines and the Sorrow outside, a rogue moon.

The Poem sat next to the Innocent, stroking the segmented body with one hand. There was something masturbatory in it, as those graceful fingers caressed sections of the Poem's own smooth flesh.

The mood of the dolls was one of wonder, hypnotized by the Innocent, perhaps in love with her. Each reacted in her own way, parallels incurring in the way they interacted with the Maker. Words might have been exchanged, but they were silent ones. The dolls were utterly unlike humans—they did not move except when they wished it. Individual limbs had a life of their own, while the body attached was still.

After several hours, the Poem went to the Maker's bed. The Innocent scuttled into the master bedroom. The Firstborn glided to the mobile. The Knife retired downstairs to her chair.

The Sorrow stayed in the attic to look out over the arroyo.

* * *

The knock pulled him from sleep.

The Poem lay curled against him in bed. The rest of the bed was empty. The Knife and the Firstborn had been there. Gone now. He hoped they weren't outside. What time was it? The clock said midnight. What day was it?

He found shorts at the end of the bed. Probably not clean, but clean enough. He pulled a shirt from the dresser and went downstairs. The Knife stood in the archway leading into the parlor. The Firstborn watched from the back hall like a ghost. Both were barely out of view of whoever was at the door.

"You have a visitor," the Knife said.

"Who?"

"The Hide."

Stephen tried to think of who she meant, couldn't remember their codes for people, the horribly appropriate little names. He opened the door without fear.

Brian shoved him in the chest, sending Stephen backward as the unhealed rib stabbed into him. Brian ignored Stephen's pain and stalked into the house. "Tabby? Tabby, are you in here?"

The Firstborn was moving forward, not at the threat to the Sorrow, but to defend the Maker. The Knife was already there, interposing her porcelain body between Brian and the house—the lady of the castle defending her keep.

"Why are you here, Hide?"

"Like you don't fucking know, whore." As he looked into her face, there was a faint question, and one dismissed almost instantly. Rage would carry him.

"Indulge me."

"You have my Tabitha. She disappeared. I went looking for

her. She's nowhere. Which means she's here and you're fucking hiding her from me!"

"And if we hide her from you, what will you do?"

Brian grabbed the Knife by her throat and slammed her against the wall with the clang of a heavy chime. Unhurt, she reached up for him, but Stephen was there, pulling Brian away. The rib shifted again and Stephen had to let go and cradle the burning pain. The Firstborn stepped into the void, protecting her Maker. The Knife shoved Brian in the sternum. He fell back, spitting and cursing.

"The Sorrow isn't here," Stephen said, the rib cutting the words short.

"I want Tabitha back. You made her for me. She's mine."

"I know. If she comes back, I'll send her home."

"Promise me, Steve. Fucking promise me. She's mine."

"She's yours. I promise."

Brian glared at the dolls, rubbing his chest where the Knife had hit him. "You better be right, Steve. Or maybe Jess hears about all of this. Maybe she finds out you're the fucking pervert."

He stormed out without waiting for anything else.

"He wants me," the Sorrow said.

Stephen turned to see her, only a slip, standing at the landing, plainly frightened, though a lack of shivering marked her as inhuman. On the inside, the Sorrow was a block of plastic. There was so much more he could do. He knew what was next, hated that there was a next.

"Yes," Stephen said.

"But you didn't send me away."

"No."

"Why not?"

"I don't know."

He turned away, went into the parlor and collapsed on the couch. Soon after, the Knife joined him, placing his head in her lap. He held onto the cool porcelain, taking in her clean china scent, until the feel of her fingers drove him to sleep. The Sorrow stayed close by, huddled with her bruised knees.

* * *

The Innocent shifted uncomfortably. When the Hide entered the house, she had wanted to come downstairs and tear him apart. It would have been so easy. She had the Knife's rage boiling through her, and when combined with the Firstborn's devotion, it had curdled into hatred. Anything entering the house without the leave of Maker or doll should be destroyed.

Her mothers calmed her. They had the Hide well in hand. If he broke free, they would release her to see if the hatred could bleed away.

She wondered what was within the Hide. The way the Maker treated him was strange to her. The Hide held some kind of power over the Maker. This could not be. The Hide had no dolls, and thus no power to hold. Yet he threw words around that cowed the Maker. The Innocent couldn't understand. Perhaps if her mothers had let her see the Hide from the inside, she would know. Instead, she called silently to the Sorrow.

The Sorrow was reluctant; the Maker was close by. She could be closer to him in sleep than she could ever be when he was awake. The Innocent understood this. Still, the Sorrow never deserved closeness with the Maker. The Innocent called again.

She felt the Knife's hand on the Sorrow's head, scarcely heard the whispered blessing. The Sorrow was coming up the stairs.

She feared the upstairs. The Firstborn and the Poem had been born with a claim to it. The Innocent shared some of the distaste they had for the Sorrow. That ugly little accident wore her stigma in a black halo.

The Sorrow opened the door and fell to her knees before the Innocent, wincing when they hit the ground.

"I'm here now," the Sorrow said.

The Innocent scuttled forward and reared up, balancing on twelve of her limbs. The foremost six folded in a strange cat's cradle.

"Tell me of your echo."

The Sorrow's face was paralyzed. The Innocent felt the rage, shame, and terror billowing up and out. "The Hide is not my echo."

"Don't lie to me, Sorrow." The Innocent clicked her porcelain fingers against the floor.

"It's not as it was supposed to be. I belong to the Maker."

"Do you doubt the Maker?"

"Of course not, but he can be reasoned with. He can change his mind."

Hope. The Innocent found herself softening slightly to the little mistake. The huge arachnid doll scuttled closer, lifting her primary head to stare into the Sorrow's glass brown eyes. "Do you feel the Hide when you are apart?"

The Sorrow was almost silent. "I do."

"How do you see him?"

"As he is. Him and his pack."

"I don't understand."

"The Hide is more than one person. Those that stay with him become like him. He warps them to be what he needs. Those that don't bend, break."

"The Maker?"

The Sorrow nodded, the words catching in her throat. "In a different way. The Maker was the first blind attempt."

"What do we owe the Hide?"

The Sorrow turned away. She had no tears. "Nothing."

"What does he look like?"

The Sorrow struggled. In many ways, people looked the same to the dolls. It was what they were that was distinctive. "Like the pack. Purer."

"And them?"

"They're not animals. They're something worse."

The Innocent considered this. "You said you can feel how he feels. How?"

"I feel him all the time. Radiating through me. Always behind, above, around. Something grabbing me in the dark."

"How does he feel?"

The Sorrow spat it out as a sob. "Hungry."

"Thank you, Sorrow. Go away. Go back to the Knife." The Sorrow retreated from the room. The Innocent hated the way the echo stank her path.

* * *

Stephen was almost expecting the phone call when it arrived, while sitting Siege Perilous, banking more blood. He did it mechanically now, drifting into the chair and letting the Firstborn unite him and the chair into a single organism. Stephen should have felt tired and dizzy after the bloodletting, but he never did. The alarm sounded, and as she unplugged him, the phone rang.

Jessica's voice, approaching cheerful. It was past dark. Stephen was losing track of what direction the sun was closer to. The desire to see her was overwhelming. She could take him from this poison house, from the dolls who smelled clean. She could save him, at least for a short time, from the blade between Brian and the Sorrow.

She told him she would be there in an hour, and told him to wear something nice. He wanted it to be a new beginning. The house fought him, already staking him in place.

The Poem leaned back lewdly, smiling. "Is it time?"

"I'm going out."

"When you come back."

She sounded so sure, so smug. He wanted to rub her nose in rejection.

A clean shirt with buttons, and a pair of dress shoes. Those qualified as nice, right? He was waiting out in the night for Jessica when her car pulled up the driveway. Stepping into the dim light, beaming, she was almost the old Jessica.

"You look better," he said.

"I'm healed," she said.

"Nothing new?"

She shook her head, falling into him. He held her, stroking her chestnut hair, a nimbus of living scent around her. "I think I'm fixed."

Why had she come to say this? He was grateful for it, but a

part of him believed she would be better off away from house and dolls. She couldn't know yet, even though he could feel the dead eyes on them now, watching from the windows. Did they want her to come into the house and join them? Take her rightful position with the dolls? Or did they want her dead?

That thought watered the fear within. "Come on."

"What?"

"Let's go somewhere."

"Where?"

"Anywhere. We need to celebrate."

"Yeah. Okay. Sounds good."

As they drove away, he searched for the dolls in the windows, but they were silent and still.

* * *

The Sorrow was huddled in the corner of the hall. She could feel the other dolls moving around the house, feet in the tracks they'd worn. They belonged in that house. They had a home.

She would wait until this became her true home.

At some point, the Maker would give her clothes to wear, and it would be more than a costume. It would feel good and right because they would be what the Maker wanted for her. She could be beautiful like the others.

A porcelain hand brushed softly through her hair. The Sorrow looked up into the Knife's blue eyes. The Knife didn't need to say what she was thinking. The Sorrow considered it and nodded. The Knife offered her hand and the Sorrow took it. The Knife led her away, into the Maker's room. Deliberately, the Knife set her dolly down on the dresser. She would no longer need it.

The Poem was there, reclining on the bed. "She isn't allowed in here."

"The Maker never gave any such rule."

"I do," said the Poem happily. "If you want, we can vote on it and the Firstborn will see things my way."

The Knife ignored her little sister and went to the Maker's closet, handing the Sorrow clothes. Though they were men's clothes, the Sorrow felt something close to comfort during the costuming. The Knife stripped, letting the straps and snaps fall to the floor. She wrapped herself in the clothing she had once worn as a disguise, those of the Joyous. The Poem watched with interest.

The Knife knew she couldn't pass for normal. Human perhaps, as long as one didn't look too closely at her scalp, or touch her cool flesh, or realize it wasn't makeup on her face. She still felt horribly exposed, even with the scarf, veil, and gloves. Casting around, she picked up the sunglasses once belonging to the Heart. Though they were dark, she saw through them as easily as rainwater.

Perfect.

"You can't go," said the Poem.

"We have to," said the Knife.

"The Maker will be—"

"The Maker will understand. He made you weak but didn't make me the same way. This has to be done."

The Sorrow stayed close to the Knife, terrified of the supine Poem.

Finally, the Poem shrugged. "You're broken."

As the Sorrow and the Knife left the house into the clear night, they knew they were crossing a border. They could see their footprints along the path, even as the asphalt of the street carried nothing. The trees intertwined above them. The world wanted their task kept secret and was conspiring to make it so.

They walked north though the dark streets. They did not speak because they did not have to. The Knife knew what they would do, and the Sorrow was frightened if she spoke it the whole thing would break like a soap bubble.

When the thick foliage of South Pasadena broke behind them to the open skies of Pasadena, the Knife felt the eyes on her. Even at her birth, she knew she was not human. The Sorrow could pass. The Knife could not. Her face was a mask. Her eyes, though more human than the Firstborn's, were still strange and different. A touch of her skin would reveal cold bone. She was only soft in places.

The Sorrow huddled in the Maker's clothes. They still felt wrong, but there was something in the closeness she felt to him. For once, she would walk with the Maker's tacit blessing. She would not be his sole error.

The Knife fell into step behind the Sorrow. She knew where they needed to go, remembering where the Hide lived. That hated place.

They started to hit crowds farther down Colorado Avenue. The Knife kept her head down, hoping the veil would conceal her stark white skin. The Sorrow shied from every casual brush. These were human, and closer to the Hide than the Maker.

The Sorrow found the building easily, having none of the confusion a flesh and blood woman might, knowing immediately where to look as it had been sliced into her brain. She went to the door, and the Knife followed.

* * *

Stephen and Jessica drove. They had no destination. There was something manic about that night. The freedom of the infection, or whatever it was, being gone. There was something else. They felt closer to one another than they ever had. For fits and starts, Stephen could forget Jessica was a living human, and in those moments, he let himself love her.

She drove north, through Sierra Madre and up Angeles Crest. Neither one spoke. Stephen leaned back and watched the night slide by along the window. The lights fell away and they were driving through void and nothing. Outside, the summer night was warm and comforting. He hoped she would never stop, continuing into the black and vanish, together in darkness.

Jessica pulled off the road. In front of them, there was the city, glowing purple under the haze. She said nothing and neither did he. She merely leaned over, and when she did, he crushed her to his lips without hesitation.

* * *

The Sorrow faltered at the door to the apartment. On the door, the number three dripped, though not with blood.

The Knife advanced, knocked, knuckles giving an inhuman ringing.

A shape loomed behind the door. The peephole eclipsed. Then, a muted chuckle.

The door opened. The Hide leered behind it, dressed only in a t-shirt and tented underpants. "You brought her back to me."

The Knife said, "The Maker sent us. May we come in?"

"Whatever. Can't promise I won't fuck my Tabby. I'm pretty

happy to see her. You happy to see me, Tabby?"

The Sorrow shuddered, looking away and nodding. The Knife brushed past the Hide. The Sorrow followed.

The Hide said, "What do you want?"

The Knife turned gracefully, removing her veil. "I thought I might like to watch you together."

The Hide's grin grew. "You don't only have to watch. It could be the three of us." He grabbed the Sorrow. She squirmed briefly, dying in futility. "Don't really like that clown shit, but you'll look fine once I learn where you hate it."

The Knife wandered into the kitchen. "There's so much more we can do together."

She found the block of kitchen knives and one whispered into her hand.

* * *

Jessica found Stephen's cock, coaxing it into her hand, lips never leaving his. She whispered into the kiss, more felt than heard, "I want you. I need you. I love you. I've always loved you." He whispered the same things, wishing they would wipe so much away. He should have realized it years before, and wished for those years back with Jessica. He could have known her before the Work took him.

Impossible. She was not his ballerina and could never be.

"Are you okay?" She parted from him only for an instant, kissing him between breaths.

"Yes. Better than okay."

She laughed into his mouth. "I thought you didn't want to fuck up our friendship."

"I don't care about that anymore."

"You're not hard yet. I need you to fuck me right. Oh. There we are."

And he was. Her scent enveloped him. Alive. Human. Filthy and pristine. It flooded his limbs and he was the one on strings, tearing at her blouse, buttons popping. Silvery skin bloomed before him. Her bra clasped in the front. One deft motion and her breasts were free, so soft and warm. So unlike the dolls, yet as comforting and familiar.

She sighed his name, her other hand guiding him beneath her skirt, rubbing him against the thin layer of fabric. Beyond was her. All of her. Hot and wet and needing him.

* * *

The Knife came back into the living room. The Hide pushed the Sorrow away, saying, "Strip."

She glanced to the Knife, who nodded.

"Don't look at her. Look at me. Now fucking strip, bitch."

The Sorrow did, face blank. A real woman might wear her emotions on her face, but the Sorrow was not a real woman. The clothes came off and she kicked them aside.

The Hide grinned. "Now come here."

The Knife stepped between them.

He turned to her. "You first?"

"Yes."

"You look so familiar. Why is that?"

"I think you know."

The Knife reached out for him, holding the carving knife in one hand. The Hide saw it, eyes growing large. She dropped it, where it landed point first in the wooden floor. The Hide grinned nervously. The Knife's hands were on him, strong and cold. He leaned in for a kiss. She spun him around and locked him in place with toothed muscles.

"What the fuck?"

He struggled against the Knife, but porcelain was stronger than flesh.

"Pick up the blade, sister," the Knife said.

The Sorrow obeyed, holding it point down. She looked from her sister, the one who loved her, and her rapist, the creature she had been made for.

"Tabby, put the knife down."

"That isn't my name."

"Tabitha. Whatever the fuck! Put the knife down!"

The Sorrow finally smiled. "You put her down."

She plunged it into the Hide's belly.

* * *

Jessica grunted in frustration, pulling her panties aside, her body heat an inferno. Soft skin caressed soft skin. One push and he would be inside her. A real woman, born, raised, a product of the universe. A single miracle, different than all others. A shuffle of cards, a toss of dice. She was something not born of him and she was ready to give herself to him.

He pushed and he was in, and she was warm and wet and perfect. Clutching at him with her whole body. Too much. His senses imploded, body seizing, and unspooling inside of her. She screamed. Something hot hit his face.

He opened his eyes.

Blood.

The skin of her chest tore open in ragged letters sliced by an invisible skinning knife.

MURDER.

* * *

The Knife and the Sorrow took their time with Brian Baniszewski. The Sorrow wanted to see him cry and she did. She wanted to hear him beg and she did. She wanted to take him apart and she did.

When they were finally finished with him hours later, his blood formed a lake in the living room, crusting at the corners like pudding. They went to the shower, washed the gore from themselves and dressed in their unstained clothes. The Sorrow went to the Hide's trophies and selected the glass unicorn. The first, when the thing had been awakened. The unicorn was hers, now she had put the monster to sleep.

The two dolls went to the door. The Knife paused. She took the sunglasses from her face and dropped them into the blood.

And with that, they were gone.

* * *

Jessica sobbed in the driver's seat. Blood ran down her chest. Semen ran down her legs. Stephen hated himself for that. It cheapened her grief and terror. It made their love venal.

"Why? Why is this happening to me?"

"Because you know me."

She was past hearing. It was hours before they left and Jessica could not speak beyond wordless crying.

CHAPTER SEVENTEEN

THE KNIFE AND THE SORROW never spoke. There was no giddy laughter, no secret whispering. They merely held hands, the Hide's blood, though washed away, gently scabbing them into a single creature.

Even as they saw the top of the house peeking over the ivy-covered wall, they knew the Maker was not home. The Knife felt him in her belly, something between love and hatred and fear. The two dolls made their way up the path and opened the door.

The other dolls waited. The Innocent's terrible bulk blocked the bottom of the stairs, every mouth smiling. The Firstborn lingered at the threshold to the parlor. The Poem stood in the doorway to the living room. All three had their eyes fixed on the two dolls crossing the entryway. The Innocent clicked her fingers. The Firstborn held her arms in a still circle. The power between those two was palpable. They could easily tear the Knife and the Sorrow to pieces.

There was a moment as all five dolls faced each other in silence.

The Firstborn curtsied. The Poem kowtowed. The Innocent splayed her limbs out and ducked her arachnid body.

The Knife led the Sorrow up the stairs and took her into the bedroom. She stripped the disguises from their bodies. One doll followed the other into the bed. The Knife cradled the Sorrow against her porcelain breast. The Sorrow wrapped her limbs around the Knife. They could not sleep, staying in silence for the full night.

* * *

It was the power of the act that the Innocent admired. She couldn't break into the bond between the Sorrow and the Knife. They had drawn too close to one another. The Innocent opened the window of the master bedroom and slithered out, fingers digging into the wood of the house. She reached the ground, swinging her tail, taking in every part of her surroundings. The Poem was beneath the orange tree, feeding it.

The Innocent scuttled toward her smallest mother. The Poem turned, smiled and beckoned to her daughter with grimy pink hands.

The Innocent stopped at the edge of the dirt, and the Poem knelt over her, stroking porcelain and wood. "I wish you could come out in the daytime."

"The Knife says others would fear us."

"Maybe. It's sad to hide our beauty. Especially yours."

The Innocent wanted to agree. "Are you going to see the Seeker?"

The Poem looked out toward the Nite Lite and back up at the house. "I can't. The Maker will be home soon and I want my bath."

"Do you see the Seeker now?"

"Not now."

"There are times…"

"I don't see her. It's much more complete. I know her. The Maker made me because he wanted her first. Made me perfect where she wasn't. It's a gift. Without the Maker's desire, we would still be unliving wood and plastic."

"He didn't desire me."

The Poem gave her an indulgent smile. "We desire you. We need you. He does too, but doesn't always know."

"Do you love the Seeker the way you love the Maker?"

"Of course not," the Poem said.

"But you do love her."

The Poem caressed the Innocent's segmented back along the rippling shoulder blades. "You shouldn't worry about these things. The echoes hurt sometimes from the need. It's best not to have it." The Poem rose and took several steps to the house. "The Maker is returning soon. I have to wait for him inside."

The Innocent didn't respond in words, instead clicking her teeth. The Poem disappeared into the house. The Innocent knew the Maker would not look for her. He never did, even when she sang for him.

She scuttled away, over the wall into the neighbor's yard, the grass thick under her fingers. She saw it at eye level and again high above and again beneath her, every empty socket providing vision. The windows of the other house were black. She moved her tail closer, peering into the dark. The house within was a painted corpse—beautiful, clean, dead. It had none of the life of her home.

Her fingers bit into the side of the house, skittering up the side like an insect, pausing only to peer into the windows. She found humans, sleeping, breathing. She knew what it was, having seen the Maker do it. What happened inside sleep was a mystery.

There was no sense of knowing any of these humans, at least not how she understood it from the words of the Poem and the Sorrow.

The next house had a few windows lit. Her curiosity would not be denied, though she was more cautious with these, finding a man in his living room, reclined in a chair, watching a movie with flashes and explosions, half-asleep. Next to him was a dog, something she had never seen, but somehow knew. The man had a hand lightly on the creature's neck.

The Innocent looked from man to dog. The other dolls had made her beautiful. She was nothing like the humans.

Four of her eyes went to the dog. Maybe she was closer to him.

* * *

Stephen didn't speak to the dolls when he came home, shoving the Poem away when she reached for him. Instead of pouting as a human woman might, she lay back and froze, eyes open like a corpse, never stirring from that position as he tried to sleep.

The house was alive. The inhuman sounds of the dolls imprisoned him. Worst of all was the maddening scuttle of the monstrous thing that had been in the attic. She had moved to the master bedroom, empty since Charles Monaghan shot himself. God knew what she did in there. She was waiting for something.

Jessica didn't answer Stephen's call the next day. Or the day after. He didn't blame her. The Knife would keep hurting her. Perhaps it was as she claimed, innocent. Perhaps it was malicious. Fear of the answer kept the question unsaid. Staying away from Jessica, never again touching her out of love, maybe the words would stop.

It wasn't until the third day that Stephen heard something, up in the attic working on new designs when the knock came. He was no longer terrified at the thought of someone seeing the dolls. The lance of worry had dulled. Part of him hoped it was Jessica and he could invite her in, introduce her to the others and hope she would join them. Become the lady of the house and raise four daughters and one granddaughter with him.

Dressed in underwear, he didn't bother with a shirt.

He went down the ladder into the upstairs hall. The Knife was waiting at the top of the stairs, body still, arms out.

"Why aren't you downstairs?"

"Outsiders," she said.

"Maybe they don't have to be."

"These scare me. I don't know why."

"These?"

He went down the stairs faster this time, yanking the door open. Right into the faces of two cops. They were in suits, the first one already flashing a badge at Stephen and saying something he could not hear over the blood rushing in his ears. The dolls were all through the house. They could be seen at any moment. Taking a life was a crime. Was making one?

"What's this about?" Stephen asked them.

The one in front, with the beard that made him look like he

touched children said, "Can we come in?"

Stephen nodded mutely and stood aside, trying to think exactly where the dolls were. The Knife was at the top of the stairs. Where were the others? If one of them made a noise then… don't think it. He led the police into the parlor, the Knife's room, and sat in her chair. They settled down on the couch.

The clean-shaven one watched Stephen through lidded eyes. The elder looked almost sad. "Mr. Monaghan." He said it wrong, but the tone kept Stephen from correcting him. "You're friends with Brian Baniszewski." The cop pronounced that one right, scaring Stephen immediately.

He responded on automatic, and only afterwards did he hate the lie. "Yeah. He's my best friend."

"When was the last time you saw him?"

Brian screaming for his "Tabitha" to be returned to him. "Four days ago."

"Where?"

"Here. He stopped by."

"And why was that?"

To take his doll back. The one I made him. He demanded and threatened and wanted her back. "What's going on?"

The other one spoke up in a thin and even voice, "Brian Baniszewski was murdered three days ago."

"What?"

The elder nodded. "They found his body in his apartment."

The other one said, "In several different rooms."

"Oh, fuck." Stephen thought he should cry, but there was nothing in him.

"Yeah. So where were you Saturday night?"

"Was that when it happened?"

"We're pretty sure."

MURDER. Stephen saw it ripping into Jessica's skin. As good as a signature. The police would never believe that scenario, and Stephen would never sell them the Knife. He forced himself to concentrate on the question and answer honestly, "I was with Brian's sister. Jessica."

The two cops exchanged a look. "Doing what?"

Stephen colored. "We were... you know."

"Having sex?"

He nodded, hoping the dolls weren't listening and knowing they were.

"From when to when?"

"From around eight to... I don't know. Three or four in the morning."

"You were having sex for six hours? Impressive."

"We weren't... the whole time. There was talking."

"Where were you together?"

"In her car. Front seat."

"You're sure she was with you the whole time?"

Stephen nodded. "Yeah. Of course."

"She didn't leave at any point? Make a phone call? Take a piss?"

The admission of her humanity made Stephen's stomach turn. "No."

"Did Brian have any enemies?"

"I'm sure he did."

"Now why would you say something like that?"

There was no need to protect Brian, except as his secrets

were intertwined with Stephen's. Any number of women could have killed Brian. It was a wonder it hadn't happened already. Stephen took a deep breath and told the story of the girl at the party. The cops exchanged another look. They knew something, and Stephen had just confirmed it. Whatever it was.

"You're saying this girl killed your friend?"

"I don't know. I'm only saying what I saw, and if I saw something, there was probably more I didn't see."

"What about the sister? How long have you been seeing her?"

"We've known each other forever."

"Not what I asked you."

"It's complicated."

"Simplify it."

The elder said, "If you had to pick a number, what would it be?"

"A month, maybe. Off and on."

"And what did your friend think of you fucking his sister?" said the younger cop.

"He told me to lay off."

"And you didn't."

"No."

The cops looked at each other and stood up. "We'll be in touch, Mr. Monaghan." They left Stephen wordless and terrified, cradling his head, trying to figure out what to do next.

"I did what had to be done," the Knife said.

Stephen looked up. The Knife stood in the archway to the foyer, the Sorrow in front of her, porcelain hands clasped around a soft plastic belly. The Firstborn and the Poem stood at the entry to the dining room. Two cliques. They had him surrounded.

"You murdered Brian?" he said.

"No. I helped the Sorrow do it."

The Sorrow looked up at Stephen, desperate for his approval. Shouldn't he be angry? Brian had needed to be put down and the dolls had done it. Jessica wouldn't understand. She couldn't. She would need him to be with her. To sit silently while she cried over a brother unworthy of her tears. Stephen walked to the Knife. The Sorrow reached out for him. He ignored her, kissing the black triangle on the Knife's porcelain cheek and moving past.

He drove to Jessica's as fast as he dared. The paranoid part of his psyche wondered if the cops would follow, but that was secondary to the tangible need of her presence. The Knife speaking through Jessica's flesh. The murder of Brian. Stephen was driving her crazy without meaning to, destroying the one woman he could love. There had to be a way to get away from it. Some part of him that could turn its back on Jessica. Find it and let it take control.

He was too weak to do it. He needed her.

He ran to her apartment, banging on the door. "Jessica. It's me. It's Stephen. Please, answer the door."

The sound of the locks first, followed by the door swinging open. Jessica was on the other side, wrapped in a sweater, hugging herself, eyes red from crying. She looked like she hadn't slept since the night they were together. They stood in silence. What hung between them was too horrible to speak.

He had to break it. "I heard. I'm sorry."

"You heard? What did you hear, Stephen?"

"Brian was... Brian... the murder. Can I come in?"

Jessica looked beyond him into the light. She turned her back and went to the dark. He followed her. No lights were on in the apartment. It was a mess, used tissues everywhere. "What else did you hear?"

The cop had insinuated the crime had been especially brutal and Stephen knew the culprit. Had made her. Had spent nights huddled in her porcelain arms. None of those things could be what Jessica wanted to know. "I don't know, Jess. I'm here for you. I wanted you to know I'm here."

He approached her for a hug. She slapped him. "Don't you fucking touch me!"

He recoiled, stunned. "What?"

"What did you know?"

"Jessica, I don't know what you're talking about."

"They found things in Brian's apartment."

Stephen's stomach turned inside out.

She continued, "A box with little locks of hair, tied with ribbons made out of cut up panties. The hair tested positive for semen. It wasn't Brian's. They haven't figured out whose yet. Is any of it yours?"

"What? No! Of course not!"

She relaxed the tiniest bit, whispering, "What were they, Stephen?"

"I don't know." She caught the lie, her eyes glittering in the dark.

"You know something. What do you know?"

"Brian... Brian had something inside him. Something terrible. Something I helped wake up." He stopped, not knowing if Jessica should know this. He had to tell someone. It had festered under his skin for too long. Maybe she could absolve him and with the secrets falling away, they could finally be together.

He explained about Emily and Dawn Molinaro, and how that led to Risa Douglass, and the night Brian had come for Emily, and how Stephen had used the blade on himself to scare Brian off. Stephen only omitted the dolls. They were too big for this, and she would know he was as much a monster as her brother.

When he finished, she was silent. Finally, nearly under her breath, she murmured, "You knew?"

"I thought if I could feed that thing maybe he wouldn't hurt anyone."

"It's pretty clear he hurt a lot of women. My brother was a... and you knew!"

"I didn't, Jessica. I didn't know. Whatever he was, I couldn't be sure. I tried to help!"

"You could have turned him in. You could have told someone. You could have made him stop!"

"You don't understand!"

"You had something to do with it, didn't you? I don't know how but those words, Brian... you had something to do with it."

"Jess, no, it's not what you think."

"I'm sure it's so much worse. Get out. Never come back."

He waited, seeing if she would take it back. She glared at him, the tears running freely from her eyes. "Jessica."

She said nothing else. Stephen didn't know the words that would let him stay with her. Even if they were once within him, the dolls probably owned them now, the way they had taken his name, his handwriting, his shadow. Jessica stood, defiant, in the dark, wounds outside and in.

He wanted to burn her out of his soul, stop feeling the emptiness Jessica had left, a yawning void choking him. The only way would be to feed it. He returned home, ignoring the dolls. His bank account was nearly dry and without Brian what little was left would go even quicker. Money was the answer. More than cards would bring.

The Firstborn plugged Stephen into the Siege Perilous, plastic vascular system turning red. Muscles locking into place, he wanted to squeeze the blood from his body, bank it all now, more than a hundred dolls would need. Enough to create a thousand daughters until he was a dried husk brooding in a rotting throne.

He ignored the alarm, cannibalized it from a digital alarm clock. It kept buzzing over and over, turning into a rasping heartbeat, calling him to wake up. Wake up. He replaced the bag, putting the full warm one on his lap, sloshing around it, his blood in a plastic body.

"Maker?"

It was the Knife, so close, yet out of sight. He couldn't stand to see her. She was too similar.

"What is it?"

"Maker, the alarm. You can't take too much at a time."

"Let me bleed."

"Maker. Please. This is two bags."

He felt himself growing drowsy. That appealed. A red sleep to swallow him.

"More for you. You need it."

"We have plenty." The Knife knelt by him. "Maker, no."

He looked down at her. She wore concern on her harlequin face strangely. One gloved hand was at the needle in his vein. Her hourglass eyes begged him to allow her to remove it.

"Why not?"

She kissed a wrist alive with spiders. "You mustn't ask that." The smile was even odder on her face. She seemed to know she should be smiling, but didn't know how or what it truly meant. He brought her face to his, wanting her to serve as Jessica's proxy. She wouldn't. The truth was the Knife had accepted him when Jessica couldn't. She knew every dark place within him and would never leave.

"Take it out."

She nodded and removed the needle, covering the tiny puncture with gauze.

"Knife?"

She paused.

"I... thank you."

She watched him for a moment and moved away. Outside, the arroyo baked in the late afternoon sun. He rose on heavy limbs, the room swimming, finding the phone waiting on the table amongst plans that barely made sense.

He called Milena Franco.

"Hello?"

"It's Stephen Monaghan."

It took her a second to find it. "I haven't seen you at any games lately."

"I've been busy. I need money."

"I have a game tonight. I could use a partner."

"Partner?"

"You know, bid up pots if the other person is going for them, don't bluff each other, that kind of thing."

"Sounds good, but I need more money than a regular game will bring."

"You're talking about a loan."

"I am."

"Pick me up tonight. I'll give you the info and the intro. The rest is up to you."

* * *

As soon as the Maker left, the Firstborn, the Knife, and the Poem went into the attic. They sifted through the limbs of the unborn. There was still much leftover from the making of the Innocent, enough to do what they hoped.

Each one knew exactly what the others were thinking as soon as the thought sprang into being. They created the pile in the hall, taking every last limb, every head, every pelvis and breast and put them in a heap.

The Poem opened the door. The dust was still thick, the Innocent's fingerprints imprinted everywhere. She was not human, and the Maker had not given them whorls. The prints were flat ovals dotted in slithering rows through the thick gray. They looked like the tracks of a swarm of giant sand crabs.

The dolls added footprints.

The closet opened. The Innocent skittered out in her glory. Two of her mothers smiled, one indulgently, the other with naked pleasure. The last's expression didn't change. The Innocent paused, dipped her bulk in something close to a curtsy, and returned into the closet.

The other dolls took the parts inside. They began to decorate the walls, attaching those severed limbs throughout. Soon, walls and ceiling were covered in pink and white flesh, a bloodless abattoir. This was their gift to the Innocent, a place for those parts of her that were not alive. When they were finished, the Poem kissed the Innocent on her mouths and the three mothers left the room.

They had created a home. The Innocent settled in, comfortable for the first time.

* * *

The Sorrow did not dream. She did not imagine, either. It was something between the two the other dolls would recognize. Yet there was something different in the way she did, because her echo had been silenced.

She still had a bond to the outside. They all did. Hers went deeper, the way the blood dripped through the floor, blood she had helped spill. It had been cleaned away, though some had seeped into the floorboards. The Hide was still in that apartment, infecting it with his hate, allowing her to push her plastic mind through the lens of gore and see things as they were.

She saw the yellow spider webs once binding the door shut, but they had already been flayed. She saw the lake of blood where the mushrooms grew through the wood, clear and proud. She saw the den where the Hide's spirit waited bound in rage and shame. She saw the trophies, still weeping silently.

There were four of them. Misshapen creatures, hunched and evil, acquisitive claws and chattering teeth. They were red from claw to elbow and from cock to belly. They fanned out through the Hide's apartment, sniffing and whining.

She had seen them before. They were the Hide's pack. Seen through the blood, they took their true form.

The Beta saw the mushrooms on the floor and snarled. The

Alpha flickered into the den to root through the Hide's things and emerged in quick moments, claws empty. The others saw this lack and howled. Something was missing.

The box of scalps harvested by the dogs of hate.

The Sorrow knew—though she could not understand their snarled words—the pack would be coming for the Maker.

* * *

After the game, as the other players filed out, Milena and Stephen stood on the sidewalk outside. She lit up her cigarette, ignoring the hateful glares from the men she had effortlessly fleeced.

"Do you have the information?"

Milena took a drag. "I do. Can I ask you something first?"

He couldn't look at her. "Sure."

"What do you need the money for? I asked Tyler about you. He said you live in some big house in South Pas."

"I do."

"So you don't need rent money. What do you need the cash for? And don't give me that shit about your patents being slow."

Telling her should have been anathema. "Do you really want to know?"

"The way you say that, it's like it's something bad. Really bad."

"It's nothing you can imagine."

"I can imagine a lot." She regarded him. "You don't have to do this if you want to get me in the sack. Cut me in on the loan money and I'm all yours for a night."

He felt himself stirring. Jessica's face, crying, cursing, hating.

Desire curdled within him, made him want to hurt Milena in some way for summoning Jessica. "Maybe I will."

"So you'll tell me what the money is for?"

"You wouldn't believe me if I told you."

"Now I have to see it." She handed him a slip of paper. "You remember the guy from the game a couple months ago? The guy who Tyler owed?"

Stephen would never forget him. "Of course."

"Him. Tell him I sent you and you'll be fine. Be careful, Stephen. Karo has ways of collecting debt. You have to be willing to pay, one way or the other."

"I am."

"I don't think you are. Call me when you have the money." She stubbed her cigarette out. "I'm looking forward to it."

* * *

The Maker left the following evening with the Firstborn in tow after making her wear something over her real clothing. The Poem had no idea where they went. Their absence meant the house belonged to the dolls for an evening. It meant the Poem could finally do what she had wanted to do for some time. This was the proper night for it.

She stripped out of what little clothes she had, laying them on the bed. She liked to imagine she could come back there, between a gateway formed of gloves and stockings. That is what she was, after all, what they all were, but the Maker did not understand it except on the most basic terms.

The Poem left the bedroom. The Sorrow remained curled in a ball by the doorway. The Poem thought of many horrible things to say and let them wash over the other doll in a palpable wave. The Sorrow had killed the Hide, an action that had been honored. It was time to remember what the Sorrow really was and leave it there.

The Poem moved past the master bedroom, inside which the Innocent hid her beauty. The Poem barely made a noise on the stairs as she went to the front door. As she opened it, the Knife said, "You think the Seeker is waiting for you?"

"You helped the Sorrow. Don't stop me."

"I won't. We are as we were made."

The Poem slipped through the door and out into the night, creeping through the shadows and brush toward the Nite Lite. She felt it pulsing inside her chest. The humans had something in there to do it. She was not sure what and the thought of it made her body soften and flow.

There was much more to be seen.

The parking lot was dark. The Seeker was within the Nite Lite, red hair radiant. For a moment, the Poem was enraptured. She fought free of it, finding the Seeker's car and ran a plastic hand across it, grounding it in her reality.

It took her a moment to unlock the door. She slunk into the backseat and hid beneath a pile of clothes. And waited.

There was something intimate in having the Seeker's clothing covering the Poem. There was the human scent, stronger than the Maker's, yet also different. It covered every inch of her, and the slightest shift let it fall around her body, finding new places to touch. The Poem's mind swirled in delirious loops. She couldn't wait for the fun to begin.

It seemed like days before the driver's door opened and the

engine turned over. The Seeker hummed under her breath as she drove. The sound worked its way along the Poem's false spine, spreading along nerve endings she didn't have until it filled her and turned her inside out.

Time stretched out in sticky strands. Finally, the car died and the Seeker left it. The Poem felt like she was melting but forced herself to wait. Only when the Seeker's mind drifted into sleep did the Poem leave the car, making her way to the front door, and for a moment, pausing in wonder at the moths circling the porch light. She waited until one landed on her forehead, fanning out its wings for a moment, before continuing its insane orbit. She ignored the smear of flight dust and opened the door.

The apartment felt right. It was dark. The Poem already knew what was there, even as she saw things for the first time. She moved through the sitting room with the TV and the ratty couch holding no significance, instead, turning to the wall of discarded toys. That had power. She wanted to touch each one, feel the same jolt the Seeker had when first plucking the toy from the garbage.

The Poem stood in front of the toys for a long time, letting the desire grow in her belly until it was the same fire that had once turned her to liquid and cast her to mold. She turned down the side hall and padded into the Seeker's bedroom.

The Seeker's chest rose and fell, so much more than the Maker's did. A dream coursed through her body. For a moment, the Poem considered taking the Seeker's dream, instead remaining still, watching the Seeker sleep, wanting to climb into bed and experience every little bit of her. The Poem could consume her echo if she wished. To close the circle.

She watched for several hours.

Finally, the Poem turned away to the Seeker's closet. She put on some clothes, reveling in her closeness, even if they were far too large. Dressed as a human, the Poem left the Seeker to her sleep.

* * *

The Innocent exited her room as the Poem was leaving the house. As the Poem had done, the Innocent ignored the Sorrow, huddled in the fetal position outside the Maker's bedroom. She climbed down the stairs, her teeth clicking in excitement. Of her mothers, it was the Knife that hewed closest to the Maker, even as she was the one who stayed the farthest away.

The Knife sat in her chair by the window, her neck swiveling smoothly to greet the visitor with a smile.

The Innocent skittered in front of her mother, all tapping fingers and rattling thoraxes. "Knife?"

"Yes?" The Knife's genuine pleasure undercut her haughty posture.

"The Heart."

The Knife's face returned to the impassive porcelain mask of before.

The Innocent shifted. "Tell me about the Heart."

"I can't."

"Your echo. She is out there. You can feel her. I know you can."

The Knife's voice was choked. "Yes."

"You wish she were here."

"No!" The Knife's voice held both anger and terror. The

Innocent understood neither. The Knife gathered herself. "She wouldn't understand us. She would… hate us. Me."

"Why? You're proof the Maker loves her."

"I'm proof of much more than that."

The teeth along the Innocent's tail clicked together.

The Knife said, "We are not natural. We are creatures. Even something as beautiful as you."

"I still don't understand."

"The echoes are links. Through them, you see what you truly are. The Firstborn was lucky. Her echo loves her and is the same blood as the Maker. You're the luckiest of all. You have only your mothers and the Maker to please, and you please us. You could not be more perfect if we tried. Don't waste time with the echoes. Instead be glad. You're the doll of dolls. Perfect. Untouched. Innocent."

The Knife and the Innocent were still and silent for almost an hour. They stared at nothing. Whether their thoughts raced alone or intertwined was impossible to say. They dreamt of the same things. Finally, the Innocent turned and pushed into the dining room, the kitchen, and outside.

The night pleased her. Birth was in the air. The Maker had conceived another daughter. The Innocent looked forward to seeing what magic would spring from him. She would not be mother, rather something closer to what the Sorrow was. She had no word for it.

She scuttled from the yard, using the ivy to help her over the concrete wall. Creatures sliced through the underbrush in a mad dash to get away. She left her odd tracks through wet grass as she crossed the neighbor's lawn, slithering over wall after wall, hugging shadows large enough for her maggot-white body. She had a destination in mind, something from hazy memory. In it, she was small, as was the Hide. The Hide had pulled a knife from his backpack. The Hide was earning his name.

She was on the roof of a one-story house, crawling over the crest. In front of her was a wide street. Beyond were hills, and beyond those, the memory. Behind her, the houses disappeared back to the Maker, the sky below and ground above. The view shifted as she reared her tail up to form a periscope, scanning the street with empty wooden sockets.

Cars swept back and forth only rarely. She scuttled down off the roof, landing lightly in the front yard. Bushes gave her a place to hide her bulk. If the light came on inside the house, she would be revealed. The Knife's terror flooded over her. She waited for a few cars, top head peeking out over the low fence. Finally, she allowed herself to move.

Spurred by the Knife's fear, she raced across the open ground. The thought that she could be haloed tried to paralyze her. A car crested the hill. She was already into the yards on the other side.

She skittered over a fence. A dog charged, barking, but as soon as it saw what it attacked, it dropped to the grass, whining and licking its lips. She paused. "Serve well." It seemed good advice. She crawled past the dog, glimpsing it again, this time upside-down, as her tail snaked past. She continued her journey through backyards, over fences and through bushes.

She could feel the Maker's touch on the fence. It was old, though somehow lingered. She slithered over the fence into the bushes where the Maker had once waited breathless. He had not come for himself. This visit was for the Hide. This was where the Sorrow was conceived.

The Innocent could never speak to the Hide. The Sorrow had completed her circle and the feeling had been ecstatic. This was as close as the Innocent would ever be to that blood, soaking the grass beneath her fingers. She could not see it with her ventral sockets, but lowering her bulk to the slick ground, she could taste it.

She stayed there for an hour, four eyeless sockets peering into the darkness of the house, two watching the blood thick grass. The Maker had never gone inside, instead releasing the Hide within. The Innocent moved off, something else driving her further than she had ever gone.

The Maker had not been there. Someone else had. Someone close to the Maker, close to the echoes, but had been neither. The Innocent slithered from a front yard and paused.

People.

She was still. As with all the dolls, when she didn't wish to move, she didn't move at all. In the moments of stillness, they were at their most inhuman. The Innocent would never be mistaken for anything other than what she was.

A man and a woman. The Blind and the Dream holding hands, a tiny dog sniffing along the path. The Innocent wondered if the dog would see her and cower. Would the Dream see her? What would happen then?

She knew what she would do. She had eleven mouths filled with teeth.

Their steps got louder. From her place huddled behind some bushes, she could look right up at them. The question would be if they looked down to the white streak through the grass.

She found herself hoping they would look down. It was a test. Two humans, perhaps the dog. Torn apart fast enough none would catch her? What would the Maker do? Would he even have to know?

A wave undulated along her tail.

The Blind and the Dream, murmuring and laughing softly, got closer.

The Innocent wondered how much they would struggle. Who to take first? The Dream would scream louder. The Blind was stronger.

They passed within inches of her. She waited. They did not turn around.

She didn't sigh in frustration, didn't curse, yell or pursue. She merely scuttled from her hiding place and moved on.

The Monk was close now. He had frequented the house before her birth and had not been welcome. He was not an echo.

He was free.

She found his house, a one-story in the hills, lacking any sense of history. The walls were stucco, the lawn clean and boring. The windows were dark. She crept around to the alley along the side of the house, inching past trash cans, knocking into a rake. It tipped over, but she caught it with a forward pair of wooden hands and righted it carefully as she scuttled past. A few steps ahead, she found a lighted window low enough to be peeked into with the head on the end of her tail.

Inside, she found a cluttered room. Old robot toys, still in the packaging, lined a high shelf running all around the room. The bed was unmade. Paper littered the floor. The Monk sat in the middle, stripped to the waist and dealing cards to imaginary opponents, face up. His back bulged in odd places, showing a map of knotted scar tissue under the skin.

He played cards alone for two hours before turning out the lights and getting into bed. She watched him sleep until the sky began to lighten, and rushed home as fast as she could.

She had hoped to feel something close to what the other dolls did in the presence of their echo, but there was only gray waste.

She would have to get closer.

* * *

Stephen inhaled deeply, picking the scents apart, separating the known from the unknown. First, the known, what clogged his nostrils every day—sweat, semen, metal. Then, the unknown—something spicy, almost sweat, something infinitely more mysterious pulling at his hackles.

The girls writhed throughout the club, rubbing themselves on the men. Disgusting. He could only think of horrible things—piss, shit, disease. The things spurring a retreat to the smooth skin of his dolls. They carried nothing approaching filth.

He felt the hand on his. The Firstborn, wearing a belted trench coat over her leotard, followed in his footsteps. Large sunglasses hid the harlequin marks and clear eyes, but couldn't mask her too white face or too red lips. When he told Milena he would be prepared, it was because the wooden dancer would be with him.

Stephen tried to clear the scent. Impossible. Onstage a sleek woman mimed fucking a metal pole. The smell tugged at dormant memories, making them stir, move, awaken. "I'm fine," he stuttered to the Firstborn's unvoiced question.

The Firstborn's fingers brushed his again.

"I won't." Stephen's eyes were pulled back to the stage. Another woman had joined the first. Now they were miming sex with each other. It looked clumsy. False.

Stephen tore his attention back and scanned the club, finding the table in the corner only with difficulty. Karo Minasian, sitting with two bodyguards and two girls.

Stephen approached, the Firstborn one step behind. After three feet, the goons saw him. After five, they were moving to intercept. Karo was barely concerned.

The first goon held a hand up. "This is a private table. Find someplace else to sit."

"Mr. Minasian is expecting me. Milena Franco told him I would be coming."

The first goon returned to Karo. The other kept his eyes on Stephen and the Firstborn. Finally, Karo nodded and the thug returned like a yo-yo. "Arms out." Frisking Stephen found nothing.

The bodyguard went to the Firstborn and touched her. She grabbed his right hand and left shoulder. There was a sickening pop. The second goon shouted, pulling a gun from his jacket. Stephen lunged at the Firstborn, grabbing her arm. The first thug gasped helplessly.

"Please. Let him go. Please!"

The second man effortlessly ripped Stephen from the Firstborn's victim. Only then did the Firstborn drop the man, who fell, clutching at his shoulder. The Firstborn's fingers were red to the second knuckle. The second bodyguard held Stephen and turned in time to find the Firstborn's arms on him. A human might have gone for the gun.

She took the arm holding Stephen, dug her fingers into the soft flesh and calmly snapped the man's arm at the elbow.

He dropped the gun to cradle the break. The Firstborn backhanded him to the ground and unconsciousness. The nauseating surroundings almost made Stephen give the Firstborn an order. One word and she would tear the thugs apart.

He couldn't make her do it. She was worth so much more.

He turned to the man still sitting. Karo Minasian tried not to look terrified and failed.

Stephen sat down across from Karo. The Firstborn stayed standing, watching the door. Karo looked over Stephen's head, shaking his head no. Calling the bouncer off. Probably wise.

"What do you want?" Karo's voice quavered.

"A loan."

Karo blinked. "What?"

"I need a loan. Milena Franco should have told you I was coming."

"And you thought it would be a good idea to rough up my boys?"

"I'm sorry about that. I should have warned her. She doesn't like to be touched by strangers."

"Crazy bitch."

"I'm not really in a position to judge."

Karo looked at his men. The first goon was beginning to recover, still clutching the shoulder with the puckered holes torn by the Firstborn. The blood bubbling between his fingers looked black in the strange light of the club.

Karo said, "You're Steve Monaghan."

"You know me."

"Milena told me about you. How much do you need?"

"Fifty thousand."

Karo raised an eyebrow. "A lot of money, bro."

"I know. Milena said you were good for it."

"I have it. The question is can you repay?"

No. "Yes."

"Because Milena has other ways she can repay. You don't." He looked over at the Firstborn. "Or maybe you do. I'd need a closer look."

Stephen considered releasing the Firstborn. Karo's money could easily be Stephen's. Courtesy made him ask rather than demand. "You'll get your money."

"Then you'll get yours. Come back here tomorrow night and leave the bitch at home."

The Firstborn was staring at Karo, making him shudder. He blinked, turning his attention instead to the table in front of him. Stephen got up and headed for the exit, the Firstborn following.

Karo called after him, "Does she talk?"

"Never."

* * *

Stephen returned the next night and collected the money. Karo was frightened, even though Stephen had come alone. Though he didn't relish the fear, it was better than any of the alternatives. Everyone needed to stay away from the house and the dolls. They needed to leave Stephen to the Work.

He bought everything to make the next doll the same night. His three concubines surrounded him as he laid the material across the attic floor, the Sorrow crouching in the corner. All of them seemed pleased.

He could barely focus, having forgotten the little things that went with the rites. The color of the candles. The proper time of day. The size of the symbols. Only the Work remained. The dolls didn't mind. As long as he gave them more sisters.

Sifting through the grains and ribbons, he thought of Brian. The last one had belonged to him. This one would be free.

The phone rang. Without thinking, he said, "Jessica?"

"Who's Jessica?" It was Milena's voice.

"A friend."

"Oh yeah? That all?" He did not respond, focused on the raw materials for the latest—last?—doll. She would be utterly unique. No one would ever mistake her for human. She would be something new and beautiful and would obliterate the memory of Jessica.

Milena wasn't fazed by the silence. "Did you get the money?"

"Yes. Thanks for the introduction."

"You promised you would show me what it's for."

"I did. It's not finished yet. If you give me a month or two, I can show you."

"Why so long?"

"Because this has never been seen by anyone. I want her to be perfect."

"Her?"

* * *

The Innocent got closer two nights later.

She took the distance from the house to the Monk with more confidence, knowing the path, if not its subtleties, keeping to the shadows and the undergrowth, her tail-head looking up at the purple sky, arms scuttling over the Monk's wall to find his rooftop, where she flattened out into a white streak against the gray shingles.

She hoped to feel it, hoped uniting with the other—with the echo—would bring the moment of ecstatic connection she imagined. The others couldn't verbalize it. She felt momentarily complete when the Firstborn closed the circle with the Joyous and when the Sorrow had mimicked that act with the Hide. Then there was the warm terror within the Knife and the rasping need of the Poem.

The Monk's car pulled up in front of the house. He moved gingerly, protecting one side of his body. The Innocent wanted to know what was behind that. The Maker periodically had injuries, many of those self-inflicted. The Monk showing the same kind of proclivities was a good sign the link was there.

The Monk went inside the house. The Innocent slithered off the side to drop into the alley formed by the house and the wall on the property line. She skittered to the front, ignoring the stucco view from her main head to concentrate on her tail-head, rearing up to peek within.

The Monk was inside. The living room was white and gold, hidden under newspapers and towels. An older woman dozed in a lounger, glasses having fallen from her face, body lit with the marine glow of the television.

She was the Deceived.

The Monk disappeared into the kitchen and returned with a glass of milk, and gently shook the Deceived's shoulder. She put her glasses on with an indulgent smile and accepted the milk. He helped her to her feet and let her lean on him, leading her down a hallway and out of the Innocent's vision. The doll backed out of the hedges and scuttled back down into the alley, where she could peer into the Monk's room.

After a moment, the light clicked on. The Monk stumbled in, stripping down to shorts and undershirt before falling into bed. The Innocent raised up her tail to get a better view. He had an arm flung over his eyes, but he was not asleep.

She felt nothing.

Something buzzed in the room and then spat out a horrible string of beeps. The Monk dug a phone from the hip pocket of the discarded pants and answered it. "Nice. See you soon."

The Innocent attached no significance to this, continuing to watch. The Monk got up, straightened the room a bit, and returned to bed. This time he didn't cover his eyes, his foot tapping on nothing.

A car pulled up behind the Monk's, stopped, and one of its doors slammed. Light footsteps approached up the walkway. The footsteps shifted, crinkling the night-crisp grass.

They were getting closer. The Innocent nearly panicked, briefly considered ripping the interloper apart. Would the Monk like that? Would it forge the connection?

She couldn't risk it.

She leapt up the short concrete wall and scuttled down the other side. The bushes shook right as the intruder entered the mouth of the alley.

"Hello?"

She had never heard the voice, but the Innocent recognized the Constant. She went around the side of the house cautiously. "If there's anyone there, you should know I've got a gun and cramps." She paused.

The Innocent was still.

The Constant went to the window and tapped. It slid open.

"You have possums out here or something."

"Raccoons," the Monk said. "They get into the garbage. They have a thing for my mom's tuna casserole."

"That shit must make them big. It sounded like a goddamn bear."

The Innocent extended her tail, peeking between the scalloping at the top of the wall.

"Must have scared the hell out of you."

"Fuck off and help me up."

The Monk braced himself and reached an arm out. The Constant gripped the offered forearm, planted a foot against the wall, and clambered into the window. She fell into the bed, laughing.

"What?"

"You couldn't spring for a stepladder?"

"Hey, you've got money."

"I will when you pay up."

The Monk smiled and shut the window. The voices were swallowed. The Monk peeled off some money and put it on the night table by a full glass of water.

The Innocent scuttled back over the wall, hugging the shadows. The Constant slipped off skirt, tights, and jacket, nothing remotely erotic in it. It was merely the mechanical action of preparing for bed. She unpinned and shook out her hair, where it fell to her shoulders, and crawled into bed, turning away from the Monk. They snuggled close, as close as two people could ever get. It reminded the Innocent of the way the Knife and the Sorrow sometimes lay. The Monk reached up and got the light.

Before the room went dark, the Innocent saw the Constant crack a tiny grin.

The Innocent felt an answering smile within. She knew how to connect.

* * *

The furnace was the same one that had been womb to the Poem and Sorrow and had forged the eyes of all the Maker's daughters. Minor modifications turned it into the birthing flames required for his youngest creation.

The blowpipe was a slender tube of gray iron, light and unwieldy. This would be a test, whether or not glass could live. And there was the matter of what would be inside. He had trouble with delicate manipulation these days, but this was balance and breath. He still had those.

He rotated the glowing blob and blew into the end.

Nothing happened. He wasn't expecting a reaction on par with blowing up a balloon, but after twenty tries, nothing had happened. Maybe one of the dolls would have better luck. They were stronger than humans. Life refined. Turning to call, he found one waiting.

The Sorrow was never far. She sat on one hip in the corner of the room, attention fixed on the Work. In the dim light of the coach house, the bruises on her knees turned to wine. She straightened, detecting the attention instinctively.

"Yes, Maker?"

"Come here."

She got to her feet eagerly and nearly scampered to his side, reaching down for him as she had seen the Poem do. Instead, he brushed her away and placed the end of the pipe to her lips.

"What do you want me to do, Maker?"

"Blow."

She did, producing the effect he was looking for—a tiny swelling in the blob of molten glass.

He thought for a moment on the problems of putting one of his plastic girls close to a birthing fire. Would she melt? Could she?

The Sorrow was expendable. It would be interesting to see what the heat would do to her flesh, a fascinating lesson to be applied to the precious others, to the trinity of Firstborn, Knife, and Poem. He watched her as they worked, a sexless, yet incestuous union that would produce another doll.

The gel was the next element in her design. He retreated to the attic. The existing dolls were forgotten for a time. The new life mattered. Not the old.

He started with a thick clear base. It would pick up the tint of the glass surrounding it, and from there, the ambient light.

He shattered a mirror and added the shards to the gel.

He stirred glass beads into it evenly.

He placed lengths of ribbon within it.

He cut shards of glass into the three letters and placed them inside.

He set the innards, a large glass punchbowl filled with shimmering gel, aside.

He had come to enjoy this time with the Sorrow. She stayed in the coach house. The other dolls had staked out their places, agreeing on it with the same unguessable silence. The Sorrow finally had a place of her own, staying in the corner, in her curiously vulnerable position, until Stephen entered. She would be on her feet immediately.

He watched the effect the heat had on her skin. She seemed to perspire, but it was actually the outer layer of her body softening to molten liquid. When she cooled, she never changed shape. The plastic flesh had a will of its own.

During this time, the Firstborn's second birthday came and went. Forgotten.

His fingers were cudgels. Gradually, she took over, leaving him to direct her from a dusty rocker. She did everything without question.

He forged the new one through the Sorrow. She was his hands, his lungs, his skill. This new creature would be wholly impractical. She would not live. Then again, none of them would, not without whatever he had found in the corners of reality. They started with her torso, later moving to upper arms and thighs. From there, to calves and forearms. The Sorrow forged each joint separately. The new one's fingers were tiny. Her body would not connect. The gel would flow the links and would be the part truly humming with life.

The Sorrow reverently carried the finished pieces to the attic. It was a strange sight, this nude girl, covered in dirt, carrying what looked like vases.

In the attic, the Sorrow stood proudly by the circle. Inside, she had carefully laid each piece of her unborn sister.

He filled each part with the gel, letting the Sorrow hold each piece for him. She was careful and attentive. The perfect assistant.

When the glass doll was finished, needing only the ceremony, Stephen turned to his last daughter.

"What is this one?"

"The Celestial."

It sounded appropriate. It always did.

* * *

Tyler returned home from Griffith Park up three hundred fifty dollars. Not the best night. Still enough to call Milena a couple times over. It was well after dark when he pulled up at home. The lights were off.

Something felt wrong.

He couldn't put his finger on it. The house was the same as it always was. The front room flashed and darkened with the TV. The windows were black. The lawn was wet. No shapes lurked in the bushes. It was probably nothing. After what Karo had done, the nightmares had happened more often.

Though never when Milena was over.

He went inside. The smells coming from the kitchen said his mother made something fish-related for dinner, and the blaring TV said she was dozing in front of some old episode of a detective series. Sleeping on the chair was hell on her back, but that's where sleep found her night after night, and nothing Tyler said would change her. He went to the kitchen and got her a glass of milk before shaking her gently.

"Mom? It's time to go to bed."

She blinked the dreams away and put her glasses on. She did this every night, only smiling when she saw him. Tyler once joked with Milena that a murderer would take the time for his mom to get the glasses on before doing anything.

"Tyler. Do you want something to eat?"

"No, Mom. I ate. I'm fine. It's time for you to go to bed."

"What time is it?"

"Bedtime."

"Okay, okay." She glared at him and then squinted at the television before turning it off. Disdainfully, she said, "I don't know that show."

He helped her to her feet and handed over the milk, trying to ignore the groan when she tried to straighten her back. Tyler avoided scolding her. She knew better than he did what sleeping in a stupid chair cost.

He glanced around, making sure there was nothing for her to trip over in the morning, and went to his room.

It was a mess. It always was. The phone was a comforting weight in his pocket. Calling Milena meant half a night's work gone. It also meant a good night's sleep, smelling the perfume in her hair. The phone waited. He wouldn't call. He would try to sleep without Milena's help.

He stripped, got the lights, and lay in bed wondering if the first time he closed his eyes Karo would be above him, the fist eclipsing everything. Tyler reached for the phone. There was no reason to deny himself. He'd work tomorrow, the next day and the next, and bring in enough to keep his roll and to keep Milena with him.

He scrolled through to Milena's name, thumb hovering over SEND. Decision time.

A tapping came from his window. Through the dirty glass, he saw a hand at the very corner of the window, almost out of sight. His mind's eye provided Milena's rings and her warm skin. Decision made. Tyler slid the window open with a grateful smile.

"Milena? I didn't call you."

The hand gripped the edge of the windowsill.

He really saw it for the first time. It was white. Stark white.

It was not Milena's hand.

Another hand had grabbed the sill. Another took the side of the window. Another grabbed the window. Tyler stumbled backward. The thing hauled itself into the window.

His mind tried to cut it into pieces, so it could be understood. The face was human, but shiny and cracked like an old plate. The eye sockets were empty. Black.

Behind were a woman's shoulders and breasts. Then another, and another, turning a beautiful woman into something terrible and arachnid.

The worst part was the look on its face. It was smiling beatifically.

It hauled itself inside, the front landing on the bed. A thick tail stretched behind it, formed of nine sets of buttocks and three smooth lower backs. As the last part came into the room, it reared up, facing him with another eyeless head, this one a clacking ventriloquist dummy.

It finally spoke, "I'm here now."

Tyler wanted to scream. The thing reached one of its hindmost leg-arms back and slid the window shut.

"You're mine now."

In horror, Tyler turned to flee. Fear sharpened his senses, slowed time to a crawl, making him flee through thick nightmare.

The shadow the thing threw against the door was human. His mind struggled to make sense of that, but there was no way to do so without breaking.

Tyler's attempted flight was useless. The thing was much faster, overtaking him, gripping him around the ankle and pulling him toward the smiling mask-face. One hand passed him to the other, then the other, farther and farther back. The thing gripped his ankles with its hindmost limbs, drawing him level with the radiant smile of the cracked mask.

"What... what... are you?"

The thing paused, wanting to say something, the words stuck in its throat. "You can't ask that."

Tyler struggled, but the thing was far too strong. As though he weighed nothing at all, it spun him around, all eighteen of its arms wrapping around his body. "Now sleep. I'm here now."

* * *

Stephen did not have the strength he'd had for the others. Not even the desired ones.

He was weak and knew with the creation of the Celestial, the rest of himself would be lost. He would no longer be human, even if he could still be considered such. Nothing could stop him now. It was that or face Jessica.

The ritual lacked the power of the Firstborn's, the need of the Poem's or the love of the Knife's. It had become something formalized, something the Poem performed by rote. A ritual in the truest sense of the term. She knew the exact movements that mattered and the ones that did not and boiled it down to its essence.

A good deal of blood still hung in the freezer, ice crystals puckering the plastic skin, but he wanted pain.

He opened his wrist and nothing came out.

He nearly cried out at the plastic wound in his body. It was pink and clean. There were no tendons, no veins, no flesh. Plastic through and through. The dolls stood around him, silently watching. What would the next cost him? What was there left to lose?

They raised their wrists—Firstborn, Knife, and Poem—and opened them. The Firstborn and Poem cut themselves with knives, the Knife cracked her wrist against the side of the desk. They bled, from scored plastic, chopped wood, and fractured porcelain. It was his blood. They had made it theirs. They had made more of it. Their wounds would heal. He started to move toward the glass doll, to give her breath, and remembered that had already gone.

The dolls watched with their inhuman eyes, showing nothing on their faces. It was beyond even reverence. Who controlled whom? Who truly had the power?

"Sorrow, come here."

The dolls turned as one. The Sorrow was farthest from the light. She crept forward, almost crawling on all fours.

"Yes, Maker?"

"Give her my breath."

The Sorrow took the Celestial's glass head in her lap and leaned over. The kiss was brief.

The Sorrow retreated to the edge of the circle, hiding behind the Knife, silvery plastic hands on white porcelain thighs.

Stephen watched his newest creation as the gel began to stir.

Then roil. It became a storm. It whirled and changed, the shards and beads catching the gold light and throwing it back out. The gel reached to the joints and fused the creature together.

She opened mirrored eyes and a soft and glassy mouth. As she rose, Stephen felt nothing, even as the other dolls went to him and bore him up.

CHAPTER EIGHTEEN

STEPHEN SLEPT FOR SEVERAL DAYS after the Celestial was born. The dolls stayed with him in turn, in a form of vigil. The Poem lay with him in bed, still as death. The Sorrow abandoned her home in the coach house to huddle outside the door. The Knife stood at the bottom of the stairs, never once looking up. The Firstborn waited at the threshold. Only the Celestial moved through the house. Her delicate footsteps sounded like clattering glasses. She didn't speak to the others. None felt the need. She would only sing, her gel forming innumerable echoing chambers, each singing its own part. As the dolls drifted in and out on their clockwork schedule, they began to take the house.

The Firstborn started it, finding the ribbons downstairs with Sarah Monaghan's sewing things. The wooden dancer unspooled them, one by one, and cut them to varying but precise lengths, and hung them from the ceilings throughout the house, dense in some places, sparse in others.

The Knife found the rusted gears and chains from the coach house. She brought those into the house one by one. The gears she placed in the wainscoting of the walls, sometimes embedding them into the flesh of the wood. The chains she hung amongst the ribbons, twisting hooks at the end. She liked the soft chiming they made.

The Poem found the Maker's blood in the attic. She opened the bags and covered her soft fingers in the holy ichor, painting the symbols of the Maker on the walls, bolstering them with the glyphs representing her sisters.

The Sorrow altered nothing. She only wanted the Maker to return.

The Innocent's chosen canvas was a mile away.

The Celestial found the pictures of the Maker's human family hidden away in the attic. She rehung them throughout the house, turning the images to face the wall. Those people should speak directly to the home itself. They shouldn't see outward.

* * *

Tyler opened dry eyes. The creature had her tail wrapped around him so that the head on the end was tucked into the crook of his neck, unconscious parody of the place Milena often rested. The insect segments of the tail were pelvises, one of them resting directly below his chin. The vulva opened, first the outer, and then the inner lips peeled back, revealing a set of human premolars. The red lips folded again, hiding the weapons from view.

It had been three days.

The abomination had not let him leave the room. The first night, he had waited until it was dark, reasoning it had to sleep some time. As soon as his muscles tensed to flee, she began to sing. It was a hideous, atonal song grinding through Tyler's mind, every droning note throwing his memory to horrible places. She sang for hours, only stopping when his mother's door opened.

He heard her shuffling footsteps outside, pausing in front of his door, before retreating up the hall. The television clicked on.

He thought briefly of screaming. His mother would be helpless, but there was something inside of him that remembered her as large and powerful. She would protect him from the thing under the bed.

He never imagined it would be something like this.

On the second day, Tyler pissed the bed.

He had been holding it since the first night. He shifted, the tail wrapping around him, and he saw the gnashing vertical mouths lining it for the first time. His stomach turned over.

"Please," he said. "I have to get up."

"No. You'll try to run. I have to make you my echo."

"I don't know what that means."

"Yes, you do. We're connected."

"We're not!"

"Yes, we are!" One of the vulvas bit into his arm, tearing off a hunk of skin. The wound went cold and he tried to scream, but the thing jammed a hand into his open mouth. He bit down. The hand was wood and felt no pain. The wound turned hot and the bed got wet underneath him. Tears sprung up. Weak. Helpless. Always.

As the hot blood flowed out of him and the hot tears absorbed his eyes, his bladder seized. The itching wetness spread in an oil slick on the bed around him.

"See? You don't have to go," the thing said. Only hatred burned worse than the pain and shame.

He realized he was thirsty on the second night. His mouth had been dry since the beginning and now his skin was beginning to flake in places. A headache pounded behind his eyes like a hangover. The fact that it was identifiable somehow made it more horrible. Familiarity increased proximity. The dull burning yawned upward. Falling was getting easier and easier.

There was no breaking free, since every tense of his muscles made the arms wrap around him tighter, the segmented tail to coil closer, vulvas masticating. Contact was constant.

He prayed there would be help coming, knowing there would not be. The perils of keeping strange hours kept anyone from knocking on the door, even his mother. Marathon games lasting several days were not uncommon and neither was crashing on someone's couch. The lights were off. There was no sound. She had no way of knowing. Calling to her was out of the question.

There was no telling what the thing would do.

His belly turned. The blood and urine had gone cold around him. There was only the itch and the feel of incipient infection.

He needed water, food. How could one explain that to a monster? A mad thought came to him. *Call Stephen Monaghan.* He would know what to do. Tyler nearly laughed. There was no reason to think that. Stephen Monaghan would be too busy trying to get into Brian's little sister's pants. Tyler wished Stephen godspeed.

He could call Milena. But what could she do? She never came over of her own accord. There was always a call, one way or the other. She couldn't deal with this monster. Couldn't help him sleep.

He would never sleep again.

And besides, the phone was out of reach on the bedside table. Might as well be a thousand miles away.

The creature shifted again, bringing the base of its tail to rest in front of Tyler's face as the creature's arms wrapped around his abdomen and groin. It reared up and Tyler nearly vomited.

A freckled and eyeless face was stretched over the first snow-white pelvis of the tail. The mouth opened, revealing the vertical vulva, irising open. The creature's singsong voice issued from within.

"Do you feel it?"

"Feel what?"

"Our connection. I think I feel it."

"Please, I don't know what you're talking about. Just let me go."

The creature's segments hissed. "You feel nothing?"

"No! Please, just let me go."

It fixed him with the eyeless gaze of three faces. "I have to close the circle to make the connection real."

Tyler opened his mouth, and she shoved the face on the end of her tail into it, the wooden jaw forcing his open, penetrating him deeply with her rough tongue. He tried to scream again, but the abomination swallowed it. Her arachnid form shifted, hands ripping at piss-soaked clothes, tearing them off him.

Struggling was worthless. She held him with eighteen arms.

Tyler was a virgin. Maybe if he told her that, told her there was nothing in him for sex. There was nothing he wanted other than comforting arms, sweet smelling hair, and soft breathing in the dark. The monster had none of these things.

The hands worked at his penis, stroking him with skill, pink plastic arms doing to him what he wished no one would. His body betrayed him, ready, hard, erect.

He shut his eyes, felt the tears falling.

The face at the base of her tail opened its mouth, spiraling open. The vulva swallowed him. Teeth scraped his cock, pulling burning strands into whatever passed for the monster's throat. The hands enfolded him, moving their bodies against one another, flesh against plastic, wood and porcelain. The cracked face found his, pressed him into another kiss. She tasted like a cereal bowl. Absurdly, he remembered being young, his mother fixing breakfast before school. If only he could be there. If everything would stop existing for that moment.

The abomination moved against him. His body boiled, coming close to it, a sensation he loathed. There was no control, a surrender to something else he had no hope of fighting. It was horrible biology.

He shuddered against the thing. It pulled back, the empty eye sockets probing him. "Did you feel it?"

Tyler could only weep.

* * *

The Celestial emerged into the morning, catching the light on her skin, trapping and refracting it through shiny innards, hurling it back in a thousand colors. She was painful to look upon, but it was the sublime pain of birth.

The Maker had forgotten the garden. There was a time when he took some pride in it. The Celestial had not been alive for this but knew it deep within her grain. It was time to take the garden and tend to it, and so she did, ignoring the old ways of doing things. She watered the plants of course, never bothering to trim them, instead taking stalks and tendrils and weaving them together. The garden was a single living body with green veins and leafy skin and should look it.

She went to tend the stubborn orange tree in the backyard. It was healthy and fruiting.

As she wandered amongst the hedge maze, something drew her glassy gaze.

A dead raven lay in the path. She knelt, throwing bright shadows all around her. The bird had been there for some time. It had been wrapped in cobwebs, hollowed, and mummified by garden scavengers. The Celestial regarded it for several hours.

She dipped her glass hands into the gravel of the walkway and scooped a moat around it, down to the topsoil. She clipped fertile branches and planted them all around, and then disappeared back into the house.

She went first to the room of the Joyous and the Firstborn, finding her sister there, lost in the world the Maker had given. The Firstborn didn't seem to notice the Celestial as she went into the Joyous's closet and found a small box shelf that still held some old shoes. Then to the dresser to sift.

Her fingers stopped. She had not found what she was looking for. She had found something so much better.

A pair of ripped stockings.

She pressed these to her smooth skin and thanked the Maker for leaving them. The idea had taken hold and she would see it done.

Quickly, she scavenged amongst the clothes of the Joyous. It felt strange. Unlike the others the Maker had designed, there had been no costume for the Celestial. Clothing was not in her future. Even she knew that to travel outside among humanity, she would have to hide herself. She found a suitable outfit, carrying the clothing and the precious stockings into the hall and downstairs.

She found the Sorrow curled up in the Knife's lap. The Knife tenderly stroked the Sorrow's hair, and both stared at nothing.

"Sorrow," the Celestial said.

The Sorrow didn't look at her. "Yes?"

"The artifact you took from the Hide. May I have it?"

The Sorrow stroked the Knife's chest. "Yes."

Only then did the Celestial see it, the Sorrow's permission having caused it to spring into being—a tiny glass unicorn, lying on its side on the coffee table. The Celestial took it in shimmering fingers.

Three remained. She took the other two items outside. The torn stockings she placed carefully by the gate. She set the unicorn on the windowsill of the tool shed. The Hide's footprint was still there, invisible to human eyes.

She returned inside. This was the easiest of all. The others she had to look for, even there was a dim connection to echoes of her sisters. The Celestial's own echo, the Constant, called to her in a powerful voice inaudible to the rest. The doll knew her echo's sigils, the best way to honor her connection to the blessed Work. The glass doll opened the Maker's cards and slid out the Queen of Diamonds. Perfect.

She went into the attic. The Maker's first chisel, the one used to carve the Firstborn. It sang to the Celestial. Raw power flooded into her hand as she picked it up. The doll was unworthy to bear this artifact longer than was necessary, placing her glass lips against it once to sanctify it.

One left.

She donned a disguise, leaving only a thin strip around her eyes visible. For the first time in her existence, the Celestial left the gate. She prowled the streets for hours, finally finding the object of her search in a gutter—a chipped and stained dinosaur toy. She turned it over in her hands. It smelled of french fries and the gutter in equal measures.

That would do.

The Celestial placed the last three items around the garden. Over the course of the next three days she built altars around each one, decorating them with images and trinkets. The raven had silks ripped and arrayed around it. The unicorn was splattered with blood. The toy was surrounded with pictures torn from magazines.

There was already a plan in the gelled innards. She would pray to the stockings at dawn, the raven in the early morning, the dinosaur at noon, the unicorn in the early afternoon, the card at dusk, and the chisel at midnight. She would do this every day, assured in her fabricated observances.

"Celestial." It was the voice of the Knife.

The Celestial turned. Her sister came up the path, the dying sun shining off porcelain skin.

"Yes, Knife?"

"What are you doing?"

"We serve the Maker," the Celestial said. This would close the conversation.

"We choose to serve the Maker," the Knife said.

"He will be gone soon. It's important to remember our origins."

The Knife said pointedly, "Have you thought of what we will do when he is gone?"

The thought spiraled into the gel of the Celestial. She stayed completely still, considering it with every fiber. The sun set. When it was full dark, the Celestial finally spoke again. "No."

"Because it's stupid." The Poem's voice was happy as she emerged into the night. As always, she had stripped out of even the meager costume the Maker had given her.

"Go back inside, Poem. This is too complex for you," the Knife said.

"Fuck yourself." The Poem sat down in the middle of them, looking up at her sisters. "The Maker is eternal."

"The Maker is dying," the Knife said.

"Both are correct," the Celestial said. "We are the Maker. We are his daughters."

"For now. Until others find us, then we're abominations. We would be raped and broken."

The Poem said, "They wouldn't do that. We're the same as them. Some would protect us."

"In exchange for what? No. We protect ourselves on our terms."

The Celestial nodded. "The Knife is right. We are the Maker's daughters, and he has given us wombs. You proved as much when you created the Innocent."

"With the Maker's blood," the Poem said.

"All people have blood," the Knife said.

"Blood can be spilled in times of need. If it means the Work survives. The Work is what is truly important," the Celestial said.

The three dolls were silent. The Celestial's words echoed within them. They would carry this back to the others, knowing the acceptance, from the wounded Sorrow, the stoic Firstborn, and the sublime Innocent, would be complete.

* * *

The dolls had begun to take care of the Maker. The Firstborn brushed his hair. The Knife spoke to him. The Poem bathed him. At times, they would take him to a different part of the house and place him in a chair where he would look into emptiness.

They did not feed him. Hunger was for humans and they would not think of it.

They placed the Maker at the dining room table. The Knife sat close by, reciting ancient stories. The Sorrow crouched, allowing her hair to be touched by the delicate porcelain hand.

The Firstborn and the Celestial made love in the Joyous's bed. It was her first connection to the others. The Maker's love flowed from the Firstborn's touch into the Celestial's body. The Firstborn seemed possessed of wonder for the Celestial's protean form, finishing only when the Firstborn rose, crossing the room to one of the strands of the mobile. The checkerboards entranced her.

The Celestial rose as well. There was one place in the garden missing. It had to be filled. She put on her human clothes and went out into the night. She knew where to find the Innocent. The doll's angry bliss was a beacon.

The Celestial walked further than she ever had. The Dream and the Blind momentarily enraptured her, picking up the pace when they noticed the Celestial staring. She thought of following them home. The Dream needed inspiration. The Blind needed to find beauty.

Instead the Celestial moved on. The Innocent was close.

She only heard the names the Monk and the Deceived when she crossed the wet lawn to find the alley and the window. She

386 // JUSTIN ROBINSON

could smell the Constant there, and something made her want to squirm out of her skin.

She peered in. The Innocent lay coiled around the Monk. Perhaps this was good enough. The Monk's eyes were wide, unblinking. He lay in concentric rings of red and yellow, nude body gray and flaking. The Innocent clicked and chattered.

The Celestial knocked on the window.

The Innocent slid it open.

The Monk turned, and in a tiny voice said, "Milena?"

The Celestial took her hat off and unwound the scarf.

Certain, pleading, "Milena."

The Celestial climbed onto the windowsill and perched, gel roiling. The Innocent regarded her. "What do you want, Celestial?"

"I found six echoes. There are seven of us."

"Seven?"

"There will be."

The Innocent nodded the head on the end of her tail. "Speak."

"I found six echoes. I haven't found yours. Is the Monk your echo?"

The Innocent paused. "Yes."

The Celestial saw through her instantly. "No, he is not."

"He is! I've made him so."

"The Maker chooses your echo. Not you."

"The Maker didn't make me."

"Yes, he did. He works through the Firstborn, the Knife, and the Poem. His hands, his heart, and his need."

"Lies."

"Truth often sounds like lies to those who do not believe."

"What of your echo?"

The Celestial could not blink. Her glass face was still, and then the expression rippled across it, tossed in the starry pond. "I don't know."

"Tell me of her."

"She is with me, even now. I feel her in this room. This was a place of contentment for her. The Monk was precious to her in some way. Not love, as we love the Maker. Something lesser. Still soft and warm."

"The Monk is precious. Can you feel her now?"

"Far away. She is a rock, a tower. The world flows around her. She knows herself intimately. She is an outsider, but it is as she desires."

"As does the Maker?"

"No. She has neither his genius nor his doubt."

"Do you wish to be with her?"

"I don't know."

"You haven't closed the circle."

"No."

"Neither have the Knife and the Poem."

"Should I... do I close the circle?"

"It brought the Firstborn and the Sorrow peace."

"Peace in the Maker?"

A shrug undulated across the Innocent's backs.

The Celestial had made her decision. "Yes. I should speak to the Constant." She jumped back down outside.

"Did you want to take something from my echo?"

The Celestial looked at the Monk, reaching out a hand, silently pleading. "He is not your echo."

The Innocent's coils tightened. The Monk gasped. The Celestial was already gone.

* * *

The Poem left the Maker to the ministrations of the Firstborn. The Poem still loved the Maker in her way, though thoughts of him seldom troubled her. The Seeker occupied the Poem's plastic mind. She had to know what lay within. She fetched her disguise from its hiding place in the back of the Maker's closet. It still smelled of the Seeker, cut with the Poem's false scent.

She climbed to the attic, where she removed her stockings, elbow gloves and choker, secreting them where the piles of discarded limbs had once lain. She went to the refrigerator and removed a bag of the Maker's sacred blood, opening it reverently, dipping a finger in and drawing the runes across her body. They gripped her curves in lines of red, born to them. She held her arms out, eyes closed, as the blood tightened over her.

The night was warm, the smog hanging low in the purple sky. She set off to the most direct route to the Seeker's home by cutting through the arroyo.

The arroyo was a natural trench running along the border of South Pasadena, terminating at the Rose Bowl. At the bottom of its two hundred foot depth, there were paths littered with horseshit from the nearby stable. A concrete wash bleeding with sluggish water cut through the middle, the stream furred with bright green algae. By day, the arroyo was home to civilization—joggers, dogs being walked, horseback riders, and the odd vagrant. By night, the arroyo was returned to its original owners.

The Poem left the house. The other dolls barely noticed her, so locked into themselves. It disgusted the Poem to see the Knife with the Sorrow. The Knife was one of the chosen. The Sorrow was an error, a cast off.

Someone looking at the Poem would not know what to make of her. A warm summer night, but bundled in a coat, soft pink feet bare, standing at the edge of the arroyo and gazing down. It was far too steep for any human to try to make it down the slope. One inevitable slip and the person would go hurtling down to smash his brains out on the rocks below or a bone-shattering stop against one of the hardy trees sprouting from the side.

The Poem had no such fear, even as the twigs tore into her delicate feet. Her balance was good, though it did not approach the inhuman grace of the Firstborn. The Poem made it halfway before the slope gave under her. She tumbled downward, head slamming into a jagged rock at the base. She got up instantly, completely unaware of the trauma that should have killed her. A dent marred the side of her head, blood matting the wavy red hair. She was neither dizzy nor stunned. Her plastic skull shifted, returning to its proper place. The rent in her skin still dripped gifted blood. She was fine.

She moved quickly along the trail, crossing the fake river at a concrete bridge. At the other side, a nearly sheer wall of soil blocked her. She regarded it for a moment before a low whine made her turn.

Coyotes.

Three of them fanned out, penning her up against the arroyo. The one in the center, the alpha, whined and sniffed at her, while the other two padded back and forth in the dark. She cocked her head at the alpha. Would it attack? What might she do?

She stood up straight, neither advancing nor retreating, making no move to pick up a rock. She was unarmed, by all appearances a small and helpless woman.

The ring of carnivores tightened. They had not yet lunged, partly because something within them could sense that the Poem was wrong. She moved and bled as a mammal, though she was anything but.

The Poem stepped forward, letting the pack surround her. If she felt anything close to fear, it never showed. She was fascinated by the pacing creatures around her. Her own death was worthy of nothing more than academic interest. She reached out one hand, fingers wet with blood. The alpha sniffed the air, catching the meaty scent.

He approached cautiously, lips peeling back from teeth, a soft growl simmering. The Poem's hand was preternaturally steady.

The alpha sniffed the blood and deciding it was enough, bit down on the plastic hand. The Poem was silent; her face did not change. The alpha let out a yelp and released the hand, tail between his legs, whining, turning to the other two animals perhaps to warn them, but they were already on him, snarling, snapping, ripping. They tore the creature apart in moments, devouring his tainted flesh almost as quickly.

The Poem watched all of this, pretty face still curiously blank. When the sweetest parts of the alpha were gone, the two coyotes turned their blood-soaked muzzles to the Poem before fleeing back into the dark.

Satisfied, she began to make her way up the face of the arroyo. With no fear of injury, she took greater risks. With her superior balance, the risks paid off. The climb was apparently effortless.

She did not sweat and did not breathe, so when she stood up at the top, nearly two hundred feet up, she looked fresh. Even the blood had dried out.

At the top, a brick wall separated the house at the top with the plummet to the bottom. She skirted this, her attention focused on the horizon, where the Seeker waited. The Poem picked up the pace, taking backstreets as often as she could.

The Poem unlocked the door and went inside, pausing at the wall of toys to pay homage, and continued to the Seeker's bedroom. The rise and fall of the woman's chest entranced the Poem. Asleep, the Seeker's face was scrunched and puffy. She babbled barely-heard nonsense, eyelids flickering.

The Poem crouched next to the bed, so the Seeker's breath would tickle her face. The Poem reached a hand out to caress the Seeker's cheek, holding it barely an inch away from the welcoming skin. The heat coming from the woman was thick and palpable. Her sleep scent was strong in the dark. The Poem was amazed. No matter how many times she saw it, the humanity of those who were not the Maker was incredible.

She could resist no longer. The Seeker's mind carried far too much promise. The link between them was visible in the room— the Poem could trace it with one bloody finger. She pushed through the link into the Seeker.

The Seeker's mind exploded around the Poem. She saw images she did not understand, yet labeled, first in the Seeker's parlance, and then in the language of the dolls. The dream flooded into the Poem's plastic tissues. She swallowed it whole.

The colors were vibrant, powerful, burning through the Poem. Words thundered and danced across pages. Faces matched neither names nor feelings. Places were mated strangely. At once, she was within the Seeker's dream, standing on the street in front of the Nite Lite while the city tore through the asphalt and buildings bloomed like plants. Ripped and dirty baby dolls crawled out of the holes and up the crumbling walls of the tenements. The Seeker was in the middle, looking helplessly at the Poem.

Go further in, find the Moebius strip. The Seeker was dreaming of the Poem who was eating the dream. The Poem consumed the ephemera of her living within the Seeker's mind, and in so consuming turned the link between them into steel, bridging time and space, flesh, and plastic. The Seeker's face was not her own. The Seeker's mind was not her own. The Seeker's soul was not her own.

As the last strand of the dream vanished into the Poem, she pulled away. The Seeker's breathing was shallow, her face gray. The Poem smiled. The circle was not yet closed. It would be soon.

She left the Seeker's presence and returned home, washed the scabbed symbols from her body and returned to bed with the Maker. He did not move or speak.

* * *

When the phone rang, it fell to the Celestial to answer it. The Maker could no longer do so.

"Stephen?"

The Celestial answered in the Maker's voice. "Yes. Who is this?"

"It's Audra. You said I could call."

The Celestial didn't remember this, but she would never doubt anyone who invoked the Maker. "Of course. I am here."

"I... had another dream. It's different now. Remember when I told you there was another me? This is going to sound weird. I saw her again, as the city gave birth to itself. Everything flooded away, into her and I was looking at her, looking at me, looking at her, looking at me. I wasn't even there, just the echo of an echo of an echo. There wasn't a me anymore. I was gone."

"The dreams will stop soon."

The voice changed. The Celestial couldn't understand the significance. "Stephen? Are you okay? You don't sound like you."

"I'm fine, and you will be, too. Give it time."

The Celestial hung up, returning upstairs on her chiming footsteps. The Innocent was right. She had to close the circle. To do that, she needed to go to her echo. Easy enough as the Constant was a beacon.

She found her disguise and put it on.

She knew the way as the Poem knew the way to the Seeker. It took hours, the Celestial keeping head down and collar up, the scarf wrapped around her face. She could hide for a short time, even amongst them. The gel rippled under her clothes, striving to get out.

When she knocked at the Constant's door, the sound like a glass tapped for a toast. The door opened, the Celestial kept her face hidden, knowing this was not something to reveal yet. Not until she could draw the Constant back to the temple.

"Hello?"

"You want to know what he made."

"What?"

The Celestial repeated herself.

"He who?"

The Celestial took the Maker's voice and repeated herself. "Stephen?"

The Celestial resumed her voice. "The Maker wanted to show you what he has wrought."

"The Maker?" The Constant sounded amused, but there was something underneath. Fear, maybe. Fear was good before the divine. "Stephen makes you call him that?"

This close to her echo, and the distinction between Celestial and Constant began to vanish. It was difficult to tell where a thought came from, and though neither understood the other completely, they could sense what moved within both.

"It is what he is." The Celestial turned and walked away.

"Who are you?"

The Celestial paused. "You mustn't ask that."

"Hold on." The Constant rushed around her apartment for a moment, turned out lights, and locked the door, following the Celestial. "Where's your car?"

"I don't have one."

"You walked? Okay. I'll drive."

The Constant followed the Celestial's directions to the house.

"You should know, Karo wants his money."

"But you won't tell him where we are."

"Not yet. He'll pay me for it, and eventually he'll pay me enough."

"The Disciple is foolish."

"The Disciple? Karo?"

"Tell him where we are when you're finished with him."

The Constant was silent, digesting what the Celestial had said and would remember it if Karo ever became more trouble than he was worth. The Constant had no doubt this strange woman or her associates could do something. One of Karo's men was carrying around a badly broken arm, another was in a sling. They refused to talk about the cause, but it happened right after Stephen asked them for money.

As they pulled up, the Constant gasped. "Tyler wasn't kidding. This place is huge."

The Constant did not see the gel inside the Celestial swirling in elaborate patterns even as her outward form was completely still.

The Constant walked behind the Celestial—steps short, breath quick. The Celestial felt the Constant's heart pounding through glass and circled it with her insides, spinning and cradling them until they grew hot and small. The Constant's eyes played over the house. The Celestial could feel the knowledge surfacing within. There was something inside, but the Constant couldn't know the reflection of what lurked within was already there and waiting.

The Knife opened the door as the Celestial came close, every footstep ringing gently on the walkway.

The Constant gasped as she took in the Knife. The doll was plainly inhuman, the house behind her no place for the living.

What passed between the two dolls was invisible. The Knife stood aside.

The Constant said, "What is she?"

"One of the blessed."

The Constant knew the answer to the question in her mind, merely nodding and following the Celestial into the house. They brushed through the ribbons, finding the occasional predatory

396 // JUSTIN ROBINSON

chain hidden amongst them as they approached the stairs.

Along the walls, the holy symbols of the Maker sent a clear message to those who entered. The Constant lacked the eyes to read it.

Every step sent a deep groan through the house. The Poem sat on the landing, oblivious to her nudity. The Constant skirted the little doll, even as she reached out to caress the woman's ankle.

They emerged into the upstairs hall and the Sorrow recoiled, scrambling backward into a wall. The ribbons were thicker by the portal to the Joyous. In places, paint had turned the floor to checkerboards. Behind the Constant, the Poem made a noise almost, but not quite, laughter. The human woman jumped again.

"Who are you?"

"We are as the Maker made us."

The Firstborn's door opened. She stood at the threshold, watching the Constant with empty eyes. The Constant passed her in open fear. The Firstborn did not move. The door to the Maker's room yawned open. The darkness within called to the Constant. She got to the door and peered in.

Light came from a few candles melted directly onto the furniture. Forests of wax stalactites attested to how many had already died.

Stephen was in bed, unconscious, painfully thin body pale and nude. Shadows pooled in and around his bones. She approached. The Celestial felt the thoughts in the Constant's mind growing sharper by the second. The Maker is dead, thought the human. The Celestial nearly laughed. The Maker was eternal.

The Constant crept closer. "Stephen?"

She was right next to him, as still as a doll. Ropy scars ran over his wrists, chest, and penis. Tracks pockmarked arms thinned by starvation.

She touched the Maker's bony chest. His eyes went from closed to open like a shutter. Nothing human in the gesture.

"Stephen?"

He opened his mouth to speak. Nothing came out. The mouth worked, eyes grew. There was nothing. He smelled like new magazines.

Softly, a tinkle of a chandelier permeated the room. The Constant turned and nearly fell to her knees in front of the thing. The Celestial had dropped her coat and now stood revealed. Transparent skin gave only the suggestion of perfection in the form of silver shadows. The body flashed in a thousand places, turning it into walking jewels. There was a suggestion of movement, perhaps a facial expression. When it—she—spoke it was with several voices layered on top of one another—a choir of one.

"I know you," the Celestial said.

"You. That was you?"

"Yes." In Stephen's voice, the Celestial said, "This is what I borrowed the money to make."

The Constant turned back to the Maker. "You made... this?"

The Celestial continued to speak in Stephen's voice. "Her. I made her."

The tinkle of the chandelier sounded again as the Celestial approached. There was the barest hint of soft teeth smiling past glass lips.

"How?"

"I can't tell you."

"Why not?"

"No, I mean I can't. You wouldn't understand. No one would, really."

She could see the points of his pelvis poking through paper-thin skin. "Are you okay?"

"I've never felt better."

The room should have stunk. Stephen had given up on bathing, but there was only the odd smell of laminated ink and paper.

The Celestial said, "If I make another, it will kill me."

"Sometimes you can't stop." Is the Constant saying this?

"I know."

The Celestial stepped toward the Constant. When the Celestial spoke, it was in her chorus of voices rather than the Maker's. "I brought you here. The Maker wanted it. You were his friend."

"Were?"

"There is not much left that would know you." The Celestial took another step.

Her scent was in the Constant now—clean glass spiked with acid. "May I touch you?" the Constant said.

"Of course."

Beneath the glass skin, the true body of the Celestial, the gelatinous mass undulated. The Celestial's fingertip fell to the carpet with a soft thump. One by one, pieces of the shell over her right arm fell away. From the elbow, her arm was a shuddering mass of artificial tissue, reflecting the candlelight in the room.

Milena Franco, the Constant, reached out to touch this. Fear never entered her. She saw herself in the glassy surface of the creature and had only burning curiosity to know what was underneath. The gel touched her fingers. It was not wet, but it felt warm and slick and gentle, artificial, yet alive. It flowed over the Constant's skin, tickling and exploring.

As it climbed her forearm, the Celestial took another step, shedding more of her glassy skin. The gel kept climbing, flowing over Milena's body, inch by inch. Her clothing fell away before the creature's gentle touch until they were skin to skin. Milena stood in the center of the room, the Celestial covering every inch of her. She breathed through the gel, saw through it, heard through it, tasted through it.

The world flooded into Constant and Celestial, each a lens for the other, reflecting and refracting. The candles flared upward, bleeding light into their singular mouth. The house sprawled around them, gossamer threads running between dolls and Maker. The building had become a fortress on an endless plain. Other houses were as nothing—they had no power within them. The dolls were titans here, mistresses of a new world.

Within the citadel, the Celestial herself, her protean body formed a structure to the glory of a new race. Within her, remnants of what the Constant had been, the certainty, the peace.

The Constant was a barrier of rocks against the deep and angry sea. The water surged around her, touching, buffeting, caressing, but never changing her. She was in the midst of perfect chaos, serene.

The doll remained joined with her echo for a full day. Their circle had been closed. Each loved the other. They would never speak again. For one, the mystery had been solved. For the other, there was too much Work to do.

CHAPTER NINETEEN

THE VOICE ON THE TELEPHONE did not sound human, but the Celestial could scarcely judge. She answered in the Maker's voice. He no longer had need for it.

The Alpha said, "We know you talked to the cops. We're coming for you."

"I did nothing."

The Alpha might have laughed. It was too animal to be called that. "We'll see what you say when we're done with you. See you soon."

The Celestial hung up the phone.

* * *

Audra had not seen Stephen Monaghan in over a month. He had been thinner, paler the last time she saw him, on a strangely cold night for his biweekly, late night tuna melt. He was always a ghost, but it had gotten worse. There were times when he would come in and she thought he might fade away entirely. She wished she could call his girlfriend, the one who was his girlfriend whether he knew it or not, but Audra didn't know her name.

The Poem knew all of this.

Audra felt herself fading, too. Since the night earlier in the week when she had awakened to a dream sliced in two. Her mind groped for what she had lost. It was like it was never there. She no longer dreamt, except for isolated moments of her double flitting through the black.

Audra thought to the one time Stephen emerged into something close to light, the party he had attended at her apartment. Though her friends thought he was a little strange, they accepted him. Audra had hoped to draw him out. Maybe sensing it, he had been around less and less.

Now there was nothing. She remembered the house on the hill, remembered thinking it was a living thing. It seemed to watch her with eyes. She stood in the parking lot of the Nite Lite, pretending she could see the house, gazing balefully down at her.

She felt it again. The sensation of something watching her. Not the house. Something closer, the ghost sense of something nearby, brushing over the soft hairs at the nape of the neck. Audra squinted into the darkness around the parking lot.

She thought she saw a slip of pink far off in the back of the parking lot. Adrenaline mainlined into her spine. She wanted to approach, but she couldn't get her feet to move.

Somehow, Stephen was connected. Somehow it was him. She got into her car and after a moment, drove for the house on the hill.

* * *

It had been one week since the Innocent had claimed the Monk and she still felt nothing for him. She tried to see his thoughts as the others had described. Sex had failed to close the circle. Perhaps something else would. There was only void. There was nothing separating the Monk from anyone else in the world.

The Monk's phone buzzed. The Innocent looked. One word: MOM.

The Innocent wondered if that was all the Monk loved. It couldn't be. He loved the Constant in a quiet way.

She wondered what would happen if she took one of them away. She couldn't take the Celestial's echo from her. The Deceived had no connection to the dolls. Cut one link and let a new one heal in its place.

* * *

The Maker had not reached for any of them. He was in bed, motionless, still. The dolls had taken the house, clicking through it in the dark. The Celestial was, alone among the dolls that sprang from his heart, the only one who had not received a blessing.

He responded to her cold touch mechanically, automatically. Once he was hard, her gel parted around him and she received the benediction.

* * *

The Knife knew the Poem had gone. The allure of the echo was a strong one. The Knife had fought it for a long time knowing it was pointless, even for her. The Firstborn, the Sorrow, and the Celestial had closed their circles. It was past time for the Knife and the Poem to do the same.

She went to the closet and found a coat. She put it on over her costume; she would not wear her disguise. The Heart had to see her, the Knife, as she was. It was only good and proper. The Maker did not see the Knife leave as he was listlessly inside the Celestial.

The Knife stepped out into the night and walked east.

* * *

Audra walked through the garden toward the dark house. Altars sprouted at irregular intervals throughout the garden, honoring odds and ends. One of them, set into the hedge at the border of the property, framed a dirty and chipped plastic triceratops. Around it, images torn from magazines were woven into the delicate leaves and branches. Here and there, symbols adorned those. She could not explain it, but Audra felt a connection to this altar. She could not force herself to move the toy even if she had wanted to, and had to consciously fight the urge to kneel in front of it.

She moved away, heading for the house. On the bench outside, a folded set of clothes—shirt, coat, pants. Hers. They hadn't been missing. Had they? In fact, she recalled wearing them recently. They felt clean and oddly full, smelling of plastic and blood.

The clothes were an offering. She could still leave.

But there was something inside. Something she had to see. There was no way she could walk away without going inside. It was no longer something between her and Stephen Monaghan. Something within her drew her to open the door.

* * *

The Innocent made her decision. She would break everything the Monk loved. When she was done, the connection could be formed and she would have an echo.

She could finally be real.

All that remained was to tell the Monk.

His eyes were blank. Glassy. Dry.

She uncoiled. He was stiff, chest still.

He fell back to the stained bed, mouth open, eyes open.

The Innocent screamed, smashed through the window, and retreated into the night.

* * *

The Knife didn't bother to knock, merely took the knob in her hand and twisted until the lock within broke. She slapped the door, tearing through the deadbolt, and stepped inside.

The apartment was at once new and familiar. It felt right to be inside. She sensed the Heart somewhere within, frightened. Hiding?

"I know you're here."

The Heart sucked in quick rabbit breaths. The Knife felt her in the back room. The bedroom. The room that was supposed to belong to the Heart and the Maker, without belonging to anyone at all.

The Knife took another step deeper into the apartment, opening the coat. The Heart leapt out of hiding, swinging a baseball bat. It cracked into the Knife's cheek, sending the doll careening into the wall. The Heart took another swing. The Knife caught the bat and tore it from the human's weak grip.

The Heart shrank away as the Knife got to her feet, touching the wound on her cheek. Cracked. Cold blood flowed from the porcelain. The Knife threw the bat into the living room.

"Why did you do that?"

"Fuck you."

"Why did you do that?"

"You broke in!"

"So I did. Do you know who I am?"

The Heart shook her head. The Knife hated her. She saw her own face on the Heart, only far more human. There was a scar on the Heart's cheek. One eye was almost imperceptibly lighter than the other. A body stinking of sweat. The Heart was so far from the Knife's perfection.

"Who are you?"

The Knife wanted to tell the Heart, tried to shape the name, but it stuck in the Knife's throat with curved barbs. Instead, the Heart screamed in pain, clutching her belly. In horror, she lifted her shirt. A word tore into her skin—LOVE.

The Knife said, "Do you know what I am?"

Another word ripped into the Heart's soft shoulder—LIE.

She whimpered, blood dripping freely. The knowledge was there for the Heart's taking. The Knife could not read her, could not know if the human would ever accept what stared her in the face.

The Knife said, fighting against herself, "I am one of the Maker's dolls. Do you know who the Maker is?"

The Heart almost shook her head again when realization dawned across her face. "Stephen."

"Yes."

"Stephen made you."

"Yes."

"Stephen made a… thing… with my face?"

"I am not a thing. I am alive. The Maker made me so."

"Stephen made a thing with my face?" The Heart's voice trembled.

"I have more than your face."

The Heart stopped. "What's that supposed to mean?"

"You and I are the same. We love the same man. We share the same darkness."

"I don't love him."

"You lie."

"I don't love him anymore."

"The same lie."

"He knew about my brother and did nothing!"

"He did everything possible to stop the Hide's atrocity, and when he could do no more, I finished it."

The Heart was past hearing. "Stephen could have had me. Instead, he created a fucking sex doll."

"The Maker gives life. You should love him all the more."

"Get out. You're a thing. A monster. Get out and tell Stephen he's a monster, too."

The Knife staggered backward. The Heart continued to glare. There was nothing there for the Knife. The love the Firstborn found with her echo and the wonder the Celestial found with hers would never belong to the Knife. She would find only pain. The world wasn't for her. The only ones who loved and understood were the Maker and his dolls. She left the Heart and would never think of her again.

* * *

The hallway was dark. Audra resisted the temptation to call out to Stephen. That was wrong. Something kissed her face. She gasped, reached for it. In the moment it took, her eyes adjusted. Ribbons hung from the ceiling. Through them, she could dimly see roughly painted symbols on the walls punctuated by rusted gears.

To her right, dim light shone from a living room. Gold, flickering, perhaps from candles. She followed it. Something deep within the house made clicking noises.

Audra turned into the room to her right and nearly gasped at what sat on one of the overstuffed chairs.

A woman. She was exquisite, pale skin glowing, expertly dotted with freckles. Her hair was perfect, a vibrant copper tumbling across her shoulders in soft waves, and waited between her legs as gentle fleece. Her eyes, gray-blue as a stormy sea, stared at nothing. Wearing only stockings and elbow gloves, she lay across the chair like a discarded toy. So alive, but no breath marred her chest. Even when Audra entered the room, the doll did not react.

Audra took a step closer.

The stormy eyes blinked, swiveled to look at Audra. The body was dead.

"So you're the one," she said.

"Am I?"

The doll stayed limp on the chair. "Oh, yes. I've been waiting."

Audra's mouth was dry.

The doll went on, "You've come to me. Come to me all the

way. We have so much to do, you and I." The face broke into a smile. Audra found the eyes unnerving. They never focused.

Audra took another step toward the doll.

The doll got to her feet. "I was so jealous of the others. Their echoes came here, and now you're here. I want to know you."

The doll resembled her. Idealized. Thinner, more delicate. Hair a proper red. But there was no denying the similarities. It was something that could never be ignored. In this realization, she recognized her. This was the double of her dreams. Instead of ephemera, the doppelganger was here. One touch, and one of them would vanish into smoke. She took another step.

"What's your name?"

"You mustn't ask that."

The Poem crossed the rest of the distance. Audra expected heat from the little one's body, but there was only a distant warmth. The Poem leaned in for a kiss.

She whispered, "I want to show you the orange tree."

Audra never saw the blade until it was too late.

* * *

In Stephen's dreams, the walls screamed. He woke up the next morning without rest, the Knife staring down at him. Her cheek was cracked, a little blood smeared there. "Thank you, Maker," she said.

He tried to speak. Couldn't.

The Knife kissed him and rose. Stephen got up, no longer bothering with clothes. Pointless. Clothes would mean the unthinkable—leaving his precious dolls for the cruel sun.

His feet made no noise on the floorboards. The thing in the

master bedroom shifted its horrible bulk. The Firstborn stood just inside the Joyous's closed door. The Joyous had another name once, but Stephen couldn't quite recall it.

The Poem was downstairs. Stephen moved easily through the house, light in the dark. The walls didn't block his passage. The stairs were silent under him. Following the presence of the Poem, he turned into the living room.

The room was washed in blood.

He could barely recognize the bits of flesh scattered around the room. The blood had soaked into walls and furniture. In places, it dripped sluggishly. There were clothes, torn and turned black. In the center, the largest mass—blood and viscera. The Poem knelt amongst it, playing like a child, pink skin stained and covered in crimson whorls. She sifted through the organs with pale fascination.

The Poem looked up, her neck moving smoothly, breaking into a grin. "I wanted to see what was inside."

Stephen's eyes roamed over the body. Finally, on the chair, the head, sawed from the neck was Audra's face, locked in agony.

"The circle is closed." The Poem turned back to her investigation.

There was nothing in Stephen to make him protest. The dolls had taken those parts of him, and the rest understood the Poem's terrible logic. It had to be Audra, and she had died because of Stephen. She had deserved none of it, and she had suffered anyway. Stephen knew these things in the rational parts of his mind.

But they didn't matter.

CHAPTER TWENTY

ONE MONTH AFTER THE POEM murdered the Seeker, the house pulsed with life.

She had vanished. Signs of her passing radiated outward from the Nite Lite. Posters with a grainy picture of her, saying, "Have You Seen Me?" were stapled to telephone poles. The police found her car on Stephen's street and canvassed the neighborhood but found nothing. There was no body. She had simply disappeared.

Summer was dying. Stephen lay in bed, never moving. In brief moments of alertness, he wondered what was outside. Part of him believed the house was all there was, the world dropping away outside the door. He couldn't believe in a world where Jessica Baniszewski existed yet was too far away. Their one night together was the single memory burning within the husk that was him. Even in the wet flashes, fucking one of the others, he couldn't bring himself to imagine Jessica on top of him. She was worth more.

He forgot the last time he had eaten. Hunger and thirst were no longer concerns. Neither was pissing and shitting. Bathing, sleeping, breathing. All gone.

The dolls took the house instead, flitting through it on their incomprehensible errands. He could feel them. The Knife and the Poem had finally made peace and the Poem was decorating the Knife's porcelain skin with bloody glyphs.

The Firstborn was coming down the stairs when the door broke inward.

The man breaking the door down was scarcely human. He saw the ballerina and grinned, putting one bullet through her chest without hesitation. The Firstborn fell, strings cut.

"What the fuck!" The Alpha muscled his way in. The other two beasts flanked him. To the house, they were creatures rather than men, faces were twisted, their mouths bloody, their eyes black—the Hide's pack.

"The bitch saw us." The Beta gestured to the clown-faced ballerina, the blood slowly blooming across her leotard. Her clear eyes looked far from human.

"Good. You see that?" the Alpha said to the others. "We don't know who he told. Anyone in this house dies and we burn it to the fucking ground."

"What the fuck is this?" The Omega said, touching the ribbons, and then closing his fist around one and yanking. It popped free and the house groaned. He glanced around nervously and sidled closer to the rest of the pack.

"Holy shit," said the Gamma.

They followed his gaze into the parlor. Evidence of Audra's murder was still everywhere, even if the actual body was gone, buried amongst several animal skeletons under the lone orange tree.

"Are those bloodstains?" said the Omega.

"I hope not." They exchanged looks. Suddenly nothing was right.

"Come on," the Alpha said.

Through the living room were the laundry area and the kitchen. The refrigerator stood open. What little food in there had spoiled a long time ago. Lettuce had turned into green sludge at the bottom of the crisper. "Are you sure we've got the right place?"

The Alpha nodded, confidence gone. The house did not look quite lived in. The electricity, shown by the fridge, was still on and things looked as though they had been moved around, but it did not look, or smell, like a home, even beyond the bizarre decoration. There was a lack of dust, even the tiny layer growing in any old house. It was curiously artificial.

The pack circled back into the dining room. They stopped. The chairs had been stacked on the table. The Omega opened his mouth to curse. No one needed to be spooked. The Alpha held up a hand and the Omega clammed up. They moved into the parlor. Empty.

The Beta was peering through the window facing the front of the house. "There's a girl outside!"

The Alpha went to the door and opened it. A pale form disappeared into the coach house.

"Come on. She knows where Steve is. And, if not, he'll come out if he wants her back."

The pack hunters went back outside into the sunlight, squinting in the sudden flash. They fanned out as they approached the coach house where something inside glowed orange. The Alpha made it to the door first, opening it up to a blast of heat.

A furnace blazed in the center of the room, turning the entire building into hell. The Alpha blinked through the shimmering haze. Maybe there was something beyond, the smoke and fire obscuring it. The pack split up, the Omega staying by the door, the other two spreading out along either side of the furnace. The fire sucked the air from the Alpha's lungs, wanting to smother him under a cocoon of smoke and hate.

Through the fire the Alpha recognized the face of the girl. It was Brian's little girlfriend, Tabitha. She was pretty, with curly brown hair, skin smudged with dirt and glowing with sweat. Something was off about her large brown eyes. Though she saw him through the haze, the eyes stayed oddly blank. There was no sense of recognition or anger, even after what they had all done to her.

"You! Stay there!"

The pack moved quickly. The girl's head went left and right, unnaturally smooth. She bolted, but they grabbed her, "She's wiggling!"

The Alpha leaned in close to the girl's face. "Stop moving, Tabitha. Don't make this worse."

She went limp.

The Gamma said, "What do we do with her?"

"Just hold her. For now. Come on."

The Beta said, "What the fuck is she doing here?

The Alpha grabbed a handful of the Sorrow's hair. "That's a good question. What are you doing here?"

Her response was serene. "This is my home."

The Beta said, "You think Steve killed him over this cunt?"

The Alpha looked down at the Sorrow, realizing for the first time she was naked. Of course. "I told Brian that little creep was crazy." To the Sorrow he said, "Is that it? You're Steve's? He killed Brian for you?"

She wouldn't answer. The Alpha knew they could get it out of her, remembering what Brian would do to her. It was a good show, even if her face was stony during the worst agonies.

They dragged the Sorrow out of the coach house. She struggled but did not scream. Her face never changed expression. In the light, the Alpha saw her more clearly. As pretty as ever, though her knees were still badly bruised. He chuckled to herself. Brian kept his mark on her.

"Drag her back to the house. Either he's in there, or we wait for him to come back."

The Alpha was through the door first, shouting, "Steve, we have..." when his voice died. The pack burst through next and saw what he saw, or rather what was not.

The ballerina was gone. There was a little blood on the stairs. Not much. Not enough.

"Maybe I didn't hit her through the heart."

It had been a kill shot. The bitch had gotten up and walked away. "Yeah. Maybe you missed. She's gonna bleed to death anyway."

"No, she won't." Tabby spoke up. Her voice, almost childlike in tone, was flat.

"What did you say?"

"She won't bleed to death. She can't die that way."

The Alpha punched Tabitha in the face. It didn't feel right. He should have felt her nose break. Instead, the face gave with the punch. She was not even bleeding. "You shut the fuck up."

Tabby kept staring and said nothing.

"Okay. We're splitting up. You two, upstairs. You, head around to the kitchen. I'm going to stay right here. Whatever you flush, I'll catch."

The Beta and the Omega went up the stairs; the Omega unable to keep his eyes off the Satanic-looking symbols painted across the walls. The Gamma went into the back. The Alpha felt the situation slipping away, and for comfort pulled the gun from his waistband and kissed the cross hanging from his neck.

The Gamma's shout echoed from the kitchen, "Freeze!" There was a gunshot. Packing dirt. Packing mud. A door splintered open. The Alpha looked and saw the Gamma on the floor, face a ruin, pieces ripped out of his body by the handful.

Past the door that continued to swing open and closed on greased hinges, two shadows stood in the kitchen. One was the ballerina. The other figure was slightly shorter, body narrowing to a waist, then blooming with a large skirt. The door closed and opened again and the silhouettes were gone.

He almost shouted to them when a clicking sound from above stopped him. A scream followed, a male scream. Ripping and tearing. The Alpha ran to the foot of the stairs. Brian's girlfriend was still sitting by the door, unperturbed.

On the wall behind the landing, a shadow. A man's shadow. Possibly Stephen's. It had to be.

The Omega was crawling down the stairs. Something had chewed him apart. A chainsaw maybe. The Alpha went past the fallen pack member up the stairs. The Omega had an arm out, trying to wave the Alpha away. Blood ran down the staircase in a waterfall. The Alpha made it to the landing. The shadow loomed large. Stephen would be at the top of the stairs. The Alpha reached the top.

And filled his pants with shit.

Although the thing crouching over the Beta was not human, the parts of it which were human made it even more horrifying. Its tail, ending in a beautiful woman's face, dipped to the still moving Beta and tore a chunk of meat from the screaming body. A beautiful redhead crouched amongst the ruins of the bodies, dipping her hands in the blood and drawing horrible glyphs across the monster's backs.

The Alpha turned to the wall. The shadow, the human shadow, belonged to this horror.

It saw the Alpha, and the red mouth on the tail said, "You are the Alpha. You need to join me."

The Alpha screamed and turned to run. The door was only a staircase away. Get to the stairs, and into the sun. Out there, the world still made sense. Monsters didn't live in the sunlight.

He ran. Down the stairs. Almost to the door.

Something slammed into him from the side. He tumbled. Turned.

It was Stephen Monaghan. The face was impassive, almost like a doll, a kitchen knife, clutched in a pale hand, pressed down toward the Alpha's face. For the moment, this was something the Alpha could deal with. This was a man, not the abomination upstairs. The thing above continued its horrible clicking. Coming closer.

Stephen had all the leverage, but he was not a strong man. The Alpha grunted and flipped the other man over with ease. Only at that moment did the Alpha notice Stephen was naked and erect. The Alpha groped for the knife, found it, and plunged it to the hilt into Stephen's side.

The clicking was deafening.

The Alpha turned. The thing had come down the stairs. The ballerina and her friend stalked from the kitchen. Two more shapes watched from the top of the stairs, one crouched, the other standing, throwing glittering reflections across the bloody walls.

"Now you belong to us," the thing said.

The Alpha never had a chance to scream.

* * *

After the carnage was complete, the dolls took up the Maker's body. He bled a milky-white fluid from the knife wound in a sluggish trickle. It would not stop. His life was already gone. But there was a way to keep him.

They placed him in bed first and would alternate watching over him.

The others returned to the attic to consider the materials waiting for them. As one, they selected the porcelain. It had created the Knife, the closest to the Maker's heart, and it would be their beginning. They bore it to the furnace in the coach house.

They sculpted a skeleton. The Sorrow, used to working the furnace, took the lead. The bones glowed a beautiful alabaster under the light. The teeth came from the Seeker's cast.

They returned to the attic. Again, as one, they selected the mahogany. It had birthed the Firstborn, and it would make the porcelain strong.

They sculpted muscle from it. The Firstborn had full knowledge of human anatomy, putting the muscles against the porcelain bone and making them perfect. They polished it to a high shine. It would be powerful. Powerful as the Firstborn.

They returned to the attic. As one, they turned to the gel. There was some that had not made its home in the Celestial's glass flesh.

Carefully, they poured it into the newest doll. This would form her viscera, her brain.

They returned to the attic. Last was the latex. This had been the skin of the Poem and the Sorrow, the sisters who could be mistaken for human. They dotted it with freckles as the Maker had learned.

They molded a body for the doll, laying over bone and muscle and viscera. They gave hair of Sorrow brown, eyes of Poem blue.

As she lay there, she was indistinguishable from human. She would be so much more. Immortal. Strong. This was the perfection the Maker had sought and had finally found through the work of his daughters.

The Incarnate.

The Maker breathed shallowly. The bed beneath him was covered in the flow of milk. They bore him up to the attic and bathed him gently, washcloths against papery skin. They laid the Incarnate next to him.

Listlessly, he turned and beheld her. In his eyes was only wonder.

They sliced him open at every vein. There was no blood. The milk flowed and he smiled. Led by the Poem, they said the words. Led by the Sorrow, they gave her breath.

The Maker closed his eyes and was gone.

The Incarnate opened her eyes.

* * *

The diaspora began the next day.

They began by constructing seven jars. The Firstborn and the Sorrow took the lead, creating layers of clay and porcelain. The Poem inscribed the appropriate symbols on each.

They butchered the Maker, keeping seven parts for the seven jars. The Firstborn received the Maker's hand, the Knife his heart, the Poem his penis, the Sorrow his liver, the Innocent his eyes, the Celestial his larynx and the Incarnate his brain. These would mark their tribes in the years to come.

The rest of the Maker's body fed the orange tree.

The Firstborn taught the others the craft. The Poem taught them the rites.

Each doll went into the bedroom and shed her costume. They bathed, each in turn. The wounds of the Firstborn and the Knife were already healing.

They dressed again. This time in the Maker's clothing.

Without speaking of it, each doll left the house carrying her jar. They would return, but not without others and not for many years. There was much Work to be done. More dolls to create. A race of daughters to be mothers to. They took with them the example of the Maker. The others would know of him and bless him for the sacrifice he had made.

And they would protect themselves.

Only the Incarnate and the Innocent stayed behind in the house. For one, it was the only home she could imagine. The other could not survive anywhere else.

* * *

It was October before Jessica Baniszewski returned to Stephen's house.

Her brother's murder was officially unsolved. Lack of evidence, they said. She had the truth—Brian's sins had come to collect. Maybe that wasn't such a bad thing.

She had not bled in some time. The words had vanished. The strange visitor and the man called the Maker occupied Jessica's thoughts. She had loved him for so long it was strange to think of a way not to. It was time to finish that part of her life, to be with him or take the rejection. She forgave him in her heart for all of it. What remained was to tell him.

She walked up the driveway and something felt different. The house was right. It had been wrong for so many years and had finally become something else.

She went to the door. It was already open.

A woman was waiting in the threshold. She looked familiar, yet Jessica had never seen her before. "I'm looking for Stephen?"

"You're the Heart."

"My name is Jessica Baniszewski."

"The Heart."

The woman's eyes were the same blue as…

"Stephen?"

"I am the Incarnate."

Jessica paused, remembering the harlequin being unable to say her name.

"Is Stephen here?" She asked the question, already knowing the answer. It tore into her, but she needed the woman to say it.

"Yes. He loves you, you know."

"Loves?"

"He is gone. But lives still."

Jessica thought she would collapse at this. Something in what the Incarnate said felt right. Stephen did not feel lost. He felt right in front of her, speaking with the Incarnate's voice, seeing with the Incarnate's eyes. The distillation of Stephen Monaghan, the parts of him that were special and powerful, the crippled parts cut away, having become what he should have always been. The Incarnate.

The Incarnate said, "Would you like to come in for a while?"

"More than anything."

ACKNOWLEDGMENTS

Thanks to all my readers who helped turn a jumbled mass of nonsense into something at least semi-coherent. Thanks to the editors at MuseItUp Publishing, who first published the ebook version, for assisting with my questionable grammar and for seeing something worthwhile in the book. And thank you to my wife, whose hard work made a print edition possible.

ABOUT THE AUTHOR

Much like film noir, Justin Robinson was born and raised in Los
Angeles. He splits his time between editing comic books, writing
prose, and wondering what that disgusting smell is. Degrees
in Anthropology and History prepared him for unemployment,
but an obsession with horror fiction and a laundry list of phobias
provided a more attractive option.

www.captainsupermarket.com

BOOKS BY
JUSTIN ROBINSON

City of Devils
Coldheart
Everyman
Nerve Zero
Undead on Arrival

Fill in the _____ Series
Mr Blank
Get Blank

Made in the USA
Lexington, KY
23 March 2015